The Waking Up

Blessings to you, Jill!
Much Love!
Melanie

The Waking Up

A frontier girl stirs to life
during an early American revival

Melanie M. Meadow

RA Publishing
Clarksville, Tennessee

Published in the United States by RA Publishing
RAPublishing.com

Library of Congress Control Number 2013931204

Cover design: Dawn Lombard
Cover photograph: Marcy Martin
Map of 1870s Logan County courtesy of Logan County Public Library
archives
Scripture quotations on pages 17 and 155 from the NIV Study Bible, 2011
edition.

ISBN 978-0-9829120-2-7

For the believers
in Logan County, Kentucky,
and northern Tennessee.
May you re-till the spiritual ground
that was so carefully
plowed and planted
more than two centuries ago.

The Waking Up

Introduction

Telling the story of Rev. James McGready (pronounced Mc-Grady)
grew on me gradually as a fire that was slow to start. The first flame
caught a few years ago when I read a friend's old, banged-up copy of
"Fire in the West: The Logan County Revivals," a magazine article written by Stephen Mansfield. It briefly summarized the seeding of the Second Great Awakening in Kentucky (which then spread throughout the
nation) and pinpointed the main "players" in this event.

Presbyterian McGready was one of those mentioned.

Not long afterward, I learned that McGready, who ministered in the
late 1700s to early 1800s, actually lived a mere forty-or-so miles up the
road from my home. As I began to study in-depth, I sensed more and
more the power of the minister of God during those formative years of
our nation. It was the time of the circuit riders, primarily Methodist ministers who traveled throughout the East Coast and Ohio Valley regions
preaching the Gospel anywhere they could park their horse.

I believe most scholars would agree that a multiplication of circuit
riders came as a result of the Second Great Awakening, a series of revivals that occurred in the early 1800s. While some would say the revivals split congregations and were a negative force, others would say
new denominations formed and the Gospel was furthered. Regardless of
your take on it, the numbers clearly show that religion in the new territo-
ries took off following these meetings. The key event was held in Cane
Ridge, Kentucky, during the summer of 1801. Early Presbyterian minister Barton W. Stone oversaw this meeting where more than 20,000 fron-
tiersmen, women and children gathered – an astounding number
considering Kentucky had a population of only 221,000 at that time. Mc-
Gready and his co-ministers most likely assisted Stone in preaching.

Yet the awakening didn't just crop up overnight.

The Waking Up

McGready and his followers had been laying the groundwork since the late 1790s when he established "societies" to pray for revival in their area and the nation. Surely he had great hopes of the Spirit of God moving over people, but I doubt he ever fully understood the enormity of what God did during this time in our nation's history.

Many of the people who inhabited this "wilderness territory" were known as revelers, rogues, robbers and drunkards. Others were fiercely independent souls who came from hearty stock, self-reliant individuals who often exhibited great resolve through hardship and a bold sense of adventure. McGready and men like him had their work cut out for them. They were pioneering the Christian faith, moving their families and all their belongings into a dangerous wilderness to preach the Gospel to those who needed it most.

Let me clearly state that the book you hold in your hand is not an academic work. As you may imagine, dozens, if not hundreds, of papers, articles and books have been written about the Second Great Awakening – some of which question whether what occurred was an "awakening" at all! It is not my intent to debate semantics or dogma.

My purpose is threefold:

First, I feel it is imperative that people understand the origins of the Second Great Awakening. The Lord sent His Spirit in a mighty way. Perhaps He will have mercy on America and do the same thing again. Naturally, it would be helpful to know how it happened in the past.

Second, McGready lived a life that begs to be known. Those who heard him called him a "Son of Thunder," a man of a powerful spiritual as well as physical presence. It is my opinion that he was a true pioneer of the faith and deserves to be known as such.

And, finally, everyone loves a good story!

The main character, Sarah Elizabeth McMillan, is completely fictitious; however, many of the Port Royal Settlement townsfolk named in *The Waking Up* actually lived and worked in that tucked-away area. Her life is typical of many during that time – and I hope I did those like her justice in my descriptions.

Conversely, McGready, his wife, and his fellow ministers are as true to life as I could make them. Thanks be to God, several people during that time thought enough of them to leave us detailed descriptions that have spanned time. McGready himself wrote several articles for "The New York Missionary Magazine and Repository of Religious Intelligence for the year 1803," which outlined the happenings in Kentucky and its surrounding areas. I relied almost entirely on these primary documents to describe the meetings Sarah McMillan attended. Most of the portions of McGready's sermons in this book are directly from his spoken words. The power in them still resonates more than 200 years later.

Believe me, you will want to disbelieve some of the occurrences detailed here; don't do it. It really did happen.

Also, the title, *The Waking Up,* is a phrase taken from an autobiography of Peter Cartwright, one of the premier Methodist circuit riders during the early 1800s. He was converted at one of McGready's Red River meetings. In his autobiography, he writes that there was a great "waking up" of those present.

Blessings be on you for believing this to be a work that is worthy of your time. May it so prove to be.

Melanie Meadow

Postscript:

The front cover photograph was taken at the confluence of the Red River and Sulphur Fork Creek at Port Royal State Park, Tennessee. At this location, baptisms have occurred for more than 200 years.

The back cover photo shows the inside of the Red River Meeting House replica that is located off Highway 663 between Adairville and Schochoh in southeastern Logan County, Kentucky. The original cemetery remains there with many tombstones from the late 1790s, early 1800s. You can drop by anytime for a self-guided tour. More information can be found at **www.redriverrevival.com.**

1870s map of Logan County, Kentucky

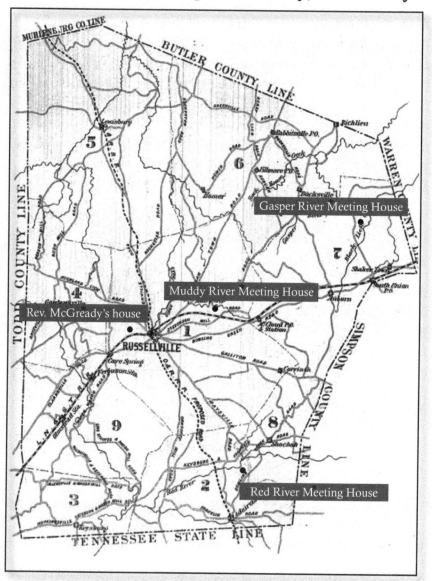

Gasper River Meeting House

Muddy River Meeting House

Rev. McGready's house

Red River Meeting House

As one of the oldest known maps of Logan County, this reproduction is not as clean as desired, but better than anything else, it displays the roads of the time. Seventy years earlier, roads would have been even less developed.
* Note: Even though the Gasper River MH runs next to Black Lick Creek, not the Gasper River, folks at the time called the creek "Gasper River."

Prologue
Orange County, North Carolina
1793

If they hadn't been so silent, you might not have known the three men were intent on evil. They appeared innocuous enough – two tall and lanky, one short and broad – tri-cornered hats pressed securely on their heads in the cool of the night air, their feet crushing spring grass and rotted leaves with each step. One held an axe, swinging it to and fro. Another bobbled the lantern as he tripped over an exposed root. Other than a muffled oath, the trek was as quiet as the night.

A solitary structure sitting atop a grassy pasture was their destination. The leader held out his hand for the axe when he entered the building. As its hickory handle slapped his palm, it created a dull thud, echoing in the cavernous room. Followed by the others through the unlocked door, he walked resolutely up the aisle to the cedar podium that stood front and center. Wordlessly, his companions picked it up, hefting it high enough to walk, their breath creating clouds of effort. The axebearer followed and began swinging almost before the pulpit was thrown to the ground. Within minutes, it was in pieces.

A flask of whiskey appeared from a breast pocket, and after two quick swigs, the remainder was shaken over the broken cedar planks. A twig plucked off the ground, held to the lantern, thrown on the pile, and, as if by magic, the deed was done.

As the blaze from the podium climbed higher into the night, the men merely watched, drawing somewhat closer to the warmth of the flame. They had no fear of discovery. It was too late and too remote a place, this Stony Creek Presbyterian Meeting House. They knew it well. In fact, all three would be back here Friday night when the meetings started again. But then ... well ... they would look different.

Flames began to die as the shorter of the men reached into a coat pocket, withdrawing a sort of scroll. Picking up a stone and a nail from the smoldering remains, he stepped to the front door, found the center plank, and nailed the parchment securely to the facade. The other two kicked dirt over the dying embers, not watching the scene behind them. They knew the words written there. They had watched as the hand had dipped the pen into the inkwell of chicken blood and scrawled out the edict of warning. Even the great Reverend James McGready couldn't ignore this.

Embers of red cedar faded into blackness as the men turned their backs on the meeting house, stepping off the hill and away, the front door closed tightly with a bloody bulletin nailed into its planks.

"Fire! Fire! There's been a fire at the meeting house!"

The Reverend James McGready jerked his head up from the Bible that lay open on the table. As was his custom, he had risen before dawn, stoked the fire and lit a small lantern that sat in the middle of his family's simple kitchen table. Because it was Thursday — March 4, to be exact, he would spend precisely half the day completing his study for the message he would deliver tomorrow night at Stony Creek. The other portion of the day would be spent with his pupils at his house.

Reuben McNair's body caught up with his voice at McGready's front door where he began banging heedlessly.

"Brother Reuben!" McGready chastised the man as he whipped open the poplar door. "Contain yourself, man. Has the Lord returned?"

"No, Reverend, sir. But someone's been up to no good at Stony Creek. They pulled out our pulpit and burned it clear to the ground. There's nothing left of it, and I found this upon the door." McNair pulled the dew-covered scroll from his front pocket and handed it to McGready. The preacher opened the door further, allowing McNair access to the warmth of the crackling fire in the hearth as he turned the paper over in his hand. "Have a seat, son. Mrs. McGready's not yet risen, but may I offer you a warm cup of coffee to ward off the chill of this morning?"

McNair moved easily to the kettle, a man accustomed to finding what he needed, as McGready shifted closer to the lantern. Smeared red letters, rudely scripted, assaulted his eyes.

"The Reverend James McGready is hereby called upon, by certain families in the county of Orange, Carolina, on this, March 3, in the year of our Lord, 1793, to cease and desist preaching doctrine that creates unnecessary alarm in the minds of those who are decent and orderly. He must stop running people distracted, stop diverting their attention from their necessary avocation. If he chooses not to desist, we demand he leave Orange county at the peril of his own life."

Signed, Concerned Citizens of God's Kingdom

A small grunt was McGready's only reaction. He slowly lifted his head, watching McNair curl his chilled hands around the pewter mug, settling in by the fire. McGready's black hair and brown eyes, gifts from his Scots-Irish ancestors, gave him the appearance of darkness and, perhaps, a touch of violence. But the glow of his countenance far outweighed any earthiness in his expression.

"Did you read this?"

"No, sir. I saw it nailed to the door with your name at the top and brought it right on here. It doesn't bode well, does it?"

McGready shook his head and opened his mouth to reply when he heard the creak of his bed and his wife call his name. Quickly, he shook his head at McNair, finger over his lips, and called out, "It's alright, Nancy. Reuben's just come by for a spell. Take your time. We've got our coffee."

McGready joined McNair by the fire and bent his head toward the younger man, one of his five students of theology. That's how McGready thought of them. Each pupil worked here in the Orange County community—McNair was apprenticed to the local blacksmith—but McGready saw them as future ministers of the Gospel of Jesus Christ. Every spare moment they had, he poured into them. It had only been five years ago that he, himself, had received his license to preach at the Presbytery of Redstone in Pennsylvania. He had followed God's call into the northern part of the Carolinas – but not before taking a detour and spending time with Dr. Smith at Hampden Sidney College in Virginia.

That's where the fire had started. Not set by amateur hands in the middle of the night. No. This fire was from above, and as McGready would testify, came straight from the hand of God. Through the leadership of Smith, revival had broken out among the students of the college; and, as McGready traveled through the area, he felt himself drawn to stay awhile, to catch some of that "spiritual" fire and bring it with him to Orange County. His reputation as a gifted preacher and a fervent man of prayer had preceded him, and many of the people in Carolina reveled under his direction. Others found it an irritation – or worse.

Nevertheless, the calling of God was upon him and he now found himself overseer of both the Stony Creek and the Haw River congregations. Under his powerful preaching and unwavering stance on the holiness of God, revival had broken out.

"What does it say?" McNair asked, his fiery red hair framing his face.

"That I am causing disturbances, and I must leave the county."

"That's not anything new. I've been hearing that around the countryside, mostly from those Carter people. They don't like the meetin's, don't like the way God seems to be moving. Mostly don't like the fact that you want them to give up their liquor and dancing."

McGready smiled ruefully. "Preaching the Gospel always comes with a price, Reuben. The question is, how do I respond?" A large ember shot out of the fireplace, a piece of burning oak popping off a dry log. McNair kicked it back into the hearth, waiting for McGready's answer. He knew this man, knew his ways and had already anticipated his response. "I reckon I will have to deliver them a message tomorrow night. They will be expecting it, and I would hate to deny them their expectations."

"But what if they get rowdy?" McNair frowned, his ruddy countenance bothered. "Should I gather the others and let them know there might be trouble?"

"Wouldn't hurt, I suppose. The Lord tells us to be wise as serpents and innocent as doves. Wisdom would say be prepared for anything. Innocence would tell me to preach the Gospel in season and out of season, without hesitation. That is what I intend to do." McGready straightened in his slat-bottomed chair, pushing the thick, unruly hair from his brow. "Now tell me about the damage. Was anything torched other than the pulpit? Is the meeting house marred otherwise?"

As McNair reported all he knew, Nancy McGready emerged from the only other room in the small cabin, carrying the McGreadys' first-born daughter who cooed and gurgled when she saw the men at the fire. Business was laid aside until a later time, when McGready would go back to his Bible on the table and find the book of Jeremiah. Friday night's message would focus upon judgment and retribution to those who had attempted to stop the word of the Lord. McGready wouldn't bend—and a pulpit fire certainly wouldn't run him out of the area.

Part I
The Seeds of Revival

"When I shut up the heavens so that there is no rain,
or command locusts to devour the land
or send a plague among my people,
if my people, who are called by my name will humble themselves and pray
and seek my face and turn from their wicked ways,
then I will hear from heaven,
and I will forgive their sin and will heal their land."
II Chronicles 7:13-14

Chapter One

Port Royal, (recently formed state of) Tennessee
May 1798

Mud and muck. Sarah was sick of it. Ever since they moved out west, she felt like she'd been walking in sticky goo. She lifted her apron and skirt a bit higher, sidestepping a long, narrow rut left by a wagon wheel, and topped the last rise before the Red River. Lying out before her was her new home. *Port Royal in all its glory.* Her thoughts were laden with sarcasm. Were it not for the beauty of the river curling lazily around its edges – and the smaller Sulphur Fork Creek joining in at the head of the compact settlement – Sarah would proclaim she'd been brought to an untamed, barren wilderness, filled with godforsaken, vile people and nothing worth salvaging. Half the time that thought occupied her mind anyway.

"Good morning, Sarah!" Samuel Johnson waved from the front porch of Port Royal's trading post, a smallish building that seemed more concerned with carrying corn and indigo seed rather than staple goods like flour and meal. Sarah had already been frustrated mightily with him. She threw up her hand in response.

"Morning, Mr. Johnson."

Her father's tin lunch bucket hit against her leg rhythmically as she walked down Market Street toward the river, still dodging mud holes. Public Square lay directly ahead, bordering the bluffs of the Red, where a few men and one or two boys sat on tree stumps whittling and chewing dried deer strips. She made a sharp right, bypassing younger children playing a game with rocks and sticks in the street, and set her eyes on Mr. Wilcox's public warehouse. It stretched out ahead, a long, wooden structure nestled at the confluence of Sulphur Fork's joining to the Red. Her father had forgotten lunch when he left the cabin before dawn, and

19

she knew he'd be expecting her to bring it down. As a cooper by trade, he would have been cutting oak barrel staves all morning or hammering out hoop poles which encircled the barrels, holding the staves together. Eventually, those barrels and pails would find their way down the river. Most likely, he was in a foul mood, but that was nothing new. When Sarah was around, he was always foul.

She stepped up on the edge of the overhang that ran parallel to the work building. Since Mr. Wilcox's blacksmith shop was housed in a side portion, she covered her ears to blunt the ringing blasts of metal against metal and kept them covered until she approached the opened double doors of her father's shop. Voices rose from the darker room, and she'd learned enough in her fourteen years to know not to interrupt her father – ever.

As she turned from the entranceway, she wondered what to do with the pail – should she leave it at the door or wait for the conversation to end? If she left it, she would avoid having to talk to her father, which would be best for now. But if he was more foul-tempered than usual, that plan could backfire when he arrived home and demanded to know why she didn't give him his lunch directly. That, of course, could lead to accusations and wild guesses as to what she was "hiding." Really, there was no good answer.

Sarah allowed her eyes to travel down the river, squinting in the bright spring sunshine in an effort to see as far west as possible. She knew the Red eventually flowed into the Cumberland River in the settlement of Clarksville, just a ways downstream. But in her month of living in the frontier, her father never had need to travel farther. She wished he had, but then again, if he did, she probably wouldn't be taken along.

"Heads up! Heads up! Logs on the river!"

Sarah jerked around in surprise as a bevy of activity erupted. Where Port Royal seemed quiet and almost deserted a few seconds ago, it now practically bustled. Men poured out of the dry goods store that fronted the river. Children appeared from houses and streets and dashed down Spring Alley, whizzing past her to be the first to count the logs. Even women put their heads out of doors, all focused on the Red River upstream. Sarah's eyes turned up to the east now, locking on to lines of long, cut trees that were lashed together and floating downstream. After a minute or two, a small flatboat emerged from behind the logs, two men guiding the bundles as best they could. River traffic! She moved farther away from her father's shop and sat on the edge of the porch, glad to be here, glad her walk into town coincided with a happening.

"Never gets old."

Sarah turned in surprise as a fiery red-haired George Wilcox ambled up and leaned against a squared wooden column. His heavy blacksmith apron was dark with use and carried an odor of wood smoke and pungent metal. *Not altogether unpleasant*, Sarah thought.

"Pardon me?" she spoke aloud.

"Watchin' river traffic," he half turned, gazing down at the newly transplanted girl. "Don't matter that I've lived here for nigh onto to five year now, the excitement that comes from the river never wanes. What's it gonna bring today? News from up at Rogues' Harbor? Mebbe some mail from back East? New friends or old acquaintances? Or, Heaven help us, mebbe some coffee!" Mr. Wilcox snorted and slapped his leg. "Now that'd be truly Heaven sent."

"Yes, sir." Sarah wasn't sure what else to say. She'd never exchanged two words with this man. She glanced behind her into the dark barrel-maker shop. Her father had yet to make an appearance and when he did, she wasn't sure what he'd say about finding her talking with a man. But surely even Matthew McMillan wouldn't have an issue with her conversing with someone who had three children and was at least twenty years her senior. She lifted her chin unconsciously. George Wilcox noticed – and wondered why the young woman with the uncommonly green eyes suddenly seemed so determined and fierce.

"Logs on deck! John, give us a hand here!" Voices continued to ring out, the words carrying clearly over the river, as the two men in the flat-boat yelled out instructions to those on shore. Back and forth commands flew, steering logs into the bank, working against the heavy flow of the river to anchor in a holding area a bit downstream from the main docking point. Sarah watched awestruck as men ran across logs that spun precariously in the water. It was as though they were on dry land and the tumbling, whirling logs merely stone steps. Time stood still as George Wilcox pulled a heavily used pipe out of his side pocket, packing and tamping the tobacco tightly down. Striking the match on the bottom of his boot, he drew a deep draught of the leaf and sighed contentedly.

"Been workin' at the side of your father for near 'bouts five week here. Matthew's a good man. Proud of his work. Proud of his past. You should be pleased to have such a father."

Sarah kept her eyes locked on the river, but Wilcox saw her full lips draw into a narrow line. He pushed on.

"Yep. I've seen many a barrel-maker in my time, but Matthew's work is the best that I've run across. Talented man. Cryin' shame about your Mama. 'Course, I hadn't asked him what happened but we all know she's been gone to glory for well nigh onto ten year or so now. Must be tough it bein' just the two of you."

Wilcox saw only the back of Sarah's head now. Her auburn, curly hair escaped the cap in wild tendrils that flew randomly in the breeze. Although her expression was hidden, he saw the firm set of her shoulders and the ramrod straight back and knew he had probed deep enough. Maybe too deeply. No one in Port Royal knew much about the McMillans. Getting any information out of Matthew was like drawing blood from a turnip, and the girl was rarely seen downtown. As far as Wilcox knew, Sarah had no friends – not a good proposition for a young, pretty girl.

"What's Rogues' Harbor?"

"What's that?" The sound of her voice surprised Wilcox.

"Rogues' Harbor. You said the men could bring news from Rogues' Harbor. What's that?" Sarah's tone was tight and crisp, her back still facing Wilcox.

"Oh, that's just up there in Logan County, past the line into Kentucky. It's not an official name of a settlement, per se. The county seat is Russellville, but Rogues' Harbor is what that area is. Yes, sir. That's what it is." Wilcox drew again on his pipe as men at the river began hauling up the flatboat to tie off. "You'd be hard-pressed to find a more derelict society than up that a way. Gamblin', vulgar speech, drink – oh, the strength of whiskey up there! It's mighty powerful. No real sense of the fear of God. Men and women alike don't care nothin' for God, don't want to learn nothin' about Him. Why, it's just filled with rascals and rogues, Logan County is. And there's nothin' for it."

Voices that had been muted from the porch grew louder as Matthew

McMillan and his visitor emerged from the doorway. Sarah heard and jumped to her feet in response while Wilcox watched with interest. The girl's stance was almost masculine, legs apart, empty hand fisted. She held the lunch pail like a weapon and her squared jaw was set firm.

Matthew merely seemed surprised to see her, then a flash of understanding crossed his face as his eye caught the lunch pail. For a split second he appeared remorseful, but it passed almost before it could be seen. It was as though a shutter drew and the window was tightly closed. He held out his hand, his face void of all expression.

"Give me the pail and get on home." His eyes never locked on his daughter, rather, they scanned the two men standing on the porch, sweeping past and out to the activity on the river. "Logs coming down?" he asked Wilcox, pushing past Sarah to walk to the edge of the porch. Matthew McMillan's short stature could have made him appear smallish and weak, but a closer examination would make any man hesitate to start anything with this man. His frame was compact and tight, power amassed in muscle; and the prominent nose, brow and dark beard added to the impression of subdued strength – and perhaps a raging temper at times. Both Wilcox and McMillan's customer stepped aside to let him pass.

"Appears to be loggers from Logan County. Probably came out of Mortimer Station," Wilcox remarked, tamping the used tobacco out of his pipe and following McMillan. "Looks like a fairly big run, but with the river up, I expect we'll be seein' more and more over the next few weeks."

McMillan grunted his reply as his sharp eyes took stock of the haul. If these two Logan Countians were planning to continue their run to the Cumberland, they might be meeting up with more loggers – might be gunning for the Mississippi if they were the adventuring sort. Might need storage for their flatboats. Might need some barrels.

McMillan turned and shook the hand of his customer, set his lunch pail against the side of his shop, and trod off toward the river and its possibilities. Sarah had remained in the background at full attention, waiting to see what might be required of her. As she watched the back of her father stride purposefully toward the riverbank, she unconsciously let out the breath she'd been holding. She felt Wilcox's eyes on her but refused to meet his gaze. Turning back toward Spring Alley, she decided to leave Wilcox there and walk home a different route. She would have liked to stay and see the logs anchored in, hear the news from the two men who traveled in from the east, see what, if anything, they might have brought with them. But she knew better. Her father had told her to go home. She'd best be gone.

Spring Alley wasn't much of a street, not like Main or Market; it had too much of the blacksmith and cobbler-type trades housed there, but Sarah liked it best of all the streets in Port Royal. Odors of tanning leather and blazing fires settled on her like the comforts of home, reminding her of Spartanburg, Carolina, and better times. Most times there were better, but not all.

Spartanburg had weathered a mighty wet winter, and the town at the base of the Appalachians received more than its share of water run-off in February. The timing was horrid as far as Sarah was concerned because that's when Matthew McMillan heeded the call of the frontier and its stories of fertile lands and new beginnings. He decided to move. Now.

Sarah really blamed William Prince, a former citizen of Spartanburg who had settled in Port Royal. Prince had returned to Spartanburg a few years earlier as a widower seeking a wife. During that time, the two former friends, Prince and her father, had reconnected, leading Matthew to consider again taking his father's Revolutionary War grant of lands in the region. Matthew had chewed on the idea for a few years, then suddenly, right after those drenching spring rains, he decided it was time. Within the week, the McMillans' belongings were strapped to pack horses.

It took two months of hard travel, inconvenience and mud — up and around mountain after mountain, drudgery, rivers, streams, soggy undergarments – before they finally arrived in Port Royal, right in the middle of a spring rainstorm. Of course.

"Pow! You're dead, Sarah. You have to die now," a tiny, high-pitched voice shot from around a corner.

"And wham again! That makes two shots. You're really dead, Sarah," another voice chirped. "You got a big ol' arrow stickin' out of your heart. You bleedin' all over the street. It's just plain ugly."

"I can't die here," wailed Sarah. "It's too muddy. I'll get my apron and petticoats all dirty." She leaned dramatically against the side of a building, propping her hand against her brow. She changed her voice to a slower drawl, that of a coastal Carolinian. "Why, I do believe I feel faint and quite undone. Whatever shall I do?" she moaned, sagging into the wall.

Two urchins shot out from behind their hiding places, giggling and pointing at Sarah with glee. One child, a boy, jumped and hopped from foot to foot, while the other, a taller, thin, colored girl, laughed uproariously. She pushed the boy aside to hug Sarah around the waist. Her head barely reached the shoulder of the tall Sarah McMillan.

"You make me laugh, Sarah," she announced. "Sammy and me was playin' pretend games. He was the Indian…"

"And I shot you with my flint-tipped, poisoned arrow," Sammy explained dutifully.

"…and I was the sheriff usin' my powerful rifle to defeat the wicked Injuns!"

"Oh my! The two of you are mighty fierce," Sarah responded as she stood up straight and continued to walk slowly down Spring Alley. "Good thing I am a law-abiding citizen so I do not have to be hunted down by a sheriff. And good thing the Injuns have moved farther out west or I would be hiding from you two," she laughed, tousling Sammy's stiff blonde hair affectionately. "How did you get away from chores this afternoon? You both look like you are up to no good thing."

"Daddy's workin' the back fields with David, and me and Hagar decided to make ourselves scarce," Sammy's cherub-like face turned up to Sarah. He was anything but angelic, but he had the look.

"Yeah. If we don't find somethin' to do, they'll find somethin' for us," Hagar added. "As long as we stay hid, we can play more and work later. We figured we'd best not go to the docks right now. We'll check out the logs later." The incongruous three reached the end of the alley and cut a right toward Main as Hagar continued. "Did you know me and my Pappy done joined the Baptist meetin' house last week?"

Sarah glanced at the dark-skinned girl in surprise. "You mean Red River Baptist? The one that meets at Mr. Frank Prince's spring?"

"Uh huh. We sho' did. Brother Prince said that me, Pappy and Mammy can come on in under the hand of Mr. Neville, seeing as how Pappy belongs to him," Hagar continued while Sammy nodded seriously.

"So now we is members of the church, and I can sit with Sammy every month that we meet."

"That is nice," Sarah smiled at the two friends, marveling at their differences in the face of their unity.

"How come you don't join the Baptist church, Sarah?" Sammy asked, kicking a rock out of the way as they neared Main Street and Sarah's turn-off toward home.

"Father does not believe in church. We have never attended. He says religion is just an excuse not to be independent and make your own way in the world. We do not need it, and we have done well so far."

Little Sammy's face scrunched up, deep in thought, while Hagar's eyes flew open wide, filled with disbelief. She reached out and clutched Sarah's arm, dragging the older girl to a standstill. "You can't go on that a way. Everybody needs to know God. Why, if you don't, you'll go to the bad place, I mean, the really, really bad place."

"It's true," Sammy nodded quickly. "It's a bad place, Sarah. We don't want you to go there."

A wagon slowly moved up Market Street, forcing the three friends to stop and wait for it to pass. Sarah would turn and follow it as it left town and moved south, but her journey would end about a mile down the road at the McMillan cabin. The wagon would continue along the trail.

"Not to worry. I reckon the McMillans can take care of themselves. We always have," she smiled and turned in the wake of the traffic, stepping to the side of the well-worn trail to avoid the staggered puddles and mud pools along the way. She'd dawdled enough and had to get back home in plenty of time to finish chores before her father returned. There was still much to do.

Chapter Two

The shadows lengthened as the end of the day approached. Sarah watched the long shade of a sycamore tree in front of their cabin stretch and eclipse the pathway her father would walk any minute now. The familiar dread began rising in her chest — that odd combination of fear, love and anger that would bubble up in her as soon as she laid eyes on him. Family in Spartanburg had claimed Matthew McMillan hadn't always been this way, but Sarah had seen nothing of the man many of them described.

Grandma McMillan had been adamant with her. "Sarah," she had declared one evening as she sat at her spinning wheel, "Matthew has a hurt deeper than life itself and without the Lord's help, that hurt will keep on festering and growing. There's not much you can do about it but endure it, God help you. It's your cross to bear until the Lord takes it away, and I can't tell you when that might ever be." Sarah's eyes grew moist as she remembered, longing to be with her wise, loving grandmother again. "In the meantime, all you can do is pray and love your father in the midst of his grief. Hang on to the Lord Jesus with all you have." Matthew had entered Grandma's house then, and the moment was snatched away.

How does a girl hang on to God anyway? she wondered.

The problem was Matthew's grief was tied to her. If it hadn't been for Sarah, Matilda – her mother – would still be here. Because when Sarah came into the world, her mother had left it. As the doctor pronounced Matilda dead, a live, screaming baby fought her way into the world. She would try to love and fill the void left by Matilda in Matthew's life – as best she could -- but after fourteen years of trying, Sarah had learned she wasn't enough. Actually, she had learned that early on. Nothing would ever be enough, but perhaps Matthew's deepest punishment was seeing the living, breathing duplicate of his wife every day … and knowing

The Waking Up

Sarah wasn't Matilda.

She glanced over her shoulder at the blackened pot hanging over the fire. The stew should be plenty warm, but not too hot. Ready for her father the minute he arrived. That's the way he liked it. Supper right away, then to chores outside until darkness drove him back in. Their single table, set near shelves, had a wooden bowl, one pewter spoon, a water cup and a small plate of hoecakes positioned for his meal. Over the years, Sarah had found ways to avoid eating at the table with him. There might be more weeding to do, or on wash day, she had to clean out the barrels or bring in the clothes she'd hung over bushes.

There had been something else back in Spartanburg, something that people wouldn't or couldn't say about Matthew McMillan. Sarah always had sensed it but had no idea what it was. Grandma McMillan had called it his "Great Sadness," and while Sarah assumed that meant her, she felt as though that wasn't the full story. But she never asked, and now she would never know. Spartanburg was far away, and Grandma McMillan, although alive, was as dead to her as her mother. Other than a possible letter or two crossing the mountains, Sarah would never hear from her again. There would be no going back.

The tell-tale step, shuffle, step, shuffle of her father's feet announced his arrival. Sarah moved back inside to stir the stew, her back to the open door. The lunch pail rattled and clanged as Matthew tossed it to the table. Walking over to the keeler, he began washing his hands. He glanced toward his daughter, seeing her back, her unruly curls escaping her bonnet in force. His expression was a mask as he pulled out the chair and sat at the table. Sarah swung the cooking crane away from the fire and picked up the cast-iron kettle. She walked over, spooned out a heaping pile of venison, potato and carrot stew, then carefully set the pot back over the fire. Matthew immediately began eating while Sarah shifted the hoecakes closer to him. As she turned to go outside – she decided today she needed to weed their young garden – Matthew stopped her with a word.

"Sit."

Sarah immediately turned, then sat across from him, hands folded on the table, chin raised and defiant. She had no idea what she'd done now.

"I got this today from the men who came from Logan County. It is

28

from your Aunt Charity," Matthew said between bites. He pulled a letter from his pocket, tossing it toward Sarah. "Read it. You will leave within the week."

"Leaving? But why? We just got here."

"I said, read it. I have worked out some help from town. The garden won't go to ruin. Neville is sending Sally's girl out to cook for me, and Sally will get up the crops till you get back."

Sally. Hagar's mama, Sarah thought, her mind racing, having difficulty focusing on his words.

"But I do not want to go anywhere. I am tired of moving and…" What she wanted to say was, I didn't know you hated me so badly that you would send me away.

"I did not ask what you wanted. Read the letter and let me be," Matthew's stony glare robbed Sarah of any courage to ask further questions. She picked up the letter and walked out the front door into the clean swept yard. Taking the trail toward the spring, she moved as far as a fallen oak, found a spot sitting on the thickest part of the trunk and opened the yellowed note. Parts of the ink had been smeared, probably from the Red River — or sweat. Who would have imagined that today's log runners carried a letter for the McMillans?

Logan County, Kentucky, April, in the year of our Lord, 1798
Dearest Matthew:

> *Greetings my brother! News from Spartanburg tells me that you and Sarah have made the trek out West, not an insignificant journey! Obediah and I send you our love from Kentucky, knowing that it must be the hand of Providence that sent you so close to our home.*
>
> *Perhaps you are surprised to hear that we are in Logan County and not farther north, into the Ohio River region as we had anticipated. Through a series of unexpected events, we are determined in mind to stake our claim here, believing the Lord's hand is what settled us. Over the years I sent you several letters to Grandma McMillan's home, but she replied for you, saying you weren't interested in correspondence. I understand your grief over Matilda still rages, as does my own, brother. A kinder, truer sister one couldn't ask for. Her loss echoes within my heart*

daily. Our prayers continue to cover you, and I can only hope that this letter finds you — and finds you well.

I know Sarah must be fourteen by now, and all reports tell me she has become the mirror image of Matilda. Certainly, she must be a help to you. However, I write with great urgency and am about to make a tremendous request. I have no other recourse and am greatly humbled by my current needs.

Obediah has found a sure occupation and business in surveying, yet it takes him a far distance from our home for weeks and months at a time. The bulk of survey work is still back east and he must travel during the easily passable months.

We now have our Matilda, age seven, Milly, age five, and Josiah, age two. I am currently with child and am due to give birth in October. Our good doctor from town is waiting outside for me now, as I hurriedly write this letter, to deliver it to Mortimer Station for passage down the river. He has ordered me to take to bed until the birth of this, our fourth child. Obediah is in the lower Virginia region, last I heard, and has no chance nor plan of returning until the fall. We have but little money and the new crop is upon us; I need a strong hand to tend it and bring it in.

I know you have your own needs, but could you see fit to spare Sarah for a time and allow her to come to me? It would feed my soul to see her, since I haven't laid eyes on her since she was a baby, but the great need has fallen upon me, as you must realize.

Please respond, Matthew. I lean into your mercy.

I remain your loving sister-in-law,

Charity McPherson

Postscript: The carrier of this note will provide ample description of the situation of our home in Logan County.

It seemed to Sarah as if the week had taken flight following her Aunt Charity's letter. Her father continued to work daily in town, sunrise to sunset, leaving Sarah to prepare the house, garden and fields for another to take over. Each day he arrived home with another piece of the puzzle as to how this thing might happen.

"Sally's girl will be doing the cooking for me. When she comes over, be sure to tell her what I like and what I do not." That was on Monday. "Twice a week Sally will be here, cleaning and washing. As the crops come in, she will stay on longer and store up what there is. I told her to come tomorrow afternoon for you to show her about. Be sure to be at the cabin right after lunch." That was Tuesday. Then, finally, "You leave Thursday morning with Neville and his family. They are riding up into Logan County for some sort of church meeting. He has agreed to let you come along and ride one of their horses. No need to take much. They don't have room to spare."

And so her fate was sealed for Thursday. As she swept the hardened dirt floor in their cabin on Wednesday afternoon, she allowed herself – for the first time – to wonder about life in Logan County and what her mother's sister might be like. Charity had left Spartanburg so long ago, far too long for Sarah to remember her; but she couldn't deny the antici-pation of meeting her aunt, to be close to someone who was once so close to her own mother.

"Whoo! Anybody home?" Sally's light, gentle voice sailed into the yard.

"Yes, in here," Sarah called back, setting aside her straw broom and wiping her hands on her apron. Sally and Hagar came down the path, laughter and joy emanating from their deep brown faces. Sarah smiled back, suddenly glad to see them.

"So you's off to Rogues' Harbor," Sally stated matter-of-factly as Hagar moved up beside her mama. "It's not no Injuns you gotta worry 'bout up there; it's them white folks that are so plum rotten. Stories I done heard," Sally shook her head, her linen kerchief tightly wound around her wiry hair. "Why I heard tell Mr. Neville talkin' to somebody a few weeks ago 'bout how they's murderers, horse thieves, highwaymen – all sorts of bad'uns that done staked a claim up in Rogues' Harbor. Some folks callin' it Satan's Stronghold. Oh, hallelujah! What the good Lord makin' you do?" Sarah glanced at Hagar who had stepped behind her mama and widely rolled her eyes, but Sally went on. "The honest folk up that way are havin' to band together just to keep the rogues from comin' and stealin' from 'um. Law! It be a frightful place."

"Mama," Hagar broke in, grabbing Sally's arm. "Don't be a'goin' on and on 'bout it. Sarah can't hep what her pappy say. No way 'round it now; she's a'goin'."

"Mercy sakes, you is right," and Sally laughed suddenly, bringing the sunshine back into the day. "Come on, girl, and show me what your pappy wants me to do. I gotta say I'm a wee bit nervous 'bout workin' here, but Mr. Neville done give me my marchin' orders. Just like you, I reckon. Ain't nothing to be done for it but do the thang."

Sarah found, as she worked alongside Sally and Hagar, that having other women in her home wasn't a bad thing, not at all. There was laughter and joking, camaraderie, six hands working at once – it not only made the work lighter, but more pleasurable. She was sorry to feel the heat of the day ebbing away, knowing that suppertime drew near.

Both Sally and Hagar were quick learners, not that they didn't know how to do all the chores that Sarah managed anyway. The real issue was teaching them Matthew's ways so they wouldn't get on his bad side early on. (Sarah knew they would eventually. Everyone did, but she didn't tell them that.) The garden grew green and healthy – squash plants, beans, tomatoes, potatoes, carrots, onions, turnips. Each was in a different stage, but so far, she'd been able to keep the deer, coons and rabbits from devouring it. Behind the cabin on a small stretch of a knoll stood a one-acre field lined with row after row of foot-high stalks of corn. The McMillans' first corn planting. Sarah had been lucky to get all the seed planted within their first week in Port Royal. If all went well, the corn could be harvested in early July; and then Sally could put in a second planting in the same field.

Together the girls finished all the washing, supper was cooking over the cabin fire and all that was left for Sarah was to pack up her few belongings and be ready to leave at first light.

"There can't be much to take," Hagar sat on the cool dirt floor, leaning into the frame of the cabin door. Her tightly braided hair hung in two tails down each side of her head. She stretched her bare feet out. "I mean, sounds like all you goin' be doin' is workin' and slavin' up there for your aunt. Sounds like us, like you goin' to be belongin' to your Aunt Charity. Three chil'rens and a baby on the way. Best carry you some work clothes is all I gots to say." The tall, leggy girl scratched her chin thoughtfully, dark brown eyes shining with mischief. "You goin' be glad to be coming back to ol' Port Royal when the time comes. You think yo' pappy is hard work? Lawd. You ain't seen nothing yet."

Sarah, who had flopped into one of the two slat-backed chairs, grimaced, her green eyes flashing. "I am no stranger to hard work and leaving father is no hardship," she lied, wanting to believe it. "Who knows? Perhaps I shall never return. Perhaps I shall find a man in Logan County that will honor me, and I shall marry him." She defiantly cocked her head, daring Sally or Hagar to contradict her. Neither attempted. Instead, Sally stood and stretched, surveying the compact cabin and its occupant.

"What's this?" Sally leaned toward Sarah, reaching for her neckline. In the effort and bustle of the day, an etched silver locket had slipped from the folds between Sarah's apron and dress, where it hung now. It glistened in the dim cabin light, catching the sun's rays streaming through the door. Sarah's hand jerked toward the locket, quickly sliding it back under her dress where it nestled against her skin.

"Nothing," she retorted quickly.

"Was too somethin'," Sally snorted. "A mighty pretty somethin' too, I might add. Let us see it. We'll keep it secret, if that's what you want."

Sarah hesitated. Until now, no one in Port Royal had seen it. Even her father had no idea she wore the locket, much less possessed it. It was a secret between Grandma McMillan and her, and that's how she wanted it to stay. Revealing the truth of the locket, and the honest emotion of her heart felt so … personal. It was too much. "Perhaps later. I need to set the table for Father, and you two best get on home before he comes back. He wouldn't like finding you still here."

The thought of Matthew McMillan not being happy was enough to deter Sally from her quest. She nodded briskly, touching Hagar on the sleeve. "Let's go, honey chile. Time's a wastin'."

Sarah watched them trail down the path, the soft tread of their barefeet fading into the forest. As her fingers mindlessly moved over the locket, her brow was furrowed in deep thought.

The dream began simply. Sarah stood on the banks of the Red River, staring quietly upstream, watching and waiting for something. She stood alone. Port Royal stretched out behind her, the sounds of wagons rolling, voices, calls, muted in her mind. High in the sky hung a bright sun, illuminating the dried up riverbed with slashes of light, and its reflection catching lingering puddles. There was no muddy cascade of water running down. Instead, where the river should have been were patches of dry, pallid death. Dead fish littered the river bottom; she spotted one close by her feet, its lifeless eyes were open, staring back into hers.

She felt the heat of the day and smelled the odor of rotten fish and rancid mud. Suddenly, she heard a trickle of water, as though a rain barrel had reached its peak and the water was slowly dribbling over. The sound grew and the trickle broadened into a steady stream. Sarah watched a tiny rivulet of water running toward her from the east. The watering turned into a steady flow, then to a rushing, then to a powerful flooding. Within seconds, the narrow channel of water had transformed into a mighty, swelling tide, pouring, rolling, thundering down the riverbed. In its path lay the tiny town of Port Royal – and Sarah. She screamed as she watched the wave stretch high above her head, blocking out the sun – and suddenly awoke, her hair drenched in sweat and her bedclothes twisted around her body.

It was pitch dark in the cabin, the sounds of her father's snoring not missing a beat. She lay still, panting, trying to catch her breath, trying to discern the time. Dawn felt hours away, so she lay back and closed her eyes. It wouldn't be long before she would leave to meet the Nevilles at the warehouse. She willed herself to sleep again.

Chapter Three

Sarah left the cabin in the dark, carrying a saddlebag filled with the barest of essentials; one extra gown, two petticoats, two pairs of stockings, two aprons, one shift – and the locket. It never left the secure place around her neck. The photo inside had become her salvation, her charm against all manners of evil, including her father. She had left him managing the fire, tamping it down to safe embers until Hagar would arrive later to prepare his meals.

"Goodbye, Father." Sarah had stood at the doorway, her earnest, square jaw set tight against emotion. She hefted the saddlebag to her shoulder, one side hanging down the front of her dress, the other swinging to and fro behind her.

"Obey your Aunt Charity and don't be a bother. Be sure to earn your keep," his voice reached around his turned back.

Sarah hesitated, waiting for words she knew would never come. "Yes, Father." Matthew McMillan's broad back remained firmly set in her view as the silence magnified in the room. Sarah's thoughts were so loud she was surprised they didn't voice themselves without her permission. It crossed her mind to say them all, to unleash all those years of pent-up questions, anger, pain, rejection. Instead, she turned silently toward the dark pathway, illuminated by a rapidly dropping moon, and began the trek into Port Royal settlement.

It didn't take long for the light of the rising sun to reveal the well-worn wagon trail leading into town. Sarah passed by towering tulip poplars, broad oaks and massive cedar trees, each housing its own set of song-singing birds. A red-headed woodpecker beat incessantly against the bark of an elm, blue jays dashed in front of her, chasing any sort of smaller bird they could find. The woods were alive, and remarkably, so was Sarah's heart. She wouldn't have said she wanted to leave her father, quite the opposite even though her life was lonely and empty. It was a life she understood and had become accustomed to.

Yet she found her heart beat expectantly at this new adventure. Fear, determination, weakness, strength – she felt them all this morning – intermingled with … hope. A new emotion. A new concept. She wasn't even sure what she was hoping for, but there it was. Hope. Her feet stepped quickly and lively as she reached the town, carving a direct route to Wilcox's warehouse and the edge of the Red River where the Neville family waited.

John Neville, proprietor of Port Royal's cobbler shop, smiled broadly as Sarah came into view. He led a tangled, confused party of travelers gathering at the river's edge that morning. A small, uncovered wagon sat to the side, two mules already yoked, a few barrels and bags stacked haphazardly on the ground. Waving her on enthusiastically, Neville turned back toward his wife to argue about loading.

Sarah knew of the Nevilles, of course. Mrs. Neville was a proper lady; Sarah had seen her walking in Public Square several times, looking over local produce and bargaining with storekeepers. Her fancy mop caps and hats reminded Sarah of the Spartanburg ladies with their store-bought goods. They had two daughters; Esther, the rowdy one, and Ann, who seemed a bit frail. Ann looked to be close to Sarah's age, while Esther had to be a few years younger. This morning, both girls sat quietly to the side as their parents argued, but it was a light-natured argument. Sarah could see that at once. An oddity to her mind, but interesting. She lay the saddlebag down on the ground and waited for instruction.

It promised to be a warm, clear spring day with the Red River running a bit high, but slowly. Sarah saw no debris in the few minutes that she watched the flow move from east to west. Directly below the wagon, the Port Royal ferry was anchored to a small dock while Mr. Anderson tinkered with the thick, corded rope that stretched across the river. He and Neville would use it to set the course and pull the mules, the wagon, the Nevilles, Sarah, and all their goods across the water. The opposite bank taunted Sarah with its accessibility — it was only about thirty yards away — but she knew the depth of the river was deceptive. Ferrying across was their only option.

Mr. Neville approached. "Is this all you have?" he pointed toward

Sarah's lone saddlebag.

"Yes, sir."

"Maybe I should have you teach Mrs. Neville how to pack her bags," he said with a laugh. "Rachel? You need to study packing from Miss McMillan here," he shouted, the timbre of his voice slicing through the peace of the morning. Rachel Neville glanced up from her task, saw Sarah standing there, and immediately came over. Her vivid blue cap matched the fabric of her gown and added even more color to her startling cornflower blue eyes. She appeared genuinely pleased to see Sarah.

"Welcome, my dear! I do hope you were warned about traveling with the Nevilles. We are a lively bunch." She glanced toward her girls with a flash of a smile. "Well, Mr. Neville and I are lively. Girls?" she raised her voice, waving her hand toward Sarah. "Come over and meet Miss McMillan. I don't believe the three of you have had an opportunity to get to know one other."

Dutifully, both girls rose and walked toward them. Sarah had heard stories from Sammy and Hagar about most everyone who lived in Port Royal. Because Sarah's ventures into town were rare – and she had only been here two months – she hadn't seen many of the people the children described in great detail. Nevertheless, she held a sort of list in her head describing many things she'd never laid eyes on. The Neville girls had a fairly large entry.

Ann looked frail because, indeed, she was. According to Hagar, Mrs. Neville often missed monthly church meetings because Ann was ill and didn't have enough energy to make the trip. Her skin was translucent yet strangely beautiful. In her eyes, Sarah saw kindness and the gentleness of her mother. She was nowhere near as tall as Sarah, but Ann stood with confidence and a subdued strength. Sarah had the feeling her strength lay more in character than in body. "How do you do?" Ann curtsied lightly.

"Hello," Sarah responded with a nod. Esther was the polar opposite of her sister, the children had declared. "She looks all sweet and nice when she's around her papa," Hagar had stated one day when the three of them glimpsed the Nevilles from a distance, "but that Esther is a rascal!"

"Yeah," Sammy chimed in. "She let a toad frog go on the bench at church one Sunday right during the preachin'. Nobody knew where it come from, but I did. I saw her do it! Some of the ladies had a real fit, and Reverend Fort made all sorts of threats about the boy that might'a done it. It weren't no boy."

Today Esther didn't look so eager to set frogs loose anywhere. Her brown eyes blended with her lightly tanned skin, very different from Ann, and she looked as healthy as a horse, yet tired and perhaps grumpy.

Sarah was thankful to see that neither girl wore a fine gown. The material was good, of course, but Sarah had been afraid that she would seem poor and destitute in the same traveling party. If one inspected closely, he would see that the girls' gowns – and Mrs. Neville's – were of higher quality; but, on the surface, Sarah's plain gown was at least comparable.

"Boarding the wagon!" called Mr. Anderson in warning. The girls stepped back several paces while Neville took one last look at the loaded wagon, tugged on the mules' harnesses again, and then led them gently onto the ferry. The wagon and mules would cross first, and then Mr. Anderson would ferry back over to pick up the passengers.

Sarah watched with keen interest as the weight of the load pushed the logs halfway into the river. The raft had been constructed by thick logs lashed together with rope. It was large enough to hold the mule team and wagon – along with Mr. Neville and Mr. Anderson – but it certainly wouldn't have held more. As the load inched its way across the river, Ann spoke, her voice light and soothing. "Have you ever ridden a ferry, Miss McMillan?"

"My father and I rode several on the way to Port Royal from Carolina. I liked it," Sarah offered. Ann smiled.

"Mama is always afraid I will fall into the water and be swept away forever." Esther giggled at this. Mrs. Neville stood a few feet to the side, watching the progress and not paying attention to the girls. "I suppose she thinks I would not be strong enough to swim to the shore, but I have always loved ferrying. In fact, sometimes I wish the rope would break, and we could just float down the river and find out what lies around the next corner."

Sarah looked over at Ann with surprise. She wouldn't have labeled her the adventuring sort, but appearances can deceive. "Not me," declared ten-year-old Esther sternly. "I don't like water, and I'll have nothing to do with it!"

"Not even baths, right Esther?" Ann joked. Esther snorted in response and moved toward her mother to have a better view of the raft anchoring on the opposite shore. Neville gently led the mule team onto dry land, the wagon laboring behind him. "I am awfully glad you are coming with us," Ann said quietly. "It is not often I get the chance to talk with a girl my own age." Sarah stared at Ann in amazement. Of all the young girls in Port Royal, why would Ann Neville want to talk with her? She remained silent. "Mama is so protective of me that it is hard sometimes to meet anyone. If I'm having a good day, like today, she still wants me to stay close to home – or even better – inside the house so I will not pick up an ailment that might be floating around." Ann laughed ruefully. "I suppose I get lonely, but I understand you are in town some, Miss McMillan, shopping or visiting the warehouse. Do you find Port Royal to your liking?"

"Sarah, please call me Sarah. And Port Royal seems nice, although I do not get into town that much. I have a lot to do on our farm and with the cabin. But that is fine. I like being alone," Sarah rushed her words, perhaps a bit too quickly. Ann's quick eyes, mirror-images of her mother's, glanced at Sarah in understanding. Mr. Anderson was moving back across the river with the empty raft to pick up the four ladies while Neville pulled the wagon and mules up the far bank toward the road.

"All aboard, ladies," Mr. Anderson called as he pulled closer to their bank's edge. "The day won't wait for nobody." It wasn't until Sarah stepped onto the raft that she realized she wouldn't have to ride a pack horse at all. It appeared that all of them would be on the wagon, setting their path toward Kentucky and Logan County.

It didn't take long for Sarah to hear why the Nevilles were going up to Logan County, how long they would be there, what they all thought about it, how they might travel back. In fact, Sarah likened them in her mind to a mess of chattering squirrels, but it wasn't unpleasant. The trip reminded her of times in Carolina with cousins and the fun they would have at gatherings. It had been a long time since Sarah had felt a part of a group, but this day she did. It created a warmth and peace in her heart that showed itself in the ease in which she laughed and practically reveled in their conversation. She was a sponge, soaking every moment.

They had ridden directly north, up the trace towards Renfro's pond as they left the Red River. Although the sun shone brightly, it wasn't high yet; and Sarah knew they would have a full days' journey to reach their destination. She wished she could be sure that someone would be meeting her there, but her father's response to Aunt Charity may not have reached her by now. He had sent it immediately after receiving the letter, but Sarah didn't trust the stranger riding through town to deliver it. It was quite possible she was riding into a place unannounced and unexpected, albeit hoped for. She tried not to dwell on it.

As the party approached the midpoint of the trace, Neville swung his mules – Jack and Jill – toward the east on Keysburg Trail, and they began toward Logan County in earnest. He hoped to reach the town of Keysburg by early afternoon, if the wagon trail was completely passable. Port Royal had seen a mighty spring storm come through about three weeks earlier, and Neville said there may still be trees down along the way.

"I am quite excited to see Lettice," Mrs. Neville declared, swinging around on the wagon seat to view Sarah more clearly. Their bodies swayed back and forth in rhythm as Jack and Jill plodded along. "Lettice is my first cousin on my mother's side, Sarah. She and her husband live near Russellville and have invited us up for a week. We never get to really visit, so I am thrilled."

"They're good Presbyterians," Mr. Neville inserted. "Got something going on with their church up there, and Lettice has been practically swept up in it. She insists we make it up by tonight so we can be rested and ready for Friday's meeting. She knows we're good Baptists, not Presbyterian, but she says her Reverend McGready doesn't pay any mind to such things. All are welcome."

"And so we must be welcomed, too," Mrs. Neville jumped back into the conversation. "There is nothing more fun than a good church meeting. Would you not agree, Sarah?"

Sarah had been watching the land move by slowly as she listened. The forest was thick here with huge-trunked poplars, their blooms decorating the forest floor with muted yellow and orange petals. Weaving through the midst of them were acres of brambles and saplings. She didn't want to appear rude but neither did she agree. She thought for a moment.

"I suppose so. We did not attend many meetings in Carolina, and Father and I have not had much time to since we arrived in Port Royal," she answered slowly. Mrs. Neville's radiant smile revealed nothing as she glanced at Sarah again, and for a time, they rode along in silence hearing only the sound of mule hooves clopping on packed ground. But that was only for a time. Suddenly, and without warning, Mr. Neville's solid baritone voice boomed out:

"On the Lass of Richmond Hill hill there lives a lass
More bright than May-day morn
Whose charms all other maids' surpass
A rose without a thorn.
This lass so neat, with smiles so sweet
Has won my right good will
I'd crown resign to call thee mine
Sweet lass of The Lass of Richmond Hill hill."

His gaity begged the others to sing along. Apparently, the Neville girls were used to such behavior because all joined in immediately with enthusiasm. Sarah wasn't sure what to make of it but found the singing became contagious, and mile after mile was completed to the rhythm of song. Every once in a while, the party met up with someone else traveling, usually a lone man on mule or horseback; and, with caution, Neville always pulled up the reins to stop and converse a few minutes. Sarah was thankful for the breaks for it gave her time to stretch her legs and feel like a human being again.

The settlement of Keysburg sat on the northern edge of the Red River, bigger and busier than Port Royal; otherwise, Sarah would have said it was a mirror image of the town, only higher upstream. Business bustled near the river and also in the market square as the Neville wagon labored through. They had eaten a full lunch in the wagon, their only real stop since Port Royal had been to water the mules at a creek crossing. Mr. Neville said if they wanted to make it by the end of the day, they had no time to dawdle.

Since leaving home, Sarah had learned that Ann was a surprising mystery of a girl, and she liked her very much. She and Ann had settled in the bed of the wagon, farther back than Esther, who nestled up closer to her parents sitting on the seat. In fact, Esther had somehow slept much of the way, giving Ann and Sarah a chance to get to know one another. Although their backgrounds were completely different, it didn't seem to matter. Sarah's hands were rough and calloused; Ann's were smooth and fragile. Sarah's curly hair, which always escaped her bonnet, flew about wildly today, blowing strands across her mouth as they talked. Ann's blonde hair hung long and straight down her back, neatly woven in one thick braid. The girls appeared to be polar opposites in every way, yet they had found a quick kinship during the journey.

"Matthew said he wrote directions from what the letter carrier told him about Logan County, Sarah," Neville called as they moved out of Keysburg. "What kind of directions does it have?"

Sarah reached into her pocket tied under her apron and pulled out the wrinkled note. "He wrote that Aunt Charity's house is down past Mortimer Trace in the Red River settlement. Father said once we get to Mortimer Station, you can drop me there, and I can ask around for the road the McPhersons live on. He said it should take only a mile of walking to reach the farm, and my saddlebags are not heavy."

"Did he note any landmarks?" Neville continued.

"Only the Red River Meeting House. He said if we see it by the river, we have traveled too far."

"Red River Meeting House, eh? That'll do. In fact, I do believe, Rachel, that's where that McGready fellow is preaching tomorrow. Lettice's place is on farther toward the east, but you never know…" Neville threw his voice back to Sarah again, "…we might just see you at the meeting, if your Aunt Charity is one of McGready's disciples too. 'Course, she's bed bound, but with all those young'uns, you might be having to bring them on. We can sure hope so, can't we, Rachel?"

Mrs. Neville didn't respond immediately; she seemed preoccupied by her thoughts. Finally, she answered quietly. "You know, George, I'm not taking to the idea of just dropping Sarah by Mortimer Station. I know it has a fairly good reputation among our kinfolk, but this area continues to be quite unruly, and just leaving a fourteen-year-old girl there…"

Sarah listened intently, ears straining to hear the subdued conversation over the creaking of leather and wood.

"Yes, dear, I see what you mean," Neville replied thoughtfully.

"Surely Matthew didn't think that prospect through when he told Sarah to tell us to drop her off."

Surely, he did, thought Sarah ruefully, but she kept her mouth shut.

"What do you propose?"

Mrs. Neville chewed her bottom lip as the wagon dipped over a rut in the road. "Let's go ahead and stop in Mortimer Station and ask around for the McPherson house, but not leave Sarah alone. We can either take her directly to the house, depending on the time, or we can take her on with us to Lettice's place and get Sarah over tomorrow when there is more daylight and more time to get the lay of the land."

"Excellent proposition, Mrs. Neville," the jovial wagoneer responded.

Sarah could only hope there would be no one available in Mortimer Station to be of help to them this evening. One more day with the Nevilles would be pure joy to her thirsty soul, not to mention the prospect of prolonging her agony of the unknown with Aunt Charity. She was willing to wait another twenty-four hours to see what fruit would grow from that tree.

Approaching dusk had cleared out the workers at the mill as the Neville group rode into the station late that afternoon. More traffic was leaving the area than coming in, but Neville continued forward, his wife and the girls beginning to sag in weariness. Ann had fallen asleep long ago, curled against Sarah in the back; and while Esther was now wide awake, she hadn't been nearly as talkative or rambunctious as Sammy and Hagar had said she would. Sarah felt tired in her bones but was far too anxious to sleep.

Beside the mill, a lone wagon stood empty while a young man fed a mule, his hand holding a small heap of corn kernels. He was scratching it behind its ears affectionately as the Neville wagon approached.

"Evenin'," Neville called from his seat.

"Evenin'."

"Wondered if you know anything about where a Obediah and Charity McPherson might live?" Neville drew the reins in tightly, allowing Jack and Jill a chance to stop and rest their weary legs.

"Sure do. Mr. Obediah lives about a quarter of a mile as the crow flies from my pap's house. Right there — down Mill Road." Neville looked in the direction the young man pointed, seeing a narrow wagon trail veering off to the left of the main road through the station.

"Is it a far piece from here?" Neville asked.

"I wouldn't say so. Maybe about a mile or a bit. Mind if I ask you why you are wanting to know?"

"Miss McMillan here is Mrs. McPherson's niece, come to lend her a hand in her time of need. We wanted to make sure she reached the McPherson home safely."

The young man lifted his head in interest then. His curious gaze swept the back of the wagon, glancing over Esther, who would be far too young to be a great help; Ann, who still lay sleeping against Sarah's shoulder; and Sarah, chin lifted slightly, eyes daring him to make any sort of remark about her person. One side of his mouth lifted in amusement at her expression, and his eyes traveled back to Neville.

"Looks like you still got a ways to go, and I am heading right down Mill Road. I will be glad to escort Miss McMillan to her aunt's house. It is right on my way."

Sarah hoped Mr. Neville would surely not allow such a thing; she didn't like the looks of this haughty boy. She didn't figure he was more than seventeen, yet in his eyes, he treated her as though she were a child. "Why, I'd be much obliged for it," Neville replied, crushing Sarah's hopes. "You must have been sent by the Good Lord Himself. Miss Sarah," he said, spinning around in his seat, "why don't you wake Ann up and hop on out with your bag? This young gentleman will see to it that you reach your aunt safely tonight."

Doing as she was told, Sarah gently shook Ann, who woke long enough to sigh deeply and shift her head onto the coverlet Sarah moved under her neck. She was back asleep before Sarah disembarked with her bag, her long blonde braid draped across her shoulder. Sarah had hoped for a chance to say goodbye.

"Thank you for driving me this far, Mr. Neville," she said, handing her saddlebag to the young man who came over to assist her.

"Our pleasure, Miss McMillan. We surely hope and expect to see you at the Red River Meeting House this weekend. It seems to be the source of excitement in this area. Hopefully, your Aunt Charity will agree,"

Neville replied as he started the mules on down the road.

"Yes, dear. Do keep in touch. I do believe our Ann has made a friend," Mrs. Neville called over her shoulder. Sarah watched the wagon ease away and felt a tug. She'd rather not like the Nevilles; it was easier that way. But her heart wouldn't allow that – it had been softened by them.

"By the way, my name's Daniel. Don't worry. I will get you to the McPhersons' farm before you know it," the young man eased Sarah's saddlebag into the bed of his empty wagon and came around the side to help her up into the seat next to him. As she felt her heart lurch, watching the Nevilles go around the bend, her tongue loosened.

"I am not worried," she snapped. "I just want to get there."

Daniel's dark eyes opened in surprise at Sarah's tone, noting the lines of creased dirt on her face and the fatigue in her eyes. "Been a long day?" he asked kindly.

"You could say that," and Sarah sat tall, staring straight ahead. It was true. She just wanted to be there now, to get this over with. Her ideas of excitement and adventure from early this morning had faded. It was as if the Nevilles drove off carrying her hope, and all that lay ahead appeared dark and unknown.

Chapter Four

Logan County, Kentucky
(Rogues' Harbor)

Reverend James McGready sat in stillness upon his horse, surveying the Red River Meeting House from the head of the lane. Behind him the river ran lazily around tight bends making its way west toward the Cumberland River. The meeting house certainly wasn't an imposing structure, nor pretty, for that matter. But useful? Absolutely. McGready had learned that usefulness to God didn't equate with beauty – in fact, it often was quite the opposite. He gently kicked his sorrel mare, easing farther into the deserted clearing. As he tied her off on the hitching post, McGready's countenance grew focused and determined. He began walking toward the back of the meeting house, then turned left at the corner seeing the open clearing behind the structure, then turned again, completing a full circle. Rather than stopping, McGready continued walking, circling the building again and again. His voice rose full and strong against the breeze that blew on this warm May morning.

"Father God, Most Holy, Most Majestic God. And our Savior, the Lord Jesus Christ, I come to You this morning in humility and unworthiness, knowing that my request comes from tainted lips and a tainted heart. You alone are good. I, most certainly, am not. And yet, I come with boldness before the throne of grace, beseeching You for Your presence to descend upon this place tonight, to come and pour out Your spirit on Your people, to bring sinners to salvation and the complacent to action for Your Kingdom," McGready's voice boomed in power, seeming to rattle the new sassafras leaves that hung on trees behind the meeting house. "As the Psalmist said, Oh God, we cry out for You. We desperately need and desire Your presence…"

The sound of a wagon rattling down the lane broke the singleness of

McGready's voice in the forest, but McGready didn't miss a beat in his petitions. A lone mule-drawn wagon pulled up beside the mare; William Hodge positioned the brake and waited. He bowed his head. He'd been in this situation before.

"...and if You don't come and bring salvation to Your people, to this people of this county of this new state and nation, we are surely lost. Lost forever. Oh God, bring revival to us. Strike the hearts of men, women and children. Let Your presence be seen in this place. Bring lost sinners here tonight. Pull them from every tavern, roadside and drinking station in Logan County. Bring the thieves, the rowdies, bring them all and pour out Your power of conviction and holiness on them. Come, Lord Jesus, come." McGready's powerful voice broke as he rounded the last corner of the meeting house and his prayer grew quieter. Upon seeing the wagon, the tall preacher paused, focused, then approached.

"Good morning, Brother Hodge. I decided to begin without you," McGready's solemn expression disappeared as he addressed his old friend and colleague.

"Ah James, the day may be young, but alas, I am not," William Hodge laughed ruefully as he eased down from his wagon seat. Fastened in the bed of the wagon were several tools – a scythe, shovels, rakes, hammers and nails. "While you prepare the house for the Lord to arrive, He told me to prepare the grounds for the people to arrive." Hodge pointed to the wagon bed. "If we don't get this area cleared, every man, woman and child could run up on a serpent; and that surely wouldn't aid the Lord in His work."

McGready's dark eyebrows lifted in amusement. William Hodge was one of several of McGready's apprentices who made the trip to the western wilderness after McGready got the call from God to leave Orange County. All of them – Hodge, John Rankin, William McGee and his brother John McGee – agreed that North Carolina already had the spark of revival lit. Ministers were crowding into that area, bringing the true word of God. When McGready read the letters of former Carolinians who had moved out west and saw they desperately needed ministers of the Gospel, he didn't hesitate to respond. It had been several years since the war with England had drawn to a close, and word had traveled to the Carolinas about fertile soil and clear streams. Lands toward the west. It remained, in part, a vast, untamed region beset with darkness and uncertainty. Indian attacks upon the isolated stations had been frequent and brutal. However, a new day was dawning among the scattered settlements, and McGready felt the push to be a part of the light coming from the east.

Back in the Carolinas, he had been accused of "running away" from those in Orange County who had threatened his work and his very life; but, in fact, McGready had continued to minister at Haw River and Stony Creek for two more years after the 1793 pulpit burning. And he'd preached on the coming judgment and repentance! No. No one who knew McGready would ever say he ran away. He simply followed a call.

"You finished preparing your message for the communion meetings?" Hodge continued, tugging the scythe out from among the other tools.

McGready leaned against the back of the wagon, thankful to God for Hodge's persistent service. Although Hodge was a minister in the Tennessee region of Shiloh, he had agreed to assist McGready as needed and had recently journeyed to Logan County. "Finished last night," he responded. "I feel the Lord would have me focus on the 'Divine Authority of the Christian Religion.' We will see what He does. Did you happen to attend the prayer society last Saturday?" McGready asked, changing the subject.

"Yes, I did. We held it at Sister McPherson's home since she's now bedridden till the baby comes. Most of the signers of the covenant were there. And of course, all had fasted and prayed throughout the day, as agreed," Hodge glanced at the sky, anxious to begin work as he felt the heat slowly rising even in the shade. With a quiet sigh, he resigned himself to laboring in the hottest part of the day. McGready was oblivious.

"Yes. And was there a presence of the Lord there?"

"Most certainly, as always," Hodge nodded, then stated more forcefully. "When do you think it shall fall upon us, James? We all have been fasting and praying for revival for the souls of Logan County well nigh onto two year now, and with the exception of those few souls touched at Gasper River, we've not seen the Lord move. I have to tell you, some of the ladies are getting a bit frustrated. Oh, they keep on praying, but when will the Lord move?" Hodge's normally easy-going demeanor had shifted to frustration, his voice rising concurrently. It was plain to see his method of preaching. He was almost there.

"Patience, William. God hears. He knows. Sometimes I think He simply wants to see how serious we are, how much we long for the things He longs for. We continue the path we are walking, stepping in the light of His direction, and He will come. He has said it, and I believe it," McGready stated firmly, then laughed. "Come to think of it, He probably does not care whether I believe it. He promised to come when His people pray. So He will come."

Hodge knew all this, had preached it himself from the Shiloh pulpit, while McGready delivered the message from the Muddy River pulpit and here at Red River. In fact, McGready oversaw three Presbyterian meeting houses, and as a co-laborer with him, Hodge would be expected to preach in each location – if need be. Strategically, it seemed, those three congregations were spread to separate corners of Logan County. Red River fell to the southern border, Gasper was over toward the east and Muddy River sat north of Russellville. McGready often made note of this, saying that God had positioned the locations for revival so when the Lord began to truly move in Rogues' Harbor, He would squeeze sin and debauchery from the outside in, until it was crushed.

"Yes, my spirit knows it, but my mind of flesh fights against the spirit of God within me," Hodge admitted with a sigh. "Were it not for the faithfulness of those who covenanted to fast and pray once a month …"

"Indeed," McGready interrupted. "By their sacrifice and determination, they will usher in the presence of God. Of that I have no doubt. And how did you find Sister McPherson on the Saturday last? Is she managing without Brother Obediah?"

"Barely," Hodges slapped a mosquito that had lit on his arm. "She has written to her brother-in-law recently moved to Port Royal, west of here. Apparently, he has a daughter who may be of age to come and help her cope until Brother Obediah returns. She has yet to hear back but is hopeful and praying about it daily."

"And God will most assuredly hear her prayers," McGready stated. "In the meantime, make sure someone checks in on Sister McPherson once a day."

"Consider it taken care of. One other thing," Hodge tossed out as McGready turned to resume his circular path of prayer, "the Wilson brothers have been talking in town again about coming out tonight and stirring up trouble. Ever since Sister Wilson saw the light of Christ at Gasper River, her brothers and husband have given her no rest. She's been a saint through it all, but they are making life difficult for her. Charles is mighty addicted to strong drink, and word is that he gets meaner the more he drinks. If he goes on a bender tonight, he just might show up here."

McGready's eyebrows rose a fraction as he pondered Hodge's words. "Tell the others to come prepared, perhaps come a little before dusk, to oversee the roads and entryways. Be mindful during the meeting to be positioned – two near the front, two near the back. Possibly, we can grab a few other men to keep watch in the yard while the service is going. Be vigilant, William, the devil, our adversary, prowls about like a roaring lion, seeking whom he can devour." Not waiting for a response, Mc-Gready spun on his heel and began praying before his foot set down another pace, beseeching the Lord of the harvest to come and gather more into His Kingdom.

Sarah woke slowly, sensing someone watching her. Just as the light penetrated into her consciousness, she found two staring eyes situated on a tiny, heart-shaped face, resting only six inches away. She jerked back and gasped.

"Sorry, Cousin Sarah," the tiny, thin voice said. "I surely did not mean to scare you, but do you not think it is time to get up? Dolly has been waiting for you to wake up for ever so long." At that, Millie McPherson shoved a homely cornshuck doll into Sarah's face, making Sarah blink in surprise. She flopped her head back down and groaned. It had been a long time since she had ridden in a wagon all day, and today she felt every jolt from yesterday's journey. The sun peeked through the floor-boards of the loft in which Sarah and two of the McPherson children slept, and she knew that, indeed, she should be up. She looked to her left. Matilda was already downstairs, and Sarah could hear the baby, Josiah, cooing and gurgling.

"Yes," Sarah turned back toward Millie. "I should be up and so should you and Dolly. Why don't you come with me, and we can get breakfast going?"

"Oh, Mattie already did that. Didn't you hear her banging the pots? I think we should play first, then go down later," Millie danced the doll on top of the quilt. Sarah laughed.

"We'll play later, cousin."

"Promise?" the simple, serious girl questioned.

"Promise."

Because Daniel had dropped Sarah off after dark the night before – with not much spoken between them except a brief thanks and goodbye – Sarah had not had much time to take in her surroundings. Aunt Charity had greeted her with great kindness and vast relief, proclaimed over and over how much she looked like Matilda; and then she had little Matilda – or Mattie as she was called – spoon up a plate of stew, and promptly sent Sarah to bed in the loft. All this was accomplished from Aunt Charity's bedroom which was located on the other side of the fireplace. Apparently, she ran a tight ship, even without the advantage of moving about, Sarah considered as she dressed.

She had slept remarkably well considering Millie's two feet stuck in her back all night long, and Mattie snored. In the past twenty-four hours, Sarah had been around so many people that she found herself feeling overwhelmed and a bit disoriented. It would take her a while to re-acclimate to relating to people. She stumbled on the last step of the wooden ladder, catching herself before falling.

"Good morning, Cousin Sarah," seven-year-old Mattie greeted her from the table. She was eating a large bowl of corn mush, the steam rising high into the room.

"Yes, dear. Good day to you," called Aunt Charity from the bedroom. "Come see me and tell me how you are feeling this morning. Did Millie kick you all night?" Sarah rounded the corner to find her Aunt Charity propped up in bed, a vast array of linens and clothes arranged all over the room. She stopped short to keep from stepping on a pair of trousers stretched along the floor. Aunt Charity laughed, a sound like joyful, tinkling glass. "Do not mind all this, Sarah. What else is a woman to do who can do nothing? I sew. I hem. I repair. I embroider. I expect I will have half of Logan County clothed by the time this baby is born," she laughed again, moving aside a sock and patting the side of the bed. "Come sit here a bit while Mattie gets your mush up. Tell me all about your trip. Was it eventful?"

"I suppose so. It was not as strenuous as coming across the mountains."

"Ah yes, well, that was no trip to me. It was a journey, an expedition of sorts. There is no telling how many poor women have been dragged out to the frontier because of our adventuring menfolk," she carefully placed her needlework to the side. "Tell me. How is your father?"

Sarah knew these questions were coming, but she had hoped to have some breakfast in her stomach before she had to answer them. She already felt a bit queasy. "About the same as when you left him, I would imagine," her laugh was like a short, hiccup of a sound. Charity simply smiled and waited. Sarah heard the children in the other room, talking and moving around. She suddenly wished she were with them. She tried again. "He is … healthy, works in town making barrels and such, seems to like Port Royal …" Her voice trailed off as Charity decided to have mercy on her.

"Yes. I see," she sighed and shifted slowly in her bed. "Well … you have much to learn today and I do not need to keep you from your morning meal. Mattie will be your primary instructor," Charity said with a smile, "which she will simply adore. Makes her feel quite special, you know, to be teaching her much older cousin things. But I must say, Mattie has been my salvation – other than the Lord Jesus, of course." Her eyes shone brightly, her face radiating a soft, peaceful joy. "But, yes, Mattie has carried a heavy load, and it is becoming far too much for a child. So, Sarah," Charity gently put her fingers under Sarah's square chin, turning her eyes to look directly into hers, "having you here is truly the sign of Providence. May God bless you for your willingness to help, and may He bless Matthew as well."

Sarah held her tongue.

"Mama," Mattie called from the other room, "Sarah's food is ready."

"And so it begins," laughed Charity. "Go, enjoy your breakfast and entertain the children. I hear Josiah toddling in there. Tell Millie to go ahead and bring her brother here while you girls eat. Mattie will then begin showing you around, and you will quickly see all that needs to be done. You came in the nick of time, Sarah."

As she left her aunt's bedroom, Sarah felt an odd shifting. It was nothing she could see, but it was as though a weight settled over her – of responsibility, of being needed and trusted, of being treated as an adult, of being appreciated. Surely it was a solemn thing, but at the same time, was a welcomed thing. Sarah walked taller as she entered the main section of the house and was greeted by a wooden bowl filled with steaming mush.

Life on the McPherson farm was busy that day. Sarah found a few acres of corn and close to one acre of wheat in fairly good shape. The corn needed to be tended to within the week, but for now, with the rains they had been receiving, the growth was on track. Affairs in the house weren't quite as good. While the McPhersons had the blessing of a milking cow, her milk appeared to be drying up – when she had calved only a month ago. Sarah was no animal doctor, and she knew it; but, she had a few tricks up her sleeve and would see what adding river cane leaves might do for the cow's milk production.

Thankfully, the children were a joy. Josiah, full of red hair and a temper to match, trailed the girls all morning as they went from location to location, his fat legs struggling to keep up. Millie and Mattie kept a running dialogue of important issues – "We're down to only a few cups of cornmeal in the house. Mama says she'll ask God to fill our stores, but we think we just need to go to the store." – to less urgent situations – "Our cat Billy got real fat, real, real, fat, and then he just ran off. We're afraid a panther might'a got him. We haven't seen him in days."

It was an exhausted Sarah that collapsed at the table after supper dishes had been cleaned and cleared away. Although she had found enough food in their storage shed to be creative with, she knew a trip to town – or someone delivering some goods – was essential in the next few days. Before she walked into the bedroom to tell Aunt Charity, she kicked the logs on the fire to knock down the heat a bit, and moved closer – just for the comfort of it. Propped up on the mantle was a formal-looking document, lying sideways but in easy reach. Her curiosity aroused, she grabbed it and flattened it out. She read its flowing script:

The Covenant

"When we consider the word and promises of a compassionate God to the poor lost family of Adam, we find the strongest encouragement for Christians to pray in faith – to ask in the name of Jesus for the conversion of their fellow-men. None ever went to Christ when on earth, with the case of their friends that were denied, and, although the days of his humiliation are ended, yet, for the encouragement of his people, he has left it on record, that where two or three agree upon earth to ask in prayer, believing, it shall be done. Again, whatsoever you shall ask the Father in my name, that will I do, that the Father may be glorified in the Son. With these promises before us, we feel encouraged to unite our supplications to a prayer-hearing God for the outpouring of his Spirit, that his people may be quickened and comforted, and that our children, and sinners generally, may be converted. Therefore, we bind ourselves to observe the third Saturday of each month, for one year, as a day of fasting and prayer for the conversion of sinners in Logan county, and throughout the world. We also engage to spend one half hour every Saturday evening, beginning at the setting of the sun, and one half hour every Sabbath morning, from the rising of the sun, pleading with God to revive his work."

Several names were scrawled across the bottom, in signatures as ornate as ever Sarah had seen, to one or two simple "Xs". Positioned halfway down were the names, Obediah and Charity McPherson. Sarah thoughtfully placed the paper back on the mantle as Charity called from her room. She left the girls at the table working on replacing Dolly's dress and went back to report in on her day's findings.

Chapter Five

About two miles down the narrow lane, a steady stream of mule-drawn wagons and lone men on horseback began crowding down the worn path toward the Red River Meeting House. As was the custom in a Scots summer communion, McGready had put out the word that the meeting house would be open Friday evening, around dusk, for the initial meeting. On Saturday, they would have an all-day preaching, and then on Sunday McGready and all visiting ministers would have several communion meetings. Brother Hodge had prepared the tables outside for Sunday's meals where all those who attended would join together. Finally, early Monday morning, a thanksgiving service would wrap up the communion session, allowing the people time to get home and begin the week's work. It would be a busy weekend, but McGready was ready.

So were the Nevilles.

Ann had already begun craning her neck as they rode into the yard of the meeting house, trying to spot a curly-haired young woman hauling three children. She knew Sarah wouldn't be hard to miss with her height, but as her eyes scanned the crowds, she saw no sign of her new friend. Mrs. Neville patted Ann compassionately on her leg as the wagon drew to a stop.

"Not to worry, dear. It is quite possible that it has been too busy a day for Sarah to manage tonight's meeting. Perhaps she will come tomorrow, and in the meantime, know that regardless, you have a new friend." Ann tried to hide her disappointment as her father helped the women out of the wagon. Her mother was right. Hoping Sarah would be here tonight was a bit far-fetched.

William Hodge had positioned John Rankin and William McGee at the entrance to the meeting house lane in the late afternoon. Both men were acquainted with the Wilson brothers and their friends and were prepared to stop them from entering the grounds, by force if needed. Word had passed quickly among the men attending about Rankin's and McGee's station, and all had committed to come to their aid, if need be. Womenfolk were aware – and praying – while the children were oblivious.

The Red River Meeting House had two identical entryways set about ten feet apart, and the wooden structure held approximately one hundred people, if all wanted to be seated on a bench. McGready had seen a rise in attendance at last month's Muddy River meeting up north but wasn't sure if that trend would continue at Red River. The open field surrounding the house gave ample space for wagons, horses and mules, and the benefit of having the river within easy walking distance provided fresh water for both man and animal.

McGready stood at the left doorway, welcoming people as they entered, his booming voice and solemn greetings setting the tone for a night of persuasive preaching. There was a sort of electricity in the air, and all who entered felt it. McGready appeared comfortable with it, speaking and moving in authority and complete control. Ann thought at once that he seemed both intimidating and comforting, although she couldn't have said why. His large, strong hand engulfed hers as he helped her up the last step into the dim, but comfortable, building.

"Reverend McGready," Aunt Lettice spoke from over Ann's right shoulder. "Good evening to you. I would be pleased for you to meet my cousin and her family from Port Royal, Tennessee, come up just yesterday to participate in our meetings." Ann stood to the side as introductions were made all around. Esther sidled up next to her, suddenly shy in this unknown place with strange people. Ann gazed around the room, seeing all sorts of folk, young and old, filling up benches and settling in together. Most seemed to know one another, although there were a few other introductions going on around the room.

"…and wondered if you had heard from Sister McPherson of late?" Ann caught the end of Aunt Lettice's sentence. She turned back to listen more intently.

"We have," McGready's voice cut through the chatter in the room.

"Brother Hodge met with her just last week and says she is praying for her niece to come and assist. Is that the girl you are speaking of?"

"Indeed," Aunt Lettice beamed. "Rachel and George brought her up just yesterday afternoon, and I, well, we had so hoped to see her here tonight. Sarah McMillan is her name."

"Very good," McGready responded, stepping to the side to let another family pass by. He waved a greeting to them, calling each by name. "Perhaps Brother Hodge can attend to the McPhersons tomorrow and see if he might be of help to the girl. We will be gathered for the next three days, so do not despair," he shot a glance at Ann in particular. "We will try to get Miss McMillan and her young cousins to the meeting if Sister McPherson is agreeable."

And with that, as though he had heard a voice no one else in the room knew, McGready spun on his heel and strode toward the pulpit, his voice rising in volume and intensity, the prayer unfolding from his lips as though he had been talking to God non-stop all day long.

Outside, at the front of the lane, McGee and Rankin heard McGready's voice lift from the meeting house, his prayer echoing and bouncing across the open yard.

"It has begun then," McGee said, straining to see down the road in the growing darkness. Rankin had located a downed tree next to the road and was sitting comfortably on it, chewing a blade of grass.

"May the Lord attend to our cries and bring His presence to His people," Rankin responded. Neither man was large in stature, but both were large in presence. Hodge had chosen well in placing them as the gatekeepers. Each had his rifle filled with powder, both fists at the ready, and the presence of God on their side as was evidenced by their just cause and the sense of power extending toward them from the meeting house. Because the doors were propped open to ward off the early evening heat, the men heard clearly each word coming from McGready's lips. They had listened to the man preach for years, first in the Carolinas, now in the Kentucky frontier, but neither ever tired of it. If anything, McGready's passion and fervor had risen concurrently with the increase of the sinfulness of those listening. Not only did the men sense they were on the edge of a move of God, they believed it had already begun – at least it had in the spirit.

They heard horses' hooves a few minutes after the sun had completely set and darkness lay thick on the road. Behind them, lanterns broke into the night – Hodge had made sure the yard would be lit during the entire meeting – and each man also held a lamp to ward off the dark. Coming out of the shadows just ahead were one, two, three horses, cantering neatly down the road. McGee and Rankin stood with their lamps, blocking the lane, forcing the horsemen to a sudden stop.

"Ho! Who goes there?" McGee bellowed, holding his rifle ready.

"None of your business," David Wilson shot back from atop his horse.

"Indeed, all who pass this road tonight are our business," Rankin responded. "For this road leads only to God's house, and we feel sure that you are not here to participate in the communion." The cadence of McGready's voice rose and fell, escaping from the house like ocean waves, allowing the men to hear snatches of sentences and phrases.

"Stand aside, Rankin," Wilson growled. "We ain't come to bother you nor nobody else here save that McGready. He's got to pay for his meddlin' in other people's business and families. He got no rights here, and it's time he learned that." David Wilson's two brothers, one on each side of him, nodded fiercely but said nothing. Their faces were partially covered by the shadows that fell from the brims of their hats, hiding all expression. McGee could feel the tension rising the longer they remained there. His hand gripped the rifle tightly.

"David, your wife's salvation is a work of God's Spirit, not of McGready. If you have issues with that, your fight is with God, not man..." Rankin started to explain but McGee broke in.

"...and I'd advise you not to fight with God. It always leads to a hard road."

"I didn't come here to have a talkin' to," Wilson shot back, shifting his horse. "I done said to stand aside, and I mean it. We're shuttin' this meetin' down." As Wilson kicked his horse to spur him on past McGee, Rankin and their rifles, the rolling cadence of McGready's voice rose dramatically, as if the very man himself stood before the Wilson brothers. The sound of it stopped Wilson short.

"And the Lord would say, 'Surely you are sinners in the hand of an angry God! Do not dare to cross me again. My anger will be turned against you unless you humble yourself and repent! Turn away from your wicked ways and acknowledge me as God. Then, and only then, can you be saved!'" McGready's voice rolled through the yard, around empty wagons and up the lane to pierce the hearts of the men on horseback. Wilson held his horse, still hesitating, and his brothers followed suit. The current in the air was almost visible.

"Some of you within the sound of my voice are just about at the end of your rope. The Lord is impressing upon me that someone here has even ridiculed a family member who has found the saving light of the Lord Jesus. You have scoffed, cursed and kicked at the feet of the God of the universe. You have made life a living hell for your own flesh and blood, and yet you do not care!" McGready's voice shot out like lightning. "Beware of your ways! The King of Glory bows to no man! Again, I say, turn back now and repent or your soul will burn in fiery flames of hell for all eternity."

McGee and Rankin stood still in the electrified night, hearing the word of the Lord go forth and drive like nails into the hearts of the men before them. David Wilson's face reddened and then turned pale as McGready's words danced around him. His brothers backed up, almost as though they had been struck, while Wilson remained frozen. Just as quickly as McGready's voice had risen, it now fell into soft persuasion, easing back into the house and leaving only the sounds of clamoring cicadas and tree frogs.

Eyes wide open, David Wilson turned his horse back toward the road, and saying no words, cantered off into the darkness with his brothers close on his heels. Rankin and McGee's shoulders relaxed, the tension of the moment disappearing as quickly as the horsemen.

"I have seen many a thing in my day, but never have I known David Wilson to back down like that," McGee laughed.

"Surely, the word of the Lord is sharper than any two-edged sword," Rankin agreed. "We will not have any more trouble from the Wilsons tonight. It almost felt like a storm brewing out here, did it not?" he questioned as he set down his rifle and again found the tree stump seat.

McGee laughed, hooking his lantern to a low-hanging branch. "Wait till we tell Brother James who his words were really for. Perhaps tonight, more than ever, we can justify why people call him the Son of Thunder."

Laughter drifted down the lane, back around the empty wagons and gently into the meeting house as McGready continued to quietly persuade his sheep that God was their protector and they should never fear the wolves as long as they were part of His flock.

Chapter Six

Sarah never made it to June's communion meetings at Red River, much to Ann Neville's chagrin. The Nevilles, instead, had enjoyed their time with Cousin Lettice, listened intently to this Presbyterian Mc-Gready, packed up their wagon and mules, and headed back west to Port Royal without ever laying eyes on Sarah. Sarah knew all this, of course, as different friends dropped by to visit her Aunt Charity and as she received correspondence from Ann. Yet it didn't make the fact any easier that she longed for friendship and especially Ann's presence. Sarah felt, for the first time in her life, that she had met a kindred spirit.

The warm milk shot from the cow's teat into the wooden bucket, striking with sharp, hollow sounds as the sun eased past the horizon of the field. It was hard to believe she had already been here three months. In that time, she had fiddled with the cow's feed enough to bring a resurgence of her milk supply, the spring corn had been harvested, the wheat was just about ready, and she had firmly entrenched herself in this family. How could a place feel so much like home so quickly?

Yet, her other home in Port Royal crossed her mind frequently. As any good daughter, she had written her father several times but had received nothing in reply. Such things merely added fuel to her love and her hatred for Matthew McMillan. Last week, she had sent another letter downriver to Ann. She hoped it would reach her soon.

The only strange part of her life was Aunt Charity's devotion to prayer and church, and while Sarah didn't mind preparing for the once-a-month prayer society held at the McPhersons' cabin, she felt a bit like a fish out of water. Out of honor to her aunt, she sat in on these prolonged times of pleading with God, as did all the McPherson children except Josiah, who was already down for the night. Yet she often found her mind wandering and her eyes struggling to stay open. She had yet to meet this Reverend

McGready but had heard so much about the man that she thought she would be able to point him out in a crowd.

Last Saturday happened to be the third of the month and the talk was all about his most recent meeting at Muddy River. Apparently, the last day of the meeting, Monday, had been quite solemn and serious, and – as Sister Campbell had said – "there was an awakening of a great number of persons." Ohs and ahs and clapping ensued in Aunt Charity's tiny bedroom at that report. (If only ladies attended, that's where the prayer society had to be held. Sarah always sat in the main room out of courtesy, leaving the chairs in the bedroom open for the guests.) In truth, Sarah wasn't sure what an "awakening" meant, but she didn't dwell much on these things. There was too much work to be done.

The light, airy sound of Millie's footsteps pulled Sarah from her reverie, and she turned on the milking stool to face the child. "Good morning, Millie."

"Sarah," Millie stood firmly in the doorway of the barn, a most solemn expression on her face. She held a squirming black and white kitten. "Billy's kittens are wandering too much. I found this one right outside the mule pen, and if I hadn't rescued him, he'd be smashed. We need to fix a cage for them."

"Oh my," Sarah responded in a similar serious tone. She picked up the bucket, threw a small tin of feed in the cow's trough, and made her way toward the child. "How do you propose we do this?"

"I don't know. You're the grown-up." Millie's chin tilted higher as Sarah drew closer, her eyes following the tall girl.

"I am?" Sarah smiled easily. She had turned fifteen in July, and probably grown another inch in the past year. "Yes, well, we could perhaps use a crate from the barn and place the kittens inside it for a time, but they are quickly growing, Millie, and will not be kept in such a place for long." Millie trotted behind Sarah as her long strides moved her toward the house. With the rising sun came quick heat, the portent of a mid-September day.

Before the girls reached the door, Sarah heard wagon wheels rolling down the road. She paused to watch the horizon, still holding tightly to the milk bucket. A bareheaded young man sat atop a narrow wagon seat moving his mule along at a quick pace. Sarah frowned in irritability. She hadn't seen much of Daniel Townsend since her arrival, but for some reason, he always seemed to put her in a bad mood. Millie watched quietly, still holding the now docile kitten. The wagon drew to a stop.

"Mornin' Miss McMillan," Daniel spoke without disembarking.

"Good morning," Sarah responded curtly.

"Wondered if Sister McPherson might have need of anything from Keysburg. I am headed that way today and have extra wagon room. My Pappy gave me a shorter list than usual." As much as Sarah hated to be beholding to Daniel, they did need several items. She had just checked their stocks last night. This was too easy, too good a chance to pass up. She sighed audibly, which made Daniel seem even more eager to help. He smiled and waited.

"As a matter of fact, I do think we could use a few things," she admitted. "Won't you come in while I double check our stores?" To her surprise, he declined, saying he would borrow their trough and water his mule one more time before the trip. She had no time to waste on thinking about Daniel, so she moved on in the house, calling to Aunt Charity as she walked through the door.

"He's here now?" Aunt Charity responded to Sarah's news.

"Yes. He's watering the mule while I get a firm count of our stores."

"Good. Mattie?" the seven-year-old stood beside the kettle where she had been stirring their breakfast.

"Yes, ma'am?"

"Run outside and ask Mr. Townsend if he might come talk to me briefly before he gets on his way."

"Yes, mother." And Mattie was out the door, apron flapping in her haste. Unlike fair-headed, serious Millie, Mattie's long, straight hair held the color of raven's wings and her eyes were just as dark. Although it was difficult to see in the small oval-shaped picture on the mantel, Sarah knew Obediah must be the darker McPherson and Mattie's looks must come from her papa. Aunt Charity was right. Mattie was far older than her seven years, and she had been Sarah's right arm since coming to Logan County. Baby Josiah whimpered and held his arms up to Sarah as she crossed the room. She picked him up without thinking and moved toward the back of the house where the McPherson's kept their stores of meal, wheat, salt, lard, sugar and corn. She heard Daniel's heavy tread as he entered the house. Although the voices were muffled, she could make out most of the words.

"...so thankful that you dropped by, Daniel," her aunt was saying. "... didn't know when we'd be able to get some of the things we need. How's your father and mother? I've missed seeing them."

Josiah pointed to a spider on the floor, loudly exclaiming until Sarah stomped it. Daniel's answer was lost, but apparently his parents were fine.

"Good, good," Aunt Charity continued. "...hoping you might could pick up Sarah and the children for the next communion meeting. The baby will come within the month and I'd hate for Sarah to go back to Port Royal without attending at least one. She's been so dependable, such a help, she deserves a little fun."

Fun? Sarah thought wryly. If her Aunt Charity wanted to provide fun, she could think of a dozen ways, none of which would be attending a church meeting. So far, God hadn't done her – nor her father – any favors as far as she could see. Josiah turned back toward the front of the house, pointing and grunting his desires, and the two of them made their way back toward the voices. Both Millie and Mattie sat at the table, digging into their mush, while Daniel stood respectfully at the doorway to Aunt Charity's room.

"...would be honored, Mrs. McPherson. I'll be by on Friday near dusk." Daniel turned away, catching sight of Sarah entering with Josiah planted on her hip. He kept his expression neutral, but his eyes grew warm as she handed him the list. "I'm beholding, Miss McMillan," he said. Pulling Mattie's pigtail, he had the girls laughing as he left the house while Sarah stood alone by the fire, chewing her bottom lip in frustration.

"Two Sabbaths, James," William Hodge sat outside of McGready's house in central Logan County. McGready's wife Nancy cooked inside with their youngest girl, while the other two girls played under an elm tree nearby.

"We've seen God's spirit pour out at Muddy River during both the July and last week's sacraments. It was a goodly number brought to Christ in both meetings, wouldn't you say?"

McGready nodded, his expression thoughtful. "Indeed, William. July and then the first week of September. It feels as though the dam is about to burst. Even this small start has appeared to overspread the country with the greatest rapidity."

"Everywhere, people are talking about the state of their souls, even on the busy streets of Keysburg and Russellville. In fields and mills, I am hearing tell of the Gospel and what it can do for a man," Hodge spoke in excitement. "Surely we are beginning to see the fruit of our labors and the results of the prayers of God's people."

"I believe it to be so," McGready agreed, glancing up at the girls under the tree. They were tossing stones, then hopping on one leg. "Now if the Lord would also bring an awakening to our children. I long to see the children know him, William. It is simply not enough for me to have adults awakened; I want the children as well."

Hodge nodded enthusiastically. "It is as John and I were discussing just the other day. Children on the frontier have been abandoned, neglected by us all. Even in our churches, it is the adults who enjoy the sacrament. The children raised in this new country know nothing of the formality and reverence in our churches back East. They were born on the trail or in the frontier and have never been exposed to religion. It is a massive mission field, just waiting to be harvested for the Lord and his Gospel."

One of the girls, a petite wisp of a thing, chose that moment to dash to her father, jumping into his lap. McGready caught her, laughing heartily as he sought to catch his balance. "I won, Papa," she crowed. "I got the most points!" The older girl leaned against the elm tree, a smile on her face. "It is true, Father," she called out. "She beat me, fair and square." Hodge's kind eyes crinkled in laughter as the scene played out before him.

"For the joy and passion of our children, James," Hodge said as McGready stood and lifted his daughter high in the air, her shrieks of laughter ringing into the woods.

"Yes," McGready's voice boomed in reply. "May God hear our cry and bring the children into His house."

The Waking Up

Sarah hugged her shawl closer to ward off the chill of the late September air. She had decided to walk a spell before Daniel Townsend came in his wagon to take her, Millie and Mattie to the Red River Meeting House. A gust of wind picked up her ever-straying hair, blowing it across her face. Preoccupied, she tucked it back under her cap as she walked toward the cornfield. The tall, gangly stalks were beginning to turn brown, and she and the girls had spent the last week stripping the ears off. Her job here was almost complete. Aunt Charity had received a letter just yesterday from Uncle Obediah who wrote he was on his way back to Logan County after a productive few months. The baby in Aunt Charity's womb had grown to the point that she was uncomfortable, even in bed, and Sarah knew it would be only a week or two before it would make its way into the world.

And then? Perhaps even before then, she would be sent back to Port Royal and a father who cared nothing for her. In a rare moment of weakness, she allowed a tear to slip from her eye, the wind dragging it across her face, leaving a trail of salt. Being in Logan County had been much like living in Spartanburg near Grandma McMillan. Sarah had found laughter, joy, peace, and most of all, love in the simple McPherson home. Mattie had been such a help these last few months, and Millie spoke in plain ways that never failed to touch Sarah's heart. Josiah, who only wanted to be held as much as possible, had awakened a need of touch that Sarah didn't know she had, the simple act of touching in love. Her heart was full, and now she faced isolation again.

Sarah's tall figure was outlined against the sky as she rose to the top of the rise, head lowered, shoulders set against the increasing wind. She knew she had to turn back toward the house before Daniel came, and she fought against the desire to continue walking. After all, once Obediah returned home, the McPhersons wouldn't really miss her. As for her father, she was sure Sally and Hagar could continue cooking for him, and that's all he would need. He'd probably be grateful she was gone so he wouldn't have the daily reminder of who she wasn't.

Lightning flashed in the distant west, at once making Sarah aware of how dark it had become. Resolutely, she turned back toward the house, knowing she couldn't walk away and she would go to this ridiculous meeting riding on a wagon with a boy who frustrated her highly. As she neared the house and heard the wagon approaching, she felt a creeping sort of deadness take root in her heart. Mattie and Millie raced out the door in joy as Daniel's wagon came into view.

Once again, the Red River Meeting House was jammed with the faithful, the committed – and the curious. The girls led Sarah to a bench set about halfway back from the front as Daniel took a seat behind them with some neighbors from down the road. They had missed meeting Mc-Gready face-to-face – he had been in deep conversation with another man – but Sarah could have pointed him out. He dressed plainly, no ruffles on his shirt. His coarse black breeches were neat, and his long waistcoat held no adornment other than simple pewter buttons. Although his voice was lowered in conversation, he had the look of power in speech and intensity in delivery. Overall, his appearance was solemn, and Sarah found herself a bit anxious and intrigued at the same time.

Outside, the lightning Sarah had witnessed a mere hour before had found its way into Logan County. Rain began pelting the small meeting house just as it filled up; perhaps God decided to wait till His people were set before unleashing the heavens, Sarah considered, half believing it.

The chatter ebbed as the big man strode toward the front, his voice rising above the rain on the shingled roof in immediate prayer and supplication. There were no introductions or explanations — which took Sarah by surprise — but Mattie and Millie lowered their heads in reverence. Sarah's gaze remained ramrod straight as she watched McGready take his place behind the podium. As he prayed, he, too, kept his eyes open while he searched for Scripture in his battered Bible – he could pray and read at the same time. Finding his place, he then lifted his eyes toward the rafters, continuing his petition without missing a beat. A sort of energy fell over the room, and in spite of herself, Sarah felt drawn into the man's prayer for repentance, regeneration and faith to be extended to the people. McGready went on for several minutes before wrapping up his plea to God. Then, opening the worn Bible, he read his Scripture verse for tonight.

"We take our text from the Gospel of John, chapter three, verse three," he intoned. "Except a man be born again, he cannot see the kingdom of God." McGready's voice began softly, vying with the rolling thunder that was moving away now, the rain settling to a slower drizzle. Sarah subtly glanced around the crowded room, catching sight of many of the women she had met at her Aunt Charity's cabin during the prayer society – and some of their children. She had not the acquaintance of most of the men except, of course, Daniel, who continued to sit behind her. While she couldn't see Daniel, she was very aware of his presence.

"The Savior lays great success upon the importance of the new birth," McGready was saying. "But how different with many in this age of the Gospel light, who call themselves Christians, and who rarely call in question their hopes of Heaven – they spend their strength and time in quarreling with other denominations about controversial points, and disputing about matters of small concern to the neglect of this great and all-important inquiry – Am I born again? Have I been made a new creature? Is Christ formed within my soul, the hope of glory?

"In that awful day, when the universe assembled must appear before the judge of the quick and dead, the question, brethren, will not be, Were you a Presbyterian – a Seceder – a Covenanter – a Baptist – or a Methodist; but, Did you experience the new birth? Did you accept of Christ and his salvation as set forth in the Gospel?"

Sarah found herself immersed in McGready's words, his questions pounding against her beating heart, one at a time. She felt her face begin to flush in red heat and wondered if all eyes in the room were cast upon her countenance. As he continued, she squirmed a bit, trying to squeeze more comfort out of the hard bench.

"My dear fellow creatures, if you would be the followers of Christ, here your religion must commence. You must be regenerated before you can live a spiritual life. If you neglect this one matter, all your endeavors will be in vain, how strong so-ever your hopes of Heaven may be. No difference how fair your profession; how upright your conduct and conversation, unless you have been born from on high, death will rob you of your religion, and the wrath of God, like a mighty deluge, will sweep you to the lowest hell – for, 'except a man be born again, he cannot see the kingdom of God.'"

For more than an hour McGready preached, cajoled, pleaded, rebuked and persuaded. Sarah walked every path he took them down, feeling his passion and weighing his arguments. Although the power of the storm had passed outside the meeting house, a new storm began brewing within as many people began to respond to McGready's words. His voice escalated with each new point he hammered into hearts until his glistening coal hair was soaked with sweat. All eyes were transfixed to the energy and power exuding from him; the truth sinking deeply into their souls. As he drew near the end of his sermon and began applying it to their everyday lives, spontaneous prayer broke out among the communicants. Sarah listened as one after another prayed, begging God for forgiveness, and seeking for this thing McGready had called regeneration. Millie and Mattie had fallen asleep somehow – that baffled Sarah to no end! – their heads on each side of her lap.

Finally, McGready ended the formal service, and Sarah felt Daniel's hand on her shoulder. "Are you ready to get the girls home?" he whispered in her ear, his breath warm on her neck. She nodded, easing their heads off her lap. Daniel came around the bench and picked up Mattie gently, gesturing for Sarah to do the same with Millie. As she lifted the small girl to her shoulder, Sarah was able to look around the back of the room and see the full extent of McGready's work. People were praying everywhere now, kneeling beside the benches, beseeching, tears flowing, and a few were even laughing quietly. McGready moved around the room, laying his hand on heads or shoulders, praying with them, seeming to care that their souls were burdened.

Sarah had never seen or experienced anything like this, and while she found her heart strangely moved, she had no inclination to join those praying at the bench. Daniel led the way out the door and she followed, carefully shielding Millie from the cool night air.

Chapter Seven

The weekend communion services continued with the blessing of warmer than usual weather on the back of the soaking rain of Friday night. Many of the faithful of Red River gave God the glory for it, acknowledging that He was the giver of the rains for their crops as well as the sun to bring forth fruit. The late corn harvest appeared to be bountiful, and the rains came in perfect time to water the recently planted rye grass seed.

"Blessing, James, it is all the blessing of the Sovereign Lord," William Hodge declared Monday after the final communion service. The last wagonload of people had just disappeared around the bend in the lane, while the men stood, watching and pondering. "I had hoped that the Spirit would see fit to move upon the Red River communicants just as he did with those who were gloriously awakened at Muddy River, and truly He has."

McGready turned to close both doors of the meeting house. "The Lord did pour out His Spirit in a very remarkable manner, did He not?" He pulled tightly, assuring each door was firmly fastened against any woodland creature who might try to inhabit the house during the winter months. From now until spring, meetings would be held in homes. Getting out was simply too difficult with cold, snowy Kentucky winters. Hodge would depart this afternoon for Tennessee and his own flock at Shiloh.

Taking a moment, McGready began to walk the property one last time before heading back to his own home where Nancy waited with the girls. Hodge followed, continuing the conversation with gestures and inflections of excitement.

"I am hearing of more people turning their thoughts toward religion. In both settlements and on farms, the faithful tell of a sense of revival.

Even Sister Wilson says her husband and brothers have become more solemn since their encounter with the Spirit of God in July," Hodge explained.

"Indeed?" McGready's eyebrow raised.

"So she says, although none of them have accepted the saving grace of the Lord, they have, at the least, stopped berating her daily. She has great hope that the fervor of the meetings will continue to spread and eventually sweep the whole of her family into it."

"Out of your mouth to the ear of God," McGready declared. "We begin to see the fruits of fasting and prayer, William. I think God has begun His unchallengeable work of deliverance." The men continued their walk , each deep in his own thoughts, until the perimeter of the meeting house had been assessed. All was set for a long winter's sabbatical. McGready untied his mare as Hodge followed suit. "Have you set the October meeting of the prayer society at Sister McPherson's again?"

"Possibly," Hodge said, settling in his saddle. "The baby's to come any day now, but she insists that no matter the circumstances, she'll be ready to host them all. Her two oldest girls were here Friday night with the cousin. You saw them?"

"I did," McGready replied. "I noted that Miss McMillan seemed somewhat uncomfortable in the presence of the Lord."

Hodge laughed spontaneously, surprising a crow that had settled on the roof of the house. "Yes, well, she'll be in the Kingdom before long. I cannot see Sister McPherson having an unbeliever under her roof. The girl has no chance of escape."

McGready's laughter echoed down the lane as both men mounted their horses. His eyes still twinkling, McGready leaned over and rested his hand on Hodge's shoulder.

"Again, I thank you, William, for your service. I could not have met the needs here were it not for your willingness to travel and assist. Please relate to Anna and the children my gratitude."

"I will certainly do so," the stocky man replied. "Twas really no bother. I would pay to see God's Spirit move in such a way." He waved his arm northward. "Now ride home and be with Nancy. We will pray and corresponde and, Lord willing, see each other in the spring."

McGready hesitated only a moment, then spinning his horse around, he lifted his voice in prayer. As he trotted the mare in the opposite direction, Hodge could hear the booming voice ebbing away. "Thank you, Lord God, for Your unwavering servant, William Hodge, who left hearth and home to attend to me and see the power of Your Spirit move over Your people…"

As his mare rounded the bend, Hodge kicked his horse into action. Smiling broadly, he moved south, toward Tennessee and home.

Word of a new Presbyterian minister in the region reached McGready Wednesday afternoon as he rode into Russellville. He had spent the morning preparing for a meeting to be held Friday night in Brother Smith's home while Nancy had assessed their stores. As always, money was scarce, but McGready had corn with which to barter for flour and sugar. Nancy had pressed upon him the hope of finding coffee, but McGready's expectations for the luxury were low. Autumn winds blew hard against him as he rode toward Main Street into the bustling part of town. The blazing sun in the brilliant blue sky did nothing to alleviate the bitter cold that had quickly swept in.

It was as he rode by Hadley's Hotel on Third Street, between Main and Summer, that he was stopped and questioned. "Reverend McGready!" a young man called from Hadley's porch. It was Hadley's oldest boy, Jed, who helped run the hotel. "Did you know of Mr. Balch's comin' to town?"

McGready pulled up the reins, slowing the wagon to a stop. "A Mr. Balch?"

"Yes, sir. Says he's a good Presbyterian minister. Done heard about some of the things happenin' at Muddy River and such. Says he come down from North Carolina to start a new work."

"He just arrived, I take it?" McGready asked.

"Yesterday evenin'. He come in and got him a room and board for a time. Didn't say how long he'd be stayin' or if he'd bought some land. I just supposed you'd know." Jed swept the dirt off the final, bottom step and turned to go back in. "Last I seen him, he was walkin' towards the town square," he tossed over his shoulder, slamming the door behind him.

McGready clucked his horse forward, deep in thought as he rolled towards the mercantile establishment of Stewart, Dromgoole & Co. If he didn't run up on Balch there, he'd at least hear about him from Stewart, the proprietor.

As usual, the mercantile held a steady stream of moving people, ladies wearing finer caps than they would at home, children tagging along, hoping and praying for a peppermint treat at the end of their mama's shopping, men carrying seed or 50-pound bags of corn. McGready always thought of the store as a beehive, the home nest for Logan County. There was no other store in the whole of the county that sold such a variety of goods; therefore, it was more than just a place to purchase. It was a general gathering hub for all Logan Countians, even more used than the Cedar House where court was held for western Kentucky. He drew the mare to a halt, tying her and the wagon off to a hitching post before moving toward the mercantile steps.

"Afternoon, Reverend," a man spoke, shielded from view by the shadow of the roof obscuring his face. One or two others called out similar greetings, but the bulk of the men either ignored him or appraised him with disdain. Rogues' Harbor was becoming more settled with good folk, such as the nest of Presbyterians that came from the Carolinas, but there were still more rogues than good citizens. The anonymity of frontier life had been a draw to criminals such as horse thieves, drunkards and even murderers, and McGready knew the only way they would change would be from the inside out. The Gospel was as a sword to many of these men, bringing violence and division, and McGready counted on the protection of God to do his work. His foot was on the top step when John Rankin emerged from the store carrying a large bag of seed. His face lit up when he caught sight of his friend and mentor.

"James," he hefted the bag to the side of the porch, allowing it to fall heavily to the floor. "What providence to see you here! Has Sister McGready sent you on expedition to bring food for those hundreds of girls at your house?" Rankin laughed, slapping McGready on the back.

"Hardly hundreds, John, although some days it certainly feels that way," McGready countered, just as pleased to see Rankin. "How goes the flock up your way? You know we had the meeting at Red River two days past, and the presence of the Lord saw fit to descend upon us again?"

73

Rankin nodded enthusiastically, pulling McGready over to the side of the porch, away from the crowd of men sitting and whittling. "Yes, yes, my heart rejoices in such news, but have you heard tell of a Mr. Balch coming into town?"

"Only just so. Jed Hadley told me as I was driving by the hotel."

"I encountered the man here not more than an hour ago. He has come from the East to take a presbytery in our area – and I must say, James, I fear he brings no good with him." Rankin turned his face away from the group on the other side of the porch, effectively shielding his words. "He is on the Old Side of things and has much to say about the seeding of our revival. None of it good. When he found out I was a McGready disciple, he began berating me loudly, calling a crowd and attention to himself before I had rightly discerned his purpose. A group gathered quickly, and I found myself defending the work of the Lord to this man – as well as to a goodly number of locals. Ears were attuned my way, James, and I began to sense the heaviness of the spirit with which Mr. Balch carries. It is dissension, I fear. And there is no other way to describe it."

McGready's prominent brow creased in displeasure. "It is as I feared," he replied. "I wondered why the man did not make my acquaintance before descending on the townspeople. Do you know where he went from here?"

Raucous laughter erupted from the other side of the porch, causing McGready and Rankin to glance that way. It died down as quickly as it began, and the two men turned back toward each another. "Not for sure. He seemed to be attempting to find places in Russellville where men gather. Perhaps he has moved on to the Cedar House. I hear tell court is in session this afternoon."

McGready glanced toward the vibrant blue sky, assessing how much afternoon was left and silently asking the Lord for His direction. Rankin's clear blue eyes watched his mentor with a bit of anxiety. McGready wasn't known as a man who would back down – his stint in Carolina had sealed that – and he wasn't sure how he would respond to ministers who might be attempting to steal his flock. To his vast relief, McGready's countenance lightened. "First things first," he said smiling now. "If I do not get Nancy's goods, she will bar me from the house. I will see to this. Then, if there is time and Providence allows it, I will find this Mr. Balch and question him on his motives in our community. Many thanks, John, for bringing this to light. Are you back toward Gasper River, then?"

Rankin felt a burden lift from his shoulders and found he could relax again. McGready had this covered, and he could again turn his energies toward the flock he attended northeast of Russellville. "I am, James. I still have the meeting house to lock up before winter, but I will keep in touch as much as possible through correspondence. Do you still hope to travel up before Christmas?"

McGready answered Rankin's questions quickly and finally entered the mercantile. As always, he was greeted warmly by the owner who was a parishoner, yet while he visited with others who were shopping – and made sure Nancy's goods were gathered – his mind was set on Mr. Balch with intent. God willing, he would find this man before leaving town and shake him, if necessary, until his purposes fell out, open for all to see.

Word had come of Obediah McPherson's impending return. Aunt Charity had received a letter just yesterday, Tuesday, that told of his travels and expected arrival in about a fortnight, if all went well. Sarah had read it herself, the document that sealed her fate more than any spoken word. She found her heart heavy as she flipped the dough again, releasing a powdery dust. She was waiting for the inevitable news that she would be on her way back to Port Royal any day now. Even the girls were sad; Josiah was too small to understand, so he simply continued to love her.

"Sarah," Aunt Charity called from her bedroom. "Come in here, dear, for I need to speak to you of serious things. Millie? Mattie? Take your brother to the barn and let him play in the warm hay for a bit. Perhaps hold a kitten or two, but for Heaven's sake, don't let him squeeze them. You must watch him at all times, understand?"

The girls sat at the table pulling seeds from cotton, their small fingers dexterous and nimble, while Josiah played happily at their feet. Sarah flipped the dough one last time then moved it closer to the fire to rise. When Mattie reached for her coat, Josiah jumped up and down in anticipation, a jumbled tumble of words falling out of his mouth. He loved nothing better than to go outside, even when it was cold. The children moved out the front door, bundled warmly in coats, hats and mittens, leaving the room empty and bereft. Sarah wiped her hands on her apron and entered Aunt Charity's room. *Here it comes then,* she thought dismally.

She found her aunt in her usual disarray, clothes spread far and wide, a stack of already finished garments and cloths piled neatly to the right of her bed. These would be delivered to friends and acquaintances as they came to pick them up. Charity's sewing had become a business of sorts as community-folk paid for her darning, stitching and embroidering. Sarah had found Aunt Charity's income to be most helpful in the last two months as she had taken over the household books until Obediah returned. As Sarah studied her aunt's bloated belly swelling high above her body, she considered that this baby may arrive before Obediah – who knew? Charity shifted and squirmed to get more comfortable, her plaited hair lying in a single strand over her pillow. Finally, she situated herself with a deep sigh of relief.

"I have much to say to you, Sarah, before you go back to Port Royal," she began, her green eyes sparkling. "Such gratitude I have. You have been more than I could have ever dreamed of these four months. I had prayed for someone to help with chores and child rearing. What I had not planned was finding a niece that I genuinely like and love, one who also brought joy to our household." Her words faltered then as her eyes filled with emotion. She cleared her throat and continued. "But that is not why I called you in here today," she smiled gamely, catching her breath. "No. All that can come later. More importantly, I need you to hear a story that I believe you have not been told. One about your father. Why he walks with a limp, why he is ... well, the way he is. Please understand that none of us wanted to hide anything from you, but Matthew made his mama swear that she would never disclose this part of his past to you. And so, as his mother, she had no choice but to agree. I, however..." Charity smiled secretly, "I made no such promise, and having seen your maturity and wisdom, but also seeing the cloud settle over your spirit when your father's name is spoken, I have decided it is time you knew."

Sarah's heart was racing, her palms sweating, and she was divided. Part of her longed to dash from this room and out the front door, past the fields and as far away from this disclosure as she could race. The other part of her yearned to hear this, must hear it, in order to survive. Sensing the girl's discomfort, Charity patted her on the hand, then held on, squeezing it gently.

"It is no secret to you that Matilda died in childbirth, and yet you, this bubbling, wonderful child of promise, survived and thrived. Oh, such a mixture of grief and jubilation we had that day," Charity's eyes filled with tears as she looked over Sarah's head, remembering it all. "Life and death came all at once, and none of us really knew how to cope with it. But Matthew was not there when you were born, Sarah. He had not made it to the house yet and we could not fathom why.

"You see, your father was completely and utterly devoted to your mother. At times, we felt he drew his very breath from her presence. The two of them had this love, this amazing, profound depth of love that we felt could only come from the hand of God. It consumed them both, and truly as the Scripture says 'they became one flesh,' so your mother and father were." Tears rolled heedlessly down Sarah's cheeks. "I remember one time meeting up with your father and my sister at the spring close to our house. I was younger then, and they were courting…soon to be married. They were walking together by the edge of the stream, hand in hand. Matilda was laughing at something Matthew said, and I have never again seen such joy in a face as I saw when Matthew watched her laugh. I cannot put it into words, Sarah, but it was as though Heaven came down and the perfect, pure love of God's kingdom was right there. I quietly turned back toward home, not disturbing them, because the purity of the emotion was too raw. I didn't understand all that then, of course, but I sensed something too precious to interrupt. I'm sorry to go on about this, but you need to have a certain depth of understanding of what your father lost the day you were born."

Sarah lifted the corner of her apron to wipe her face. "Are you able to continue?" Aunt Charity asked kindly. Sarah nodded, not trusting her voice to speak. "Very well. On to that day." She again looked off into the distance, seeing nothing – and everything.

"There was a family that lived about two miles away from Matthew and Matilda who had two children and one newborn baby. Your mother, especially, had become great friends with the Williamses and being pregnant with her first child, had learned much from them. Their small cabin lay in the path of your father's way home. Your Uncle Billy had ridden quickly to the mill where Matthew worked when Matilda went into labor, gone to fetch Matthew home of course. Billy came on back, leaving Matthew to saddle his horse and make his own way. But right off, your mama was having a hard time of it. No one knew where Matthew was, but we could not worry about him then. Matilda was the main concern.

"Billy rode on to the east to find the doctor while Grandma McMillan and my mama did as much as they could to help Matilda. Her labor was intense…" Charity drew a deep breath, steadying herself, the telling wearing on her heavily, "…and I helped as much as any fifteen-year-old could. The contractions were so close. Matilda could barely draw a breath before she was pushing again. The baby's head – your head – was crowning but not coming forth and Matilda was weakening. Finally, Billy arrived with Doc but there was still no sign of your father. After dropping off Doc, Billy tore off in the opposite direction to track down your father. We knew something bad must have kept him away.

"Of course, you know that having Doc there did not help your mama, but his presence did allow for your entrance into the world. Without him, you would have died, Sarah. We treasure him to this day for that." Emotion overtook Charity and for several minutes, the only sound in the room was weeping. Once again, Charity gathered herself.

"We found out later that Billy finally ran up on your father where he lay wounded in oh-so-many ways. The Williams' home, that your father always passed, had caught on fire – we think it was a hearth fire gone amuck. Nevertheless, by the time your father was galloping by on his way home, the house was filled with flames, and Mr. and Mrs. Williams were out in their yard, covered with soot and having only two of the three children. Your father told Billy later on that he wanted to ride through and get home to Matilda, but he knew he must stop to help; that is what God would want him to do. So he pulled up on his reins and ran to Mr. Williams, who sat coughing and wheezing from the smoke in his lungs. Apparently, he had just hauled their middle child from the cabin, but the baby was still inside. He was trying to go back in but could barely walk for gasping.

"Of course, Matthew went in for the baby. There was no other choice for him. He told Billy that the cabin was so filled with smoke and so hot, that he immediately dropped to his knees and began crawling toward the area where he knew the baby's crib was. I don't know how long he felt around in there, but he eventually found her, reached inside, and snatched up the Williams' baby. Now crawling with only one free arm, his progress was slowed, and he began to be overcome by the smoke as well. Your Uncle Billy said your father almost did not make it out, but as he prayed and cried aloud for God to help, he felt a push from behind and practically fell over the threshold. At that same moment the doorposts fell in, one of them landing on your father's left leg. Had it not been for the quick response of the Williamses, your father would have been lost then. But there they were — Mr. Williams pulling your father away, Mrs. Williams taking their baby girl, and one of their children dousing your father's leg with water to dissipate the flames. It must have been horrifying," Charity shook her head.

"Before he even reached the Williams' cabin, Billy ran up on the oldest child riding a mule toward Doc's house. Mr. Williams had sent the boy to get Doc for Matthew … but not the baby. She didn't make it." Sarah gasped incredulously. Charity wore a sad smile. "I know. So sad, is it not? Billy pointed the boy in the direction of Matthew's house where Doc was, then went on himself to the Williams' place. He found Matthew in great pain with Mrs. Williams attempting to pull his burned trousers off that leg. The moment he laid eyes on Billy, all thoughts of his pain left, and he tried to get up to go to Matilda. When Billy told him she was having a hard time of it, Billy said he thought Matthew would go mad trying to walk and mount his horse. But it was impossible." Aunt Charity drew a deep breath, gaining a little more energy to finish the tale.

"As you can imagine, by the time they found a wagon and got Matthew positioned on it to get him home, Matilda was gone. He arrived to find her dead, just like the baby at the Williams' place, but you were alive and well. I will never forget the look on his face that day. That bare, naked grief still pierces my heart. We all grieved Matilda greatly, still do, but Matthew? Well, Sarah, he simply died. It was as though a door dropped down in front of him, and his soul perished while his body lived on. We had hoped the joy of having you would somehow overcome the grief after a time, but it never did. Grandma McMillan had many talks with him, but she says his only response has been that he did God's will, he stopped when he wanted to go on home, and he selflessly gave according to God's will. God's response to that was to kill Matilda, wound Matthew for life, and even allow a baby that he attempted to rescue to die. Matthew says …," Charity paused, "Matthew says that if there is a God, He would never allow such things to happen to His children. And since that day, Matthew shut himself off from all who love him, refusing to return any love. I have always believed he is afraid to love you, Sarah. If he does, he might lose you —- just like he did Matilda and the baby."

Charity lay back on her pillows, completely spent, the tendrils of her brown hair wet with sweat, while Sarah felt as if her mind would explode. She'd had no idea, no hint of any other event on the day of her birth except her mother dying. It was as if someone just rewrote the story of her life, and it was too much to comprehend. She found her legs couldn't move, and although a million questions swarmed through her mind, she couldn't formulate one of them.

Charity glanced at the girl, very nearly a woman now, and felt her heart lurch in compassion. Sarah's usual stoic countenance was softened and tender, full of grief and pain. While Charity knew that the truth will set you free, according to Scripture, she also knew that the truth is a hard taskmaster, sometimes allowing no kind place of retreat. She smiled tenderly, squeezing Sarah's hand. "Take some time, dear niece. Go walk the field you so love and try to digest what you have heard. You will be going home soon and may find a compassion in your heart not felt before."

Chapter Eight

McGready and his loaded wagon had just passed by Caldwell's Leather Goods when he spotted the crowd in front of the Stewart House. In the center of a small gathering stood a tall and commanding figure who was draped in a long black waistcoat, matching knee britches, stockings and a wig. The contrasting beaver skin hats and deer hide coats made the man in the center stick out like a buffalo among raccoons. McGready had found Mr. Balch. He pulled up on his reins and sat motionless, allowing the man's words to carry through the air. He clearly heard it all.

"And what is the Gospel of Christ? Is it but bare emotionalism? Ranting and raving? Weeping so uncontrollably that one's heart is driven almost to the point of madness? I say no! The Apostle Paul wrote that our God is a God of order and not confusion. These services run by Rev. McGready are full of confusion, not order. How then can these be the work of an orderly God? Stay steady and calm in the Scriptures, my people, and don't find yourself wrapped up in an emotional state that could only be of the devil," Balch proclaimed from the street corner. McGready had heard enough. He leaped from the wagon seat and strode toward the gathering. Men and women separated like the waters at the Red Sea as he approached.

Balch turned in surprise, catching sight of the towering McGready moving toward him with intent. He unconsciously straightened his shoulders to stand his ground while the townsfolk who had gathered waited expectantly. "Mr. Balch, I take it?" McGready demanded, a wry smile on his face.

Balch matched his expression, already assuming this was the much-talked-about McGready. "Yes, indeed, sir. And may I inquire as to your name?"

"I would be the Rev. James McGready who is running good Presbyterian services filled with confusion and not order, as I believe you stated."

"Ah yes. It is so, then," Balch dipped his head in greeting, an implacable expression on his face. "Well, sir. One must teach and preach the truth, and that would be the truth I've learned, lived and taught these many years."

"Your truth, Mr. Balch. And, forgive me, but did I see you at Red River? No? Perhaps Gasper River? Or Muddy River? No, indeed, no. If you have not attended one of our recent communion meetings, how then can you presume, sir, to pass judgment upon the Spirit?"

Balch didn't hesitate while those watching dared not breathe for fear of interrupting. "There is no need to witness firsthand what I have heard a full fifty miles away. It is obvious that you are a lively exhorter of the faith, but it is said that your people are high in the spirit with unusual manifestations seen in your meetings. It is not only a breach of good manners, but a spirit of the devil himself has infiltrated in your midst. I find it my duty, sir, to come warn the good people of Logan County of this deception."

McGready was constantly aware of the crowd surrounding them. He and Balch stood as a hub on this ever-expanding wheel of people. Whereas McGready was completely comfortable debating him and knowing the righteousness of his cause, he also knew the heart of man was easily swayed, and Balch's arguments would sound convincing to the newly converted souls. He restrained his anger and cried out to God for self-control. He tried a different tactic.

"Mr. Balch. Would you care to accompany me to Hadley's Hotel where we might sit with something warm to drink and discuss these matters further?" McGready attempted.

"I have no issue with the location of our discussion, kind sir, but do you not know that it is imperative for the good citizens of Russellville to hear the truth that your enthusiastic preaching does not equate with solid doctrine?" Balch asked determinedly, ignoring McGready's darkening countenance. "Why, I have been in meetings where some of the people have affected these outbursts, then commanded them to cease – and they did so! Surely, were it a work of the spirit, no man could control the movement?"

McGready reacted incredulously. "You say I teach no solid doctrine, yet you admit you have never set foot in a meeting I have run. You admit that you have stood in the way of the move of the Spirit among a congregation, and even take pride in that admission. I know not what spirit you are of, Mr. Balch, but it is not the spirit that I have witnessed in these gatherings here. Your doctrine is a hindrance to the work of the Lord that is being wrought in this area, and I will thank you to take your philosophy somewhere else."

"But Mr. McGready, the Cumberland Presbytery has offered me this position in Logan County, and I mean to fill it. If this territory needs anything, it needs educated ministers who can teach and preach the sure Word of God, not excessive exercises of meetings and gatherings," Balch spread his arms wide as if to embrace those standing around him. "Surely we can unite in this cause?"

"That the Gospel of the Lord would go out to the farthermost parts of the earth, yes, on that we can agree," McGready acquiesced. "But in the sense that you ridicule and reject the work of the Spirit among this people, no matter how strange you may find it appears, on that we must disagree. Indeed, I would say you must see firsthand the proof of changed lives and repentant hearts. Hear the stories told of gamblers converted, drunkards dried up, women whose hearts have turned back to their husbands and homes. God has come and you would miss it!" McGready's voice had risen in volume as he spoke. Bystanders had not left but found themselves in rapt attention to the ministers. They knew this was a showdown of some sorts, but many weren't quite sure about what. Nevertheless, this exchange would be repeated over kitchen tables and beside fireplaces for days to come. When McGready finished speaking, Balch shrugged, glancing skyward, his manner dismissive.

"I feel sure I shall not miss the Lord since He walks beside me daily," he laughed. "Now, the sun sets, Mr. McGready, and I must be on my way. Perhaps we can resume this discussion another time, but I have a supper appointment I must keep tonight. Good day, then," and he was off, people parting the way for Balch to make his way back to Hadley's. McGready stood silently, watching him leave. Several men slapped him on the shoulder as the crowd dispersed, and McGready smiled in return, said a few words of greeting, but all could see he was quite preoccupied.

Finally, McGready stood alone in the street and slowly turned toward his wagon. "Alas, the devil has his plan deeply laid," he said to himself, easing back up to the wagon seat. "Prayer is the only recourse." As he clucked his horse forward, McGready's voice rose, alone on the street, in supplication to his God.

It was the following Sunday, the first week in October, when Aunt Charity found a way for Sarah to return to Port Royal. Daniel Townsend and his father were traveling by wagon to the mighty Cumberland River and said they would go right through Port Royal on their way. Sarah had longed to attend the birth of the fourth McPherson child, but Aunt Charity had said they must take the first opportunity they had of getting Sarah home. "For another one may not avail itself," she explained, pausing to catch her breath. The weight of the child had shortened her sentences to brief spurts of information. "I know Obediah will be here early in the week, and all will be well. My only regret is that the two of you would not meet, but we will remedy that soon enough. I am praying Matthew will again allow you to come to me in late spring of next year. Would that be acceptable to you, Sarah?"

If possible, Sarah had grown even taller these last few months in Kentucky. As she stood in the threshold of her Aunt Charity's doorway holding Josiah on her hip, she appeared almost as tall as a man, yet her features were striking and beautiful. Sarah smiled in response. "More than acceptable, Aunt Charity. I need to return to chase this boy around the chicken coop again, right Josiah?" The red-haired child giggled, tugging playfully on a ringlet that escaped Sarah's cap.

She had resigned herself to the return to Port Royal, and in fact, was excited about seeing Ann Neville again, their friendship now sealed through correspondence. Sarah knew Ann would be pleased she had returned, and she would have to find a way to visit Ann in her home. Apparently, Ann had become sick again, and her mother had confined her to "the prison," as Ann had written so sarcastically. Sarah's concern was that her father might not allow such visits; in the past, he had kept Sarah in her own prison at their cabin, but Sarah felt sure she would be able to find a way – even if it had to be hidden from Matthew McMillan.

"...tomorrow morning at first light," Aunt Charity was saying. "Mattie will be able to manage until Obediah comes, and Sister Townsend will drop in on me two times a day. I feel sure that the Lord will supply all my needs according to His riches in glory. I pray He also is an anchor for you, Sarah." She paused again, those green eyes piercing and questioning.

"Yes, Aunt Charity," Sarah tossed out as she turned back toward the kitchen. "And supper is just about ready."

Daniel Townsend's father appeared to be a most agreeable man – jovial, laughing, his long beard shaking with each witty comment he made. How unlike the son is from the father, Sarah thought crossly as she handed over her now-stuffed saddlebag. Aunt Charity had made sure Sarah had enough food to feed an army for this one-day journey, and each child had made Sarah a special going-away gift. Mattie's contribution had been a corn shuck doll just like hers, complete with a homemade apron. "Her name is Mattie, too," the solemn seven-year-old announced. "That way, you can talk to her just like you talk to me, except she won't answer back." Sarah could see the raven-haired girl knew the weight, again, of managing the household. Were Sarah a praying girl, she would ask God to bring Obediah even more quickly so Mattie wouldn't have to be so serious.

Millie had worked long and hard knitting Sarah a new scarf. No matter that it hung a bit sideways or the threading missed loops here and there, it was done by her own hand and in colors that brought the startling green out of Sarah's eyes. Sarah wore it this morning as she loaded up. "Don't forget Josiah's present," Mattie had said earlier.

"Josiah has a present, too?" Sarah had stared at the chunky boy who had mush stuck all over his mouth. The four of them shared breakfast together as Aunt Charity finished up one more sewing item for the Townsends. "Show her, Joe," Millie urged. He gurgled happily and reached into the side of his wooden high chair, pulling out a large rock. Holding it out to Sarah, she could see it was part quartz and had lots of clear and silver stripes in it.

"Why, it's beautiful, Joe," Sarah said with a smile. "Did you find it out in the field?" Josiah bounced up and down in his seat, saying something akin to "rock for Sarah, love Sarah, hold me, Sarah." The three girls laughed, enjoying the moment.

Just as the Townsend wagon drove up, Aunt Charity had called Sarah to her room one last time. She had prayed over the girl, much to Sarah's embarrassment, and had given her a small stack of garments for Mr. Townsend to take to town for her. Apparently, he was returning some pieces she had worked on during the week.

All talk of Matthew McMillan had ended that day last week when Aunt Charity had released her secret, and for that, Sarah was grateful. It had almost been too much to digest, and she wasn't sure how she was to react to her father now. Letting him know that she now understood his pain – or at the very least, was privy to the situation – was out of the question. Not only would he rail against her, for he would think she saw him as weak, but he would most certainly close the door between Sarah and her Aunt Charity, an event which must never occur. So Sarah found herself in the unenviable position of knowing too much and wondering how to hide it. She could only hope her father would be as uninterested in her thoughts as he usually was.

After much embracing, Sarah turned to leave Aunt Charity's room, tears threatening to fall. "My dear niece?" she had stopped her. "One last thing, child. I have noted you wear a locket; it slips out from your dress occasionally, though you do well trying to hide it." Sarah's hand flew unconsciously toward the silver locket nestled against her neck. Charity smiled. "Yes, I have seen it. And I know it. It belonged to Matilda. There were two images painted inside – one was of Matilda, the other was a rough sketch of Matthew. She was never without it around her neck. You received it from Grandma McMillan, did you not?" Sarah nodded, afraid.

"Yes, it is as I thought. After Matilda passed, someone took it from her neck and left it there, in the cabin she and Matthew shared. Grandma McMillan said she returned some days later, and while Matthew sat out in the sun, recuperating, she entered to clean. Lying on the floor in a corner was the locket. It had been crushed, but not to the point of uselessness. The image of Matilda remained inside, but Matthew had pulled his own sketch out and attempted to destroy it in the fire. Grandma found it, partially burned. She pulled it out and retrieved the locket. She pocketed both, thinking of you I believe, and never told Matthew what she had done. I am sure he wondered what happened to it but never raised the question." Sarah was astounded. Once again, something she thought she understood had another complete life of its own. She pulled the locket from the folds of her dress, examining it closely.

The etching of the rose on the front seemed perfect, and the only sign she could see of the attempted destruction was a few nicks on the sides. She had assumed that had come from wear and tear. "Yes, it is exquisite, is it not?" Aunt Charity read her thoughts. "Grandma McMillan had it repaired by a local silversmith who did a glorious work. But the piece I have is here, and I had hoped that you might somehow desire to have this as well." She reached beside her on the bed and picked up a tiny strip of singed paper. As she placed it in Sarah's palm, the sketch of a younger, clean shaven Matthew McMillan peered at Sarah. Only a portion of the oval had been singed; in fact, it might still wedge into the left side of the locket. Sarah looked up confused.

Charity sighed. "Yes, I know. You may not be ready to add him to your treasure, but regardless, it is yours to keep. Grandma McMillan was uneasy with the thought of holding on to the sketch, and I believe she hesitated to give it to you. So it became mine ... for a time. Hold on to it, Sarah. One day, it may join the image of your mother and lie next to your heart." Sarah took the small paper and placed it carefully in her pocket. She didn't want Aunt Charity to see the disgust on her face – the very idea of placing that in the locket with her mother! She would deal with this "gift" later, after leaving the McMillans' home.

So it was that Sarah found herself wedged between Daniel and Mr. Townsend – reviewing the morning in her mind — as dawn broke over the horizon of the cornfield. Waving goodbye to the children standing in the yard, she looked past them and saw the tied stalks of corn left for Obediah to finish up. She felt for the tiny sketch in her pocket. So much to take in ... and on top of it all, she had to sit next to Daniel all day.

Chapter Nine

Sarah was thankful the overland road back toward Keysburg often ran parallel to the Red River so she could watch the swollen, muddy waters and the swinging bends. They had come out of the McPhersons' lane then turned due west, but not before Sarah caught sight of the Red River Meeting House. She hadn't had time to dwell much on her night there, the persuasive preaching of Rev. McGready or that strange sense of another world she had felt in her heart. Perhaps religion was an acceptable thing – she could see where it brought hope and a sort of release from the hardships of life – but she still couldn't see the hand of God anywhere in her life. If He truly did exist, He must have dismissed the McMillans from His mind long ago.

Mercifully, Daniel and his father had much to discuss, and although Sarah was a bit uncomfortable with the two of them talking back and forth to each other over the top of her head, she became accustomed to it and was glad to sit, think and stare at the river.

She was bundled warmly against the chill of the day having been told that early October in the Ohio Valley region was unpredictable. It may be fairly warm and comfortable, or she could be surprised by an early snow. This day was overcast and grey with large, billowing clouds moving rapidly through the sky. Still, it didn't have the damp feel of rain yet, and she thought they would make it to Port Royal without getting wet. She pulled the blanket tighter around her shoulders as they rode around a bend, the wagon pressing her into Daniel's left arm.

"Are you cold?" Daniel broke out of his conversation with his father about the price of tobacco on the current market. His hazel eyes were kind and concerned.

"No, I am fine," Sarah responded in clipped words, hoping he would continue to let her be, but Mr. Townsend decided otherwise.

"Miss McMillan, it is certainly our pleasure to have you joining us on our journey," the older Townsend remarked. "And I've been noticing you watching our river. Nothing like it, is there? My pappy brought our family here well nigh onto twenty years ago from Virginia, and I've loved it ever since. The river is like a friend to me, part of the family somehow." He reined in his horses for a moment as the road and the river drew closer together. They could hear the sound of the rushing water now, the color a typical cloudy red. Weeks of rain and runoff had turned the sometimes ambling river into a careening mass of water. All river traffic had ceased until the current ebbed; it was simply too dangerous for flatboats. Sarah smelled the damp mosses that grew around the edge, an odor that transported her back to Port Royal while Daniel sat still beside her, his eyes roaming up and down.

"Yes, I admire it as well," Sarah responded, in spite of her unconscious attempt to keep quiet on this trip. "It runs right next to Port Royal; it is the first thing I see when I top the hill to come into the settlement, and I find solace in its greeting."

"Indeed?" Townsend turned toward this solemn girl in surprise. Apparently, the waters ran deep in her as well. "Both Townsend men feel the same way, don't we, son?"

Daniel's eyes crinkled in amusement at his father as he nodded in agreement. "It is a common thing, I think, to respect the river for what it brings to us – much needed water, energy for our grist mills, the best way to travel in this wilderness," Daniel said thoughtfully. "But I have often thought I love the river even more for what it brings to our spirits and souls, a peaceful sense of God's provision, beavers and otters and other critters that reveal his creation, a chance to explore and seek out new opportunities – yes, Pappy, I do love the Red." Daniel paused, watching a stray log tumble through the waters. The three of them sat transfixed for a time longer before Townsend clucked the horses forward. They rode into Keysburg quiet and thoughtful but not uncomfortable in one another's company.

The day moved along much the same as the threesome passed through Keysburg settlement and down the trail toward Port Royal. They had lunched on the way in hopes of beating the rain to Port Royal — the billowing clouds had darkened slowly as the day progressed. It appeared to be slow-moving, but moisture in the air had increased steadily and now, in late afternoon, Sarah began to feel her damp garments sticking to her skin. There was no doubt about it; rain was coming. Townsend predicted about one more hour of travel as he urged his horses forward with haste. Sarah's head had begun to nod as the wear of the ride took its toll when the wagon rounded a sharp curve in the road. The simultaneous jerking of the two men on each side of her woke her abruptly. Townsend pulled tightly on the reins to keep from running over two Indians who stood firmly in the center of the dirt trail. He swore under his breath as Daniel reached behind her for the rifle lying in the back of the wagon.

"Whoa, whoa there," Townsend bellowed, all frivolity gone. "It's dang Chickasaws," he mumbled under his breath. The two Indians each held long-barreled flintlock muskets in their hands and from their waists hung sharp-bladed knives and powder horns; their faces showed intent but were unreadable. Sarah was relieved that they did not appear to be part of a war party, but she had heard tell of many instances of Indian trouble even when they wore clothes of the settlers' style. Their dress fell somewhere in between. Both wore leggings of deer skin, a lone shirt and a short coat. Their faces were smooth. The larger of the two spoke broken English.

"Need help," he stated simply, showing no signs of using the old British musket he held. "Woman hurt river. Need doctor. Need wagon," he pointed to the back of Townsend's almost full wagon while the three stared fixedly at the two Indians. Sarah knew enough to realize this could be a ploy and she felt the tension in Daniel's body as he leaned into her, partially blocking her. While there had been no rumors of Indian attacks on the settlements in the past months, one could never be sure. Relations had improved since the Creeks and Cherokee had signed a treaty, and these more northern Chickasaws said they only desired peace, but it was fragile at best. There remained rogue Indians as well as rogue white men. Townsend responded warily.

"Bring her to us, and we'll see what we can do."

"No, you come," he pointed with the old flintlock to Daniel and Sarah. Daniel leaned even more into Sarah, laying his weapon in his lap.

"I will come," Daniel replied, "but we leave her here," he said, nodding toward Sarah. In a quick assessment, Sarah realized she'd rather take her chances with Daniel and a rifle than be left in the wagon with Mr. Townsend and the other Indian. She couldn't have said why, but that was her instinct.

"No," she said, turning toward Daniel. "I will go with you."

The usually calm façade of Daniel Townsend had disappeared, and Sarah saw a boy – no, a man – she had not encountered before. His face was set like stone, and his eyes snapped toward her in anger.

"You will not go with me," he whispered through clenched teeth. "You will stay here with Father where it is safe. He has a pistol."

"No," she repeated, her square jaw tightening. "I am going with you."

"Sarah ..."

"Stop!" the Indian spoke sharply. "No time for argue. Come." He raised the aging musket, pointing it in the direction of Sarah and Daniel. Instinctively, the other Chickasaw mirrored his companion, raising his musket and pointing it toward Townsend. The older man slowly slid his hand behind the wagon seat, trying to reach his loaded pistol, but the Indian observed his shift. He took a step forward, bringing the musket up and pressing it against his cheek. "No move," the speaking Indian directed. "You," he swung again toward Daniel and Sarah, "come now."

"Fine. We will come," Daniel said, "but I bring my gun."

"Yes, yes, yes." The speaking Indian pointed toward the bluff overlooking the Red River while the other had taken a step back but still kept his musket fixed on Townsend.

Sarah led the way through briars and brambles, following the directions called out from the Indian who walked behind Daniel. Sounds of rushing water greeted them as they approached the bluff; the Red River lay in front, snaking toward the west. "Down," the Indian pointed. "Go big rock." Sarah inched her way down the slippery trail. Leaves had begun to fall on top of footpaths, creating ribbons of slick mud. *Again,* she thought. *More mud and mire. What a fitting way for me to die.*

As she neared the base of the ravine, Sarah spotted what looked like a white cloth bundled near the edge of the water. Wet hair was flung over the ground, and a boot lay to the side. "Dear Christ," she heard Daniel mutter behind her. She ran the last few steps toward the very still, very pale woman. She was young, maybe a little older than Sarah, her skin as white as new-fallen snow. Daniel dropped to his knees, putting his ear to her mouth. "She is breathing," he declared, "but barely. We've got to get her to the wagon and get her warm. Here, Sarah, hold this," he thrust the rifle into her hands as he leaned down to lift the girl. The Chickasaw merely stood to the side, watching and waiting. Sarah held onto the weapon as she glanced up and down the river. There were no other signs of people – no grounded boat, nothing to tell this girl's story. As she stooped to pick up the boot, she realized she had been left with the Chickasaw. Daniel's back was disappearing up the path, the head and feet of the girl swinging with each step. She looked back at the Indian who continued to stand still, watching her every move. *So much for protection,* Sarah thought wryly. She shrugged, hefted the musket to her shoulder and followed Daniel up the path. She could have sworn the Chickasaw smiled.

They were able to wedge the girl into the back of the wagon between tobacco and barrels. The blankets that had kept Sarah so warm throughout the day now covered the still figure, wrapped and tucked tightly around her body. While the men looked the other way, Sarah had stripped as many of the wet clothes off as she could, then wrapped her much like a worm in a cocoon. Not once did she stir, and Sarah feared greatly for her life.

The braves stood silently for a short time observing the movements in the wagon, the larger speaking to the other in their native tongue. Finally, they turned in unison and started walking in a northwesterly direction. In a gesture of goodwill, Townsend had given them several sticks of dried beef and a small portion of cheese to ease them on their way. They appeared grateful for the food and, by the time they moved on, had lost all fierceness in their demeanor. Their straight, proud backs quickly disappeared into the dense, wooded forest.

Now the threat of impending weather was coupled with the need to get this girl to Port Royal – Townsend barked his horses into motion, and they set off with speed. The wind blew directly into the faces of the three on the wagon seat, and without her blankets, Sarah was cold to the bone within minutes. She gazed at the sky with trepidation. She would put up with the cold. Much better to be cold and dry than a little warmer and soaking wet. She hoped the Townsends were praying for the rain to hold off.

The final hour of the trip flew by in a montage of images for Sarah – the silent, pale girl who already looked as if she was wrapped for burial; Townsend's horses, frothing at the mouth, sweat and steam coming from their bodies; the constant jolting and tossing of the wagon on a rutted road; rolling, billowing clouds hurling themselves closer and closer as they neared Port Royal. Finally, they topped the last rise, and the settlement lay before them. Sarah was able to see the town for the first time from the north rather than the south, the Red River curling in front, its rolling waters appearing to deny them entrance. It was not yet dark, but close, and the rain had held off. She felt the tension ebb somewhat in her shoulders.

Townsend began yelling for the ferry before they even reached the river. It was anchored on the north side this evening, a fact for which they all were grateful. The Townsend men thanked God for his provision as they moved the girl out of the wagon, and Daniel carried her onto the ferry. Mr. Anderson began hauling them over the river immediately while Sarah and Townsend waited by the water's edge, watching them inch across the dark waters. The moment the raft hit the opposite shore, Daniel jumped off and ran toward the Public Square, the ragdoll figure of the girl bouncing awkwardly in his arms. Apparently, Mr. Anderson had told him where to find help, and he disappeared around a corner before the ferry had reached the north side of the river again.

As Sarah watched the men load the wagon and horses aboard the quivering raft, she began to feel the weight of home settle over her. In her pocket was the letter from Aunt Charity, asking Matthew to send Sarah again to Logan County in the late spring. It was Sarah's promissory note of hope. If her father denied her this … she simply couldn't dwell on it. Right now, she had to face him, had to walk the mile to their cabin in the dark.

Daniel still had not returned by the time Sarah and his father landed on the Port Royal side of the river. Townsend was a complete gentlemen, offering to carry her home, but Sarah knew the horses were spent and needed their stable, food, water and grooming immediately. Plus, she wasn't sure how her father would feel about this man taking her home alone. She declined his thoughtful invitation, lied that her cabin was right around the corner, and hefted the saddlebag to her shoulder. She had hoped to see Daniel again, although why she didn't know. True, he had been kind and tried to protect her, but his way of treating her like a child was immensely irritating.

In fact, Sarah felt frustrated at the thought of him. *Why was he so pushy and controlling?* She stomped down Spring Alley, head into the wind, watching her feet. *And then he left me with the Chickasaw – alone. After all that talk about keeping me safe. Once we found the girl by the river, it was as if I didn't even exist! And I'm glad about that,* she thought, trying to convince herself. *Maybe now he'll leave me alone. Maybe she'll live – oh, I hope she lives! – and they will join in marriage. Then Daniel Townsend won't bother with me anymore.*

Sarah reached the edge of Port Royal proper and turned down the south trail toward home. Rather than feeling relieved, she felt somehow bereft … and it began to rain.

Chapter Ten

The winter of 1798-99 was bitterly cold, and McGready found it difficult to maintain his congregation during those months. Meetings popped
up in various homes across the county, but it was well nigh impossible to
gather all his flock in one place – even if he broke it down into areas.
Those communicants in Gasper River were almost too far north to be
reached when the weather turned. Thankfully, John Rankin was covering
that section, and McGready liked what he saw in his disciple. He felt
sure Rankin could handle the congregation on his own fairly soon.
Muddy River, however, seemed to be floundering.

And then there was the damage done by Mr. Balch. McGready stared
thoughtfully into his fire this early morning, jostling the baby on his knee
while Nancy prepared breakfast. The other girls had yet to rise, and the
house held a cozy, early morning serenity. A gentle stirring and sloshing
told him Nancy was almost ready to put the Johnny cakes over the fire.
As she leaned close to fix the kettle lid over the flames, thereby creating
an oval, flat area for the cakes, she squeezed his shoulder and gave him a
brief hug. "Where are your thoughts this morning, Mr. McGready?" she
said with a smile.

He hesitated briefly, "Where they always are, my dear."

Nancy sat in the empty slat-backed chair beside him, taking the baby
and nestling her into her shoulder. As she gently patted the baby's back,
Nancy found her eyes drawn to the flames as well. Last night had delivered a hard freeze, and she knew the older girls would not look forward
to the outside chores this morning. But as she watched her husband lean
down to toss another log on the fire, she set all other thoughts of household duties aside. *He looks tired,* she thought. *Always tired and always
working.*

"James?" her voice broke the silence. "You know, dearest, that the winter months are the most difficult. It is then that Satan throws despair and discouragement over your spirit – every year you find yourself thus. I pray for you, my husband, but also encourage you to not allow it a foothold into your heart."

McGready's dark eyes never left the fire.

"In a practical sense," Nancy continued, "I hear tell of the grand results among the faithful. Sister Wilson maintains her conversion experience, and although her family has yet to embrace the Gospel, I feel sure they will. The Townsends remain ever faithful. The Princes and Johnsons continue home meetings in spite of bitter cold and snow. The fruit is remaining, James." She leaned forward, flipping the cakes over.

"And yet, you cannot deny the fact that Mr. Balch's party has deeply opposed the working of the Spirit among us," McGready sighed. "The county has been filled with contention and disputation. Within weeks of his arrival, every appearance of conviction seemed to be lost! There has been scarcely a sentence heard about religion from many who, only weeks before, gave great attention to the work of their souls' salvation. I find it a dismal state of deadness and darkness," he shook his head sadly, a blackness of spirit settling over him like a cocoon.

"And yet again, dear husband, the prayer society continues to pray for revival steadily and with conviction. Why, we met only last week at Sister McPherson's home, with dear Obediah finally present and working their farm, and cried out to Heaven for revival among our children and the people of Logan County. God surely will hear our cries," she stated firmly.

The steady, rock-like man appeared almost broken as he hung his head. "What if Balch is right, Nancy? What if we have only seen emotional excesses and not the move of the Spirit? He is certainly a man of God, a minister of the Gospel who knows the Scripture as well as any other man of faith. Perhaps I have been deceiving myself and others by believing something that is of the devil and not of God."

Nancy McGready's solemn eyes looked in sadness on the bent figure of her husband. She prayed silently for a moment then responded. "I think you know the real answer to those questions, James, but I also think you need to spend time with your Lord today. This darkness of spirit is only that – a blinding oppression sent by the enemy of our faith.

How many times have you seen it on me and prayed for me and called me forth, back into His marvelous light?" She smiled, tiny wrinkles curling around her eyes. "So many I cannot begin to count." McGready glanced toward his wife, the baby nestled warmly in her arms, sleeping contentedly. "I will pray for you – and I will attend to the children's lessons today at our house. I can teach them a few things and review their memorization. I would that you attend to your soul, perhaps walk the land or go to the river. I have no doubt our God will meet you there."

McGready didn't want to leave his wife handling his affairs – what man would do that to such a woman? And yet, he knew the wisdom of her words and felt the draw in his heart from the Lord. He must reconcile the truth again; he must stand on a firm foundation and the only rock he had found in this life was that of his Lord. "If you are sure?" he asked.

"More than," Nancy replied with a nod. "You are always the strength of our family. I am honored to stand in your stead for a short time." They heard the older girls stirring in the back room, looked at one another and smiled in silent agreement. Truly they were blessed.

Winter in Port Royal was much the same. Sarah easily slipped back into her routine of solitude, although she often found herself talking out loud to the McPhersons at the lonely cabin. Like McGready, despair threatened to overtake her at times, but then she would find a reason to walk into town, hoping to meet up with Ann or hear news of Logan County from the docks.

That was how she had heard the rest of the story regarding the girl by the river. Her father had never mentioned the river-soaked girl nor asked any questions about the journey, the Townsends or the McPhersons; but Hagar and Sammy Pace were full of information and questions when Sarah walked to the trading post a few days after her return.

"We done missed you, sho nuff," Hagar pronounced that day with gravity. "Me and Mama worked yo' cabin, mindin' yo Pappy like we wuz his own, but it tweren't easy. He's a hard man, he is." As usual, Sammy had no time for these gossipy female sorts of conversations. He jumped from one foot to the other as the three of them walked together through the settlement. They had been waiting for Sarah to come to town for two days – while they shot robbers and rogues in the alleyways.

"Tell her, Hagar. Tell her 'bout that girl," Sammy panted, out of breath from his antics. Without waiting for an answer, he shot out, "An' you got to tell us, Sarah, 'bout how you found her and what the Injun was like!" he spun around, staring into Sarah's green eyes. "There was an Injun, weren't there? That's what we heard. We don't see many Injuns round here. My Pappy says they used to be 'round here all the time, but they moved on. Was he a big Injun? With big, round eyes, holding a hatchet, ready to chop off your …"

"Sammy!" Hagar shushed the boy with her hand over his mouth. "You watch what you be sayin'! Lauds a'mercy, boy. Yo' mama would swat you good if'n she heard yo' nonsense." Sarah continued to walk, swinging an empty tin pail by her side, smiling broadly at her two young friends. Perhaps it was good to be home.

"Now, Sarah, here's what happened," the three moved over to the side of the road to let a wagon pass. "Next day after you'uns brought in the girl, yo' friends moved on early, headin' through to Clarksville and leavin' her with Mr. Skinner and his wife. Mr. Skinner told Mr. Neville he didn't 'spect her to make it, but she began to wake up and talk a little bit. Mr. Skinner say he was most surprised person on the face of the earth. He say he don't know much 'bout doctorin' and such, but he's seen plenty folks in a bad way."

Sammy interrupted. "How you know all this, Hagar?"

"I done stood outside Mrs. Skinner's window when she opened it, lettin' in the air to clean out the room. Mr. Skinner, he was talkin', talkin' – loud too. Meantime, down the river late yest'day mornin' comes a flatboat, but tweren't pushin' no logs. Had two men, three women on it. They's lookin' for their sister, the women says. She got swept up in the current way upriver, and they's lookin' for her body somewhere's, but had no luck. They's plannin' to go on to the Cumberland, if'n they could.

"Well sir, just imagine their surprise when they find their sister laying on the bed at Mrs. Skinner's all as pretty as you please. Course, she tweren't nowhere near healthy, but she was alive. Oh the rejoicin' and celebratin' coming from that place. 'Bout near made me cry," Hagar wiped an invisible tear from her light brown cheek. "I hears theys a goin' stay in Port Royal till she well enough to travel, then they goin' on back up to Kaintuck, which is where they was headed in the first place."

"So they all are still here then?" Sarah asked.

"Yep. So I heard from the window," Hagar nodded, crossed her arms around her chest and jumped up and down a bit to warm up. The clouds from their breath hovered around them as they talked.

"What about Ann Neville?" Sarah changed the subject. "How is she?"

"Why you want to know about Ann Neville?" Sammy tossed out as he stomped the ice in a shallow puddle.

"I just do. We talked some on my way to Kentucky," Sarah responded vaguely, not sure she wanted her young friends to know how much she really cared about Ann.

"Well, she been sickly again ..." Hagar began.

"An' she ain't been to no meetin' house at all since they started burnin' the woodstove," Sammy finished. "Mama said the other day that she was afeard for Mrs. Neville, that maybe she might lose Ann." His bright cherub face fell as suddenly as a cloud covers the sun. "I sure hope not. Ann's nice."

"Ho there!" a wagoneer's voice broke through their conversation, forcing the three to once again step to the side of the road. Sarah longed to hear more, to know more about Ann, about the Townsends leaving town (Did Hagar see Daniel?), but she knew she had already pushed her luck in the time she had taken to catch up. While her father was at the warehouse, he had eyes all over town, and he would sure enough know if she stood and talked in the road for more than a few minutes. She gave the children a quick hug.

"I had best be getting my goods and then back to the cabin before it is too late," Sarah looked at the sky. Hagar understood immediately.

"Yep, you'd best do that, Sarah. We'll tell you more next time you come in," she said, pulling Sammy back toward Spring Alley.

"But wait!" Sammy tugged back. "I ain't heard the Injun story."

"Next time we hear it. We got to let Sarah go," Hagar instructed.

"That's not fair!" And the two of them left — Hagar dragging Sammy by the shirt collar, Sarah watching for a moment in amusement. Then she was off to Johnson's trading post.

The Waking Up

The night she had returned, Sarah had handed her father Aunt Charity's letter requesting her presence again in the spring. Matthew had taken the note from her hand and tucked it into his pocket. Sarah never saw it again that winter, never heard anything about it. Her newly acquired knowledge about the tragedy her father experienced never threatened to be exposed because she simply couldn't reconcile the man Aunt Charity had described with the man she served in their home. Nothing had changed. He showed no signs of affection (perish the thought!) or even interest that she had returned. Sarah found their old pattern both routine and stifling. Living with the McPhersons had given her a taste of normalcy, and now she wasn't sure she could survive in this prison created by her father.

And the charred sketch Aunt Charity had placed so tenderly in Sarah's hand the morning she left? Sarah surprised herself by not throwing it away – or better yet, burning it in the fire! She tucked it in her box of keepsakes that she kept nestled underneath her bed. She couldn't have said why she bothered, but she did. Maybe all hope wasn't gone.

At times, she recalled parts of Rev. McGready's sermon she had heard that night – she almost could hear his voice resonating in her mind. *The child experiences a wonderful change when ushered into life; but that is a much more wonderful change which the unregenerated sinner undergoes when transformed into the image of God. Indeed, it is so powerful and extraordinary, that nothing but the Almighty power of Jehovah can effect it. In Scripture it is expressed by a "new creation."*

Certainly, she understood nothing of this spiritual change McGready talked of, but that phrase — the new creation — those words banged and rattled in her spirit daily. To be a new creation, to start over as something else, that was a concept Sarah could grasp and long for with everything in her. What would it feel like to be new and start over? She could only imagine.

Over the frigid winter months, Sarah found two instances where she was able to visit Ann Neville in her home. The visits had to be there because, as far as Sarah knew, Ann had not left the house since the weather had turned bad. Thankfully, Matthew did have to leave the house; in fact, on those two particular days, he'd had to leave the settlement and ride west to Clarksville to find white oak for his barrels and pails. He'd soaked plenty of hoop poles during the spring, but he was running low on wood. On those days, she had sneaked through town, avoiding being seen by many people, and gently knocked on the Neville's front door. Mrs. Neville somehow knew all without Sarah saying anything. She welcomed her in quietly and led her to where Ann would be resting, either in bed or sitting by the fire in their fancy sitting room, a wool blanket thrown over her lap.

And then, for a blessed numbers of hours, Ann and Sarah talked, laughed, sometimes cried a bit, and enjoyed all the treasures of a kindred spirit friendship. Sarah always felt guilty when she noticed that food had been brought into the room for them or a nice pot of hot tea had been situated on a nearby table. She and Ann were so caught up with one another, the rest of the world – and those responsibilities – disappeared. What Sarah never would have guessed was that Mrs. Neville was so thrilled with her visits that she told the house help to do anything to keep Sarah there as long as possible. There was no doubt that Sarah's visits revitalized Ann. The color returned to her cheeks and laughter was heard in the house again.

But Sarah had no knowledge of such things and would have been the most surprised because, in her mind, the visits to Ann were her lifeblood and gave her the impetus to keep going in her solitary life. And so the two fed off each other without leaving the other drained.

Sarah's last visit that winter was actually closer to spring. It was early April when her father had to take another trip to Clarksville, and Sarah and Ann had regaled one another with stories they had heard and gossip Sarah had picked up from Sammy and Hagar on her infrequent trips to town. Ann's cough seemed worse that day, and Sarah noticed spots of blood on her handkerchief. She immediately became concerned.

"How long has this been happening?" Sarah prodded, trying not to give way to panic. Ann smiled wanly.

"Quite a while, really, but not daily. I go through periods of it, but please do not tell Mama, Sarah. It overly upsets her, and there is no need for it."

"But surely she finds out when she cleans your handkerchiefs?"

"Yes, she would, but I give these to Sally who washes them without Mama knowing. We have an agreement of sorts. Neither of us sees the need to alarm Mama who already lives on pins and needles with me," Ann replied quietly. "The truth is, I am dying, Sarah, and I know it. I can feel the life draining from my body, but it is alright. God and I have come to an understanding, and I know that Heaven is my home. The longer I remain in this frail body, the more I want to be with my Lord Christ. I become tired." As if to highlight her words, Ann laid her head back on her chair, closing her eyes for a moment, taking deep breaths. Sarah's Irish green eyes opened wide in alarm, disbelief struggling with truth on her strong face.

"Do not say that out loud, Ann!" she urged. "It is not true. You will be fine, just wait. The spring will come. You will be able to get out and enjoy fresh air. It will strengthen your body and spirit. This is just a temporary illness, and I will not hear anything else about it," Sarah's shoulders snapped in decisiveness as Ann cracked open her eyes, smiling in gentleness and kindness.

"If only it were so, Sarah. But even Mr. Skinner admits he has done all he can, as have others in Clarksville. Mr. Skinner fears it is consumption – my coughing continues to worsen and I simply cannot hold any good food down these days." Ann shifted in her chair, leaning forward to place her hand on Sarah's knee. She peered deeply into Sarah's eyes, as if to will her to listen and listen well. "Sarah, my greatest hope is that you, too, will find the Savior so that we will be together in eternity – forever. My greatest fear is that you will not. Please, Sarah, will you not reconsider the goodness of the Savior, the kindness of a God who sent His Son to die on the cross for your sins. I know your past and the horror of it all, but that does not change the character of God or His love for you. If only you would open your heart to Him, you will see these things clearly. But you cannot see Him until He enters. You cannot fix yourself first, Sarah. He must do the repairs to your soul." Ann flopped back onto her chair again, spent from the effort to keep her friend from the gates of hell.

Sarah simply stared silently as the Neville's sitting room walls threatened to squeeze her until she couldn't breathe. She heard the ticking of their clock, smelled the fresh corn pone coming from the table beside Ann's chair, felt the brocade needlework on the quilt lying over the arm of the chair in which she sat. Her senses all tingled at once, proving she still lived; and yet, she felt another part of her heart begin to die. She heard Ann's words, and honestly, if anything made her want to embrace Ann's Gospel, the thought of being with Ann forever did. But Sarah knew there was even more at stake than that and this wasn't a decision to be entered lightly nor would she deceive Ann by lying and telling her the commitment to Christ had already been made. Ann deserved more than that, and she would know if Sarah was telling the truth anyway.

Sally entered the room, her soft footsteps bringing a sense of sanity. "Miss Ann?" the dark-skinned woman questioned. "You needin' yo' bed?" Ann sighed deeply and shook her head. "No, Sally. While Sarah is here, I will sit. I will make her talk to me so I can listen and not overtax myself. Would that be acceptable?" Ann smiled, still with her eyes closed, and Sally glanced at Sarah sadly.

"That's fine, Miss Ann. I'm thinkin' Miss Sarah here will take good care of you." Sally's hand trailed on Sarah's shoulder as she left the room, somehow taking part of the sadness with her. Sarah mustered herself to think of a funny story. She decided to tell Ann how Millie and Mattie were convinced Billy the cat was fat, and how surprised the girls were when Billy had kittens.

Quiet laughter rolled out of the Neville's living room for another hour or two before Sarah knew she had to leave. The girls fiercely embraced, Sarah promising another visit as soon as it could be done. As Mrs. Neville closed the front door behind her, Sarah began running toward home, feeling as if a thousand demons were chasing her.

Chapter Eleven

Logan County
July 1799

Sarah stretched her arms high over her head, drawing the pungent smell of fresh corn deep into her lungs. All around her, she heard shifting sounds of corn stalks bending and breaking as men, women and children moved in and out of the rows, quickly snapping off ears of ripe corn and tossing them into baskets. Even Aunt Charity, a much smaller version of the woman Sarah had left last October, moved quickly, the new McPherson baby swaddled next to her breast with a cloth tied around her midsection.

Sarah had been making her bed in the loft at the McPherson home for almost a month now and was thrilled to be back. Once the early planting had been accomplished in Port Royal and the summer months had moved in, her father had announced she would be returning to Aunt Charity as soon as could be arranged. Apparently, he already had spoken with Mr. Neville and, once again, Sally and Hagar would manage things at their small cabin. Sarah, of course, had been overjoyed but allowed none of that to show on her unyielding countenance. She felt sure if her father knew how much she loved her aunt and cousins, he would find a way to stop her trips. She even attempted to appear chagrined. Who knew what he thought?

Within only a few days, Sarah was back on the old trace east to the settlement of Keysburg with plans to meet up with Obediah McPherson. All along the trail, Sarah recalled her earlier journey with the Nevilles and longed to be with them again; but beggars couldn't be choosers and riding with Mr. Wilcox and his apprentice was her only option. She had been allowed about ten minutes to say goodbye to Ann, who had improved with the coming of spring. Since her arrival in Kentucky, Sarah had written three letters and received two in return. Every once in a while, the fear that something may happen to Ann while she was gone would rise in Sarah's heart, threatening to take over and throw her into a wild panic. But she would squelch it, reminding herself how much Ann trusted in a God who was merciful and kind. Sarah relied on the fact that their relationship was so close; He wouldn't allow such a thing.

After only a week at the McPhersons' home, Sarah's uncle Obediah once again mounted his horse and rode east to survey. Having only heard stories about him from Mattie and Millie, Sarah was pleased to get to know him better and fully understand where Josiah's fiery temper and red hair originated. In many ways, Obediah reminded Sarah of her father but without the bitterness and barely suppressed anger. Where Obediah ranted and raged over finding the cow out of the split-rail fence and eating the corn in the field, he inevitably found something to laugh about in the process. Her father would have thrashed the cow half to death; Obediah gently rounded her up, gave her extra grain, and complained all night about the stupidity of certain animals. Sarah found he was the perfect balance to the McPherson household and understood why tears fell when he left to travel.

"Sarah?" Aunt Charity interrupted her thoughts, passing her another empty basket. "Here, use this one and when you have it filled, go ahead and take it to the corn crib. We have only a few more rows, and the field will be picked clean." Sarah took the basket and used the corner of her apron to wipe the sweat from her face again. It was a typical blazing hot July day. Mattie had been sent back to the cabin a few minutes ago to prepare mint tea for the workers. Knowing that Obediah had to leave – and the corn hadn't yet been harvested – many of Aunt Charity's neighbors had come out that morning to help clear the field. As Aunt Charity said, the least she could do is offer them a cool glass of mint tea after sweating all day. Sarah thought longingly of the cool drink – Mattie was using water from the spring house – when she glanced up and spotted Mrs. Townsend through the corn stalks. The gentle lady with a perpetual smile on her face was showing Josiah how to pull the ear off the stalk without injuring the plant. Sarah liked her very much and longed to ask where Daniel was today. She hadn't seen him nor heard from him since her return to Logan County, but she hesitated to ask. She had tried to see if Mattie or Millie might know where Daniel was — thinking the girls wouldn't wonder why a pretty fifteen-year-old was asking about a handsome young man — but they knew nothing.

Sarah wouldn't allow herself to wonder why she cared.

"I think that's your last basket, Sarah," Aunt Charity labored up behind her, lugging her own full basket and a sleeping, perspiring baby. Sarah took the basket from her and poured the corn into the bulging crib. "Whew! What a bountiful crop the Lord has provided," Charity leaned far back, hands on her hips. "I am not sure my body will be straight ever again."

"Indeed," Mrs. Townsend eased up, hauling her last load. Sarah took it from her hands. "I think we should make the children pick the corn from now on while we recline in the shade," she said, half in jest. Daniel had three younger siblings, Sarah had learned, all of which had worked diligently in the field that day. His grandmother, who lived with them, remained at home. "I hear tell that women in the deep South have big houses and are only concerned with their upkeep. Perhaps they know something we do not."

"And perhaps they have slaves to help," Charity said with a hint of bitterness, "and we do not." Mrs. Townsend nodded.

"Yes, Charity, you are right. Better to work all day and night in our fields and not have the onus of slaveholding on our consciences and our spirits. I fear the judgment of God is coming to our good nation," Mrs. Townsend pulled out a soiled handkerchief and wiped her face, squinting toward the sun. Charity saw her fatigue and gently put her hand under Mrs. Townsend's elbow.

"Come, Joy, let's move toward the spring where it is much cooler. Mattie has mint tea, and there are several stumps on which we may rest. Sarah?" she looked back over her shoulder. "Would you mind telling all the others that they may come to us after they unload their last baskets? We have cool drink and a shady place to rest."

"Yes, Aunt," Sarah smiled, watching the two good friends move toward the woods.

She completed her job quickly as all the children finished the picking. Two older gentlemen and their wives also had come, but decided to head home without refreshment, thanking Sarah for the offer and assuring her they would see her again at the meeting house in a week or so. Sarah smiled, graciously thanked them for their help, and felt her stomach twist oddly at the thought of another McGready sermon at the crowded meeting house. As she walked into the shade a few minutes later, she found Aunt Charity and Mrs. Townsend deep in discussion over the very same thing – much to her displeasure. Meanwhile, the Townsend and McPherson children had found the cool creek to their liking. Boots and socks were strewn all over the bank and the creek was filled with splashing and laughing. Sarah was a bit envious.

"Pull off your boots as well, Sarah," Aunt Charity said, reading her mind. "Dangle your feet in the water while we talk. It is pure bliss," she smiled, wet strands of hair falling out of her cap. Sarah imagined working the field while hefting a nine-month-old couldn't be easy, but Aunt Charity had a mighty strength in her tiny frame and sweet baby Matthew didn't seem to mind. She was nursing him now, her own feet hanging over the side of the spring branch. Sarah quickly unlaced her boots, joining the women. The feel of the ice cold water was an immediate, powerful relief. Aunt Charity was right – pure bliss.

Mrs. Townsend had been silent through this exchange and began speaking, apparently picking up where she and Charity had left off. "I agree, Charity. I do believe this week's communion services will be most powerful. We have sensed the presence of the Spirit of the Lord in our covenant prayers, and Rev. McGready says that a move of God is imminent. Oh, how I long for our Savior to move among his people," she had pulled a small paper fan from her front pocket and was rapidly cooling her face. "It feels as though we have survived the winter of the burial, and resurrection Sunday is on its way."

Sarah watched Millie catch Josiah before he landed face first in the shallow water, only half listening to Mrs. Townsend. Mattie was on the other side of the creek trying to catch a crayfish. She was considering walking through the water to help her when Mrs. Townsend asked her a question.

"Did you ever get to know Elizabeth Holland, Sarah? I know she recuperated quite a few days in Port Royal before she and her siblings came to Logan County."

"Do you mean the girl we pulled from the river?" Sarah asked. "No, I never met her. I heard that she stayed in the settlement for about three days, but I was busy at our farm and never made it in to see her," Sarah attempted to appear casual when, in fact, her father forbade her to try to establish any sort of friendship. He said it would complicate matters and he needed her to be at home. Hagar had reported to Sarah the general facts of the girl's health, and then she had left. Honestly, Sarah had not thought much of her since.

"Ah well. She is certainly a dear girl – she and her brothers and sisters. With the death of their parents and grandparents, they have come to claim war grant land in the north of the county and plan to start farming there. Daniel has been helping them get settled and find the materials they need to begin building," she stated, matter-of-factly. Aunt Charity gently moved Matthew to her shoulder, patting his back and waiting for the burp. The splashing and yelling coming from the creek began to fade into the background as Sarah's mind grasped what Mrs. Townsend had just spoken. Daniel … helping beautiful, frail Elizabeth Holland? Sarah fixed her eyes on the children, willing herself to reveal nothing.

Aunt Charity seemed not to notice. "I am sure the Hollands need much assistance, coming to such a new place and needing to be settled by winter. Are none of them married?" she asked, moving her feet out of the cold water. She stretched them out on a rock as she moved Matthew to the other breast.

"Oh yes. I say siblings, but there are two married sets there. Elizabeth and two of her brothers are yet unwed, but the others are full sisters and brothers-in-law. They came from Virginia through the Cumberland Gap, longing for adventure and freedom from restrictions, as we all do. I expect Daniel will have more to say of them when he returns. He's been gone well nigh a fortnight now, and his father needs him back soon to begin our own harvest. He seems to be quite taken with the young Miss Holland," Mrs. Townsend smiled knowingly. "I would not be surprised that he bring other news as well."

Sarah felt herself begin to choke and tried to suck the hot July air down into her lungs. She coughed and gagged, the beating of her heart almost overcoming her good sense. Aunt Charity patted her on the back, searching her face for signs of distress, but Sarah managed a weak smile, saying she must have swallowed too much tea. She was fine, she assured, but knew she was not. A powerful wave of knowledge had struck her between the eyes and Sarah felt deep within her soul that she really cared for Daniel Townsend – that the irritating, overpowering, bossy, kind young man had stolen her heart. Not only did she not know what to do, but even if she did, it was too late. Such comprehension left her stunned and quiet; her soul bereft.

Slowly, the awareness of a continuing conversation came to Sarah, and she heard Aunt Charity speak her father's name as she patted Sarah on the back. "…realizing the sad state of his soul, Obediah and I agreed that we would name this young one after his Uncle Matthew, in an attempt to redeem the name and pray God to seek and save both our Matthews. "

"Oh my," Mrs. Townsend said knowingly, "truly only the grace of our loving God can redeem a man's soul." She, too, leaned toward Sarah, gently patting her knee. "I will pray for your father as well, young Sarah. What is it for a man to gain the whole world but lose his soul?"

It was simply too much. Sarah jerked her leg away from Mrs. Townsend, practically leaping to her feet in distress. "I need to check on Josiah," she blurted as she stumbled toward the shallow end of the creek, holding her skirts high. Mrs. Townsend stared after her in confusion while Charity watched the retreating girl thoughtfully.

McGready had been preparing for this fourth Sabbath in July for over a month. His right-hand men, John Rankin and William Hodge, were scheduled to teach during the Friday through Monday services; and of course, McGready himself would deliver several of the messages. He removed his coat as the heat inside Red River Meeting House threatened to overtake him. Although he had left both doors wide open while he knocked down wasp nests and drove out the bothersome creatures, the heat was stifling and oppressive.

He had survived the "dismal state of deadness and darkness" of the winter – as he termed it – and even regained his faith in the move of God over Rogues' Harbor. Mr. Balch continued to minister as well, having drawn many of the new converts back to a sedentary faith, as McGready viewed it. But even in the oppressive heat, McGready felt a coolness of the Spirit in the meeting house, an anticipation of God's move in the place. His pack of covenant prayer warriors had not ceased laboring in the Spirit to call forth God's presence, and he knew God would hear their prayers eventually and come to move among them. Perhaps it would be this week, this meeting.

"I have fixed the front step, James," Hodge barreled through the door, hammer in hand. "Once these devil wasps are driven out, we should be prepared for the people tonight. Perhaps God in His sovereignty will have mercy on us and visit us again, as he did last summer."

"It is our only hope," McGready acknowledged. "Are you prepared to bring the word on the morrow during the morning meeting?" He stepped down from a bench, an empty wasp nest in his hand.

"Most certainly. The word of the Lord burns in my soul; may it come forth with clarity and power," Hodge declared solemnly. "I hear rumored through the countryside that many souls plan to attend all services –perhaps even some of Mr. Balch's followers – but I have heard of no trouble yet. The Wilson brothers have settled down quite a bit, and because it has been so long since this meeting house has operated, we may be covered, as under the wings of our heavenly Father."

McGready strode quickly past Hodges, tossing the paper thin nest into the dirt yard. He took two jumps down the front steps and smashed it with the heel of his boot. "Just in case I missed one," he said, turning toward Hodge. "And may our heels stomp the plans of the enemy of our souls in the same way." He spun back toward the open door with determination.

The crowds arrived early for all meetings that weekend, even on this, the last day.

Steady, McGready thought on that Monday morning before the gathering of the last communion. *It has been a steady, solid time of meetings.* In no time, the late July sun burned off what little dew covered the grass. Though it was still early, the people had returned for a final sacrament of the Lord's Supper to be administered before they left for a week's worth of labor. The McPhersons – and Sarah – returned as well, taking their places on the fourth bench on the right, sitting quietly and solemnly as

McGready began his final message which he offered to the consideration of the young.

"Now, in the bloom of youth, in the morning of life, you enjoy the most precious and favourable opportunity of salvation. You have the fairest chance of eternal life of any other class of the human race. Your hearts are young and tender, they are susceptible to good impressions, and they are not yet seared and burdened by long habits of sin and wickedness," McGready's voice rolled effortlessly. "Jesus comes as a suppliant to the door of your heart, and prays you by His groans and bloody sweat – by His torments and dying agonies – by all the joys of Heaven – by all the blessedness of the celestial Paradise – to give Him your hearts while young and tender – to honor Him with the first fruits of your lives."

Mattie, Millie and Sarah sat side-by-side, pressed tightly against one another, listening with all their might. Sarah felt a warm heat begin rolling down from the top of her head, through her body, to the tips of her toes. She was completely uncomfortable and awkward and excited and breathless at the same time. It was as though McGready spoke to her and her alone.

"Yea, the whole Trinity, God the Father, Son, and Holy Ghost come, as suppliants, and court you with all the arguments which an infinite God can use, to fly from the wrath to come – to seek your salvation, and escape as for your lives, to the outstretched arms of a bleeding Jesus. My dear young friends, it is your best, your eternal interest, to forsake the ways of sin, seek salvation and come to Christ, now in the time of youth." McGready continued in this vein for a time, unfolding his words slowly as a woman unfolds a blanket for a baby, section by section. Sarah sat transfixed.

"Another consideration, we would offer to induce you to come to Christ is – while out of Him, in an unconverted and careless state, you are in dreadful danger, although you are spiritually blind and do not see it; spiritually dead, and do not feel it; and this renders your case more pitiable and distressing," McGready's voice began to rise and beat against the thin, wooden walls. "You are in unspeakable danger from the Old Serpent, who tempts you to sin and rebellion against God: he tempts you to postpone the work of repentance and salvation to some future period – to middle age, to old age, or a dying hour. He tells you that it would sink you into contempt and disgrace, and forever destroy your respectability in the world if you were to have a serious look or shed a tear under a sermon; and that you would be ruined and undone, if you were to become the humble, praying, brokenhearted followers of Jesus. He endeavors to persuade you that there is no reality in religion, it is all hypocrisy, enthusiasm or foolishness – and that your highest glory is to be bold and open in his service –that it is only necessary that you observe what the world calls politeness and support the name of a good citizen."

McGready's words tumbled through Sarah's mind, picking up pieces of his earlier sermon from last year when he spoke of being a new creation. *I am spiritually dead,* she thought, repeating his thoughts. *And I long to be a new creation. I have been persuaded that there is no reality in religion. I have listened and believed my father, a man who turned his back on religion and his God, and I have allowed him to do the same for me.* The realization struck her with a force that threatened to take her breath away. Mattie and Millie faded away, and she suddenly felt all alone in the meeting house, just her and the presence of a God she had not seen nor believed – until now. McGready's voice bellowed as the Son of Thunder concluded his communion message.

"Coming to Christ is the same as believing, receiving, looking and flying to Christ. Would you come to him, you must pray and never faint – you must lie at the footstool of the Sovereign God, crying for mercy; and this must be your last resolve – I will go to Jesus, as a lost, condemned, hell-deserving wretch – If I perish, I will perish at His feet; if I am lost eternally – if I should go to hell at last, I will go from the feet of Jesus, crying for mercy," he thundered. Sarah felt hot tears coursing down her face, her body began to tremble violently of its own accord, and she found herself kneeling upon the floor, weeping as a girl without hope coming to a God whose name was Hope.

Chapter Twelve

Friday, the second of August,
the year of our Lord 1799

Rev. James McGready's Journal

On Monday at Red River Meeting House, the solemnity was very great during the time of preaching: many of the most bold, daring sinners in the country were brought to cover their faces, and weep bitterly. After the congregation was dismissed, a considerable number of people stayed, lingering about the door, as if unwilling to depart. Solemnity appeared in every countenance, and some of them were bathed in tears. Some of the ministers told me that we ought to collect the people into the house and pray with them, which was done. It appeared evident that the power of God filled the house – Christians were filled with joy and peace in believing, and sinners were powerfully alarmed under an apprehension of the horrors of an unconverted state. At this time, I hope, there was one soul sweetly delivered from a burden of guilt and distress, by a believing discovery of the glory and sufficiency of the merits and mediation of the blessed Jesus. Some had their convictions revived and quickened, and in a few days were filled with joy and peace under blessed discoveries of the glory and suitableness of Christ. Others, who had lived quite careless and thoughtless before were filled with such distress under a sense of their sin and guilt, that they freely disclosed their cases to ministers and praying Christians. About this time, a remarkable spirit of prayer and supplication was given to Christians, and a sensible, heartfelt burden of the dreadful state of sinners out of Christ; so that it might be said with propriety, that Zion travailed in birth to bring forth her spiritual children.

McGready leaned back at the table, rereading his entry. *Sweetly delivered from a burden of guilt and distress ...* he paused, recalling the bucket of tears Sarah McMillan unleashed at the meeting house that morning. He remembered her from the previous year, her face set like stone against any sort of wooing by the Spirit of God. Charity McPherson had told Nancy a bit of her story, but at best, he could only piece together small sections of fact. What he knew in the Spirit was much more complete. Certainly, until last Monday, she had been unconverted, a sinner stuck in the muck of this world, but he also sensed her deep wounding in her own spirit and the piled-on pain of her circumstances.

As he had preached, he had felt the power of God go forth, but it wasn't until Sarah fell to her knees that McGready knew she was targeted to come to a saving knowledge of Christ that day. Charity had quickly reacted, dropping to her knees beside her niece, weeping with her, directing the way to repentance and salvation. In fact, the two women – for that's what Sarah had become, a woman – knelt together while the service concluded and many walked toward the door. McGready and Hodge had no problem allowing congregants to pray in the meeting house while others began to make their way home. Finding the way to God took more time for some than others.

Yet that morning, many didn't want to leave, so Hodge and Rankin encouraged McGready to re-enter the house and call for prayer. Sarah and Charity continued to kneel as others began to seek the Lord for their own distresses. It wasn't long before some began singing and laughing in joy, others wept as did Sarah, while others sat quietly and reverently under the power of God. McGready, Hodge and Rankin moved among the flock, praying for them, encouraging them on their journey. It was McGready who found his way to Sarah and Charity, and once he knelt beside them, he sensed the work of the Spirit already had been done.

Sarah met his eyes levelly as he knelt, and he saw joy and peace emanating from the green depths. Her determined, squared face had softened into peace. "It is done," she said softly, her Aunt Charity's hand resting protectively on Sarah's arm. "I have seen the Christ and I am His."

As McGready leaned into the back of his chair and crossed his hands behind his head, he remembered the incredible contentment he had seen in Sarah that day. Smiling, he reveled in the pleasure of her new birth.

Nancy eased up behind him, wrapped her arms around his neck and leaned down to brush her lips across his cheek.

"What has my husband sighing so contentedly this morning?" she whispered.

"Miraculous things, my dear one," he grabbed her hands, squeezing gently. "Recalling the move and the power of God merely whets my appetite for more of His graces. I feel as if we dangle on the edge of His move again, and I pray God it is not quenched by any scheme the enemy has planned."

The routine of life continues, Sarah thought philosophically as she milked the cow a few days later, *but how is it that I can be a completely different person than I was only a week ago?* She slapped the cow's leg as it attempted to shift. Pressing her shoulder into its haunches, Sarah leaned in closer, squeezing and drawing out the milk. Finally, she could testify that Christ could make someone a new creation, that her thoughts, her motives, her heart had been completely transformed.

After Monday's meeting, Aunt Charity had opened her Bible and explained many wonders to Sarah's hungry ears. It was as though a veil had been lifted and suddenly all the Bible stories Sarah heard as a child from Grandma McMillan made sense. Colors seemed brighter, the air smelled fresher, even the sun slipping up over the horizon this morning seemed to bring an uncommon joy to her heart. As she hefted the pail of warm milk and walked toward the barn door, she breathed another prayer of thanksgiving for her new life. She didn't realize she could be this happy.

Aunt Charity was working over the fire and instructing Mattie and Millie in their schoolwork when Sarah entered the house. Charity had begun teaching the girls to read in the past months; Sarah's job had been to impart her knowledge of numbers and arithmetic. Mainly, the girls read in the mornings and worked with figures in the afternoons. Sarah loved the time spent with them and labored diligently to come up with unique ways to explain the principles. Today she planned to have them assist in determining how much grass seed to buy to cover the back pasture. Mr. Townsend – sadly, not Daniel – was to come by on his way to town for their dry goods order. She hoped he would bring seed back as well.

"Sarah, would you mind rousing Josiah from his slumber?" Aunt Charity turned from the fire holding a steaming kettle. "Let us eat and have our devotions. It promises to be a busy day." Sarah's heart leapt at the thought of devotions, which had been such a mundane experience only a week ago. Aunt Charity reading the Bible by the fire first thing in the mornings was now her greatest joy. She shook her head, smiling again. *A new creation, indeed,* she thought.

The sun was waning, easing the heat of the day, when Townsend returned from Russellville with his wagon full of supplies. Only a small portion was to be dropped off at the McPhersons' home, the rest making its way further down the road. He reined in the horses, his face breaking into his characteristic smile. "Ho there," he shouted, even though Sarah, Millie and Mattie stood under the elm tree watching him ride in. "How are my favorite McPherson girls today?" He jumped off the wagon, moving toward the back as he spoke over his shoulder. "I've got quite the load for you all –and even perhaps a surprise or two from town."

"A surprise?" Mattie yelled, leaving her game of hopscotch to dash over to the wagon. Millie followed, her bare feet slapping the well-worn ground.

"Why, of course! Surely you don't think I would go all the way into Russellville and not bring a surprise for my two girls?" he cut his eyes toward Sarah in amusement. "How 'bout a treat for you ..." he leaned down, handing Mattie a piece of hard rock candy, "… and another for you." Millie held out her hand, taking her piece with the solemnity the occasion required.

"Thank you, thank you," both girls called over their shoulders as they ran to the house to tell their mother of their good fortune.

Sarah laughed, her eyes twinkling in joy. "You do spoil them, you know," she said as she held out her arms for the small loaf of sugar. This sugar brick was better than any piece of candy in her eyes.

"What's not to spoil?" Townsend replied unashamedly. "They are dear children, as you are, Miss McMillan. And I have a treat for you as well." He set the bag to his side and reached for his pocket. Drawing out a letter he passed it to her. "A gentleman coming from the Cumberland brought this in to Stewart's Merchantile and left it for you. I'm assuming it's news from Port Royal. Nothing like news from home, I always say." Sarah reached for the letter excitedly and tucked it carefully in her pocket. It had to be from Ann; she would savor it later. Townsend saw the expression on her face.

"Why don't I unload all this for Sister McPherson while you go read it?" he asked kindly. "The Good Book says news from a distant land brings refreshment, or some such thing as that." He laughed heartily at himself as he turned back toward the wagon. Aunt Charity was moving out the door to assist, and Sarah decided to take him up on his offer. She simply couldn't wait.

Waving her letter in the air to show Aunt Charity what she was about, Sarah turned and began walking back toward the shade of the elm tree. She stared at the envelope, not quite recognizing the writing, but seeing the Neville name in the top corner. With a question on her brow, she unfolded the paper.

July 29, the year of our Lord 1799

My Dearest Sarah,
    It is with great sadness that I tell you that our precious angel of God, Ann, has gone home to be with her Savior tonight.

Sarah felt the ground shake beneath her as her legs completely gave out. She fell to her knees in shock, her wails piercing the air before she knew they were coming. Within seconds, she felt the strong arms of her Aunt Charity enfold her, vaguely heard Townsend say something, but couldn't put form to the words coming from their mouths. Ann. Her dearest, most kindred friend Ann, was gone for well nigh five days, and she hadn't even known it. Heaving, shaking sobs drove her face into the ground, her grief threatening to completely overtake her. The letter fell out of her hand, and Charity picked it up, quickly scanning the contents.

"Dear Jesus, Lord Christ," she whispered to Townsend. "It's her friend Ann. She's dead to this world, and I know not how Sarah will stand it." Charity's light green eyes rose, meeting Townsend's concerned countenance. "This will be a mighty grief to carry, Mr. Townsend. Can you help me get Sarah inside?"

The gentle giant of a man nodded solemnly as he bent to lift Sarah from the ground where she had now spread out completely, her face pushed into the packed dirt. As he picked her up, her body sagged into his arms like Mattie's ragdoll, without form or life. By now, the McPherson children had heard the commotion and stood in single line beside the door of the house, eyes wide with wonder and gravity. Mattie held baby Matthew, tears falling from her cheeks, not knowing why Sarah was distressed but instinctively feeling her pain as if it were her own.

"Watch out, children," Charity spoke as Townsend carried the weeping girl over the threshold. "Pray, pray for your dear Sarah. It is the only thing that will help." Their eyes followed Townsend as he placed Sarah on Charity's bed. The moment he backed away, Sarah rolled over and curled up in a ball in the corner. She had never spoken, never ceased sobbing and wailing. Townsend shook his head sadly, his heart broken for the young woman.

"Do you need Mrs. Townsend, then?" he nodded toward Sarah.

"I'm not sure," Charity hesitated. "Perhaps she could check in tomorrow? We will cover the night with her."

"I'll bring her over first thing in the morning," he assured her. "Meanwhile, we'll be praying for the girl. Such a great sadness for such a young lass. And let me finish the unloading for you. I'll put your goods right beside the front door where you can store them later."

"I thank you, Mr. Townsend, for all your assistance this day." Charity briefly touched his shoulder as she turned back to her room and Sarah's grief.

It took a day for Sarah to come to her senses enough to grasp where she was and what had happened. Each time her mind had risen above the fog, the stab of grief pierced her again, sending her back to the place of a murky unknown. Even in the darkness of her soul, even when she didn't know her own name, she sensed a presence of strength that she could grasp and hold on to. She would tell her Aunt Charity later that she felt she had been on a sea voyage, the waves high and often threatening, yet her feet firmly anchored in the ship. Somehow she knew she wouldn't drown in this place, but her body, mind and soul felt cast adrift in a sea of turmoil.

Saturday morning she woke, her eyes swollen and crusty, while Charity slept in a chair beside the bed.

"Water …" Sarah whispered, her voice hoarse. Charity jerked and reached for the cup by the bedside before she had full awareness. Sarah drank long and hard then fell back to the bed, exhausted by the effort.

"Hello, dear child," Charity said quietly, pushing Sarah's hair back from her face. The usually strong, square-jawed Sarah looked weak and pale in the early morning light. "Are you awake, then?"

Sarah sighed deeply, shuddering at the end of it, the hollowness of her eyes seeking Charity's stability and love. "She is gone, Aunt Charity. Ann is gone."

"I know, Sarah. I read the letter, but now you understand where she is and what a great reward your Ann is enjoying with her Savior."

"Yes … " a tear slipped from Sarah's eye, sliding effortlessly down her cheek, "… but I will miss her so." With an effort, Sarah sat up higher in bed, determination marking her face. "Will you read the rest of the letter to me? I want to know what happened, but my eyes burn …" Sarah reached to her face, gently touching the raw edges of her eyes.

"Of course. I have it here," Charity pulled the letter from her pocket, smoothing it out on her lap. She glanced toward Sarah, hesitating. "You are sure?"

Sarah nodded fiercely.

"Very well then. It reads as follows.

Dearest Sarah,

It is with great sadness that I tell you that our precious angel of God, Ann, has gone home to be with her Savior tonight. You well know of her condition and the fierce determination she held as she struggled to keep life, but in the past month, the struggle became too great for her. We watched her slip from us, day by day, with no recourse but to make her as comfortable as possible and pray God to have mercy on her and let her come to Him without suffering. I believe He heard our prayer and gently carried her to His bosom of eternal love.

My tears fall freely as I write this, knowing that you will be as bereft as we are with her passing on to glory. For as much as we rejoice in her joining with her Lord and Savior, we also grieve, longing for her presence every minute of every day. Sally is beside herself with grief, completing her work about the house in a dark shroud of anguish. Mr. Neville wears it well, but he sleeps not at night. I hear his steps in the house well past dark and into the early morning light. Esther continues to be our bright spot although she feels Ann's loss deeply. She has the resilience of youth on her side.

And I, of course, live with the weight of her passing, my precious flower, my dearest daughter. Each day dawns with new sorrow rushing back in.

We buried her Tuesday on a bluff above the Red River just outside of Port Royal. Mr. Neville placed a lovely wreath around the cross that we made to mark her final resting place. I hope to have a more permanent marker made in the not-too-distant future.

Also, as much as it grieves me to recall, I must tell you of her last words for they were of you, dear Sarah. Our Ann thought of you as she lay passing from this world to the next. Her final plea was to, once again, present to you her Savior and beg for your consideration of the Christ. How desperately she longed to see you again in Heaven, to leave this world knowing that she would not leave you forever, but only for a short time. Therefore, I call your attention again to His grace and love for you, to know that God loves you, Sarah McMillan, enough to send His son to die on a cross for your sins. Welcome Him into your heart, my other daughter, and you will find life now and life eternal.

In conclusion, know again that Ann did not suffer at the end. Her countenance radiated with uncommon joy as she drew her last breath and her beauty was breathtaking. God heard our prayers.

We look forward to your coming home in the months ahead. Please visit as soon as you are able.

I long to see your face.

With devotion and love,
Mrs. Neville

Sarah could hear the muted voices of Mattie and Millie calling to one another as they finished out the morning chores, but inside the house the silence permeated. Charity's voice had broken as she finished reading the letter, not in sadness over missing Ann – for she had never met her – but in the universal compassion of one woman feeling another's grief. Sarah stared blankly at the wall, allowing the weight of grief to settle in over her like a woolen blanket, heavy and tightly woven, attempting to suffocate her. Reaching for the baby who was stirring from his nap in the cradle, Charity drew him close, her head tilting slightly as she gazed at her disheveled niece.

"Child, do you realize what our Lord has done?"

Sarah dragged her eyes away from the wall to rest on her aunt.

"Mrs. Neville wrote that your Ann passed into glory on July 29 … just five days ago. That would be Monday night, Sarah, Monday night. The very night that your soul became a part of glory. Do you see?"

Slowly and deliberately, Sarah's focus returned to her vivid green eyes and a subtle wonderment appeared. "Oh …" she breathed, "Oh my."

"Yes. I believe it to be the hand of the Lord," Charity stated with conviction. "The enemy of our souls would hope that you take your newfound belief in the Lord Jesus and blame Him for this grievous sorrow. Yet God, in his sovereign kindness, used His timing to show you the relationship between life and death – and indeed, true life! You have a choice, dear one, to believe one or the other. Is this the work of a God who is unfeeling, uncaring and unkind – a hard taskmaster – or a God who weeps with us and allows the pain and suffering in our lives to achieve His glorious results? It is a trial of faith for you, and so soon after your conversion."

Footsteps pounded through the door as the girls dashed inside, chasing and laughing at one another. Neither Charity nor Sarah paid any mind at all as they considered this turn of events. Obviously, Sarah gaining life and Ann gaining her eternal life – all in the same night – could be no coincidence; and Sarah didn't have to ponder long to know whom she believed.

"I would trust my Savior," she said softly but firmly. "He rescued my soul Monday night from a sure death. Why would I turn from trusting Him today? Indeed, the knowledge that Ann ushered me into His kingdom somehow makes her passing much easier to bear." Her countenance began to change, a strange light coming over her face, then a realization.

Sarah turned to her aunt, placing her hand on Charity's knee. "Aunt. This place where I am, this valley of grief, it is akin to where my father went, is it not? When he lost the life of the baby then found he had lost my mother as well. His soul was pierced with an even deeper sadness than I hold right now."

"Yes, I believe it to be so."

"Therefore, this would be the point where he would turn from God and go his own way." Sarah thought out loud. "I face the same choice … but I would not turn from God. I have seen the way of my Father and I would choose another way," she declared. "I will accept this as God's will and know I will see my Ann another day."

The laughter in the front room had ceased and when Sarah glanced up, she caught sight of two small heads poking around the threshold of the bedroom door, their dark eyes questioning. Sarah smiled, waving Millie and Mattie into the room and onto the bed with her. As the girls snuggled up, one on each side of her, Sarah gratefully held them tightly, taking comfort in their presence.

"The anguish of the grave came upon me; I was overcome by trouble and sorrow. Then I called on the name of the Lord, 'Oh Lord, save me!'" Charity quoted from the book of Psalms as she bounced baby Matthew on her lap. "He will turn your sorrow into dancing, dear child, somehow joining anguish and joy into a beautifully woven fabric."

Chapter Thirteen

McGready, Rankin and Hodge felt as though they collectively held their breath after July's visitation of God's Spirit. This was similar to what had happened only a year ago at Muddy River sacrament, but the move had been doused by Balch's accusations and finger-pointing. Would the county again be filled with contention, or would this visitation merely be the tip of an outpouring of God's favor? McGready could only pray and continue ministering at Muddy River and Clay-lick. Recently, McGready had handed off the Gasper River congregation to Rankin, saying the distance and difficulties of the road made it well nigh impossible to do its congregants justice. Still, McGready had ministered with him in late August where the power of God again fell on the old and young, white and black. They thought that at least twenty souls had been awakened in Gasper River by God's glory.

As was his custom, McGready prayed aloud and with great volume early this September morning as he rode into the clearing where the Red River Meeting House stood. The solid wooden structure appeared stout and hearty in the bright sun while mosquitoes had already begun finding their targets on McGready's arms and face. He slapped yet another as he dismounted.

"I thank you, Sovereign One, for the visitation of Your Spirit to this place," he practically shouted, smashing another mosquito against his neck, "for even though the devil and his hordes would stop the move of Your presence, they have no authority over You. They are pesky and bothersome – as are these flies of torment – but their power is small and weak." He bent down to pick up a stray feed sack that must have fallen out of one of the wagons. It would do perfectly to hold debris until he gave it to Nancy for better uses. He continued to pray as he gathered bits of pieces of refuse that littered the grounds.

"James!"

McGready, who had stripped down to his undershirt in the heat, turned to listen again.

"James! Over here!"

Shading his eyes, McGready peered into the thick vegetation that bordered the Red River. Brambles, small cedar trees and wild grape vines all but obstructed his view of the owner of the voice. He barely could make out a figure behind the thicket of thorns.

"Who goes there?" McGready responded.

"James, it is I, William," Hodge poked his head around the trunk of a towering tulip poplar.

"William? What in Heaven's name are you about, man?"

"James, I need your help. I find myself in a pack of troubles."

"Well, come out and speak to me, man-to-man," McGready said impatiently.

"I can't."

"What do you mean, you can't?" McGeady moved toward William Hodge, his feet pressing down the high grass with ease.

"Don't laugh, James, but I have lost my clothes."

"What?"

"Just now, this morning. I am coming back from Shiloh and decided to cross the river right here at the meeting house. I figured it would be easiest here, so I stripped bare and tied my clothes onto my horse's back, but I didn't reckon on my poor tying job or the swift current that hopped up over the rock midway over. My tie loosened, and my clothes are gone."

McGready's usual implacable countenance began to crack. The laughter came, first a slow rumbling, then a full-fledged, knee-slapping, contagious guffaw. He bent over at his waist, propping his hands on his knees, and let loose. Tears trailed down his cheeks while his shoulders heaved in merriment. No sound came from the brambles. Finally, McGready caught his breath enough to speak. "So … you stand there behind the tree as naked as a man proceeding from his mother's womb?" he gasped, trying to control his mirth. "William, you truly do bring good medicine. Oh my …" and McGready began laughing all over again.

"James, please," the voice pleaded from behind the tree. "Laugh all you want, but do so when I am decent again. Do you have anything with you that I may wear?"

"Yes, yes, I am sure I might find something …" McGready turned back toward his saddlebags fastened on his horse, laughing and shaking his head as he crossed the clearing. "Dear God, this friend and minister You have given me," he cried aloud. "He truly is fresh breath to my soul." The towering man of God searched through his bags, coming out with another undershirt and a worn pair of breeches. Fortunately for Hodge, when he swam the river with his horse, he kept his boots tied to the saddlehorn, thereby saving a good pair of boots from the river's insatiable appetite. Within minutes, he was dressed in an overly long undershirt and an equally long pair of breeches, clothes that didn't come close to fitting his stocky, short frame but for which he was eternally grateful. He sat next to McGready on the front steps of the meeting house, his brown and gray-flecked hair still wet from the early morning river bath. Elbows on knees, both men rested, enjoying the solitude of the place and each other's company. McGready wiped his eyes every so often, the vestiges of his mirth playing out slowly.

"If a cheerful heart is good medicine, you should be as healthy as a horse," Hodge said wryly, a bit chagrined at his early morning swim. "Would to God I had not lost my clothes. My wife will be fit to be tied, that putting me down to only two undershirts now." He shook his head. "I would rather face your ridicule than my good wife's anger. Alas. What is to be done?"

Knowing the value of clothes on the frontier, and even more, the ire of a woman who must quickly make more, McGready had the grace to feel a bit sorry for Hodge – at least he was able to quench his laughter long enough to sympathize with his plight. He held out a piece of sweet grass for Hodge to chew, a peace offering of sorts, and the two men stared together at the clearing, contemplating life and lost clothes.

"On the brighter side of things, the congregation at Shiloh seems to be growing. They are not seeing the souls converted as we did at Gasper River last week, but they are ripe for God's move and praying for His visitation," Hodge ventured. He wrung out a sock and draped it over the step, his bare feet stuck out in the sunshine. McGready chewed the sweet grass thoughtfully, then responded.

"Next Sabbath, we go to Clay-lick. Then that last Sabbath in October, we round up the meetings at the Ridge in Tennessee. That will be our last sacrament before winter sets in. May God have mercy on us and deliver more souls – then keep them through the long winter months. I would not see Balch's influence grow as it did last winter season."

"Hm … yes .. we must continue to pray – and stay healthy." Hodge glanced at McGready from the corner of his eye. "You are staying healthy, are you not, James? I know Mrs. McGready had been concerned of late."

McGready shrugged, glancing at the sky and abruptly standing up. "I will do, William. Now I must be about my business. I assume your mount is still with you, or did he, too, get swept down the river?" Laughing eyes gazed at Hodge who groaned and began putting his damp socks back on his feet.

"My mount is fine, as you well could imagine. I left him tied by the river. I will be off and will return your garments at first opportunity." Hodge laughed now, shaking his head. "I suppose if I had to run up on any man, it was best it was you. God help me. Riding naked holds no appeal for any man. Thank you for your kind assessment and help in my situation." He stood and bowed extravagantly toward McGready, and the two men laughed again, putting their arms around each other as they walked away from the meeting house door.

The second corn harvest of the year was in, and Sarah knew that meant her time in Kentucky was drawing to a close. It had been almost two months since she became a new creation – and since Ann went to Heaven. That's how Sarah thought of Ann's death now. She refused to consider the word "dead;" rather she decided that the truth was that Ann was more alive than she ever had been. When speaking of her to Aunt Charity or the girls, Sarah always placed her in Heaven, alive and healthy for the first time in her life. Her grief remained, but it was intermingled with joy.

So much had happened in her soul since she saw the Christ that last Monday in July. Aunt Charity's weekly prayer society made perfect sense now. In the past she endured them in a fog of confusion. Now she reveled in them, counted down the days, and prayed with as much fervor as the rest of the society. The salvations that had occurred in Red River, as well as Muddy and Gasper River congregations, had only excited the group to pray more frequently and with more passion.

And so it was as the days approached for her return to Port Royal, her heart grew more and more heavy. Aunt Charity wasn't without her concerns as well.

"You must find other believers with whom to fellowship in Port Royal, dear child," Charity admonished late one afternoon as the ladies were shucking corn. Baby Matthew slept on a blanket on the ground while the other children played under the elm tree. "It is a classic scheme of the enemy to isolate little ones in the faith and separate them from the flock. Somehow, you must stay connected while at home, at least until you are able to return in the spring. I feel sure Matthew will release you again, as he has been so kind to do."

Sarah allowed that piece of praise to slip by without comment.

"I have heard from Obediah that he should be here within the fortnight, so, as much as it grieves us all, I am searching for a way to deliver you back to your father. Mr. Townsend says there are few wagons on the roads these days. They will increase in about a month when harvests are taken to markets in Port Royal and Clarksville, but he did say several flatboats will be moving downriver soon. How would you feel about going home by river?" Charity held a corncob up to the sun to better see the silks crammed into its crevices. She picked quickly and skillfully at them, tossing the clean ear into a basket that sat between the women. Sarah eyed her aunt playfully.

"And how do you think I would consider the river?"

Charity stopped her careful searching to look, instead, upon her headstrong niece. In the past months, Sarah had lost all childishness in her countenance and at the age of sixteen now, she truly had become a young woman – a young woman of adventure. Charity laughed aloud. "Indeed, you are thrilled! Very well, I will see what I can do about a return trip on a flatboat." She shook her head as she reached for another ear of corn. "Most women I know are terrified of traversing rapid rivers, but then again, Sarah, you are not like most women I know."

The two laughed easily together then became silent as they worked methodically. It was an easy, companionable silence, broken only by intermediate shouts and laughter from the children. The basket was half full when Charity spoke again.

"By the by, I've heard from Mrs. Townsend that Daniel finally has returned home."

"Oh?" Sarah kept her eyes lowered, her ears open.

"Yes, apparently he assisted the Holland siblings as much as he could in developing their home and lands before winter."

Sarah waited for more. When it appeared Charity had no more to say, she attempted to draw her back into the topic. "And how did he find Miss Elizabeth Holland?" She hated asking out loud but had to have the answer.

Charity glanced at Sarah, revealing nothing in her countenance.

"I believe she is fully recovered from her dousing by the Red River, if that is what you are asking."

"Well, yes," Sarah said hesitantly, "and what of her ... her ... relationship with Daniel?" Charity looked up at Sarah with raised eyebrows. Sarah rushed on, "I mean, Sister Townsend mentioned that they ... the two of them ... I mean ... they could have an understanding of sorts as to ..."

Charity laughed, taking pity on her stumbling niece. "Oh, Sarah, dear one. You do bring me such joy! Let me set your mind at ease, child. Daniel and Miss Holland have no such understanding, and I believe that they never will. Mrs. Townsend was mistaken. Have you not seen the way he looks at you?" Sarah felt the heat rising to her face. "I am thankful that you finally have grown to care for him in return. Finally!" Charity restated with energy, swatting at a fly settling on the freshly shucked corn. "I thought you would never see it!"

"What?" Sarah stared, mouth agape.

"Ah, it is always this way. The one whose heart has been wooed by another often does not recognize it for what it is," she stated. "Be of good cheer. I am sure Daniel Townsend will find a way to visit the McPherson farm before a certain pretty young lady has to leave for Port Royal. I am praying, you know," Charity smiled, tiny lines folding into the creases of her eyes, full of kindness and understanding. Over the wild beating of her heart, Sarah felt a warm wash of peace. Her Aunt Charity was praying –

and Daniel wasn't marrying Elizabeth Holland! Perhaps, just perhaps…

Within two days, Aunt Charity had found Sarah a portage down the Red River and plans were made to get her to Mortimer Station the following Monday. Daniel had not yet made an appearance, and while Sarah at times felt almost panicked by his lack of attention, she simultaneously sagged in relief for she had no idea what their meeting would look like nor how to act. She lived each day a mixture of sweet joy and sorrow. It was the Saturday prior to her leaving that their early morning was interrupted by the sound of rattling horse hooves galloping down the lane. Millie reached the door first, jerking it open to see who it might be and why they were traveling so quickly. Daniel leapt from the saddle before the horse fully stopped and took three giant steps toward the house. Words tumbled from his mouth like a cascading waterfall.

"Mrs. McPherson! Sarah!" his eyes clung to her as though he were a drowning man. "My father! A tree fell on him. I'm going to get Mr. Taylor from town. He knows a little about injuries. Can you go to my mother?"

Charity stood at the door, her petite frame practically overshadowed by Sarah, yet strength emanated from her. "Yes! We are on our way!" she spoke, untying her apron. "Get to Mr. Taylor, Daniel, hurry!" He jumped back on the horse and disappeared before another word could be spoken. Charity began shouting out orders and within minutes, Sarah and Charity were in the wagon, riding with fury toward the Townsend farm, while Mattie stayed behind with the other children.

When they thundered into the clearing, they saw nothing out of order until all three of Daniel's younger siblings raced out to meet them. Instead of the joy of greeting visitors, their faces spoke of panic and fear. Charles, a boy of about eleven, unloaded the information in rapid-fire order.

"My pappy is still in the woods – over there!" he pointed to the right side of the main house. "Mammy is with him and Daniel eased the tree up, but we can't move him until Daniel comes back with help. Oh, do hurry, Mrs. McPherson." The boy grabbed the reins from Charity to take care of the wagon team as Charity and Sarah jumped from the seat.

"Hurry, hurry," chanted six-year-old Sally as she darted toward the woods, looking back to make sure they were following. Sarah stooped to pick up Hannah, the youngest of the children, and carried her with her as they ran down a well-worn foot path to a back pasture. Obviously, Mr. Townsend had been clearing for another field because they found a partially cleared section of land riddled with stumps. To the left rose a pile of downed trees. A mule stood by, lazily chewing grass, adding an unreal serenity to the tragic scene, while a little past the downed trees Mrs. Townsend knelt beside her husband who lay unmoving underneath a felled red oak. Apparently, Daniel had been able to put a wedge under the trunk of the tree, lifting its weight off his father until he could return with Mr. Taylor and more hands to help.

"Charity! Sarah! Thank God you are here," Joy Townsend shouted, waving them over. Sarah, still carrying four-year-old Hannah, tripped over stumps and limbs as she stumbled toward the scene. Drawing up beside them, she saw that Mr. Townsend's usual jovial face was shadowed with gray pain. He was unconscious and moaned sporadically. Charity fell to her knees at his side.

"What happened, Joy?"

"Daniel says they were clearing – Jedidiah chopping with the broad axe while Daniel pulled trees to the side using the mule and his yoke – when Jedidiah felled a large poplar. As it came down, it snatched another smaller tree along with it and the smaller of the two snapped and fell on top of Jedidiah." Mrs. Townsend spoke matter-of-factly, her face a mixture of fear and determination. "Daniel was able to lever the tree up a bit but could not get it off of him. Jedidiah lost consciousness somewhere in the process and has not come around again. Daniel fears that his leg is broken, perhaps ribs, perhaps more. I brought whiskey out but have not been able to get him to drink." She raised her eyes to the women, pleading, afraid. "All I have been able to do is pray. Oh God, what would I do without Jedidah? I am not strong enough …" she caught herself and cleared her throat. Straightening her shoulders, she breathed deeply.

"Sarah," she said, fully in control again, "can you care for the little ones until Daniel returns?"

"Yes, ma'am."

"Excellent! Grandma Ana is in the house. She can tell you what needs to be done. Charity?" Mrs. Townsend looked Charity in the eye. "I believe we will need rags, bindings, bandages. Anything with which to wrap and carry. Charles will show you where I keep those items. Can you retrieve them while I wait here?"

"Certainly, Joy," Charity stood up, searching the path for Charles. Hannah, who still sucked her thumb, much to her mother's chagrin, wiggled out of Sarah's grasp. Sarah gently placed her on the ground, and Joy held out her arms. Sarah and Charity left the clearing on their respective errands, while Joy held Hannah close to her side, praying aloud for the life of her husband.

It probably took an hour or more for Daniel to return with Mr. Taylor and two other townsmen. The four of them were easily able to lift the tree off Townsend, the easing of the weight eliciting a gasp of pain from the still-unconscious man's lips. Mr. Taylor made a quick perusal of his patient then directed the men to gently move him over to the makeshift stretcher Charity had formed from quilts. They carried him down the path and into the house, all the time being aware of possible broken bones and the whispers of shallow breathing emitting from his chest.

Inside, Charity had cleared the kitchen table to set up a temporary location for Mr. Taylor to make a thorough examination of Townsend. The men lifted him gently to the spot and simultaneously stepped back, allowing Taylor a full view. As Sarah, Charity and the two men, LeRoy and Merriwether Johnson, retreated through the front door into the yard, they heard the ripping of clothes and the quiet murmur of voices.

With Sarah's help, Grandma Anaphileda already sat under a tree, positioned near the children. She was quiet yet attentive to all that was occurring.

Finding places to sit, each began the wait for word. While Charity made small talk with the Johnson brothers, Sarah tried to distract the Townsend children as much as possible, but it was well nigh impossible to keep their minds occupied. Daniel remained inside with his mother and Taylor. Finally, Sarah despaired of any attempt to ease the children's minds, and she fell into silence along with everyone else who kept the vigil outside. Crickets, tree frogs and songbirds were the only sound makers for a long while. And so when Taylor's voice boomed from the front door, practically every one of them jerked abruptly.

"Well, then. It could be worse, could be worse," he pronounced, his eyes crinkling kindly as he took in the sight of the smaller three Townsend children huddled at Sarah and Miss Ana's feet. "I do believe, young Charles, that your father will live many more days and will have plenty of opportunities to whip you into shape," he joked heartily. His wide grin lightened the darkened countenances of those waiting, and Sarah felt her own heart lift immediately. Charity looked over her way, a smile of relief and delight on her face. "Now you will have to help Daniel a good bit for the next few months – can you all do that?" Mr. Taylor addressed all three children now, serious and sincere.

"I always help Mama," four-year-old Hannah took her thumb out of her mouth to respond. "But I don't help Daniel too much." Pop. Back in went the thumb. Taylor laughed as he walked to a full water bucket sitting near the door. As he washed his hands, he glanced up at Miss Ana, Sarah and Charity. "His right leg is broken but I have set it as best as I could. I believe has several broken ribs and has some blood coming from his mouth, but I do not think that is too much a cause for worry. It is subsiding as quickly as it began. I wish we had a doctor from the East; he could do a better job of it. But Townsend is aware now, and Mrs. Townsend knows how to manage him from here on out. I will check on him when I'm in the area … as best as I can tell, he should recover." Taylor glanced at the two men who stood back from the others, waiting politely and quietly.

"LeRoy? Merriwether? Perhaps you can talk with Daniel before you head back to your places? Not sure how much you might be able to help, but this two-man farm is now reduced to a one-man place until winter. He will need some assistance from his neighbors to keep things going here," Taylor pulled up, examining his hands in the ebbing light of the day. Wiping them on a rag tucked in his pocket, he sighed deeply. "And Mrs. McPherson? Mrs. Townsend asked that I send you in before I leave. She needs to confer with you, I do believe. Miss Ana? Are you feeling spry enough to assist your daughter-in-law?" Taylor squatted to gaze at her eye-to-eye. Her clear topaz-colored eyes shone like gems in her wrinkled, weathered countenance.

"Mr. Taylor, I doubt I have felt spry since I left Carolina, but I am certainly strong enough to pull my own weight plus one more!"

He barked out a guffaw as he stood.

"Yes, I expect that to be so. God love you, Miss Ana. You will hold your own."

The ride back to the McPherson farm was much slower and less frantic than the earlier race in the opposite direction, Sarah considered thoughtfully. She was forcing her mind to recount the last few hours in order, all in an effort to not think too much about Daniel, who sat next to her, his leg resting against hers. Aunt Charity remained with Mrs. Townsend, promising to stay the night as the family tried to acclimate to this new life while Sarah was to return home, assuring the McPherson children that all was well and taking care of them until Charity could return the following day. Sarah glanced under her eyelids at Daniel; his stern face was set forward, the stress of the last few hours could plainly be seen. Sarah sighed, thankful Mr. Townsend would recover, yet disappointed in this "first meeting" with Daniel since her conversion – since his return from Miss Holland and her family. They rode in silence until Daniel finally spoke.

"I thank you for attending to my mother and brother and sisters today."

"I was glad to do it," Sarah responded simply. "And I am sorry about your father."

"Mr. Taylor says he should be fine, although I have my work cut out for me in the next few months," Daniel trailed off, glancing now at Sarah, her green eyes striking in the fading light. "Will you feel comfortable tonight without Sister McPherson?"

"Of course, why would I not?"

"I was not sure. You will have all four children, and that is a heavy load," Daniel clucked loudly, urging the horse to go a little faster. Sarah felt the old frustration begin to rise in her chest.

"A heavy load? Indeed, it is not," she snapped. "I do not know how frail you think I am, Daniel, but caring for these children is not a heavy load. I am a grown girl. I can take care of myself." She stared at him intently, a pink hue rising in her cheeks.

"That is not what I meant," he clipped back. "We live in a dangerous place, Sarah. I just want to make sure you are comfortable with the situation."

"I was shooting a rifle before I could count; I think I will be fine."

"For Heaven's sake!" he shook his head, "it seems I cannot say anything correctly for you."

"If you would stop treating me like a little girl, I would not get angry," Sarah retorted.

"Fine, then!" Daniel jerked the reins tightly, stopping the horse in mid-stride. "Sarah McPherson, I think you are the most ornery, hard-headed, stubborn, frustrating girl I know, and I do hope to marry you one day!" he blustered, turning in the bench seat to look into her eyes. His dimple had disappeared, and, like Sarah, his face had filled out and matured in the past year. Daniel Townsend, at eighteen, was a man. Sarah felt her face go pale and the breath leave her body. She stared mutely.

"Is that something I would say to a little girl?" he asked.

She shook her head, eyes wide.

"Fine!" he clucked again, and the horse began the slow plod forward toward the McPhersons' house, the light already lit at the front window. Sarah gamely tried to recover but found she didn't know what to say. The house drew closer and closer, and Sarah saw her window of opportunity fading quickly.

"I find you quite headstrong as well," she finally stammered, "and more than a bit irritating and frustrating. However, the prospect of marrying you fills my heart with joy, and I know not why." She fixed her eyes on the oil lamp burning brightly now as they drove into the clearing then she chanced a glance toward him.

Daniel's hazel eyes had become kind once again, wrinkling in the corners in amusement. He pulled up the reins as the front door flew open and Millie charged out, yelling her greetings and a bucket-load of questions. In this last sliver of a moment, he smiled, saying, "Then we have much to discuss in the days ahead."

Chapter Fourteen

But I have to leave tomorrow, Sarah had cried out silently as Millie threw herself up the step of the wagon to find out what had happened. Josiah tumbled out the door after her and Mattie brought up the rear, holding baby Matthew in her arms. Any and all chances of a private conversation were gone, and Sarah felt as though she was caught up in a whirlwind. While Daniel unharnessed the horse, fed and groomed her, Sarah tended to the fire and supper, attempting to restore a semblance of normalcy to the children. She found they began to settle quickly after she told them Mr. Townsend would be fine. Then the night became a game of sorts for them, a special time with "just Sarah" before she left on Monday. LeRoy Johnson rode up a few minutes later to give Daniel a ride back to his farm. Before Sarah could say anything other than "thank you," the two men were gone, the back of Daniel's coat taunting her as she watched.

Aunt Charity had returned the next day with Mr. Johnson's wife in their wagon, and the remainder of Sunday was spent preparing to leave early Monday morning. Charity had mentioned that Daniel was needed at home and Sarah had said nothing about their conversation. Still, there had been a thread of hope that she would see him before going back to Tennessee.

But this morning, all hope was gone. Sarah lifted her eyes from the murky Red River's swirling patterns to gaze at the bluffs rising high above her. She was firmly planted at the bow of a flatboat, only a few hours from Port Royal, and she had not even left Daniel so much as a letter. It had been in her heart to do so, but she didn't know what to write. *Thank you, Daniel, for the lovely drive Saturday and for speaking of marriage. When can we marry, do you think?* Sarah composed in her head, a wry smile curling on her full lips. *Dearest Daniel, dear, dear,*

Daniel. Were you serious when you spoke of marriage? Do you have the courage to face my father? She shook her head sharply at those words.

"Ain't she runnin' smooth this mornin'?" A crusty voice jarred Sarah from her daydreaming. Glancing up toward its owner, she had to shade her eyes from the glitter of the early morning sun reflecting off the water. Looming over her was an older woman, standing with legs akimbo and hands on her hips. The kindness in her features juxtaposed with her stance. "The Red River is what I'm talkin' about. You never know what you're gonna get with her. Might be high and mighty one day, could be low and humble the next." She sagged onto a barrel next to Sarah. "My husband and me been runnin' her for near 'bouts five year now. Build a flatboat, pack up as big a load as we can carry, get her down to the Mississip', run her south then come on back up to Kaintuck. We walk and ride up the Trace. Rivers are funny things. Just when you think you know 'em, they change up on ya."

Sarah nodded knowingly, glancing again at the brackish depths of the river. Who knew what lay under those waters? But the thought didn't bring fear to her, rather curiosity.

"You ain't the first one we carried from one place t' another, ya know. Every little bit o' profit heps out, we always say. Who knows? We might even find another t' carry when we unload you in Port Royal." The woman stretched her feet out in front of her, gazing steadily at her worn moccasins. Thick, red mud clung to the soles, and Sarah wondered how she could stand walking on the knots of clay without scraping them clean. Perhaps she was used to it.

Apparently, Mr. and Mrs. Sherman were known as a safe ride downriver; Aunt Charity was entirely comfortable with Sarah embarking from Mortimer Station in their care. They certainly were unlike any other couple Sarah had ever met. Even in the journey over the Appalachians – a trip taken with characters of all kinds – she had not encountered such as these. Mr. Sherman sat next to the steering oar at the stern of the little boat, smiling jauntily each time Sarah glanced his way. Once he even waved, even though he sat not eight feet from her.

At first glance, the flatboat – about fourteen-by-six feet – didn't appear big enough to carry the three of them downriver, but Sarah quickly grew accustomed to the tight quarters and reveled in the ease in which the craft maneuvered. The pine boards under her feet were nestled tightly together, and the tar between them sealed any chance of leaks. The Shermans had erected a small shelter toward the stern which was filled with bags of indigo. Barrels of other goods sat in every free space on board. In fact, Sarah sat on one such barrel, having no other place to rest during the short journey.

Her hungry eyes drank in each vista that appeared around the next bend. Mighty bluffs, thick forests, even what looked like small barrens, spread out before her. They scared up otters and beavers, sending them scrambling back under the water or into lodges that were built in winding offshoots of the main river.

"I'm feelin' a mite bit hungry, Mrs. Sherman," her husband yelled good-naturedly from the stern. "How's about we crack open some of that hoecake from last night? You got you some grub, girl?" he shot toward Sarah.

"Yes, Mr. Sherman. I'm fine, thank you."

After much digging through satchels and walking between barrels and bags, Mrs. Sherman returned to her spot with a heavy sigh. "And how'd ya find things up in Rogues' Harbor durin' your stay?" she demanded in a tone that expected an answer.

"It was most enjoyable," Sarah responded. "I feel as if I am a different woman returning home. No. I know I am different."

"Is that so?"

"Indeed. Thanks to Rev. McGready, my soul has peace for the first time in my life for he showed me the Christ and He is mine," Sarah stated matter-of-factly.

"Ah…you got religion, then?" Mrs. Sherman pulled a pipe out of her pocket and began tamping in tobacco.

"I suppose most would call it that. All I know is that I saw what a wretched sinner I am and, for the first time, fully realized that the sacrifices Christ made on His cross were made for me, for Sarah McMillan. It is a joy unspeakable. My sins are forgiven, and my heart is free," she lifted her face to catch the gentle breeze blowing up from the water. Mrs. Sherman saw the tilt of her head and felt the same gentle stirring, but it seemed more than just a breeze on the water. She smiled knowingly.

"A better description I've not heard of late," Mrs. Sherman sucked thoughtfully on her pipe now, a small swirl of smoke ascending above her head. "Mr. Sherman and me found religion early on in life, and I heard tell of strange goin's on up in Rogues' Harbor. That the Presbyterians got 'em a work goin'. All I got to say is it couldn't happen in a better place. We always depend on the Good Lord watchin' over us up that'a way. Rascals and rogues oftentimes find the river a good place to disappear in. Got to keep your eyes open, your wits about you." She paused, drawing deeply. "Still, river life is the best. Makes us free, it does. The Christ freed us in our hearts; the river frees us in our bodies. Didn't have no young'uns, though we sure tried mightily," she laughed – a hard, sharp sound. "I reckon the river is most like our young'uns – but like our parents, our aunties, uncles too. Family, it is." Mrs. Sherman looked up then, her steel blue eyes meeting Sarah's, a little embarrassed, perhaps, at her philosophizing. "What about your family? You pleased to be goin' home?"

The question took Sarah aback, transporting her thoughts abruptly from the serenity of the river to her father's anger and isolation – and worse, to the thought of Port Royal without Ann. She had successfully dealt with Ann's death while in Kentucky, but the closer she drew to Tennessee, the heavier her heart became. How could she endure the long winter without the hope of seeing her friend? How would she face Mrs. Neville, visit the Neville home, see the rocking chair in their front room without losing her wits? She had no answers. The old, used Bible Aunt Charity had given her this morning was nestled in her saddlebag. She could only hope it would hold the secret.

Before Sarah could answer, Mr. Sherman called from his perch, "Rapids up ahead!"

Sarah and Mrs. Sherman grabbed the few items closest to them that weren't anchored well and shored up for the short run. Their boat speed increased as they fell lightly down each succeeding drop. It was nothing dangerous, in fact, Sarah found the rapids the most exhilarating part of the ride, but they did need to be alert.

Once they were back on the river proper, Mr. Sherman called for his wife, saying one of the indigo bags had fallen open. As she moved toward the stern to right it again, Sarah breathed a prayer of relief at not having to explain her "family" in Port Royal. She resumed her quiet vigil and considered the dream she had last night – almost a duplicate of the one she'd had a year before.

She was standing on the southern bank of the Red River, the settlement of Port Royal spreading out behind her. The sun, which had shone brightly in the first dream, was closer to setting this time. Shadows stretched from the tall trees on each side of the bank, casting elongated stripes across the dried riverbed. The dead fish remained scattered throughout – a macabre scene that felt haunting and eerie.

At this point, her father had walked into the dream. He eased up behind her, saying nothing. Glancing at the riverbed, he then looked intently upriver, waiting for something – as was Sarah. The trickle of water began again, running from the east, and as it progressed toward them, it grew in volume. Just as in the previous dream, it had reached a crescendo of swirling, crashing water just before it engulfed the two of them – and Sarah woke on the verge of screaming.

Thankfully, Millie and Mattie had slept through her thrashing – the quilt was twisted around her legs – but Sarah had been covered in sweat, her heart racing with fear.

What could it mean? Why was she having this odd nightmare again, and why had her father entered the picture this time?

She inhaled the pure odors of fish, water and mosses while praying silently, as Aunt Charity had encouraged her to do. "Always pray, Sarah," she had remarked one day last week. "Whether you are washing, cooking, cleaning or walking, always pray, and the Lord will begin to talk back to you. In faith, believe that He is with you – for so He is."

At times Sarah felt overwhelmed with all the new things she was learning, really a completely different pattern of living. And yet, she tasted the freedom of being a new creation. Where there were a thousand unknowns, she still felt her feet were solidly planted now – that, somehow, everything would work out. No longer was she steering her own destiny.

Chapter Fifteen
November 1799

This year, McGready felt somewhat better facing the long winter season. Mr. Balch still ministered in the area of Logan County, but the new converts – and there were many of them! – had a stronger foundation of their faith and seemed less likely to be shaken. Physically, he felt a bit worse. The periods of extreme fatigue combined with chronic stomach issues were increasing. He had spoken with Mr. Taylor about it, but there seemed to be no solution other than herbal remedies, which he undertook religiously. Still, he struggled against his physical limitations more often than he wanted – and with them came bouts of depression. He was thankful for the Lord's recent visitations, a sure catharsis for his maladies.

He glanced up, reading the sky as the sun began to sink below the horizon. It was the night for the prayer society to meet again, to continue praying for revival together. McGready was determined to attend this meeting at Brother and Sister McPhersons' home, regardless of his stomach pain. This group of believers had paid the price for revival, years of prayer and beseeching the Lord. They deserved to hear from him, firsthand, what the Spirit of the Lord had done. A stab of pain gripped his midsection, and he grimaced, propping himself against the wall of his house, waiting for the discomfort to pass.

"James?" Nancy's voice rode on the wind. "James? Supper's ready!"

"Coming!" he responded, pulling himself up straight. "On my way!"

Chairs pressed tightly against one another in the front room of the McPherson home. A blazing fire welcomed the society, and it was a warm relief on this cold November night. Kentucky had yet to see its first snow of the season, but the temperatures had dipped below freezing several times, forming thin layers of ice in animal troughs. It promised to be another long, cold winter.

Yet the elated voices and cries of greeting warmed the bitter night as neighbors and friends who hadn't seen each other in months met once again. The last Red River meeting had been in August – and what a meeting it had been! But, what with harvest and approaching winter, there had been no other organized meetings, so the faithful were encouraged by merely being together. Obediah McPherson stood and addressed the group as the last chair was filled.

"Greetings to my brothers and sisters in Christ and welcome to our humble home," he spread his arms wide, an accompanying broad smile playing across his face. "We rejoice in seeing you and being together once again, but make no mistake, we are here to seek and hear from the Lord!" Smatterings of hand claps and "amens" filled the room. "We will make time to visit and tell of our joys and sorrows, and we will pray and continue to cry out to the Lord for his Spirit to visit our country; but first, Rev. McGready has asked for a moment to encourage us as believers to the current move of the Spirit north of us. I know that I, for one, have heard threads of reports from the most recent meetings up that way but have been waiting with anticipation to hear it from the horse's mouth, so to speak." Several people laughed, jabbing each other in the side, while McGready nodded his head, smiling slightly. "So without further prolonging the matter … Rev. McGready?" Obediah found his place next to Charity, settling on the edge of his seat, eyes and ears attentive. The towering McGready dominated the room, both in body and spirit. He continued to sit but gripped each person with his intense gaze, practically forcing them to hear what he had to say.

"As you know," he began, "months ago I resigned the charge of Gasper River, giving that body of believers over to Mr. Rankin, a faithful and successful minister." Heads nodded around the circle. This was not news. "However, I did go up and assist him at the administration of the Sacrament at Gasper on the fourth Sabbath of August. The almighty power of God at this time was displayed in the most striking manner. On Monday, a general solemnity seized the greater part of the multitude; many persons were so struck with deep, heart-piercing convictions, that their bodily strength was quite overcome, so that they fell to the ground, and could not refrain from bitter groans and outcries for mercy.

"In one place, I heard an old sinner, unable to support under his burden, speaking to his wife and children in the following manner: 'Alas! We have been blind all our days – we never saw our dismal state till now – we are all going to Hell together – Oh! We must seek religion, we must get an interest in Christ, or to Hell we must go.'" Solemn murmurs accompanied serious nodding all over the room. McGready paused and shifted in his seat.

"In another place, a poor awakened sinner addressing her minister in such language as this: 'I have made a profession – I have sat again and again at the communion table; but alas! I was a poor, deceived hypocrite – I see plainly I have no religion – Alas! I am going to Hell!' In other places, many poor, giddy young persons, who, on the first days of the solemnity, could not behave with common decency, now lying prostrate on the ground, weeping, praying and crying for mercy. But time would fail to relate every particular. In a word, it was a day of general awakening; several persons on that day, we hope, were savingly brought to Christ; and in the space of three weeks after, above twenty of those then awakened gave the most clear, satisfying accounts of their views of the glory and fullness of the Mediator; and the sweet application of His blood and merits to their souls."

Spontaneous applause erupted in the small room of the house as McGready took a long drink of his tea. Shouts of "Glory!" and "Hallelujah!" punctuated the air. He held up his hand, and the room quieted again.

"Indeed! Praise be to God! But there is even more. On the Sabbath following, the power of God was displayed at Clay-lick, and then, on the fifth Sabbath of September, we went to Muddy River. Every day of that occasion was marked with visible tokens of God's presence. At this time many persons were solemnly awakened, and many distressed souls were relieved, by sweet, soul-satisfying views of Jesus. It was a time of unspeakable comfort, joy and peace among God's people.

"Then, finally, on the last Sabbath in October, Ministers Rankin, McGee and myself administered the Sacrament of the Supper at the Ridge in the Cumberland settlement of Tennessee. A very general revival took place in the congregation and still continues, so I hear. A very considerable number of all ages and description of people have, we hope, experienced the reality of religion in their own souls."

Charity, who held the hand of her husband, squeezed it tightly, seeing the joy in her eyes matched in his. Such good news! Such fruit being born from their labors! When it was apparent that McGready had completed his report, spontaneous praise broke out from the tiny group. It led into a prayer session of thanksgiving and a continued crying out for more souls to find Christ in Rogues' Harbor and even into the state of Tennessee. It was as though this group of the faithful had tasted a crumb of what was to come.

Wham! The hatchet fell true, splitting another piece of kindling off the small cedar log. Sarah bent over to retrieve it from the ground then tossed it into the basket to her right. Although it was November, and even a chilly November day, sweat shone on her brow, and she had long ago taken off her cloak, laying it over a nearby stump. Wham! She finished off this log and reached for another.

Her father had worked all fall gathering enough wood to get them through the winter months; it stood stacked neatly under the eave of their cabin roof. But he had not had enough time to split much of it into kindling — that was Sarah's job, and she preferred to split logs in the warmth of the afternoon before dinner. She found the hard work a remedy to her sick heart.

Not much had changed with Matthew McMillan while Sarah had been in Kentucky all summer. She, of course, was quite different. Somehow she had expected – or hoped – that in her state of "new creation" he would come alongside and be new as well. In reality, she wasn't sure what she had hoped, but whatever it was, it was unfulfilled. Her heart certainly was softer towards him, but nothing in his manner or demeanor had softened toward her. He was as stone cold as this cedar log, and while she prayed for his soul every day, Sarah found it increasingly difficult to feel compassion for him. Certainly, it was easier to care for him when he wasn't at home. In her isolation she could convince herself that God could and would move on his heart, and he would begin to change. Then he would return home, full of darkness and vile temper, and hope would be abandoned within minutes.

She shook her head at her thoughts, lifting the corner of her apron to again wipe the sweat from her face.

One of the first things she had done after returning home several weeks ago was to place the sketch of Matthew back into the locket she wore around her neck. She didn't know why, but she felt clearly that the action was almost prophetic, displaying what she longed for or what would happen. That somehow, God would change Matthew, and he and Sarah would become a family.

She sat to rest for a moment, pulling the locket from under her shift, popping the latch to open it and peer inside. There she was, beautiful Matilda McMillan smiling at Sarah in her simple way. Opposite was the solemn-faced Matthew with the hint of a smile forming at the edge of his mouth, a younger, kinder version of the man she knew. She stared at the two of them, fingering the edge of the locket. If they could talk, what story would they tell? Would she and Daniel ever love with the depth of her parents' love – the way Aunt Charity described it?

The crunching of her father's uneven footsteps announced his imminent arrival. Sarah quickly slid the locket back under her shift and stood up, holding the hatchet loosely in her hand. As he rounded the path and appeared out of the thick tree covering, she had a few seconds to watch his approach. Head down, limp even more pronounced – fatigue displayed itself in every line of his body. She felt her heart stir again, and then he raised his head and saw her standing there. Apparently, he didn't like what he saw in her eyes.

"Why do you look at me so?" he demanded harshly, stopping abruptly.

"I was not," Sarah lied, God forgive her. "I was only resting from chopping wood."

He glared at her in response, his eyes hidden behind his scowl. Suddenly, he strode forward quickly, reaching her before she could move. He stretched out forcefully for her neck and grabbed the locket that had not found its way to its hiding place. Disbelieving, he pulled it out, holding it tightly, a dark cloud of anguish and rage descending over his countenance.

"What is this?" he demanded through clenched teeth. Sarah's heart dropped, fear pouring into every part of her body. She wasn't able to speak. He released the locket as though it burned him and grabbed her shoulders, shaking her from head to toe.

"I asked you a question. What is this? Where did you get it?"

"It is .. a gift … from Grandma McMillan," she stammered, her breath coming out in spurts.

"This was never hers to give," he clinched her right arm, holding her tightly, his other hand again grabbing the locket. With a mighty jerk, he pulled it from her neck, breaking the chain in half. Sarah yelled out in pain as the chain pulled against her neck and she fell back from the release. He let go of her then, turning the beautifully repaired locket in his hand. A sort of fierce anger wrestled with wonder as he viewed it – then he tugged it open, staring fixedly at the two sketches on the inside.

Sarah watched as he tried to master the emotions that threatened to overtake his soul. Sharp pain crossed his eyes as he saw his wife again – a sweet bitterness, barely controlled anguish, heartache and wounding such as Sarah had never viewed. Its intensity took her breath away. He finally settled on anger.

He barely glanced at the right side of the locket, which held his own likeness. Instead, moving slowly, with purpose, he closed it back and placed it on the stump Sarah had been using as a base for her wood cutting. Snatching the hatchet from her hand, he deftly flipped it around, turning the flat end forward and raised it high.

"No!" Sarah yelled as he slammed the hatchet on the locket, smashing the fragile cover into its back and locking its door forever. He flung the hatchet to the side, pushed her away with one hand, and picked up the locket with the other. Leaning back, he threw it as far into the thicket as possible. Sarah watched the flattened silver oval spin through the air, disappearing into brambles and cedar limbs. A soft thump echoed through the woods, and then all was silent.

Eyes wide with disbelief, Sarah turned to stare at her father. She shook from head to toe with fear and anger, but suddenly, from somewhere deep inside, came a control she had never known. It was as though God washed her with grace – she knew not another way to describe it – and in that moment, she loved her father with a love that made no earthly sense. Her green eyes, which had been charged with hurt and rage, suddenly were filled with compassion and love. Matthew saw the shift, and where he had been ready to respond to anger with anger, he didn't know what to do with love or compassion. He stared at his daughter blankly.

Taking a deep, shuddering breath, Sarah smiled tremulously . "I am sorry you feel this way, Father," she said quietly. "I believe supper is ready. I should go check the stew."

Without another word, Sarah reached for her cloak and turned toward the cabin. Sweat dripped from his brow as Matthew watched his daughter walk away from him. The atmosphere that had been so full of strife and anger, spirits that he completely understood, now sat still and stagnant. He shook his head hard, looking again toward the thicket where he had thrown the locket. Then he turned his gaze back toward Sarah as she disappeared through the cabin door. His body sagged as he fell to the stump, sitting hard. Hanging his head into his hands, he remained there for a long time.

Chapter Sixteen

No other words were spoken at the McMillan cabin that night, and Matthew was up before dawn, leaving by the time Sarah rose to check the fire. After stoking it up to a roaring blaze, eating a bowl of corn mush, and straightening the cabin, Sarah wrapped up warmly and headed out the front door. A bright sun rose over the tops of the trees, bringing strong light to her quest. She had watched carefully the evening before when her father threw the locket. It had spiraled, twisted and turned in the air, through the branches of the cedar, over the tops of the spent blackberry bushes, and into the depths of the woods that stair-stepped into the hollow. She headed off in that direction now.

Her breath made tiny puffs of mist as she bent to her task. She was under no illusion that the locket could be fixed again. He had smashed it in the direct center. But still … she had to have it.

Sarah reached an open area then turned back to face the cabin. Neck arching, she attempted to relive the moment from this perspective. She imagined the silver disk flying through the air, trying to predict where it may have landed. Leaves stood thick on the forest floor as the last of the trees had dropped their burdens within the past week.

Eyes intent and brow furrowed in concentration, she knelt and began the laborious task.

After about an hour, her back hurt and necked ached, and she was no closer to finding the locket. As she stood tall and stretched again, she heard steps coming down their footpath. She stopped, not moving, silent. If it was her father and if he found her here…

"I done tole you not to make so much racket, Sammy," a voice chastened. "A dang herd of buffalo would be quieter than you. Sarah's liable to greet us with a shotgun blast and questions later."

A smile formed on Sarah's lips as she heard a tiny voice respond in an exaggerated whisper. "I'm tryin' to keep quiet, Hagar. You ain't walkin' fast enough, and I keep trippin' over yo' big ol' feet."

"Both of you just shut up," a grown-up voice, full of authority, whispered. "What good is a surprise if a girl cain't be surprised? Now come on up close to me and we'll knock on the door together. Wait. Wait. Don't be pushin' too close, Sammy. You goin make me drop the pie. Easy boy. Good Lawd a' mercy. What am I goin' to do with you?"

Three hard raps could be heard through the trees, and Sarah realized they already had made it to the cabin. Glancing briefly at her location — she needed to begin searching again near the rotten stump closest to the large pile of moss — she tromped through the woods, calling out as she went.

"Hello! Hello! I am over here!"

As she came into the clearing, Sarah saw the three — two rambunctious children and Sally — standing at her front door in a line. They turned when they heard her voice, surprised etched clearly across each face. Sally screamed and almost dropped the pie she held in her hands.

"Oh! Lawd, chile! You done 'bout scared the life out of me! I thought you was a haint — a Port Royal ghosty for sure!" Her light brown complexion was a tad pale. Sarah laughed, her spirits rising at seeing her friends.

"Don't stand out here in the cold all morning," she said, moving around to open the door, "Come in and get warm by the fire. What in Heaven's name are the three of you doing out here anyway? And with a pie?"

Sammy shot around Sarah, dashing over to the fire, hands held out, teeth rattling from the cold. His hands were bare and chapped and he hopped from one foot to the other in an attempt to warm up. Sarah dragged a chair from the table toward the flames, motioning for Sally to take a seat, while Hagar put the pie on the table then found a warm spot on the floor. The four of them shed their blanket coats and sighed in relief as they felt the thaw begin. Sammy, who was never at a loss for words, began to explain.

"It's your birthday, Sarah," he stated simply. "We decided to celebrate."

"My birthday? It's not my birthday."

Hagar smiled, "It sho is today."

"I don't understand," Sarah retorted.

"The chil'ren's been wantin' to visit with you since you come back from up Rogues' Harbor way, and they thought it'd be fun to surprise you with a birthday pie," Sally said with a smile.

"'Ceptin' we don't rightly know when yo' birthday is," Hagar said.

"So we decided to make today your birthday so we could come visit and eat pie together!" Sammy finished out with a flourish. Sarah laughed, her heart filled with joy. The tiny, isolated cabin practically ballooned with life.

"Far be it from me to turn away a good pie," she said after she caught her breath. "What kind is it anyway?"

"Peach," Sally answered. "Mrs. Neville said I could use some of the peaches stored in the cellar, and they's some mighty good 'uns from Mr. Neville's trees. She sends her birthday greetings."

"Yeah," Sammy said. "She don't know it really ain't ..."

"Isn't," Sarah corrected. Sammy didn't miss a beat.

"... your birthday. So just pretend if you see her that you had a most bountiful birthday pie." His face turned serious for a second, contemplating the consequences of such a white lie. Apparently he decided it would all work out because his smile returned quickly. "When can we eat it?"

"Now hold yo' horses," Sally cut in. "I still gots a bit of a birthday surprise for Sarah here in my pocket." Sally reached deep into her pocket, pulling out a neatly folded letter. Handing it over to Sarah, she explained. "Mr. Neville says Mr. Johnson over at the tradin' post got this here letter in yeste'day from somebody comin' down the river. It's got yo' name on it, and seein' as how we was comin' here for yo' birthday ... " Sally smiled broadly and winked, "...he said to jest bring it on to you 'stead of givin' it over to yo' Pappy in town. We done figured they's nothin' as excitin' as a letter for a present."

Sarah clapped her hands in the fun of it all. Her green eyes sparkled in pleasure as she accepted the treasured gift. Perhaps it would be from Daniel? Her eyes quickly swept over the handwriting on the front, recognizing Aunt Charity's script immediately. Her heart dropped a little – she had hoped ... — but still, word from Aunt Charity was good, too. She looked up at the three of them with gratitude.

"My sincere thanks to you all. What a wonderful birthday morning this is turning out to be."

"When can we eat pie?" Sammy repeated, his bristled, thick hair standing on end at the crown of his head. It waved back and forth each time he spoke. Sarah loved the simplicity of that angelic face while Sally merely glared at him in frustration.

"Sammy, you is the most aggravatin' thing."

"Mama, let's cut the pie and let Sarah read her letter," Hagar suggested.

"Yeah!" chimed Sammy.

Sally and Sarah laughed easily together as Sally stood up. "Good idea, you two. Read that letter, Sarah, then we'll share some birthday pie."

All three moved toward the table on the left side of the room, searching the single shelf hanging over the keeler for enough plates to go around. Sarah left them to their quest as she eagerly unfolded the note. Aunt Charity's crisp, clean handwriting stretched beautifully across the page.

November 16, the year of our Lord, 1799

My Dearest Niece,

Greetings from Logan County! Obediah has returned just a fortnight ago and all is settled and well in the McPherson household. After a flurry of activity in welcoming him back, we find ourselves hunkering down for the winter months and contemplating how much we all miss you. The girls mope about as if they lost a best sister, and Josiah cries each time your name is spoken aloud. We have begun referring to you as the "Niece" so as to keep him happy and content.

My purpose in writing today is truly single-minded. I have prayed to our Lord Jesus Christ that He would allow this letter to reach only your eyes. I trust in His ability to see that it happens that way. In no way do I want to hide things from my brother-in-law, but I know Matthew's current fallen condition and cannot see where this news would bring any easiness to his life. In fact, I have prayed heavily over whether to write at all – it is such a chance I take! But I feel strongly that the Lord would have me set your mind and heart at ease, and He will cover any transgression on my part with His grace.

The Waking Up

I want you to know, dear child, that your Daniel is fine and that his words spoken to you that last evening you spent together are sure and true. Nothing has changed on his part. He is taken up with matters at his own home. While Mr. Townsend heals well, it is not so quickly. Daniel works from sun up to sun down to maintain their property and livelihood. I know not how he does it. Young Charles has become a mighty help to him, but nevertheless, it is the work of three men that he does.

In the moments of solitude in his day, he wants me to assure you that he thinks of you and your future together. And as he said to me just yesterday, a real man would write this himself and send you a letter by his own hand.

However, he is aware he has yet to ask your father for permission, and, in fact, has yet to meet your father. Because I have explained the way of Matthew to Daniel, he refuses to write you directly in the fear that such a letter would bring great anger and rage to Matthew (and we both know it would!). So, as much as I hate to be the messenger, for this moment, I find myself thus and can only think that the Lord would have me set your heart at rest for these next few months until Daniel has time to properly court you.

I pray that God would open doors, shut doors and bring His will into your relationship with Daniel. My dear, dear niece. How I pray for you daily and long to be with you. Stand strong and lean upon the Lord. I will write more soon. Know that you are loved.

Your Adoring Aunt,
Charity

Sarah reread the letter again and again, each time feeling her heart grow with happiness. She was not forgotten. Daniel had not forgotten her. Finally she looked up from the paper and caught Sally staring at her oddly. Blushing, she folded the note and tucked it in her pocket.

"Good news?" Sally questioned, bringing a hearty slice of peach pie over to her.

"Indeed," Sarah responded. "A letter from Aunt Charity about matters in Logan County."

"Uh huh," Sally peered at her inquisitively but let the matter drop as all four of them enjoyed a slice of pie and the warmth of a morning fire.

Because Sally hadn't been to the cabin since Sarah returned, the two of them spent some time later going through the stores Sally had built up all summer. Once again, she had left Sarah and her father in a perfect condition to weather the winter. Not only was there plenty of store goods, but Sally and Hagar had found berries and nuts from the surrounding woods to add to their gardening crops of potatoes, onions and leeks, dried beans, apples and peppers. The tiny shed behind the cabin was filled with stock. As the two women stood at the open door, surveying the contents, Sarah marveled at her good fortune. Hagar and Sammy had disappeared into the woods to search for fox holes.

"It is simply beautiful work, Sally," she praised the small, dark-skinned woman. "I could not have done this good of a job. I have more than enough to prepare food all winter."

"You'll be havin' to add some corn to yo' stores 'afore spring comes good," Sally pointed out. "I done got what I could from yo' fields, but I do believe you'll have to add to it somehow. Still, I sho' am glad you happy 'bout it." The two women leaned back, shutting the shed door tightly and securing it with a wooden latch that swiveled over the frame. "You happy 'bout lots a' things, is my guess. Happy 'bout what's in that letter right there," Sally pointed to Sarah's pocket. "Wanna tell me 'bout that happy?"

Sarah hesitated. Yes. She did want to tell someone. If truth be told, she wanted to tell Ann. Her life back at home felt empty and dismal with-out the hope of visiting with Ann and sharing her heart with her. In fact, Sarah had yet to visit Mrs. Neville, although she knew the kind woman longed to see her. In her mind, she had used the excuse that she'd only been home a few weeks and hadn't had time yet; but in her heart, Sarah hadn't been able to face the house, the rocking chair, Port Royal "proper" without Ann. Each day Sarah's conscience yelled "Selfish!" and tried to persuade her to face the truth, but so far, she'd been able to block the voice with hard work and excuses.

Sally spoke again, as if reading her mind.

"You know, we cain't always be keepin' our bizness in our hearts. Every once in a while, we gots to let things go and share 'em else it jest gets too powerful big. What I's tryin' to say is: I don't got to know yo' bizness, but sharin' somehow spreads the weight of things, and you can trust me, Sarah. I be yo' friend," Sally's usual light-natured demeanor was serious now, her clear brown eyes peering into Sarah's. The women moved around to the front of the cabin, finding two stumps propped up in the sunshine. They sat and Sarah opened up – slowly at first then with words rolling and tumbling over one another.

She told Sally about her conversion to the Christ, about Daniel and his intriguing confession and announcement, about her response, about the letter. Thirty minutes later, Sally knew it all and Sarah did, in fact, feel lighter in her spirit. Sally had offered no comments or advice save for a "Hallelujah!" or "Praise to God Almighty" as Sarah told of her conversion. When Sarah had emptied her last bit of news, Sally raised her eyes toward Heaven saying, "Blessed are the feet that bring good tidings, and most assuredly, you bring good news, Sarah! Mrs. Neville will be beside herself when she hears you done found Jesus. Why hadn't you been to see her yet?"

Sarah dropped her gaze, ashamed to respond.

"You gots to do it, chile. Yo' news will bring so much joy to that precious woman. Yo be puttin' yo'self aside and go bring her joy. Jesus'll give you the strength to do it," Sally preached. "Takes no mind-reader to see you still grievin' the young Miss Neville, but we gots to get on past ourselves and do the thing we knows is right – even when it's hard. They's lots a' times I gots to do what I don't want to do, but you jest do it 'cause you know it's right."

Sarah hugged herself tighter to ward off the chill seeping into her body. Though the sun had warmed the day considerably, it remained cold if a body wasn't moving enough. She knew Sally was right, heard the truth in her voice, but she didn't respond. She had already settled in her heart that it was time to go to Mrs. Neville.

The sound of Sammy's and Hagar's voices traveling up the hollow grew louder as they approached. Although they couldn't make out the words, the pitch told Sally and Sarah that the children were excited about something – perhaps foxes or coons or even traces of panthers or black bears. The two friends could often be found exploring forest life.

"Mama, look what we found!" Hagar called out as she emerged from the forest. Sammy followed right on her heels.

"I found it first," he shot out, glaring at the leggy girl.

"Don't matter," Hagar threw back over her shoulder. "It's broke anyhow. But it was sho' pretty once."

"How'd you think it got all the way out here?" Sammy panted as he drew alongside Hagar.

The thin girl stood tall, proudly holding out the flattened silver locket in her hand. The chain was no longer attached, the once-beautiful etching now ran together in swirling lines of confusion, and its center was pressed into the back. Sarah gasped and held out her hand. "You found it," she whispered in wonder.

The three stared at Sarah, confused. She took the locket and fingered it carefully.

"I was searching for it this morning when you came up," she explained. "Had been searching for a goodly amount of time but had seen no sign of it. And now, here it is." She closed her hand over the locket, drawing it to her breast. "Thank you, Hagar – and Sammy," she tousled his hair. "You saved me much time and made my heart even more thankful, as if that were even possible. What a birthday this has been!"

Laughter rose up into the giant trees that surrounded the small, simple cabin, calling forth life that had been stolen the evening before when Matthew tossed a piece of Sarah's heart into the brambles. Sally insisted they had time for only one more story, and even though Sammy begged and pleaded for that story to be the one about the Injun and Miss Elizabeth Holland, Sally and Hagar won out. Sarah told the story about the locket and when she had finished, none of them were dry-eyed.

Glancing at the sky, Sally knew she had to get back into the settlement with her two charges. Mrs. Neville expected her to help serve lunch to the field workers. Sarah, too, had chores to complete — and preparations to make so she would have time to slip away this week to visit Mrs. Neville. It was overdue.

As Sarah watched the three disappear down the foot path, Sammy turning back to wave one last time, she realized her heart was light and she held hope. The winter would, no doubt, be cold and long, but spring was just around the corner.

Part II

The Seeds Sprout

"For we know, brothers and sisters loved by God, that he has chosen you, because our gospel came to you not simply with words but also with power, with the Holy Spirit and deep conviction."
I Thessalonians 1:4-5

Chapter Seventeen
June 1800

McGready watched the four boys run and skip down the lane that went from his house eastward toward Russellville, his usual eight students cut in half due to field work required at their farms. He would end classes for the season next week but had hoped to complete their Latin training, or at the very least, leave it in a reasonable place to take it up again in the late fall. His own girls had disappeared toward the creek, stealing playtime before supper chores began, while Nancy worked inside the house. He leaned his towering body against a post that supported the overhang at the front of his modest home, his mind racing even faster than the four boys ran.

The spring of 1800 had brought many new things. Certainly, there had been an uneasiness, a widespread fear to see the new century roll in. Would it be the end of the known world? Should we expect earthquakes, floods, signs in the heavens? Although none of the Presbyterian meeting houses opened during the hard winter months, locals found their way to homes where Bible studies or prayer societies met. McGready couldn't say whether there were conversions at these events, but surely a hunger for religion was on the increase.

Also, none of Mr. Balch's forces reared their ugly heads during the winter, and McGready felt sure those converted souls from late last year still walked with the Lord. In fact, he looked forward to seeing them at the first meeting of the year – Red River, to be held one week thence.

Feeling the weight of standing, he slipped over to the front steps and sat down heavily on the top plank. It had been a steady day of teaching and though it fed his mind, it somehow depleted his body.

"Is it your stomach again?" Nancy eased out on the small porch, wiping her hands on the muslin apron tied at her waist.

"No, thanks be to God," McGready replied, turning his head to gaze at his blonde, blue-eyed wife. The fine wrinkles creased the corner of her eyes as she smiled in response.

"Perhaps it has passed then." She moved toward him, sitting to his side on the step.

"One can only hope. I've not seen signs of the malady in well nigh two months."

"Hmm. It could be having some fresh foods again. That always seemed to make my Papa's disposition better."

"Or it could simply have been the wiles of Satan to stop the work the Lord has begun," he smiled at his wife, leaning into her shoulder. "Nevertheless, it is gone for the time being, and I have been sensing a renewed energy in my spirit as well as the Spirit of the Lord. I can't help but see the growth in our fields – seeds that have sprouted and taken root and are now producing bountiful plants. It will not be long before the harvest begins in earnest. 'The fields are white for the harvest,'" he quoted with an abrupt laugh. "Both our physical fields and the fields of men's souls. It is as though there is an urgency within me to proclaim the Gospel – even more than I have had in all my days past. The power of the Gospel rolls within my belly like a mighty ocean, and it must come forth or I shall burst."

The intensity of McGready's voice increased as he spoke, the spirit of a Son of Thunder rising in him. Nancy gazed at him, letting him speak freely.

"Have we not seen a mighty move of God, Nancy? I know this very well and am filled with praise and joy. Yet, I also hunger for more, and I would that He be pleased at this hunger. As the society continued to pray through the winter months, my faith grew to increase until now ..." he paused, passing his hand over his brow, "...now I can only hope the next week will pass quickly so that the fullness of my heart will not overflow before our first meeting together." He glanced at his wife, her heart-shaped face turned toward him, silently listening, silently believing. Abruptly, he smiled broadly, releasing the fever of his emotion in a quick second.

"Ah, but I shall endure. And until then, my dear wife, my body needs nourishment, and my feet need three little girls to complete chores for me." He stood then, reaching out his hand to pull Nancy to her feet. "Why don't I go find our wayward children while you begin those hoe-cakes?"

Brushing the debris off the back of her skirt, Nancy nodded in agreement. "Most certainly, Mr. McGready. Many hands make for light work."

Sarah grabbed the seat of the wagon frantically, catching herself before her body was pitched to the ground. The road east to Keysburg was horrible! A deluge of spring rains and then complete drought for the past month had turned the shallow puddles and small rivulets into hard-packed ruts and deep crevices. It was a miracle their tiny wagon had not broken an axle. She glanced at her father through the corner of her eye. His strong face was intently set on the road ahead, hands easily gripping the reins, confident in his ability to maneuver the trace.

Riding back to Logan County with him had not been her first choice of transport. She smiled wryly at the thought. Not even her last choice. How about not a choice at all? Yet, to her surprise, he not only was allowing her to attend to Aunt Charity again this summer, but he claimed he had barrels to sell in Keysburg and would use the opportunity to take her farther to Charity's house. It would be the first time he had seen his sister-in-law since her departure from Spartanburg fifteen years ago.

When Matthew had announced his intentions last week, Sarah looked closely into his face to see if perhaps there lay any other motive. She had been praying for him steadily throughout the winter – never letting him know that she even believed in prayer, of course — but she had watched for any sign to show God heard her. Was this a weak attempt to reconnect with family, and thereby, a softening of his heart? Or was it simply convenience?

The wagon dipped threateningly into another hole, the imbalance throwing her against her father. She quickly righted herself, turning her face toward the surrounding forest. They were in the area where she, Daniel and Mr. Townsend had met the Chickasaws two years back. She found it hard to believe it had been so long. Since then, she had seen a few Indians here and there, mostly in towns trading with settlers. News of Indian attacks had been commonplace up till about five years ago but not so much lately. Apparently, the treaty had achieved its goal. Sarah was profoundly relieved.

At almost seventeen, Sarah had fully developed into a young woman. All the childlike roundness in her face had disappeared, leaving her strong, square-jawed features prominent. Her green eyes – which darkened when she was angry – spoke volumes about whatever emotion she currently felt, and while some would not call her pretty, all would say she was arresting. Her wild, unruly auburn hair remained firmly wrapped in a topknot under her cap for the most part, but when the inevitable tendrils sneaked out of their prison, they framed her strong face, bringing a softness and gentleness to her demeanor.

Men in Port Royal certainly had noticed that young Sarah McMillan had come of age, but her father had said nothing about it, which pleased Sarah greatly. Had he been insisting on marriage, she would have had to bring Daniel into the conversation, a topic she hoped Daniel himself would address in the near future. Perhaps even today if he knew of her father's visit.

But that would be impossible. Matthew had directed Sarah to write to Aunt Charity, explaining she would return to Kentucky in early June, but she didn't declare how she would return. No. Matthew's visit would be a complete surprise, one that she doubted Charity would ever expect. The idea that Daniel would know was ludicrous.

She shook her head slightly as she thought. Anytime you add her father to an equation, the results would be anyone's guess. All she could do was hunker down, try to enjoy the beautiful Kentucky forests and barrens, and pray for how this day might end.

Because they had left before dawn, the McMillans arrived in Logan County earlier than one might expect, sometime in the afternoon when Charity and the children all were outdoors. As the wagon approached the farm, Sarah saw Charity and Mattie working with the cow near the barn. It appeared that Millie and Josiah were watching after baby Matthew, who was now toddling under the elm tree.

Home, she breathed silently. *Now I finally feel as if I'm home.* Even the presence of her father couldn't smother the way her heart leapt when she spotted them. She began waving before the wagon ever stopped.

"Sarah!" a scream erupted from Millie. "Sarah! Mama! It's Sarah.

She's back." Forgetting her responsibilities for a moment, the tiny, long-legged girl raced toward the wagon, her cap slipping off her head and hair catching the breeze. Sarah found herself laughing heartily and practically falling out of the wagon as it drew to a stop. "Oh, you're back. You're back!" Millie cried out, jumping into Sarah's outstretched arms.

"Of course I'm back, you silly girl," Sarah held her tightly, savoring the sweet smell of lilac and lye soap. "I would never leave you for long."

By this time, Josiah had reached the reunion, arms raised expectantly, a bright smile on his cherub face. Sarah bent to retrieve him as Aunt Charity and Mattie approached the wagon. She glanced up just in time to see the shock on Charity's face as she recognized Sarah's wagon driver. Mattie found Sarah's waist and clung to her, but she was silent, somehow sensing a change in the atmosphere. Charity's steps slowed, a mixture of disbelief and wariness in her eyes. Matthew had jumped out of the wagon, dropping Sarah's stuffed saddlebags at her feet. He cocked his head, a bit derisively.

"Charity," he spoke.

"Matthew," she whispered. "I cannot believe it is you." She drew closer, a longing to embrace him apparent in her face, but he stepped back. She stopped, waiting.

He laughed abruptly, hard.

"Had you begun to think I did not exist then?"

"No. Of course not. It is just …"

"I assure you, Charity, I am not as poor and wretched as you imagine. I live and breathe and conduct myself as a standing member of society."

Charity stretched up to her full five feet, two inches, mentally arming herself. Knowing her aunt, Sarah assumed she had begun praying silently.

"It does my heart well to lay eyes on you. I had wondered if I ever would again."

"As you can see, I have barrels to deliver and brought her as I came," he dipped his head toward Sarah.

"Will you not come in for some refreshment and let us talk for a bit. Or better yet, plan to stay the night here, and you may conduct your business tomorrow."

That hard laugh again. "Would you not love to have my brain to yourself for a night to pick clean?" he spoke curtly. "No. No. I promised barrels today, and they shall have them today." Matthew swung his leg wide, pulling himself back up into the wagon seat. Charity stepped closer, placing her hand on his knee. He jerked it back as though her touch was fire.

"I must tell you how grateful I am, brother, that you allow Sarah to be with me all these months out of a year. She is not only a help. No indeed, she is better than any laborer we could hire. Her work is good and precise and as a bonus we all," Charity swept her arms wide, encompassing her wide-eyed children, "love her dearly. Thank you for your sacrifice."

"'Tis no sacrifice for me," he spat out. "I am glad you find the girl a help and more than glad that she is out of my business. I will admit she is useful, but I find her presence stifling and bothersome much of the time." He didn't look at Sarah as he spoke, but she felt the dagger point of each word as though he stood in front of her, stabbing repeatedly at her heart. The familiar wall she erected when he spoke this way was mentally sliding into place, a protection she would build to ward off the pain. Yet since she had accepted the Christ, she had found He would not let her put up that wall anymore. It was as though the Lord Himself stayed her hand, whispering in her spirit that He was her protector now, and she no longer needed invisible walls to keep out the pain. She took a deep breath and whispered a prayer of desperation. Peace flooded over her immediately, and she knew she would be alright.

Sarah felt Mattie's arms tighten around her waist, and, as she glanced down at the solemn, dark-eyed child, she saw fat tears streak her cheeks. Sarah leaned down, brushing her lips across Mattie's hair, smiling and wiping a tear away in silent assurance. Charity, however, was not to be consoled.

"Brother," her voice had risen in temblor yet deepened in authority. "This is my home, and as Obediah isn't here, the Lord has given me authority over these lands. You are standing on my property, speaking evil against one of the Lord's children and a dear niece. I would convince you of her noble character, but I truly believe you already know her character is noble. In fact, I would believe that you have such a great love for your daughter that the depth of it – when you face it…if you ever have – causes your breath to cease. She stills your heart and while you may deny it until you fall into your grave, know that I see it." She stepped one step closer to the wagon.

"I also know you would have me bring up the past again so you might have a foothold to speak of your pain and your loss, but that I will not do. Matilda is long dead, and I have made excuses for you too long already! It is time to live again, Matthew. Take the bitter root out of your heart, forgive God, and accept His love and grace for you. It is a mighty weapon against the hatred in your heart."

Matthew's face blanched whiter and whiter beneath his beard. The lines of his jaw clenched tightly, and Sarah wondered if he would be gnashing his teeth against her aunt. Instead, he jerked the reins and lashed out at the horse. With a jolt, the wagon leapt forward, almost knocking Charity down. Sarah reached out to steady her, and Charity gratefully squeezed her arm. They all stood for a moment and stared at the rigid back of Matthew McMillan heading west toward Keysburg.

As the outline of the wagon disappeared from view, Charity spun toward Sarah, a look of pure delight on her face.

"Oh, Sarah! Welcome home! And with such promise!"

"Promise, Aunt?" Sarah vaguely returned Charity's embrace, a question on her face.

"Why, most assuredly. God is hearing our prayers, dear niece. Matthew is drawing closer to the Kingdom."

Mattie reached for Sarah's saddlebags and hoisted them over her thin shoulder. The group began walking toward the house, Charity explaining as they went.

"In past years, Matthew has had nothing to do with me whatsoever. No letters. No messages to pass on. Absolutely, certainly, unequivocally, no visits! He may point to his barrels in the wagon all day long, but I know that he brought you to us this time because of the pull of the Lord. He is curious. In his spirit, he longs to belong again to family, yet his stubborn heart will not face that truth. So he makes excuses, even for himself, to find the lay of the land, so to speak." They entered the coolness of the house, the children crowding into the McPherson front room, eagerly waiting for this adult conversation to end. They had so many new discoveries to show to Sarah.

"I am sorry, Aunt. I do not see what you see."

"Ah, 'tis no matter. Perhaps it is the discernment of the Lord, but I must tell you that I am most encouraged by this turn of events. My prayers for your father will increase from this day forward. Trust me when I say he is close, at the very door of the Kingdom, Sarah. Pray for him as though his life depended on it – for it very well may."

Josiah simply couldn't wait any longer. He tugged fiercely on Sarah's skirt, his round face puckered in frustration. "Sarah, come see the rock I found yesterday. It's a big one," he pleaded. Sarah laughed at the boy, tousling the top of his fiery red hair.

"Yes, Josiah. I will come. Then I want to see what Mattie and Millie have found since last fall. And … where is baby Matthew?"

"Oh!" Millie exclaimed, dashing out the door to retrieve the toddler waddling his way toward the house. Laughter erupted, and for Sarah, life had returned.

Chapter Eighteen

Four days later, McGready inhaled a deep breath, reveling in the clean smell of rain. The drought had finally broken this morning by way of a fine summer rain which fell most of the day. It was good, he thought, and hopefully a heavenly sign of what was to come in the Spirit. Blue sky had replaced the early morning thunderheads, and although the lane to the Red River Meeting House was dotted with sitting puddles, there were no deep mud holes that could bog a wagon wheel. No. The rain was providential and, McGready hoped, symbolic.

The third Sabbath of June was upon them, a time for communion services that he had prayed over, wept over, prepared for – he was ready. For the first time since last fall, the body of Christ would come together again, and he felt the urgency of the Lord for the event to begin.

Hodge was ready to minister as well – he had selected a passage out of Job to present to the congregants during the Monday morning sacrament, and McGready was prepared to deliver sermons on Friday and Saturday evenings.

Oh gracious Jehovah, McGready had written the night before in his journal, *may you pour out life like a mighty river upon this guilty, unworthy country. Show yourself to be a prayer-hearing God. Give your people a praying spirit and a lively faith and then answer our prayers beyond our highest expectations. Make this wilderness and solitary place glad, this dreary desert rejoice and blossom like the rose.*

As he ascended the steps of the meeting house, he noticed the summer rose out of the corner of his eye. Wrapped around the corner of the building, the bush held a single, fragile pink blossom. He took it as a confirmation that God's rain was pouring out even more on the dry, spiritual desert of Logan County.

Even a hermit would have known that the Red River Meeting House was the site of McGready's first meeting of the year. Hand-written signs hung on the door at Stewart, Dromgoole & Co. Merchantile, word of mouth had carried the news far into the surrounding wilderness, and among the faithful there was a palpable air of anticipation. Sarah felt it as well and had waited impatiently for Friday night, but she had added incentive. Daniel would attend.

She had learned within hours of her arrival that he had gone west to trade that week. The Townsend farm was functioning well with Mr. Townsend now working as hard as he did prior to the accident. Throughout the winter, Daniel and Charles had collected skins – bear, beaver, fox, coon – and this was the first opportunity to trade them for stores and cash. It was Charles's first trip to trade, for Daniel had taken him along. More than half the pelts came from Charles's gun.

Regardless, Daniel had told his mother he would definitely be back in time for the third June Sabbath.

Chores were wrapped up early that Friday, and Sarah took the extra time to wash her hair at the creek. She dried it in the sun, trying to pin it up several different ways. She finally settled on a loose topknot at the nape of her neck with two long tendrils framing her face. The day before, Mattie and Millie had washed all their best gowns, so by early Friday evening, the whole family – clean from head to toe – rolled toward Red River with Bible in hand. Sarah found it difficult to breathe properly, excitement pressing in on her chest.

Although they had left early, they still had a hard time finding a spot for the wagon. Tethered horses, braked wagons, mules that were tied off – it all greeted them as they approached the meeting house. It appeared that the whole of the county had turned out.

"Whoa, there!" Charity cried out, stopping abruptly. They sat for a moment, surveying the scene.

"Why not over there, Mama?" Millie pointed to a small, empty area just past a sycamore tree.

"Yes, darling, I think that might do."

"Hello there, Mrs. McPherson. I have saved you a place," a voice cried out from a crowd of men. Daniel trotted over toward them, a broad smile spread across his face. Sarah thought she had never seen such a handsome man, and he only had eyes for her. She felt her face grow warm under his gaze as she waved self-consciously. He laughed out loud then and directed them into a small space halfway between the lane and the house. Charity eased the wagon in, barely fitting, and pulled the hand brake firmly.

The McPherson children piled out like sailors abandoning ship, bodies flying every which way to try to be the first on the ground, the first to greet Daniel with a hug, then dash off to find friends. Laughing, Charity watched them dart away. Millie had passed baby Matthew off to Sarah before jumping from the side of the wagon. Thankful she had the boy as a distraction, Sarah patted his back, waiting for Charity to come take him from her hands before disembarking. Instead, Daniel came over and stood formally at her side.

"Good evening, Miss McMillan," he said, bowing at the waist. "May I take this child from you in hopes that perhaps sometime tonight you may be able to leave the wagon?"

Sarah smiled, her green eyes dancing with joy. "That would indeed be most appreciated, Mr. Townsend."

Charity had made it around the side of the wagon and accepted the squirming child from Daniel's hands. As he turned back to help Sarah out of the wagon, his tone changed.

"I am very, very glad to see you, Sarah," he reached up, taking her hand. She stepped lightly over the edge of the wagon, hit the single step, then was standing next to him. Even with her height, Sarah found herself gazing upwards. Daniel stood at least three inches taller. "The winter spanned at least three years for me. If there had been any way to see you, any way to write without causing you harm, I ..."

"There simply was no way," she interrupted. "I understand that and, though the winter was interminable – and spring felt even longer – it was worth the wait. I am glad to see you too, Daniel Townsend."

Charity had stood to the side, pulling items from the wagon bed to take into the meeting house – a few things for the baby to keep him occupied, her Bible, a few extra handkerchiefs. Even though she heard the conversation, she never responded but simply let the two of them reconnect. As Daniel linked Sarah's arm into the crook of his, he turned toward Charity and held out his other arm. "May I escort the two most beautiful ladies into the meeting house?"

"You may," Charity smiled, passing Sarah a handful of items. "We would be most honored."

As McGready rounded up those gathered for Friday's meeting, he breathed prayers of gratitude for the number of people present – many of them children. He had never understood why previous ministers to this wilderness had not encouraged the children and youth to attend meetings – why they had not gone out from house to house, farm to farm, to gather in the young. Did they not know that the Kingdom of God was made up of such as these?

Calls from parents brought them from all corners of the clearing and some had even ventured near the river, but all came running in obedience as the time neared for the meeting. The benches filled up quickly as did the back and side walls in the building. The six tall, normally shuttered, windows stood open, letting in the breeze that could always be found atop this hill, and many men stood outside those windows to hear the Gospel from McGready. There simply wasn't room for everyone to fit inside the house, much less to have a seat. It was the largest crowd to ever attend the sacrament at Red River.

As was his way, McGready began with earnest, soul-searching prayer, calling on God to come and meet with his people on this, the first occasion of their gathering for this new century. Revs. McGee and Hodge also were present, both praying fervently and watching the lane for any signs of rowdiness. Truly, those dangers had become less and less as McGready established the meeting houses in Logan County, but the ministers remained vigilant, always watching and waiting.

They didn't have to worry. The only presence to show up that first night was the presence of the Lord, Hodge reported to McGready the next day.

"Indeed," McGready responded. "I saw Christians filled with joy and peace in believing; and poor, distressed, condemned sinners brought to see the glory and fullness of a crucified Jesus."

Hodge and McGee concurred, and the meetings continued. On

through Saturday – where McGready preached a rousing sermon on "The Deceitfulness of the Human Heart" – then into Sunday's picnic and service. Sarah and the McPhersons, like all the others, traveled home in the evenings, but made their way back to the meeting house early each morning.

As was the custom, Monday was the day of the final communion before the meetings would be declared over. Hodge presided, preaching a stirring sermon out of Job, Chapter 22, verse 21. "Submit to God and be at peace with Him; in this way prosperity will come to you." He had barely begun the core of the message when a woman interrupted the flow. Sarah had been watching her for a time out of the corner of her eye. She appeared quite undone and couldn't seem to keep still on the bench. Her children were lined up on each side of her, she had many, while her husband sat on the other end of the bench. Finally, the woman – Sarah had seen her frequently but didn't know her name – jumped to her feet and began to repent.

"I am a sinner!" she cried, breaking into the middle of one of Hodge's sentences. "I cannot keep silent any longer for I have now seen the Christ! Oh, such a wicked creature I am! For many of these months, I have fought against the drawing of the Holy Spirit and have pushed him aside. Yet I knew," she laughed wryly, "oh, yes! I knew that I must be here, that the Spirit would draw me to this place and this time. As the Rev. Hodge preached, I have released my all to the Lord Jesus and am one of His! Oh, the joys of His goodness and grace. Oh, the love of the Savior!"

Simultaneously, Hodge began declaring praises with her as did many of the other congregants. Truly, Sarah thought, the heavens opened, and God Himself stepped in among them. She bowed her head, feeling the weight of the presence of God. Daniel, who sat beside her, did the same. After a few moments, the woman took her place next to her children, now quietly weeping. Hodge picked up his Bible and again began to preach.

His words gathered power like a boulder rolling down a hillside, the weight of them mightily increasing, while McGready stood at one of the back doors, praying silently. Finally, Hodge summarized his message and waited. A dread, solemn spirit fell over the room, and more people began to weep. From front to back, side to side, tears flowed down the faces of the young and old by the conviction of the Holy Spirit.

"What shall I do to be saved?" a man cried out as he knelt on the floor. His voice echoed throughout the small building. And then the move came from the children.

Throughout the room, children began to fall face down on the wooden floor, crying out for God's presence, calling for God to have mercy on them – sinners. Sarah watched astounded. When she had met the Christ last fall, it had been a powerful time, one that she would never forget, but this? Even many of the youngest children in the room were overcome.

The commanding form of McGready moved up from the back and began to minister individually. Hodge and McGee also moved in between benches, leading the repentant to the Christ. Soaking in the presence of God, Sarah, Daniel and the McPhersons sat quietly watching people's hearts change. Mattie and Millie were especially moved when two of their closest friends heard the voice of the Christ and turned their lives over to Him. Joyful tears flowing, they moved toward their mother and stood next to Charity's side as they listened and watched the sisters confess belief in God through Jesus.

For several hours even after the last communion was over, no one seemed to want to leave. The three ministers continued to pray and talk with people in the building, but the move of God extended out of the church and into the clearing. There were pockets of solemnity and periods of rejoicing. A spiritual lightning filled the air, and as people began to pull out in their wagons or on their horses, they carried with them a sense that something significant had happened.

In a spontaneous mood, Charity had mentioned to several of the prayer society that tonight might be a good time to gather again – to both thank the Lord for the manifestation of His presence and to pray that this spark of revival continue to burn. Sister Townsend and her mother, Anaphileda, as well as Sisters White and Ewing agreed. They would be at the McPherson farm immediately after supper.

Sarah was vaguely aware of the plans but found herself more taken up with Daniel. They stood off to the side as Charity began to gather the children.

"I feel as if there is too much to tell," Daniel was saying, running his hand through his thick, black hair. "We seem able to only snatch minutes here and there, and I would talk with you longer, if possible. For now, I must see to my grandmother, mother, brother and sisters; but perhaps I could call on you this evening or on the morrow?"

Sarah's eyes followed her Aunt Charity as she raced after a toddling Matthew. The boy was heading toward the creek. "Yes," she answered slowly, "but I know that your mother and grandmother are coming to the house this evening for the prayer society."

"I heard that as well. Father most likely will still have to work the fields and perhaps, I might as well," Daniel scratched his chin thoughtfully. "Tomorrow then?"

"Tuesday," Sarah stated. "Yes. I think that would be best. Perhaps for supper? I am sure Aunt Charity will not mind another hungry person at the table." The breeze picked up, pulling another strand of hair from Sarah's cap. It flapped wildly across her face, and she captured it quickly, shoving it back under the cap.

"Why do you always hide your hair?"

"What do you mean?"

"It is beautiful," Daniel said gently. "You always seem to be tucking it away somewhere."

"Yes, well…it has a mind of its own," Sarah responded, a little embarrassed.

"I think you should let it do what it wants. It is most becoming."

Sarah glanced around quickly, making sure none of the children were hearing this. She felt an odd mixture of excitement and embarrassment – and apparently, the turmoil was written on her face because Daniel laughed, not unkindly, but with understanding.

"Yes, I know. I will stop talking this way. Tell me, before you have to leave, what did you think of today's communion?"

Sarah's countenance lit up, her green eyes shining with joy. "Oh, my. It was too astounding for words, don't you think?"

"Yes." Daniel looked off over the field and down to the road, seeing the remains of Maulding's Station through the trees. "I've never been in a place where the presence of God moved such. The children … the things they saw. The reality of the Christ in their eyes. It was remarkable. I wonder what we have experienced? What will come of this? My heart still beats quickly in my chest at the thought of it all."

"I know. Although I saw them – heard the cries for mercy from others – I still found sweet communion with the Lord as I sat on the bench. His presence was active and moving among us all," Sarah replied, looking now fully into Daniel's face.

"Sarah! Daniel!" Millie ran toward them, a smile filling her tiny countenance. "Look what I found. It is a crayfish." As she waved the tiny pinchers in her face, Sarah laughed, jumping back in mock fear.

"Oh my! It is huge!"

"I will protect you, my lady," Daniel cried, standing in front of Sarah with his arms akimbo, his feet apart. "No foul beast of the creek will harm you this day!"

Millie doubled over laughing, holding her stomach with her free hand, while Daniel winked at Sarah. She smiled back, reveling in family.

Chapter Nineteen

News of that third Sabbath in June spread like wildfire throughout Logan County. Even McGready might have been surprised had he known word was reaching outside county lines farther into the wilderness of Kentucky and back toward the east and the Appalachians. But of that he was not aware. What he did know was that a spark had been lit, and God had blessed the congregation of the Red River Meeting House with a powerful move of His Spirit. Now, if only they could ride the crest of this wave as they moved toward Gasper River.

"Rankin will be ready for us on the fourth Sabbath of July," McGready reported to Hodge and McGee a week later. "I received a letter from him just this morning saying that word of the outpouring of the Spirit has reached Gasper River and beyond, and already there is an expectancy among the faithful."

The three men sat together under a shade tree next to Stewart's Merchantile. They had not intended to meet, but by chance each had been in town on separate business. It was a good time to compare thoughts.

"Indeed, I almost wonder if we ought not move more quickly, to keep the revival flames from dying out, so to speak," Hodge remarked, picking his teeth with the edge of his knife blade. "You know, there are always the Balchs out there — and others who would degrade the work of the Holy Spirit. I would hate to see yet another dousing of the fire – although I must confess that those who participated at Red River are not giving the anti-revivalists the time of day."

McGee, a short, stout man, nodded. He had picked up a small stick and was whittling with intensity. "It is the same in my corner of the county. The anti-revivalists are certainly out there – some even within our own homes and families – but this move of the Spirit seems to be the genuine article. I am not hearing of any falling away, and … how many did we have at last count, James?"

"As of yesterday, about ten persons."

"Yes? Well, the salvations of those ten souls appears to be set in stone and the fervency of their testimonies only increase as the days pass." McGee peeled off a thick slice of poplar. It was a hot day for June, and the men had met up in early afternoon when the peak of the heat beat on the hardened ground around the merchantile. Still, they sat sweating in the shade as the vast variety of folk in Logan County came and went – everyone from Indians to prosperous farmers to, more abundantly, the average wilderness dweller trying to survive. And even by this new century, there were still enough rogues and rowdies to warrant several more Presbyterian meeting houses in the area. McGready watched them all from his shady spot, his brow furrowed. Finally, he lifted his elbows off his knees and straightened, looking at McGee and Hodge with intensity.

"I hear you both and have spent considerable time in prayer over our next meeting. I believe the Lord would say that we are to wait until late July, and I cannot tell you why. Reason, it seems to me, would be to go ahead and strike while the iron is hot, but that's not the way the Spirit is leading. Perhaps there needs be a lull in the move for more people to hear the word. Perhaps there is some work the Spirit needs to do in men's hearts before they once again hear God's word spoken from the pulpit. I am not at all sure. But I am as sure as I can be that I heard to wait till the end of July."

McGee and Hodge listened thoughtfully, more poplar strips flying out of McGee's quick hands.

"Rev. McGready! What a pleasure to find you here!" a large, bustling Joy Townsend descended on the three men in a flurry of movement. The ribbons from her hat joined with the lift of her apron as she hurried toward them, giving her the appearance of flying rather than the hasty walk she assumed. All three men involuntarily drew back as they stood to greet her. She stopped short from embracing McGready, although the desire was certainly there.

"Well, bless my soul. And the Reverends McGee and Hodge as well. What a boon for me," she gushed, joy illuminating her countenance. McGready smiled at her enthusiasm.

"Sister Townsend, it does my heart well to see you this fine day," he responded. "And how is Brother Townsend and the rest of the family?"

"We are most well – I might even say, thriving and joyful! We have found it difficult to put our feet on this earth after last week's meetings. Oh, what joy and pleasure in the Lord! The prayer society has already met twice at Sister McPherson's home, and we continue to ask for even more of His presence. And do tell (she had not yet paused for breath), do I hear we are to go to Gasper River next month for a gathering? It has been spoken that might be the case and we all – the society, that is – plan to attend those meetings as well. Of course, we will have to take the wagon and some provisions for I am sure our brothers and sisters over that way cannot tend to our families as well as their own. But it is no matter. Providing for ourselves will be of no consequence if we are to experience more of the Lord's glory as was had last week. Is that not so?"

She finally had to stop to catch her breath, and perhaps realized she had rattled on a bit because she appeared chagrined. Hodge contemplated that her given name of "Joy" may well have been a prophetic christening from her parents. McGready simply laughed.

"If all have the enthusiasm of you, Sister Townsend, the July meeting will be a mighty success. Yes. It is to be at Gasper River, and it is set for the fourth Sabbath of July. Do let the faithful know of this, and, if they too want to make the trip east, they are more than welcome. Your idea of wagons and provisions is not a bad one. I could see the need for such as that."

McGready's encouragement seemed to fuel Mrs. Townsend's fire, launching her on yet another discourse of the rigors of travel and the need for solid provisions. McGee and Hodge subtly made their excuses and faded away, leaving McGready alone to weather the storm. As Hodge entered the cooler merchantile, he glanced back. James lifted his hand in a short wave, a reproving look in his eye. Hodge smiled broadly as he entered the building. McGready would get him back one day; count on it.

Between the early corn harvest, a subtle yet persistent courting from Daniel, and helping Aunt Charity grow the McPhersons' first crop of indigo, Sarah didn't have much time to think about another gathering of the church, but Charity had been planning since the first of July for the family's travels to Gasper River alongside the Townsends. It wasn't that Sarah didn't want to attend, she just didn't have extra space in her mind to contemplate it. Daniel occupied her thoughts day and night.

Yet now, as the time of their departure drew near, she found she could handle both thoughts as one, for the McPhersons and Townsends were to travel together tomorrow. She and Daniel, as the two oldest "children," would certainly have responsibilities in each household but would be traveling together – a reality that brought excitement to her heart. She scrubbed the boys' breeches over the washboard faster and harder just thinking of it.

"Do leave some of the cotton on the cloth, Sarah," Charity said, laughing as she approached the girl. They had a work line of sorts operating with Sarah scrubbing, Mattie rinsing in the nearby creek, and Millie hanging the clothes on bushes, over tree limbs, on anything that would support them while they dried. Charity carried the last load as she walked down the narrow path from the house. Josiah toddled behind her, holding his favorite blanket and yet with a scowl on his face.

"My apologies, Aunt," Sarah paused, gazing intently at the wear on the knees of the breeches. "I suppose I was lost in thought."

"I suppose you were." Charity smiled in understanding. "It is an exciting time, is it not?" She turned toward Josiah. "Come now, son. Sarah is ready for the blanket."

The scowl deepened, Josiah's fiery red hair warned Sarah of what was to come.

"No! My blanky."

"Josiah Stewart McPherson! You are never to tell Mama no!" Charity drew to her full height, a frown of frustration on her face. The toddler only gripped his blanket tighter.

"My blanky," he repeated, stubbornness etched in every part of his body.

Sarah could see a stand-off in the making. "Josiah? Did you hear that?" she whispered. The boy stopped, a questioning look replacing the scowl. "I heard a voice calling my name. Did you hear it?" He slowly shook his head, thumb moving toward his mouth. "It said, 'Sarah, will you please make me clean?'" His eyes grew wider while Charity suppressed a smile. "I think it came from somewhere over here."

Josiah looked behind him and to his side as Sarah pointed in his direction.

"Wait! There it goes again. It said, 'Sarah, help me. If I do not get clean, I cannot go on the big trip tomorrow, and I want to go oh-so-badly. Oh! It is such a sad voice. It wants to be clean."

Josiah's big blue eyes began to water a bit, his heart feeling every bit of the sadness.

"Oh, poor thing. Now it is crying," Sarah continued, reaching toward the toddler. "I think it is coming from … oh my! It is coming from your blanky!"

Josiah wavered a moment as Sarah reached out to touch the beloved cotton blanket. Threads fell from its sides while stains dotted the front and back.

"It is begging me to wash it before tomorrow so it can go," Sarah explained again, having a light hold on it now. "Will you let me take good care of it if I give it back in a little while?"

Thoughtfully, the boy hesitated, eyeing Sarah with a bit of suspicion. Lifting his blanket up, he gazed at it seriously then met Sarah's eyes again. Was she trustworthy?

Apparently, the four-year-old decided she was. He solemnly handed the blanket over, popping his thumb back into his mouth.

"Oh, thank goodness!" Sarah exclaimed, holding the blanket tenderly. "It said it is so happy now, Josiah."

Laughing out loud, Charity reached out and clasped the boy's hand. "Well done, Sarah. Josiah and I must go check on baby Matthew, right Josiah? We will return in a bit to get blanky back."

Smiling, Sarah watched the two trod back up the path toward the house as she turned her attention to the grungy blanket. If she'd had a free hand, she would have held her nose as she pushed it under the soapy water.

The tiny wagon practically bulged with provisions the next day. Sarah stood to the side, hands on hips, surveying their work. It had been a real challenge to fit enough food to last three days in one small wagon along with supplies that would allow all the McPhersons to sleep outdoors at Gasper River – all the while leaving room to travel. In many ways, it felt like she and her father were packing again to cross the Appalachians into the Western frontier.

Charity had depended on Sarah heavily the last few days. After their best clothes had been washed – and the frightful blanket finally cleaned – Sarah had been responsible for planning and packing all food. Beginning with a list of each meal and what would be needed, Sarah had used the wide kitchen table to lay out the items. After they used the large kettle for this morning's corn mush, she had sent Mattie to the creek to wash out the pot. They would use it at Gasper River for practically every meal. Last night after supper, Sarah had made another batch of hoecakes and hard biscuits to take in the wagon. They would be good staples to fill their stomachs when cooking wasn't available. She had been up at first light this morning, packing the food carefully in the allotted space. Thankfully, Charity and the girls had seen to gathering the coverings needed in case of rain, and blankets to be used to sleep on. Of course, those items had taken up the bulk of the wagon space.

"What do you think? Have we forgotten anything?"

"I certainly hope not," Sarah responded, turning toward her aunt. "I do not think we have room for a kitchen mouse on that wagon."

Charity laughed, moving to check the back latch. "I told all kitchen mice they must stay here, although if they got religion, perhaps they would stop stealing from our stores."

The two women laughed together easily as the children ran out the front door, each carrying their one item allowed for the journey. Josiah brought up the rear, clutching the treasured, sparkling clean, blanket.

The McPhersons were to meet up with the Townsends at Mortimer Station. Then they would travel together north, up the Nashville Road to Russellville, then east up the Bowling Green Road toward Gasper River. Daniel had estimated that it would take them about half the day to reach the meeting house. Hopefully, they would then have a few hours to set up camp before the first meeting commenced. As Sarah had spent some time in prayer the night before, she found excitement rising in her spirit again. It was as though she sensed God's heart for the heathen in that area of

Logan County, and her passion for the lost outshone even her anticipation of riding with Daniel. *And that is as it should be,* she considered as she and Charity loaded up the children. *If my love for the Christ does not outweigh my love for a man, I am most certainly lost. Jesus Christ must increase, and I must decrease,* she quoted the Scripture to herself.

Still, she was looking forward to spending so much time with Daniel. Perhaps they would be able to talk of their future – alone.

About ten miles north at the same time, McGready leaned down to kiss Nancy before mounting his horse for the ride to Gasper River.

"You will be alright with the girls?" he questioned for the third time.

"I have said it is so," she retorted. "You are turning into a worrisome old man. Next thing you know, you will send someone to stay with us while you are gone – as if I cannot manage on my own."

"I had considered ..." he began slowly, eyes crinkling in amusement as Nancy swatted his arm playfully.

"Oh ... you! It is only a three-night trip. I feel sure the girls and I will survive, Mr. McGready."

Laughing outright, the tall, muscular man threw his leg over the back of the sorrel mare, mounting with ease. Looking down from the horse, his eyes softened as he gazed at his petite wife, her blonde hair neatly pinned.

"In all seriousness, I will pray for you, my dear, and ask that you also would cover me in your prayers. I will return forthrightly, hopefully full of the Spirit with great things to speak of."

Nancy touched her husband's leg gently, wishing he didn't have to go, knowing he did.

"I, too, will pray for you, my dear. Be safe on the roads and know that God watches over you."

McGready kicked his horse into motion, setting off at a brisk pace, as Nancy watched him ride off. In a booming voice, he began to pray even before his silhouette disappeared over the horizon. Smiling to herself, Nancy turned back toward the house to make sure the girls had finished their breakfast.

Chapter Twenty

It was the perfect July day for travel. Billowing white clouds skipped over the sun, providing frequent breaks in the heat, and the blistering temperatures from the previous week had disappeared. In fact, it felt almost like spring with a light breeze adding another level of cooling. Sarah was relieved. Nothing would keep her from attending the Gasper River meeting now that her heart was engaged, but she knew there may not be a shady place to set up camp. The idea of dealing with the heat of last week had not been appealing.

It had taken only a little over half the day to reach the meeting house, yet as the Townsend/McPherson caravan drew closer to the clearing, they found they were not the first to arrive. At least ten other wagons had already staked claims to different areas around the building and makeshift tents flapped under just about every shade tree.

"Let's move over this way, Sister McPherson," Mr. Townsend bellowed from his driver's seat, pointing to a small area to the right. It wasn't as close to the meeting house as others were, but there would be enough room for both wagons to fit as well as extra space for tents. Charity slapped the reins lightly, easing their horse over that way. Sarah sat beside her aunt, as she had all day, while the little ones had their places in the back.

"It is not for the first time that I wish Obediah were here," Charity spoke with a sigh. "He misses so much when he is surveying, yet I cannot complain at how he cares for his family. But to miss this move of God? Well, he will be bereft." She eased the wagon up slowly, pulling the brake and sitting back in her seat. Turning, she smiled wryly at Sarah. "If wishes were horses, beggars might ride, my mother used to say. Ah well. 'Tis the way of the Lord, I suppose. Children?" Charity glanced over her shoulder. All were awake and eager to disembark. "Find your way out and let us get our tent and provisions set. After that, you may explore." Mattie flashed an excited grin and turned to help Josiah down the step.

Sarah felt a light tug on yet another strand of hair that had slipped from her cap. Daniel stood at her side, playfully holding out his hand to help her down. He had ridden back and forth between the Townsends and McPhersons all day, chatting with both parties. Sarah had enjoyed his easy banter but looked forward to spending time alone. She wasn't sure when that would happen as there was much to do before the meeting began at dusk.

"It is attached, Daniel Townsend," she shot out, tucking the loose strand back under her cap – again.

"Attached to a hard-headed girl. Here, let me help you down."

"Thank you," she said, lightly jumping onto the ground. "Not so hard-headed that I will not accept assistance."

"That you shall have and more. My mother is getting our camp well under control, as you might imagine, and has directed that I come assist those 'poor McPherson women.'" His eyes crinkled in amusement. "So, you 'poor woman,' how might I help?"

Charity came around the side of the wagon, wiping her hands on her apron. "I have no problem accepting your charity, Daniel," she spoke matter-of-factly. "First, you can stop conversing with my beautiful niece and grab those tent stakes. Here is the mallet. Perhaps we should set it up over there?"

Sarah smiled broadly, sweeping her hands toward the wagon and tipping her head in agreement. With a short laugh, Daniel gathered the wooden mallet and stakes and moved toward the open space under a large hickory tree.

Within an hour, the McPherson camp was completely set up and Mattie, Millie, and Josiah (under close watch by the girls) wandered off to investigate the surroundings. Charity kept Matthew as he slept peacefully on a quilt spread out on the ground, while Daniel moved to see who else he might assist as another wagon had rolled into the clearing just a few minutes ago.

"I have never seen such as this," Charity remarked. She and Sarah sat side-by-side on a plank stretched across two stumps. "I assumed we would be the only ones bringing wagon and provisions, but, apparently, many others had the same thought. And what a good idea to have those extra wagons for transport," she pointed to the line coming and going down the main road to the meeting house.

A constant stream of wagons barreled in and out, each bringing families and provisions, dropping them off, then leaving again to pick up another group. Surmising the July meeting would draw many, Rev. Rankin had quickly devised this transportation method for the locals and their families, thereby leaving the area around the meeting house open for those who would stay overnight. By this point, Charity counted seventeen wagons that had set up to stay and camp.

Sarah motioned to a larger wagon that was positioned close to the meeting house. "Daniel said those people over there rode about one hundred miles to attend." They saw much activity revolving around it with both adults and children moving to and fro.

"One hundred miles?" Charity asked incredulously.

"Yes. He said they came down from north of Bowling Green. It took them three days of hard travel."

"How did they hear of it, I wonder?"

"A relative lives nearby, Daniel said."

"And the word of the Lord goes forth..." Charity's voice trailed off.

Suddenly, the two women noticed a small commotion near the front steps of the meeting house. McGready emerged with his trusty cohorts, McGee and Hodge. Rankin, current minister at Gasper River, had been making the rounds through the campsites and greeting locals as they disembarked from the transport wagons. Sarah had found him courteous and quiet but attentive to their needs. Seeing McGready, Rankin ambled his way toward him and the four men shared a laugh together over something. Sarah considered again how tall McGready stood; he rose several inches higher than any man around. Yet his frame was stout and sturdy giving the appearance of great weight and bodily strength. His prominent features added a sort of fierceness to his sermons, especially when he spoke on the realities of hell and eternal damnation; yet conversely, when he brightened and smiled – or laughed as he was now doing – his countenance became joyful and fun-loving. Make no mistake, he was all seriousness, but he was able to easily banter with the common man as well.

Perhaps because he is one, Sarah pondered.

"Is it true that Rev. McGready's farm is only a few miles north of our home?" Sarah asked out loud.

"It is so," Charity was adjusting Matthew so his face wouldn't catch the sunlight streaming through the trees.

"And he works the farm as well as ministers?"

"He does. He and his wife, Nancy. You remember meeting her at Red River?"

"Um…yes."

"Small, blonde woman with the three girls. But Rev. McGready also runs a school from his home, so I believe they farm only enough to supply their needs."

"I see."

"Why do you ask?" Charity questioned as she turned back around and followed Sarah's eyes to the four ministers on the front stoop.

"Just curious, I suppose. He seems such a solemn, serious man yet is also quite humble. His dress is so plain and neat. No frills. No ruffles. I suppose I am saying he seems to be one of us and not affected by airs of importance."

Charity laughed. "Certainly, I would agree, dear niece. Rev. McGready is perhaps the most humble man you would ever meet, feeling that with those ruffles and frills come pride and arrogance, two traits that are not conducive to presenting the Gospel — at least not in his opinion."

"Why do you think his family has not come with him today?"

"He travels a good bit during these summer months. I would assume someone must stay home to care for crops and children."

"Yes. I suppose you are right."

"Being the wife of a minister would be a challenge, I would imagine," Charity scratched her chin thoughtfully. "There is the glory and honor of having served the Lord and hearing firsthand the accounts of His movements, especially during times such as these. However, I am sure that there are trying times. After all, they are people just as we are, trying to survive this wilderness." Charity paused, "I wonder… no. Never mind."

"What?"

"I just – no, it is nothing."

"Aunt? You are becoming tiresome. What would you say?"

"Well — it seems to me that you, dear one, would make quite a nice minister's wife one day."

Sarah's Irish green eyes flew open in horror, and her heart skipped a beat. Automatically, she looked across the clearing and caught sight of Daniel as he pounded in yet another tent stake. *Surely not,* she thought fearfully. Seeing her expression, Charity felt pity on the girl. She patted her knee kindly.

"Do not worry, Sarah. I don't think I spoke a prophecy," she laughed. "Be at peace and let us take one thing at a time.

McGready, Rankin and McGee were laughing outright now at yet another one of Hodge's incorrigible stories.

"And then the old gentleman said he had no idea how the mule got out of his field," Hodge relayed. "But he reckoned however he got out, he could just as well get himself back in. And he turned on his heel and walked away, leaving the stranger standing in the middle of the road staring at the mule."

McGee's stocky frame was practically bent in half as he doubled over with laughter. Rankin had tears coursing down his cheeks, and McGready leaned back, enjoying a deep, satisfying guffaw. Hodge, too, wiped the tears from his eyes as he finished up.

"And indeed it is so, gentlemen. An honest tale told by an honest man."

Hoot and howls ensued once again as the men enjoyed a moment of hilarity before the weightier theme of saving men's souls came forth.

"William Hodge, I wonder if you have ever told an honest tale," McGready shook his head, dark eyes sparkling in amusement.

"Oh, come now, James. Such a man as myself? Give a poor man some grace."

"Perhaps in the Lord, yes, but in your tales?"

Rankin and McGee stood erect again, the vestiges of mirth dying away. "If we don't give William grace in his storytelling, he may become unrepentant – choosing to tickle men's ears rather than save their souls," McGree spoke, slapping Hodge on the shoulder in jest.

"Gentlemen, Gentlemen," Hodge pouted, "I will have you know that I prayed fervently about including that story in my sermon tomorrow evening, and the Lord spoke clearly and told me no." He sighed in feigned sadness. "So, you see? I am indeed a humble and obedient servant and know how to curb my tongue when needed." He smiled then, glancing back at McGready. "It was a lovely tale, was it not?"

McGready laughed again. "Shenanigans!" he said firmly. "That's what you are about, William Hodge. Full of shenanigans. Yes, man. It was humorous – and it was a much-needed respite – but as I look out over this growing multitude, my soul grows burdened again."

McGee, Rankin and Hodge turned, and following McGready's lead, gazed out over the clearing. In the time since the McPhersons had arrived, the crowd had practically doubled, many people also walked or rode in single on horseback. The wagons continued to barrel through, each unloading more people, more provisions. Practically every clear spot had been taken by a family, and the new arrivals were forced to set camp in the edge of the woods. Wafts of stew competed with other aromas all around; supper fires were lit and the rich smell of roasted venison made hungry stomachs growl.

"Have you found the group from Cumberland who said they were coming to view the work of the Spirit?" Rankin questioned McGready.

"Yes," he pointed to a few wagons set back from the main camp, positioned next to a tree line. "They are there, four wagons loaded with at least four families, possibly more. William pointed them out to me."

"And how are they predisposed?"

"They appear to be mature and ready to hear, yet there is definitely a strong prejudice against the manifestations of the Spirit. I know not how they will respond if God continues to move in the way He has," McGready's eyes drifted back toward his ministers.

"Are they anti-revivalists, then?" McGee asked, leaning back against a handrail, propping up his dirt-covered boot on the step behind him.

Hodge responded. "They have not said as much but certainly they lean that way. Several are from my Shiloh congregation, and they have many questions. We can only wait and see."

The four stared thoughtfully again at the campsite, wondering how the Lord would address this issue. As Rankin allowed his gaze to sweep more broadly across the area, he was again surprised at the number of people present.

"How many people can this be?" he spoke his thoughts aloud.

"I would guess close to two hundred," Hodge responded.

"Two hundred souls. God help us," McGready whispered under his breath.

"Surely, only He can," Rankin responded.

Chapter Twenty One

By the time McGready took the podium at seven o'clock that evening, the crowd had swelled to more than two hundred. Men, women and children pressed in the simple structure, streamed out the doors, stood at open windows or sat outside close enough to hear the voice of the Son of Thunder as he began the meeting with fervent prayer.

Sarah, Charity and the children had managed to squeeze in on the last bench with Miss Anaphileda, Mrs. Townsend, and her two girls. Daniel, his father and brother also were in the building, but they stood against the back wall directly behind the women. A cool breeze blew in through the windows, providing a sporadic relief to the heat and making the close quarters bearable. Lanterns hung on the walls, casting long shadows across the thick wooden beams and revealing a great quantity of moths and mosquitoes. Although the house bulged with humanity, not a sound could be heard as McGready ended his prayer and segued into his message for the evening.

"Our text comes from II Corinthians, chapter four, verses three and four," he began. "But if our Gospel be hid, it is hid to them that are lost, in whom the god of this world hath blinded the minds of them which believe not, lest the light of the glorious Gospel of Christ, who is the image of God, should shine unto them." He paused, waiting for all eyes in the room to turn his way.

"The Gospel is defined, glad tidings or a bundle of good news. Indeed, it is the sweetest sound that ever reached the ears of sinners of Adam's race, for it conveys to them the blessed tidings of a door of mercy being opened for poor, guilty, condemned criminals – of pardon and reconciliation to God, and a full and eternal salvation through the atoning blood of the Lord Jesus Christ."

On and on his words flowed, stirring hearts and quickening spirits.

Sarah's soul lifted higher and higher as his voice rose in passion; she felt as though she could reach out her hand and touch the hem of Jesus' garment. Yet the air in the room – and even in the extended congregation that flowed into the clearing – remained serious and solemn. It was a quiet multitude indeed that was dismissed to their camps – or homes – following McGready's message. Even as people moved back into their respective areas, not many were heard to converse. Campfires were banked for the evening and a feeling of reverence fell over the entire area.

That same feeling extended into Saturday morning and throughout the day as yet another meeting was held, and congregants ate together, fellowshipped with one another and met new friends. Over it all hung a strong sense of power to come. Of course, the four ministers sensed it as well but were content to simply preach, teach and wait on the Spirit of the Lord.

Hodge spoke at the Saturday evening meeting – a powerful sermon on the deity of Christ. As occurred Friday, he dismissed the assembly under the blanket of an air of reverence. This time, however, several women remained in the meeting house, talking loudly about their experiences in the Lord and His power and attention to them. Over a hundred people remained as well, just standing or sitting – waiting for something.

Sarah stayed in her position on the last bench; Charity had exited to make sure Matthew and Josiah had an opportunity to sleep, but Mattie and Millie had wanted to wait and see what might happen. Their thin bodies trembled with excitement, their eyes wide open. Daniel stood behind them while the rest of his family had left with Charity. Quietly, they watched as McGready and the other ministers moved among the congregants, praying with some, speaking softly with others.

Suddenly, it was as if a flame shot out from the small group of women talking together near the front of the room. Their voices rose above the murmur, and everyone could hear their adulation of the Christ and the saving power of His grace. "It exploded through the room like lightening and would not have surprised me more had I seen it in the natural realm," Sarah told her Aunt Charity the next morning. Their fervor radiated to others in their proximity, and within seconds at least two dozen were overcome and praying loudly and passionately.

Cries of "Mercy!" pierced the darkness within the house and without; people both young and old began to pray. Many fell to the floor or the ground outside – overcome with a sense of their unworthiness and sinfulness. Sarah felt the power run through the room, almost in waves. It weakened her body to such a state that she could not have stood if her life depended on it. Behind her, Daniel leaned heavily against the wall, tears coursing down his cheeks. Both Millie and Mattie slipped to the wooden floor, weeping quietly, though they could not have said why. But while Sarah felt and knew the presence of the Lord, she forced herself to remain attentive. She wanted to watch.

On the other side of the room, a large family was overcome, and many were crying out for the saving power of God to arrest them. The mother still sat on the bench with one of her younger children – a girl – lying in her lap. McGready moved over and tried to talk to the little girl, who was in complete despair. Sarah couldn't hear what he said, but he knelt beside the woman and appeared to be praying for both her and the daughter.

Without warning, the girl jumped to her feet, her face suddenly lit with a light so bright it practically filled the room.

"Oh, He is willing, He is willing – He has come, He has come! Oh, what a sweet Christ He is, what a precious Christ He is. Oh, what a fullness I see in Him!" she cried. "Oh, what a beauty I see in Him. Why was it that I never could believe? That I never could come to Christ before – when Christ was so willing to save me?" Her voice echoed through the rafters and tripped out the windows. It penetrated even the groans and cries coming from people lying on the floor; it demanded to be heard.

In her ecstasy, she spun around and addressed the whole room. "If you stand within the sound of my voice and do not know the Christ, you must come to Him tonight. I tell you He is willing, His glory is here, and I beg you to repent of your wickedness and come to Him," her eyes shone kindly, yet full of a heavenly light. Sarah was amazed. The girl continued to plead, quoting Scripture and using such language that any minister would be proud to possess. It became apparent very quickly that this girl was speaking of divine things that she probably, in her natural state, knew nothing of. The Spirit of God hovered in the place.

As she continued to plead with those who would listen, her mother wept, and her sisters stood by astounded. Sarah heard cries coming from those lying on their faces near her. When the little girl seemed spent and practically fell back into her mother's lap, Hodge moved toward the front of the house.

"Christians and believers," he spoke loudly. "I adjure you to move toward those feeling the conviction of the Spirit of God and minister to them as you are led. There are only four of us," he continued, sweeping his hand wide to point out McGready, still near the front, McGee in the back right, and Rankin, who had stepped outside. "All are called to be ministers of the Gospel. Move now and aid your brothers and sisters as they seek the Christ."

Sarah needed no more prompting and, glancing quickly at Mattie and Millie who were both still kneeling on the floor, she moved toward the front of the meeting house. Within seconds, she stood by a young boy, talking and praying and waiting for him to come to a saving knowledge.

And so it went throughout the night. After putting the younger children down, Charity returned to the house, stepping over people lying prostrate and embracing sisters in Christ all along the way. She found Millie and Mattie curled up asleep on the hard wooden floor and waved to Sarah as she roused the girls. Sarah nodded briefly and bent her head back down to continue praying.

When at last there seemed to be a lull in the activity, Sarah noticed bright morning rays streaming into the windows from the east. Amazed, she surveyed the meeting house. Other than a few of the children, everyone remained through the night – including Daniel who sat up against the back wall, a grin of satisfaction on his strong, angular face. Moving his way, Sarah plopped on the bench, facing him. They spoke quietly.

"What a night!" she wiped her brow.

"Incredible, wasn't it?"

"Indeed. I lost count of how many I prayed with, but I know several of the girls found the Christ – and with such joy!"

"So it was with me as well. I had opportunity to move outside among some of the men who stood by the windows. I found I had to watch my step in the night for fear I would trod upon their heads," Daniel laughed quietly. "Do not think the presence of God was confined to this tiny house."

"So they were outside as well?"

"Certainly so. Rev. Rankin remained outside the whole of the night, as best as I could surmise. Rev. McGready seemed to go in and out, but I can testify that at least ten men were brought to the Lord. And … I find I am not tired this morning," Daniel gazed at Sarah thoughtfully. "Are you?"

"Not really. I felt weary sometime in the night, but it has passed and my spirit feels light …"

"And hungry?" Daniel smiled playfully.

"And hungry!"

"Then let us go find some victuals. We can hope my mother or Sister McPherson has been busy at the cooking pot." He stood easily, holding out his hand. Sarah grasped it and stood beside him, her head leaning gently against his shoulder.

"It was an amazing night, was it not?" she whispered.

"Beyond this world," he answered simply as they quietly left the building.

From their vantage point under a nearby oak tree, McGready and Hodge watched Sarah and Daniel descend the steps of the meeting house. McGready leaned against the tree's broad trunk, chewing a blade of grass, while Hodge sat on a stump. Their eyes followed the handsome young couple down the lane, but their minds were elsewhere.

"I tell you, William, I have not seen the likes of it," McGready moved the grass aside to speak again. "To hear the children describe the gracious willingness of Christ to save the very worst of sinners? Astounding!" He paused a moment, nodding his head to acknowledge a good morning greeting to a gentleman that passed near their spot. Hodge agreed.

"I prayed with many of the men outside and, though they are not children, they too used language that appeared to come straight from Heaven."

"I say," McGready continued, "to hear the children speak upon these subjects, the good language, the good sense, the clear ideas and the rational, Scriptural light in which they spoke, truly amazed me. I felt mortified and mean before them – they spoke upon subjects beyond what I could have done. I believe it to be evidence demonstration that, out of the mouths of babes and sucklings, the Lord can perfect praise."

"Yes, and good morning to you, sir," Hodge called out with a wave. Lowering his voice, he responded to McGready. "I heard just a bit of that from my perch, James. Truly God's Spirit moved among us all – both inside and outside the house." He paused. "By the by, have you heard from the Shiloh group? The learned ones who came from my region of Tennessee?"

McGready glanced toward the far right of the clearing, seeing the wagons and campsite of those who had doubted the move of God's Spirit. It was quiet there with only a few women moving about their fire.

"No one has spoken with me as of yet," he replied. "But I noticed many did remain throughout most, if not all, the night. We will watch and see. Perhaps the Lord will convince them yet."

Hodge laughed loudly, slapping his knee and drawing attention to the two ministers. "If He cannot, no one can, I say."

That Sabbath Sunday of July 27 continued to be full of grace and joy. Following campfire breakfasts and the travel wagons carting in locals who had gone home overnight, the morning sermon commenced with Rankin taking the pulpit. Although several people still appeared to be moved by the Spirit – some groaning and crying quietly – it did not interrupt or overshadow the preaching of the Word. Sunday dinner was shared by all on the common grounds, and a general spirit of fellowship prevailed. The setting of the sun found all the congregants assembled back in the house, ready to hear McGee speak. His text was the circumstances of Peter sinking in the waves.

Although the congregants had only been meeting two days and nights, they had found their "places" in the assembly and most had returned to the same benches on the same rows. Certainly the McPhersons and Townsends remained in the back area with no visible signs of weariness or fatigue. Even Miss Anaphileda sat erect and attentive. As McGee's message grew in volume and power – his voice extolling the deliverance that Jesus brought to Peter in the midst of the waves – more cries from distressed individuals were heard. By the end of the message, their shouts competed with McGee's voice. He waited a short time, and then officially dismissed the crowd for the evening. Yet no one seemed to want to leave. No one thought of sleep or food; again, they waited.

Sarah's heart thrilled as she once again perceived the presence of God in their assembly, and she strove to watch and listen as the Spirit moved. She didn't have long to wait. A voice rang clear through the back right window, the rawness of its plea ringing in her heart.

"I have been a sober professor!" the man cried out. "I have been a communicant. Oh! I have been deceived! I have no religion!"

McGready's heavy footsteps trod out the door, toward the weeping man, and Sarah could hear a lowered conversation as he approached. She strained her ears to listen.

"Mr. Hamilton, may I pray with you, sir?" McGready offered.

"Oh, Rev. McGready! I see that religion is a sensible thing," the man's voice rose in a crescendo. "Oh, my friends, if ever you get it, you will know something how you obtained it. Believe what the ministers tell you, religion is a sensible thing. Oh! I once despised this work, I thought it was all delusion, but, oh, I am going to hell. I feel the pain of hell in my soul and body. How I would have despised any person a few days ago who would have acted as I am doing now. But I cannot help it!" It sounded as though he collapsed, weeping, while McGready prayed for God to hear his cries.

"Wasn't that one of the Shiloh people?" Daniel's breath warmed her hair as he whispered from behind her. She turned toward him quietly.

"I believe it is so. Aunt Charity told me they were learned scholars and anti-revivalists as well."

"Hmph! I do not think he is anti-revivalist now."

Sarah smiled as she turned back around.

As it was the night before, the vast majority of communicants stayed until daybreak, many of them lying prostrate on the ground.

Sarah, however, slipped out sometime in the night to go sleep with the children while Charity remained at the meeting house, praying and weeping with those who sought the Lord's grace and finding incredible joy in seeing her prayers fulfilled.

Chapter Twenty Two

As the sun rose in the cloudless sky Monday morning, it was evident the work wasn't complete. No one broke camp to go home, although this was the last day of sacrament planned. After a quick consultation, the four ministers agreed to continue preaching, teaching and exhorting as long as the people had a willingness to listen. McGee and Hodge were prepared to deliver messages on this day with one taking the morning slot while another covered the evening position. A sense of camaraderie and other-worldliness had overtaken the entire area surrounding the meeting house. Sarah had passed many new faces each time she walked to the river, yet she felt as though they had been friends for life. The sense of kinship and relation was almost palpable, and Sarah imagined it was a taste of the Kingdom of God to come. She could hardly believe that a year before she believed she had no real family and no purpose. Now she had more family than she could count, and she knew she was called to a divine purpose – that of glorifying God – for the remainder of her life. *A new creation,* she contemplated again as she struggled up from the river, carrying two water pails. *It is a divine work that simply cannot be explained fully. It must be experienced.*

Remarkably, the McPherson children had weathered the past few days well. Sarah and Charity had taken shifts in making sure the little ones received enough rest and food, while Mattie and Millie had been fully engaged in the revival happening in the meeting house. And thankfully, Sarah had the foresight to pack more food than was planned – they should have enough victuals to last them until Tuesday evening.

As she entered their campsite, Sarah gazed across a veritable sea of wagons and tents, watching the smoke from dozens of campfires hover over the area. Aromas of cooked meat tickled her nose and tempted her stomach while she could hear snatches of conversations and the sounds of children playing games coming from all around. Soon, families would gather for supper before entering the house for the evening sermon.

One of the men from Shiloh had asked Daniel to help change a wagon wheel, and Aunt Charity and Sister Townsend were visiting some of the neighboring campsites. The children were playing elsewhere, and Sarah found herself alone for a moment. She stood still, savoring the solitude, praying for the next meeting, when she heard a small, wavering voice rising from the Townsend's campfire. Walking around the tent, she peered over their wagon to see Miss Anaphileda resting beside the fire, poking the embers. All by herself, the venerable grandmother sat on a makeshift bench, her cap fastened securely to her head.

"Great God of wonders!
All Thy ways are matchless, Godlike and divine;
But the fair glories of Thy grace more Godlike and unrivaled shine,
More Godlike and unrivaled shine."

She warbled off key as she sang, unaware of Sarah's presence. As she stood to position the kettle closer to the glowing embers, Sarah rushed around the wagon, taking the heavy kettle from her hands – gently but firmly.

"Whatever are you doing, Miss Ana?" Sarah asked, shifting the pot quickly to her other hand that was protected by her apron. She carefully hooked it to the ring that hung over the fire.

"Doing?" the old woman gazed at Sarah directly, as if she'd taken leave of her senses. "Doing? Why, I think that would be apparent, Miss McMillan. I am attempting to heat our supper." She shuffled back toward her bench seat and eased down carefully, patting the empty spot beside her. "Now, why do you not sit with me a spell and stop worrying about an old woman tripping over a fire? I have hoisted more kettles in my life than you have lived days. Besides, I have wanted a chance to talk. This rheumatism that was sent from the pit of Hell itself has been keeping me stowed up and not able to converse with others as I would wish."

Somewhat self-consciously, Sarah sat beside her, wondering if Daniel had mentioned his intentions of marriage to his grandmother. She had assumed the entire Townsend family at least guessed, but since Daniel had yet to speak to her father, there had been no official announcement. Sarah began to feel as if eggshells were on the ground, and she had best prepare to tiptoe.

Miss Anaphileda turned toward her expectantly.

"Now then, Miss McMillan, tell me what you think about these happenings here."

"Well, I…I am not sure what to think. It is apparent that God has elected to visit us with His presence, but I must say I have never heard of such things as I have seen in the past days."

"Um, yes. I would agree, child. Although I have heard of such tales, but they came from mouths that are long since dead."

"Indeed? What tales?" Sarah's ears perked up with curiosity.

"My father told of hearing the famous George Whitfield preach as he rode throughout the colonies. I was a young girl then, only about eleven or so, and remember hearing Mr. Whitfield's name and generally feeling the excitement coming from people, but he never drew near my home in Virginia. Nevertheless, his was a powerful preaching, father said, and it fanned the flames in people's hearts. For the first time, they began to feel the power of God and read the Bible on their own. Religion was spread from churches into homes and people began to respond with emotion toward God. Where there had never been tears in church, they began to flow. Father said it was as though Heaven came down to earth and dwelt among us." A gust of wind blew smoke into their faces, and Miss Anaphileda began to cough. Sarah looked for a drinking vessel. Wheezing, Miss Anaphileda held out her tin cup which had been beside her, and Sarah took it to the pail that was close by. Filling it with water, she came back and handed it to the lady. She took a deep draught.

"My, that's much better. Thank you, child."

"You are most welcome," Sarah paused. "I have never heard of such things or of a man named George Whitfield," she confessed.

"Mercy! Never heard of him? Why, child. Were you not raised in the church?"

"No ma'am. My father denied me that opportunity," Sarah replied, feeling the old anger rising in her heart. Her chin lifted slightly, and Miss Anaphileda saw it. Nodding slightly, she continued.

"Well, one can't help how one was reared. Never you mind, child, the

Lord has seen fit to reveal Himself to you now and you are, therefore, a part of His Kingdom. We all have our journeys."

"I suppose so."

"I remember the way our church changed after that time … it was about the time I met Thomas. It was as though a wind blew like this one is," she laughed ruefully, holding her hat tightly to her head as yet another gust came through the campsite. "Only it was a wind from God and it swept through the churches in America bringing fresh air and blowing out the stodginess of old religion. Of course, not everyone liked it. We were called revivalists then, and some of the established men in churches did not like losing their power or position, nor did some of them want mere farmers or sharecroppers reading and interpreting the Bible on their own – not to mention slaves!

"Ha! But we did. Father eagerly embraced the changes and nightly devotions became a part of life in our home. It was such a tradition for us that when I left to make my life with Thomas, I was given a Bible as well. It has not departed my hearth since, and it is read daily."

"Were there stories then of people falling out under the power of the Spirit as they are doing now?"

"Oh my, yes. Especially in the New England states. Conviction of sin was powerful strong, and many times as people are confronted with their sin – while sensing the holy power of God and His presence — they will respond in humility and reverence."

The old lady put her hand on Sarah's knee, her keen blue eyes gazing kindly at the girl. The wrinkles on her face could have told the story of her life, Sarah considered. Some were deep creases, others thin lines; they were many and varied and spanned her entire countenance. Yet they were not ugly, rather intriguing, and when she smiled, her face transformed into a visage of wisdom and kindness. Some may have thought of Miss Anaphileda as an ugly old woman, but Sarah found her beautiful – and a bit intimidating.

"So this is the first time you have actually seen God move in this way?" Sarah asked.

"With my own eyes? Certainly, yes, but I have known about Him in my heart for years. I am not surprised that our prayers have been answered in this way, and I pray it continue."

"It is remarkable, is it not, the length that some have driven to attend the meeting?" Sarah's arm swept wide, trying to encompass the dozens of wagons that were positioned over the area.

"Oh my, yes. Never have I heard of tents and wagons set up at a sacrament meeting anywhere. This is a new thing and seems to speak of the determination of the people to hear the Word of God." She laughed abruptly then continued. "Who could have imagined that this many folk would hear of a meeting at Gasper River and actually make the trip? Why, I am not certain we have this number of people living in Russellville proper."

"I feel as if we are on the cusp of something even bigger," Sarah ventured to say. "Not that I do not believe this is big, but ..." She trailed off, unsure of herself. Miss Anaphileda patted her knee again.

"Yes, dear, I know what you feel. I feel it, too, but neither can I put it into words. We pray, we watch and we wait on the Spirit to move. That is all we can do."

Footsteps on hardened ground announced the arrival of Joy Townsend and Charity, signaling the end of the conversation. Sarah was disappointed. This was the first real talk she had enjoyed with Miss Anaphileda, and she found many similarities between her and her own Grandma McMillan. She felt her eyes grow moist at the thought and pushed the resemblance out of her mind. No time now to get sentimental.

"Has Daniel not returned?" Mrs. Townsend questioned as she walked over and stirred the stew.

"No, ma'am. We've not seen him for a time."

"Ah well. He will show up when it is time to eat. Boys do that, you know." She laughed heartily, her girth bouncing in rhythm. Looking hot and bothered, Charity held Matthew in her arms.

"Are you ready to prepare supper at our camp, Sarah?" she asked. "This boy has run me ragged, and I am in dire need of sustenance."

"Yes, Aunt." Turning toward Miss Anaphileda, Sarah impulsively leaned down and embraced her tightly. "Thank you, Miss Ana. I so enjoyed visiting with you."

"And I, you, child." The wrinkles bent and twisted as she smiled broadly. "May we have many more such conversations in the future."

McGee and Hodge preached wildly that day, as though possessed by something not of this world, and many people continued to weep and cry out for God's mercy on their souls. Sarah and Charity split duties Monday night, with Sarah staying the first watch of the evening – praying for others, helping them find the Christ as she had – then Charity stepping in sometime in the night, giving Sarah the chance to sleep and be with the smaller children.

Thunderclouds heralded the advent of Tuesday, and perhaps it was the rumble of thunder that finally ushered in a close to the meeting at Gasper River. Throughout the night, more souls had found the Lord, and others remained on the grounds in various states of searching. McGready and his team again worked solidly through, appearing to neither need sleep nor food. The heavy blanketing presence of God remained strong.

But many had to return to their farms, and it was obvious that rain was on the way. A short time after dawn, McGready called everyone together into the meeting house, delivering final instructions on walking out the life of a disciple of Christ. It didn't last long, and blessing the body of people with a prayer, he dismissed the July sacrament at Gasper River. Before the ministers went their separate ways, they met one last time under the oak tree by the meeting house. McGready's usually clean, crisp appearance was wrinkled, McGee's unruly hair stood straight up in places and Hodge looked as though he'd been sleeping in his clothes for four days – because he had.

"Lord, have mercy. Are we not a sight to behold?" Hodge ruefully ran his hand over his vest, trying to smooth down the creases and wrinkles.

"What would our stodgy counterparts in the East think of us if they could see us now?" Rankin added.

"And yet … glory!" McGready almost shouted, stopping a few people in their steps. "I would rather be a wrinkled unkempt man who has seen God's glory than a vain peacock of a man who had never tasted of the fruits of the Lord."

Hodge only smiled, patting McGready on his back.

"Not to worry, James. No spirit of a vain peacock would dare to hover around you."

"What is the last count?" McGee spoke up.

"Adding up what you men told me, I believe we have seen forty-five souls come to grace this meeting – seventeen of which come from the Red River congregation," McGready responded.

"You don't say? They had to travel all the way up here to find glory?" Hodge joked.

"Apparently so," McGready smiled. "I will accept them into the fold, either way."

"And what is the next move, James?" Hodge scratched his beard vigorously. "Meet at Muddy River in August?"

"Certainly, but I feel the urgency of the Lord pressing upon me with severe weight. I believe we are to gather for Sabbath at Red River this week and not wait so long to gather again."

"For a full sacrament meeting?"

"No, just for Sabbath, but we must all be ready to preach and teach at any given moment. I believe the Spirit is on the move, and we must not be found wanting."

A solemn silence fell over the ministers as they pondered their own obedience in the midst of, what appeared to be, a new outpouring of the Spirit of God.

Chapter Twenty Three

Tuesday's journey home from Gasper River had been fairly miserable. The McMillans and Townsends packed up before the storm hit but were beaten by it all the way home. By the time they approached Mortimer Station, the muddy road sucked and pulled at the wagon wheels, and both Sarah and Charity were drenched. Thankfully, the children remained in the back of the wagon, covered securely.

The worst part of the ride, in Sarah's opinion, was the lack of Daniel's presence coming and going between wagons. Many of the men stayed behind to help clean up the meeting house and grounds, and since Daniel was a lone rider, it only made sense that he would be one of those "chosen ones." Sarah wiped the rain off her nose again. It kept hitting her cape's hood and running down the center crease. Thunder rumbled and a flash of lightning lit up the eastern sky.

"It feels as though Satan would attempt to dampen our enthusiasm, my dear niece," Charity said as she clucked at the horses, popping the reins to speed them up. "I must confess it has been a most horrid trip!" Their wagon sped up just enough to keep pace with the Townsends' wagon. They watched the swaying back and forth of the front wagon, knowing Miss Anaphileda and the children were hunkered down under the tarp, longing for the end of this ride as much as they were. Sarah glanced behind her again.

Baby Matthew had collapsed into Millie's lap, his fat cheeks flushed with the heat, stuffiness and humidity found under the cover. He finally had begun to grow hair and was stretching up in height rather than out. *He's looking more like a little boy every day*, Sarah thought tenderly.

Millie raised her dark eyes, meeting Sarah's gaze, and waved quietly. Her body bumped back and forth, but she held tightly to the side to keep as still as possible. Mattie and Josiah slept together – somehow – toward the back of the wagon. They had piled onto bundles of blankets and created a bed of sorts. The lack of sleep in the past four days had caught up with them, all except Millie. Sarah smiled then grimaced as a giant drop of water fell again between her eyes. Millie giggled quietly, putting her hand over her mouth.

"Only a few more minutes," Sarah mouthed the words.

Millie nodded, understanding, and mouthed back, "Thank goodness."

Turning back around, Sarah spoke to Charity, her voice loud enough to rise above the thunder and rain, but low enough to keep from waking the children.

"The children have weathered it all very well."

"Indeed, they have. I must say I am quite proud of them and look forward to telling Obediah what stalwart sons and daughters we have."

Mortimer Station loomed ahead, blurry and gray in the rain, and Charity drew to a stop beside the Townsend wagon.

"Will you also run inside, as Mr. Townsend is doing, and see if any correspondence has come, Sarah? I would rather not come this way again for a week or more. I believe I am ready to unload the wagon and stay home."

"Of course," Sarah quickly jumped down the steps and ran into the small structure. She returned within a minute with several letters tucked under her apron.

"How many?" Charity asked as she released the brake.

"Three. It looked like two from Obediah and one from my father." Sarah tried to appear lighthearted, but she found it hard to swallow.

Charity's green eyes flashed in understanding as she turned her face toward Sarah. "He is probably writing about your return to Port Royal," she patted Sarah's knee. "I doubt there is much more to it, but we will find out when we get home. Only one more mile to go."

Charity's hood was tied so tightly around her head that her face looked like a small, pale orb, her complexion as white as cotton. A few strands of brown hair had forced their way out and hung limply, dropping water into her lap. She clucked again, and the horse began her slow plod toward the house.

The Waking Up

It wasn't until the entire family was settled in for the day, the horses cleaned, groomed and fed, and supper plates cleared that Charity and Sarah sat down to read their letters. The two from Obediah reported on his success in surveying, his longing for his family, and his plans to begin making his way back west by the end of August. Charity read them out loud as they all sat around the fire. Wet clothes hung everywhere in their small home. Aprons and capes were draped across chair backs, hung on wall hooks and lying on the mantle. Stockings and little boy breeches lay on the floor. There was barely enough room for the family to gather around. Although it was a warm July rain, soaking in it all day had made them all long for a cozy dryness that only the fire could provide.

"Read yours now, Sarah," Mattie demanded as her mother folded the last letter, tucking it in her apron.

"Well, I am not so sure…"

"Children," Charity admonished, "Sarah's letter from her father is a personal matter. It is time to scoot up to bed and let her read it on her own. I am sure she will tell you if there is any news of import."

Sarah smiled gratefully at Charity and kissed each child on his or her head as they moved past her chair. Leaning down to lift Matthew, Charity, in turn, patted Sarah's shoulder.

"I will be back in a few minutes, child," she said, turning toward her bedroom with the sleeping boy. Sarah waited until all were busy in their own areas before opening the single sheet of paper. The strong, abrasive handwriting of her father filled the page.

July 26

Daughter,

As occurred in June, I am coming to Logan County in the upcoming weeks. My intent is to be in the county seat of Russellville the first week of September. After I have conducted business, I will come pick you up to return to Port Royal. Be ready in early September to leave.

There was no signature. *I suppose he assumed his name on the outside of the envelope was enough,* Sarah thought bitterly. She saw no signs of Charity's prediction of a softening heart, but she wouldn't be the one to tell her that. Let her aunt continue to believe there might be a change in the man. *I know better,* Sarah thought, crumpling the letter and tossing it into the fire. *I have seen God move mightily on many people in the last few days, but my father ... in such a manner? Never!* She got up abruptly, testing the dryness of the clothes and flipping some over.

"Have you already finished reading?" Charity entered the room.

"Yes. It was short. He plans to pick me up the first week of September when he is nearby on business."

"Oh? Well, wonderful then. We have you for another month." Charity came up behind her, smoothing her hair. Between the humidity and constant rain, Sarah's curly auburn waves had become a frizzy, unmanageable mane. "You may want to give your hair a strong brushing before bed," she commented.

Sarah laughed easily. "Now you see what I endure."

Charity walked to the mantle and picked up a large comb. Taking it from her aunt's extended hand, Sarah moved back over to the fire to untangle her hair before climbing the ladder to the loft. Unnoticed in the fireplace, the edges of Matthew McMillan's letter curled together as the flames completely devoured it.

The prayer society met late Friday afternoon in Charity's front yard. Although none of the ministers from Gasper River were able to attend, Mrs. Townsend brought news. It began to spill from her lips even as the small group of women searched for chairs and stumps on which to sit.

"I must tell you all immediately of the report that was brought to us today from up Muddy Creek way," she bubbled, her round face full of animation. Sarah had positioned Miss Anaphileda carefully under the best part of the shade. It was a typically steamy August day although the sun barely dipped over the horizon. Even as the ladies took their seats, fans came out, batting and swinging heartily trying to stir up some kind of cool breeze. It was impossible.

"What is it, Joy?" Charity responded, amused at her friend's excitement.

"Well, it is a most unusual event, but I believe we are becoming accustomed to unusual events these days." Nods and murmurs of agreement moved through the group, but no one interrupted.

"Of course, we all know the stories we hear from Muddy Creek are most always of wickedness and thoughtlessness. Most assuredly, theirs is a rogue settlement. Well, according to Jedediah, who ran into Mr. Rankin in town yesterday, there was a mighty move of the Spirit there." She leaned forward, almost whispering now.

"Apparently, somewhere from eighteen to twenty people all found themselves gathering at a certain house. Not one of them could say why they had gone there, but at the very same time, they all arrived. There was no minister on hand, no prayer society scheduled, no plan at all to meet, yet there they all were. So they stayed together, discussing this strange thing. As they talked, their conversation moved toward the condition of their souls."

Several "ahs" and "ohs" echoed among the listeners. Mrs. Townsend ignored them and continued.

"At length, they concluded to join together in social prayer. Then the power of God appeared to come among them and before they parted, several persons were said to obtain religion. They are now meeting in society in Muddy Creek every day, with the number of those finding the Christ up to about twelve at this point."

Sporadic bursts of applause, "Hallelujahs," and "Glorys" rang out from the little group of women gathered under the elm. Hearty laughter and joy emanated, and Sarah felt that familiar rush of God's Spirit of joy and peace all wrapped together. She locked eyes with Miss Ana, who merely sat quietly with a smile of satisfaction spread over her wrinkled, wizened countenance. Mrs. Ewing spoke up in the midst of the celebration.

"Ladies, I have been debating something." They ceased their praises, waiting for the older lady to speak. "In our sacraments – both at Red River and Gasper – we have not the ample time or opportunity to allow for water baptisms to seal the conversion of these new saints. I am most sure Mr. McGready has considered this problem, but I have yet to see him – or Mr. McGee or Mr. Hodge – respond to the need. What do you say? Should we approach our ministers with this concern?"

"With the river so close by, I do not see why a full baptism would be a problem," Mrs. Townsend said thoughtfully. "Surely the ministers have considered this issue?"

Sarah noticed Miss Anaphileda shifting on her bench while Mrs. Ewing responded.

"And that is what I thought, yet it has not happened. Again I ask. Should we approach Mr. McGready?"

Miss Anaphileda cleared her throat and sat up straight. Sarah kept quiet.

"Careful, ladies," her voice was a whisper yet cracked like lightning. "I fear if we delve too much into ecclesiastical methods we will become dogmatic and dictatorial. I say we let the ministers focus on those matters while we continue to pray for God's Spirit to move. Is the real issue whether someone has been baptized or whether a person has met the Christ? I have seen many in my day begin with a devotion to the Lord Jesus and end life as a bitter, religious old fool. We must keep our eyes on the simplicity of the Gospel and not muddy the waters, so to speak."

She sighed heavily then and leaned back on the tree positioned behind the makeshift bench. The group had listened respectfully and were now so quiet they could hear the children playing by the creek. Mrs. Ewing, known as a proud, headstrong woman, seemed to be wrestling with what Miss Ana had said and eventually must have given in.

"I suppose you speak truth, Miss Anaphileda," she finally admitted. "Although I would admonish those individuals who have not been baptized to complete their process of sanctification as soon as possible." She glanced briefly at Sarah, who fidgeted under her gaze.

Sarah knew she had yet to be immersed, and she did not know why she had not pursued that course of action. She felt in her spirit that it was not yet time. She and Charity had discussed it at length one day last week, and Charity had agreed with her. Neither woman knew why they felt the Spirit of God was saying, "Wait," but they sensed the same thing.

Sarah was waiting.

But Mrs. Ewing wasn't aware of that, and her pointed glance made Sarah uneasy, as though she were on display. Charity broke into the conversation.

"Well, ladies. It seems if we are to pray, we should begin before the sun sets when we must return to our homes," she said with a gently admonishing smile. "Mr. McGready has called another Sabbath meeting for this Sunday at Red River, and we must pray for the revival to continue and increase!"

Seeing the wisdom of her statement, they bowed their heads as one and began beseeching the Lord of the harvest to send more workers and continue to move among them.

As Sarah closed her eyes to join in, she felt a wispy light grasp on her left hand. Miss Anaphileda squeezed it gently and didn't let go.

Chapter Twenty Four

It began the same way, a familiar specter of impending doom. Sarah stood silently on Port Royal Landing by the Red River. The dead fish littered the riverbed, and a tiny trickle of water barely made it down river before it soaked into the muddy ground. She felt her heart begin to race, anticipating.

As in the last dream, her father approached and stood beside her. By this time, the trickle had become a steady stream, and Sarah peered upriver, squinting to try to see as far as possible in order to react to the coming tide. Her father stood to her right gazing upriver along with her, his presence a steady support, but Sarah's subconscious remembered he was no help last time and would probably be no help now.

The stream grew wider, the noise louder. Sarah could hear the rushing waters gathering together. She turned toward her father.

He was wearing his blacksmith's apron and his hands were dirty from bending metals. *He must have walked straight down here from the barrel-making shop,* she thought, feeling weightless and surreal. The water level increased exponentially.

She felt his gaze fall upon her as she dragged her eyes back to the roiling water. Fear and panic began to rise as quickly as did the water in the river.

Without further warning, it happened. The widening stream began to bubble and roll, and the mighty sound of a waterfall crashed into her ears. She felt her father's fear match her own as he turned toward her with eyes wide and panicked. The trees she had seen upstream disappeared as an enormous rushing tide of water cascaded in their direction.

Suddenly – and unexpectedly — she felt her fear disappear. It was as though it had been a cloak, and someone had come and taken it from her shoulders. She found herself holding out her arms as if to embrace the wave of crushing water. The last thing she remembered was seeing her father open his mouth to scream as she turned back toward the river, a laugh of pure joy bubbling from her lips.

The one-day Sabbath meeting at Red River had gone well. Sarah had been grateful for another chance to spend time with Daniel – and the Spirit of God had continued to move on people, bringing reverence and repentance. They were to discuss it at the Sunday dinner table since Daniel had returned home with them. Plans were already in place to travel up to the Muddy River Meeting House late in the month for the next sacramental gathering. Sarah knew it would be close to her time of leaving, but she should have a week between the meeting and her father's arrival.

She had told Daniel of her father's letter on the way home, and he had been relieved to know he would be able to speak to Matthew within the month. He faced her, standing next to the wagon.

"As yet, I have no substance to take a wife, Sarah; but I am saving everything I make and Father has offered me a piece of land toward the western corner of his property. It should take no time for me to build a small cabin for us to start with, and then I can continue working the fields with Father until we are established," he spoke rapidly, trying to get it all out before they were besieged by the McMillan children. Daniel had offered to unharness and groom the horse while Charity told the children she needed their help in the house.

Sarah took the reins he handed to her, hanging them over a large hook fastened to the barn wall.

"I can help with the cabin. Then we can wed sooner, can we not?"

"Perhaps," he met her eager eyes with a wry smile, "but I feel strongly that it is the man's job to provide the house – and I would have the best for my wife."

Sarah's eyes flashed in annoyance as she handed him the brush.

"Man's job? Really, Daniel! Surely you know by now that I am not concerned with the 'jobs' society places at our feet? Why not work together, be married, and enjoy the process together?" She tried to speak persuasively but couldn't keep the bite out of her tone.

"Because it is important to me to have things set right before we wed. There is no hurry for it should take only a few months to complete the cabin, and I do not see how we could wed before next year anyway. You will need to return with your father for the winter months, do you not agree?"

Picking up a smaller brush from a bucket, Sarah began to press into the mare's back haunches with great energy. She was silent a moment, her breath coming out in short grunts and gasps. Daniel, too, was quiet as he wiped the sweat from the top of the horse's coat.

She finally got her temper under control enough to speak. "You would send me back to Port Royal – engaged but still a 'blood slave' in my father's house? Do you know what that would do to me?"

She couldn't control the quaver in her voice, the tears that filled her eyes, and Daniel immediately moved toward her. Taking her face in his hands, he smoothed away the unruly curls then held her tightly.

"Understand, dear Sarah, if I had my choice, I would marry you here and now – today –in the barn! But I feel a strong leading from the Lord that I am not to interfere with His work, and you returning with your father for the winter is part of His work. Have you prayed about it? Sought the counsel of the Lord?"

Sarah buried her head in Daniel's shoulder, breathing in the strong scent of him. Leather, horse feed, sun-dried clothes. She inhaled deeply, savoring the moment and feeling the energy begin to drain from her spirit.

"No. I have not prayed about it. I have only dreaded it. I did not want to ask the Lord for He might make me return to him – to Father."

They stood together, still.

"Will you ask?" Daniel whispered softly in her ear.

Will I ask, Sarah wondered. *I must ask, mustn't I? If I do not seek the Lord's counsel, what will become of me? What would become of my future with Daniel?*

"Yes," she mumbled into his shoulder. "But give me time to wrestle with Him."

"Sarah! Daniel! Mama says dinner is ready!" Millie's tiny voice drifted through the barn doors. Daniel pulled away first, wiping a tear from Sarah's cheek.

"Are you ready to eat, Soon-to-Be Mrs. Townsend?"

"I am always ready to eat," Sarah admitted, taking a deep breath to pull herself together.

"Me, too. Head on to the house and tell your Aunt Charity that I will be along shortly."

Sarah squeezed Daniel's hand tightly then turned to pass through the barn door. A strange mixture of sadness and resolve settled over her like a heavy weight.

Letters flew back and forth throughout August of 1800 between McGready, Rankin, McGee and Hodge. Although the men saw each other individually at different times, the plans for the Muddy Creek sacrament required careful prayer and thought. As more reports of strange occurrences were heard, the men realized this next sacrament may be even larger than that of Gasper River, and they knew they must prepare accordingly.

August 14, the year of our Lord, 1800

My Dearest James:

I am certain that, by now, you have heard of the happenings near Muddy Creek when the Spirit of God drew more than a dozen men and women together at one location. Since that spontaneous outpouring, we have counted at least sixteen persons who got true religion there – and without any help from a minister of the Gospel. Truly, God is moving!

As I contemplate our next sacrament at Muddy River, I realize we must ready ourselves with wagons and provisions. I have taken it upon myself to visit the faithful around Muddy River and encourage them to not only prepare for themselves, but also look to the stranger who will appear "at the door," so to speak. Many have said they will bring an extra wagon of their own and find a way to have more than double the provisions their families would need. I can only hope and pray this will be enough.

As I pray about this sacrament and arrange the sermons required, I feel the burden of the Holy Spirit upon me. Please continue to beseech the Lord for me as I pound the very gates of Heaven to hear from Him.

> *Yours,*
> *John Rankin*

McGready thoughtfully tucked the letter into his vest pocket as he stood on his front porch, gazing over the plot of ripening tomatoes. It had only made sense to have Rankin carry the bulk of the preaching at this sacrament. Muddy River was so close to Gasper, a congregation that Rankin had taken oversight of more than a year earlier. John knew many of these people, plus McGready was tired and spent. His stomach ailment had returned, and he felt somewhat drained. William McGee also was preparing to shoulder part of the preaching burden, and McGready had sent a call out for extra ministers to be on hand. He, too, felt the burden of the Holy Spirit about this sacrament and thought it wise to plan for more people than even Gasper.

"Penny for your thoughts," Nancy whispered, coming up behind him and wrapping her arms around his waist. McGready sighed deeply and turned to face his petite wife. He had to look down on her, yet he would have been the first to admit that, many times, her faith was the giant that conquered fears in his life.

"I just received a letter from John Rankin and was contemplating the Muddy River meeting."

"Of course you were," she teased. "When are you not contemplating a meeting of some sort?"

"I fear you are right, as always," he laughed lightly.

"Will you be able to attend? Will you feel well enough?"

"Oh, I will go, and I would that you and the girls come as well. It is time they saw this move of God. "

"Then we must prepare the farm," she gazed past him thoughtfully. "There are tomatoes to be harvested, corn to be picked, the fruit trees are bearing …"

"When are you not contemplating work and harvest?" McGready jested. "Perhaps we think the same thoughts but on different planes. My harvest may not fill our storerooms, but it does fill the storerooms of the

Lord. Ah, I am thankful for you, Mrs. McGready. I could not do what I do without the work you do here at home."

"And I am thankful for you, Mr. McGready. Your harvest produces souls won to our Lord – a much higher ambition."

They turned together, his arm propped on her shoulder, each lost in thought.

Chapter Twenty Five

Friday, August 29, 1800, rolled in hot and dry. Sarah noticed the benches in the Muddy River Meeting House were coated with a layer of dirt, while particles of dust danced in the late afternoon sun that streamed through open windows. Sneezing, she reached for her handkerchief and blew her nose again. It was difficult to breath.

Having about one hundred people crammed in the house didn't help. There had to be more than twenty wagons parked outside, and another dozen or so that were empty. Mr. Rankin had arranged for extra empty wagons to be placed for strangers who came to the sacrament. It had been a wise call. While Sarah secretly prayed for one of the common late August thunderstorms to roll through and take care of the dust, she also knew that would cause all sorts of havoc with the open air tents set up and the dozens of people – many children – who would be sleeping on wagon beds or under the trees tonight.

She coughed again, then sneezed.

"Are you alright, child?" Joy Townsend leaned close to Sarah, speaking loudly into her ear. The meeting had yet to start, and there was much chattering among those present. The voice level in the house had almost reached a yelling pitch.

"Yes, ma'am. It is all this dust …" Sarah couldn't finish her sentence for coughing.

"I understand, my dear. It is a blessing that Mr. Townsend did not make this trip with us. Dust is a worrisome thing for him. Thankfully, none of the children are ever affected the way he is," she said, sweeping her hand as if to embrace the three younger ones sitting to her right.

Once again, they had arrived at the sacrament early enough to have seats. Charity and the McMillan children sat to her left, Mrs. Townsend and her brood to her right; Sarah was the middle pin. Miss Anaphileda didn't make the trip this time, a fact that saddened Sarah. And Daniel, as usual, was here and there assisting new arrivals. Sarah knew he eventually would take his place standing somewhere behind them.

The meeting finally got underway just as dusk was approaching; lanterns had been lit all over the clearing as well as inside the meeting house, and as it had been at Gasper River, people swarmed the area. There were stacks of humanity outside each window, leaning in to hear the Word of the Lord, and many even farther out. As for her part, Sarah listened attentively, knowing in the back of her mind that she would return to Port Royal in about a week and not have the blessing of Bible teaching for almost a year. There would be no way to attend meetings once she was back with her father. In fact, she didn't plan to tell him she had been attending at all.

"Mr. McGready looks a bit piqued tonight, do you not think?" Aunt Charity whispered in Sarah's ear. Sarah's eyes roved around the room looking for the unadorned man. She finally saw him in a back corner, leaning against the wall and talking to one of the other ministers.

"It is difficult for me to see him clearly."

"I noted his countenance earlier, and he is pale and thinner, I think. His wife and children are here, though. Have you noticed them?" She directed Sarah toward the right front of the room with a subtle thrust of her chin. Sure enough, on the front row sat a small blonde woman and three young girls.

"Oh, I have seen her before ... at Red River."

"Yes. I am pleased they came so far for this meeting," Charity declared quietly. "I am sure the girls will enjoy the time over the next few days; so many children are present."

Sarah nodded as Rankin's deep voice began to carry a melody over the gathering. As they sang a hymn together, then another, Sarah allowed herself to close her eyes and feel the anxiety of her future lift off her shoulders. She would put Port Royal – and her father – out of her mind for now. She simply wanted to savor the moment.

Friday night's meeting was formal and solemn, as were many of the first sacrament meetings that summer. Rankin stayed through the night, praying and conversing with many of those who encamped around the meeting house and chose to stay up rather than sleep. The McMillans and Townsends, worn out from traveling, slept hard and long and woke Saturday morning refreshed. Aromas of sizzling pork sausage assailed the area, and once again, the children played heartily, running from campsite to campsite chasing one another in fun.

The solemn assemblies continued through the day, and on Saturday night, Rankin found his text out of Acts 1:16.

"Brothers, the Scripture had to be fulfilled which the Holy Spirit spoke long ago through the mouth of David concerning Judas, who served as a guide for those who arrested Jesus – he was one of our number and shared in this ministry."

As he carried his congregation on a journey through introspection – Were they 'one of the number, sharing in the ministry,' and yet a traitor to the Lord Jesus? – some people began to be overwhelmed with conviction while others rejoiced in their saving knowledge of the Lord.

Sarah found herself as she had been at Gasper River, moved to tears over the proclaimed Word, yet moved out of her seat to minister to others around the room. The Townsends remained seated – except Daniel who was praying with a group of men in the back. As the night wore on, Rankin formally ended the meeting, but many stayed — praying, crying, laughing.

Sarah had moved up close to the Smythe family, who lived a few miles from the McMillans in the Red River area. Although she knew them by sight and reputation – they were quite wealthy — she never had met them. As she positioned herself a bench seat behind them, she realized it would be difficult to pray for the young wife from Muddy River who was seated next to her and not eavesdrop on McGready who prayed with one of Mr. Smythe's daughters. McGready was on his knees right next to Sarah, speaking quietly to the girl who looked to be about twelve years old and sat directly in front of her.

Suddenly, the young girl cried out, the timbre of her voice bringing up goose bumps on Sarah's arms.

"What is it, child?" McGready's voice was low, yet still powerful.

"Oh! I have met with the Christ. I have found that precious Jesus!"

"Indeed? He has come to you, then?"

"Oh! If I had ten thousand words, I would give them all that my dear father could but see and feel in Christ what I do!"

At that point, the girl leapt up from her seat and ran around McGready and into her father's arms. Sarah watched out of the corner of her eye. As the girl put her arms around her father's neck, she began to weep, telling him that he had no religion, but she did and she felt the love of Christ.

"Oh my Father, Christ is willing to save you. Try to seek Him and you will find Him. If you but saw in Christ that which I see; if you but saw His fullness and willingness, you would come to Him!" She lay her head on his shoulder as he began to weep as well.

Then jumping up from his lap, she went to her little brother, grabbing him fiercely and pleading with him to seek religion and the Christ who saves. He, too, began to weep heartily, and McGready moved in to pray with both the father and the brother. Mrs. Smythe sat quietly, smiling and crying simultaneously, joy emanating from her countenance.

Sarah pulled herself back to focus on the young lady at her side. While she had watched the Spirit move over the Smythe family, this young wife had also been seeking Christ, and Sarah realized she needed to focus her attention back to her. Truly, the Spirit was dancing both in the room and the clearing that surrounded.

"It has been yet another night of power and the presence of God," McGee said, shaking his head incredulously as he sat heavily on the top step of the meeting house stoop. "I thought Gasper River was the zenith of my experience, yet I find it surpassed once again. What an amazing display!" He drew his knees up and wrapped his arms around them, barely embracing his legs around his stout belly. McGready had just walked out on the stoop while a sliver of the August sun winked over the horizon.

"Yes, John, I know of what you speak," McGready concurred, sliding in next to the man.

"Tis a shame Mr. Hodge ails. He would have much enjoyed the night."

"And he has left us short one man," McGready shook his head. "We certainly could have used his ministry through the night."

"Yes …" McGee stared out over the bevy of wagons littering the grounds. "By the by, what happened with the gentleman from the east? The one who is a learned Deist. I overheard him speaking with you earlier yesterday."

"Hmm? Oh yes. He is – or was – a Deist," McGready laughed. "I am not sure what he would say this morning."

"What happened?"

"Did you see the child, the boy of about twelve years, who obtained deliverance early in the evening?"

"Which one?" McGee said, laughing yet half serious.

McGready smiled wryly.

"I agree, John. The conduct of the young converts, I think, has fastened more conviction than all the preaching so far. However, I speak of the blonde-haired child who sat near the east wall of the house."

"Yes. The Larkin boy from up Gasper River way. I saw him."

"Right after he met the Christ, he turned and found our Deist sitting on the bench directly behind him. Much to the Deist's surprise, I am certain, the boy spun around and began recommending the Christ to him in a most forcible and affecting manner. He told him of the heavenly sweetness that was to be found in Christ and religion. The Deist began to dispute with him, but the Lord opened the child's mouth to speak so affectingly and convincingly to his conscience that it silenced every argument."

"Out of the mouths of babes…" McGee began to quote.

"Truly. And I believe if the man was not convinced last night, he certainly was given solid theology upon which to ponder. He has no issue with God being in these meetings, but as the boy spoke of the Christ, well, as you can imagine, I believe he felt his foundations of knowledge quake beneath him."

"I believe that is happening all around us. I tell you, James, the children are a key to this move of God. I have yet to see an adult unmoved when the children begin telling of the wonders of the Christ. And such language that they use!" McGee paused a moment, remembering. Then he turned his head back toward McGready. "Speaking of children, what of your own family, James? Is Mrs. McGready pleased to be here?"

Morning sounds floated across the clearing as McGready considered the question. Muted voices coming from inside wagon tents, fires being lit so people could cook before the heat of the day set in. It was Sabbath – the last Sunday of the month. What would this day hold?

"James?" McGee nudged him with his elbow.

"What? Oh, yes. I do believe she is enjoying herself immensely, and the girls stayed up much of last night, watching the Lord move about. I believe they left the meeting house some time after midnight."

"Hmm," McGee responded, cupping his chin in his hand. They were silent for a time.

"You know, James," McGee spoke again. "We have seen many Deists, many nay-sayers and rogues in the past meetings; but I am grateful to say, we have not seen disruption or violence. For that, I am most thankful."

"Do not count your chickens before they hatch, John. The sacrament is not over yet."

Both the Sabbath and Monday's meetings went much the same. As at Gasper River, Sarah felt herself weary but not downhearted. She prayed for a stronger constitution to be able to stay awake longer and watch the way the Spirit moved throughout each day. Also, everyone realized Monday that the meetings would not end on time. There was a great desire to stay in God's presence, so a general word went out that the ministers would continue their work into Tuesday morning. That would be the day to break camp.

That was a disappointment and a relief, Sarah thought as she stirred the stew for Monday's supper. *I am surely feeling weary – as I know the children are as well, but to leave? That means facing my father.*

Charity walked up then, toting baby Matthew who was covered with river mud, and spoke as if reading Sarah's mind.

"Sarah, it is the first of the new month. The date came to me this afternoon," she stated, her words shooting out in breathless spurts as she carried her heavy load. "Oh, child!" she placed the boy on the ground. "You will be the end of me. Now, be still and let me get those clothes off!"

Sarah was accustomed to conversing with her aunt over whatever child happened to be in the same space.

"I know," Sarah walked over, picking up the mud-soaked breeches and taking them to the wash bucket on the west side of their camp. "I have not forgotten. I believe I have only a few days before he arrives."

"Hmm," Charity pulled the shirt over baby Matthew's head and tossed it toward Sarah. "Throw that in the water as well. Once they are washed out, we will just have to put them back on the boy wet. You, boy!" she tousled his hair affectionately, taking the sting out of her words. Catching the wet cloth that Sarah threw back at her, Charity began washing off his face. "Well, dear one, I have been praying and expecting to see even more of a change in your father. I cannot explain it," she said, pushing harder on an especially muddy spot on Matthew's cheek, "but there is a shaking in the Heavens over that man. Pray, Sarah. Pray for Matthew even more than you already do."

"Owww. Mama, owww!"

"Well, what do you expect, boy? This muck must come off. Hold still and stop squirming!"

Sarah laughed at the two-year-old's fierce expression and short red hair standing on end.

"Perhaps I should pray for this Matthew first?" she questioned as she walked over to help Charity.

"Pray for Matthew," the toddler repeated.

"I would say pray for both Matthews," Charity responded, wiping the sweat off her forehead with her apron. "Pray that the big Matthew finds the Christ and this little Matthew survives the day!" The two women laughed as they searched between fingers and inside ears for more crusted mud.

Chapter Twenty Six

The sun rose Tuesday morning, September 2, apparently forecasting the same sort of day Logan Countians had seen for the past month – hot and dry. Yet the wizened farmers knew there was an odd look to the sky, which could speak to late afternoon storms.

Still, most of the people gathered and encamped around the Muddy River Meeting House didn't seem to care. Once again, the ministers had worked through the night as congregants stayed up, praying for themselves and others around them. McGready reckoned that about fifty people had come to Christ in the past four days – a staggering amount, even in his mind. He still wasn't sure where all these people were coming from.

But Sarah knew nothing of those numbers as the McMillans took their places in the house for one last meeting. Soon the wagons would turn towards their homes, and all she could think about was her father and Port Royal. Her heart lay heavy. Daniel stood behind her against the wall. She felt his presence as a strong support, yet it couldn't outweigh the dread.

What little dew there had been on the grass as they all awoke had dissipated early on, and the heat bore down on the small structure with relentlessness. Sarah felt drops of sweat roll down her back as McGready took the pulpit and began to give directions to both new and old disciples of Christ. There were a few people who had never left the house all night; their cries and moans could still be heard underlying McGready's voice. Pockets of people gathered in corners, continuing to pray even though the meeting "proper" had started. It was as though revival must happen, had to continue, regardless of crops that needed working or congregants who had to leave.

Sarah mused on all this as she listened to McGready's voice rise and fall. In the background, she heard another wagon roll close to the house, but the sound barely reached her consciousness. Wagons were constantly coming and going.

It wasn't until she heard her name bellowed from the door that she realized who drove that wagon.

"I am here for Sarah McMillan!" her father interrupted McGready in mid-sentence. Sarah found herself on her feet.

"Father…"

He saw her then, his face dark with rage, eyes filled in anger.

"You are not where you are supposed to be," he spoke, more quietly this time and with deadly calm. Charity rose as well.

"Matthew, we thought you would come later in September," Charity attempted to smile, her lips tremulous. "We are to leave today and return home."

"Sir!" McGready spoke from the front. "You are interrupting our meeting, and worse yet, you are interrupting the Holy Spirit! I would that you take your conversation out of doors." He was firm and unbending. Matthew McMillan seemed to notice McGready for the first time – actually seemed aware of a room full of people, some still crying in corners.

"Is this what you have been doing with your aunt?" his lips curled derisively as he addressed Sarah. "Playing religious games?"

"I assure you, sir. You see no games here, only the presence of God Almighty," McGready thundered from up front. McGee and Rankin, who had been standing close to McGready, began to move toward Matthew's bulky form. The angry man saw them approach, and, while there was no fear in his eyes, he seemed to think better of fighting in this place. He looked at Sarah squarely and said, "Daughter, get out and gather your things."

Sarah lifted one foot after another, feeling as though she dragged through mud. Behind her, Charity and Daniel followed, but she only saw her father's wrath and only heard his voice. Despair consumed her. Fear assailed her. It felt as though the warm presence of God had completely disappeared, leaving her bereft and alone.

As Matthew snatched her by the arm and dragged her down the steps, a small cadre of people followed. Daniel and Charity moved quickly to catch up, while Rankin and McGee brought up the tail end. McGready resumed speaking inside, his voice rolling out the doors and chasing them toward Matthew's wagon, which sat parked near the entrance. He released Sarah's arm and spun around as Charity touched his shoulder.

"Matthew, brother, please," she began.

"Please, what? I allow you to have my daughter through several summer months each year to help – to help! – you with your crops," he spat out. "And I find that you are not working a farm, no! You are filling her mind with lies and deception. With promises of what? A safe journey in this life? That God will guide her steps and give her happiness? What a farce! You have betrayed me!"

Sarah stood by helplessly, watching the tears stream down Charity's face. She had no emotions. No feelings.

"It has been no betrayal, sir," Daniel moved out from behind Charity and addressed Matthew. His presence only seemed to infuriate the man more.

"Who are you to tell me about my family? Stay out of what is none of your business!"

"Sarah and Mrs. McMillan are my business, sir. I hope to marry your daughter one day!"

Oh no, Daniel, not now. Not like this, the words never left Sarah's lips but resonated through her mind. Her father's face grew colder; the barely concealed rage that marked it grew and expanded and his voice cracked like ice.

"I beg your pardon?"

While Daniel didn't back down, he rubbed his brow in frustration, realizing he had jumped too far ahead. He attempted to backtrack.

"What I mean to say, sir, is my name is Daniel Townsend, and I ..."

"I don't give a prat who you are! You have the gall to speak to me of marriage to my daughter before I even know your name? Your family? Your station in life?"

Charity held up her hand. "Matthew, Daniel is a good man. We have been waiting for your visit so that you could meet him and hear his plans and dreams for Sarah and for their family. Listen to him, you could find no better match for Sarah. Please!" Her tears ran unheeded now, dropping on the bib of her apron, her face a contortion of emotions. Rankin and McGee stayed back, knowing they had to allow this to play out, yet being available in case any violence erupted. They also prayed.

"I will not listen to any more of this talk," Matthew declared. "No more. Sarah?" He turned toward the tall girl, standing silently, dry-eyed, by his side. "I said to go get your things. Do it now." Matthew moved toward his wagon again, preparing to climb in, when Daniel reached out for his shoulder.

"Sir, I would beg…"

At the touch of his hand, Matthew spun around with lightning speed, his fist raised. He connected squarely on Daniel's jaw, dropping the young suitor to the ground before Daniel knew what hit him. Sarah cried out, running to Daniel's side, while the two ministers took two steps toward Matthew. The stocky man raised his arms as though to surrender, an odd smile on his face.

"Sirs, I beg your pardon," Matthew tried to look chagrined. "I am leaving your premises now, but I would say to you that this young man has been delaying my departure. And, as her father, you would certainly agree I have a right to gather my daughter and return home?"

McGee and Rankin looked at one another, realizing the truth of Matthew's words, yet unwilling to leave it there. McGee drew closer in.

"Sir, if you do not remove yourself from these premises sooner than later, you will regret your actions. There is no cause for violence nor bloodshed. Your anger is unbecoming, and your rage is of the devil himself," McGee declared unflinchingly, his body tight and ready to respond quickly.

Matthew nodded.

"I simply ask that you keep these two," he pointed to Charity and Daniel's groaning form, "away from me so that I may leave your meeting grounds. Believe me, I have no desire to stay any longer."

Daniel had pushed Sarah to the side as he struggled to stand. Blood trickled out of the corner of his mouth and he was dazed, but he clearly was ready to fight. As he swayed on his feet, Charity grabbed his arm, trying to restrain him, while Sarah reached for the other arm. The two women stared silently at one another around Daniel's weaving body — Charity's face streaked with dried tears and dirt, Sarah's countenance twisted and wounded yet strangely calm. Silently, they communicated, and Sarah knew what she had to do.

It was the hardest moment of her life, she realized later, to let go and walk away from Daniel, from the man that she loved. Yet she felt compelled to do so, and even more, she knew Charity felt it as well. Had Daniel held all his senses at the moment, she knew he would have concurred. In the midst of this spiritual storm – for that's what it was – her role must be played to completion. A heavenly resolve settled on her heart, and she stepped away from him. Speaking clearly and calmly, she said, "It will take me only a moment to gather my bag." Sarah smoothed out her skirt then addressed Rankin and McGee. "Do not worry. I will be fine with my father." And she turned on her heel to find her saddlebag at the McMillan campsite.

The ministers had moved beside Daniel and Charity, supporting him yet adding to Charity's restraint. Daniel kept trying to push their arms away and approach Matthew; it was plain that his head still wasn't clear enough to reason. Matthew ignored Daniel's weak attempts – and his mumbled words — climbed into the wagon, released the brake, and turned it around in the clearing. As the shaken young man leaned against McGee, Charity wiped his mouth, the two of them carrying on a brief, but solemn conversation as Sarah emerged toting a full saddlebag. Her cap had completely fallen off during the scuffle and her thick hair blew freely in the wind. The gusts blew dust in her face and around her body, giving her the appearance of a ghostly form emerging from the spirit world.

As she climbed into the wagon, assisted by Rankin, Sarah turned toward Daniel. They locked eyes, communicating more deeply than many do with words. He slightly tipped his head and stopped fighting restraint. Sarah allowed a brief smile, and they were off. Matthew slapped the reins loudly, sending his horses thundering toward Tennessee.

Chapter Twenty Seven

Matthew pushed the horses as hard as he dared all the way back to Port Royal. They stopped only for water in Keysburg and arrived at their cabin well before the sun set that Tuesday. From the moment they left Muddy River, he never spoke another word. The hours of hard riding bumped Sarah around so much that she felt black and blue, but it gave her plenty of time to think. Miraculously, she held the tears back – because they threatened to come more than once — when she realized she never got to say goodbye to Mattie, Millie, Josiah and baby Matthew, when she remembered the look of agony on Daniel's face as she rode away, when she considered she may never get to stay with Aunt Charity again. What would happen now?

She felt as though demons from Hell chased her all the way back to Tennessee, her resolve to leave with her father evaporating with each passing mile. What had she been thinking? Surely God would not call her to do something like this? There was no promise of escape, and she was certainly old enough now to decide to leave Matthew and make her own way. She could have made a strong case to stay, and with all those people at Muddy River on her side, it could have worked.

She must have heard incorrectly and just *thought* God impressed her to go with her father.

The steady rhythm of hoof beats competed with her thoughts and, by the time they drew up to the tiny cabin in the woods, she was utterly exhausted, spent — and wet. The rains had come as they had left Keysburg, pouring heavily for about an hour. As she stepped down from the wagon, she swayed a bit and had to grab the side to keep from falling. Her feet hit on dry, hard ground and in the back of her mind, she realized the rains never made it here.

"Take the horses and rub them down," Matthew demanded, not meeting her eyes. "Leave them in the enclosure for the night, and I will return them tomorrow."

Sarah had wondered where they had come from. Apparently, her father borrowed the mares from Mr. Wilcox who often loaned out his animals for a fee. She took the reins and turned toward the small barn.

"Do not think we will forfeit discussing the events of this day," Matthew warned, speaking to her back. She paused, waiting. "There is still sunlight, and I have the back pasture to plow. While I take the mule to work, you finish with the horses, unload the wagon and begin to prepare victuals. When I return, we will talk of this religion and the flagrant disregard for my wishes for you, daughter. While I have never been proud of you, I had yet to be ashamed – until this day. You disgraced me and disgust me."

Sarah heard every word, felt them beat in her back. Yet over his accusations she heard McGready's voice as a Son of Thunder in her mind teaching from the book of Ephesians.

He has imparted to us a shield of faith, McGready had stated. *It is a mighty shield that protects us from every fiery dart delivered from the enemy of our souls. Nothing can harm us for He who is for us will never be against us.*

As she envisioned such a shield over her back, she pictured each word from her father hitting it and falling uselessly to the ground. She heard his heavy steps plod towards the back pasture where the mule and plow were kept, and then there was silence. Sarah never moved. Holding the horses' reins in her hands, she prayed out loud.

"Father God, most Holy One, today I have obeyed You as best as I know how. I ask You now to protect me, guide me and cover me as I live in the devil's lair. Fulfill the prayers of your daughter, Charity, and meet my father where he is. Bring him back to You, for You are his only hope. And give me grace, Lord God, grace to make it until you do."

She pulled on the reins, moving again towards the tiny barn where grooming supplies were kept. In her exhaustion, she felt she could barely walk, but somehow, praying had helped. At the least, she could make it through another few minutes.

The Waking Up

Thanks again to Sally's stores, Sarah was able to have a decent supper prepared by dusk. Fresh sliced tomatoes, corn from the cob, hoecakes and cold pork were spread over their table. The wagon had been unloaded, the horses rested in the pen and Sarah had already lit the lantern that hung near the door. It was dark in the cabin and almost dark outside.

Her ears had been straining for the past hour to hear the first footstep of her father's return from the back field, but so far, she heard nothing. She sat to wait, alternately praying and thinking. Her stomach was a knot of fear and dread, yet she also felt a peace in her storm. The chirping cicadas grew louder as the night approached, a sound that comforted Sarah in its normalcy.

About an hour later, the light of the half moon lit up the clear sky and still no sign of her father. The hoecakes were cold and spongy, and while Sarah had kept the flies away as best she could, they had eaten their fill of supper. Every few seconds she stared intently at the back path, searching for any shape emerging from the darkness, but there was nothing. Even the cicadas had stopped singing. It was fully night.

As much as she hated to do it, Sarah knew she had to go look for him. If he was alright, she would certainly be chastised for leaving the cabin when he told her to wait for him. And yet, if something had happened …

A renewed Indian attack? Surely not. It had been so long since there had been any episodes.

Perhaps a bear? A panther?

Her mind jumped to every horrible scenario, producing images of a bloody massacre. Adrenalin began pumping through her body, and the enormous fatigue she had felt all afternoon evaporated.

She shook herself mentally, stood and took the lantern from beside the door. There was simply nothing to be done for it. Grabbing a fistful of her skirt in one hand and holding the lantern high enough to see the ground with the other, she ventured down the back path toward the far pasture. She decided not to call for him, hoping if she saw him first and if he was unhurt, she could return to the cabin unnoticed. Ducking her head under low hanging limbs, she walked as quickly as she could, but this path wasn't as clear as others around their home.

As she emerged from the woods, she saw the field before her bathed in moonlight. Standing on the far side was their mule, alone and still hitched to the plow. She couldn't see her father's figure anywhere, so she began walking around the edge of the field – Heaven forbid she put footsteps over the freshly plowed soil! As she drew closer to the mule, she heard moaning. A dark clump lay at the foot of the plow, and while it was unmoving, it did groan. With a tiny gasp, Sarah ran the rest of the way and fell at her father's form. Placing the lantern beside his head, she bent down to look him over carefully, his head, his chest. There was no blood. No apparent injury. Yet he was unconscious and mumbling sporadically.

Her gaze moved further down his body. He lay on his stomach, legs sprawled out, his face turned sideways and smashed into the freshly turned soil. His arms were spread eagle, as though he embraced the earth. His shoes and feet were perfectly normal. She gently felt around his head and neck. There were no lumps. She could find nothing to explain his injury.

"Father," she spoke gently.

Nothing.

"Father," she increased the volume. "Father, can you hear me?"

He moaned, a gurgle of unintelligible speech falling from his lips.

"Are you hurting? Can you move?" she tried again.

He continued to gurgle, and she leaned down to listen more closely, thinking perhaps he was choking or had an obstruction in his throat. But no. His breath, though labored, was clear.

Sarah rocked back on her heels, confused. She picked up the lantern and once again looked him over from head to toe, moving the light over his body like a sweeping beacon.

Shaking her head, she reached out and shook his shoulder gently. "Father?"

He had never moved, except to moan, and Sarah began to realize this was getting her nowhere. She stood up and glanced over toward the mule. He gazed back at Sarah, his big brown eyes unblinking in the subdued light.

"Ah, boy. What happened here?" she spoke out loud. "And what are we to do?"

The mule shifted a hoof and turned his head away from Sarah's searching gaze.

Taking a last long look at her father, Sarah knew she had to get help.

There was no way she could get him back to the cabin by herself. She probably couldn't lift one of his legs much less his whole body. She halfway considered using the mule to help her pull her father back, but getting him down the narrow path and then into the house? No, it simply wasn't feasible. She had to go for help.

Thinking quickly, she decided to leave the mule harnessed and the lantern lit beside her father to ward away any predators. As she ran back down the path, she thanked God for the moonlight and for rested horses. It took her only a few minutes to grab a bridle and one of the mares. Slipping on her bareback, Sarah kicked her into motion and headed as quickly as she could to the Neville's house. She could think of no other option.

The ride only took minutes once she hit the main road into the settlement, but it felt like hours to Sarah. When Mrs. Neville opened the front door, she was greeted by a girl whose hair was loose and wild, cheeks were streaked with blood from the scratches of tree limbs and whose speech tumbled out so quickly it was unintelligible.

"Sarah! Dear girl! Whatever is it?" Mrs. Neville grabbed her by the shoulders and shook her hard.

"My Father!" Sarah panted as though she ran the whole way from her cabin. "He is laid out in the back field – out of his mind and I know not why! Is Mr. Neville at home?"

"Yes, he's out back. Come in, child. Let me fetch him."

"I cannot. I have one of Mr. Wilcox's mares here, and I must stay with her," she said, pointing to the horse tied off at the bottom of their steps.

"John! Sally! Fetch John! Quickly!" Mrs. Neville shouted from the front door, her words catching Sally as she emerged from the back of the house. The dark-skinned woman took one glance at Sarah and sprinted toward the back, yelling loudly all the way.

John Neville appeared within seconds, anxiety clouding his strong face.

"Sarah? What is it?"

Sarah repeated her words while Neville grabbed his gun off the mantle over their fireplace. He shouted out orders as he moved.

"Sally, tell Robert to get my horse ready – now! Then have him get the older mare ready. You and Robert follow me as quick as you can to the McMillan cabin. Tell him to bring a gun. Rachel," he turned toward his wife, "send Esther down to Mr. Skinner's house. Tell him to get on out to the McMillans' cabin and wait for us inside."

"And Sarah," he shot out the front door, "mount and wait for me in the yard. We will ride back together." Neville charged toward the back of the house, carrying his rifle, as Mrs. Neville turned back toward Sarah.

"I will pray, child. I would have preferred our reunion to be on better terms," a wry smile tugged at her lips. "Do not forget that God has this all in His hands. He is your strength, Sarah."

Neville's voice rang from behind the house, horse hoofs announcing his approach. Sarah slung her leg over the mare and turned back to Mrs. Neville one last time."Thank you," she spoke firmly, yet her eyes were filled with fear. "Please continue to pray. Something is terribly wrong with him."

"Sarah!" Neville rounded the corner, reining in his horse. "Let's be off. Robert and Sally will follow."

Together they turned their mounts toward the southern road out of Port Royal and gave them as free a rein as they could in the hazy moonlight.

Chapter Twenty Eight

After leaving the horses at the cabin, Sarah and Neville raced down the narrow path, back to the pasture; and, once again, Sarah had to fight off fear and dread. What if the lantern had not been enough of a deterrent, and wild animals had come while she had been gone? She could never forgive herself. She almost ran into the back of Neville as he stopped short on the edge of the field.

"Where is he?" he barked.

"Over there. On the ground next to the lantern."

Caring nothing for the straight, freshly plowed furrows, Neville raced over the moist soil and reached Matthew's still form before Sarah did. He fell to his knees, acting out the scene Sarah had completed only an hour before. Picking up the lantern, he ran the light over Matthew's prone body, highlighting every shadow while probing gently with his fingers. Matthew was still unresponsive and mumbling incoherently. Neville glanced up at Sarah.

"Has he been this way the whole time?"

"Yes, sir. At least he was this way when I found him about an hour or so ago."

"And he has never awakened?"

"Not that I know of."

"Hooo-weee! Whar's you at, Mr. Neville?" Robert's soulful voice sounded muffled by the thick woods at the edge of the field.

"Over here, Robert. Follow my voice then follow the light," he began waving the lantern back and forth as he stood up. The mule shifted, reminding Sarah that he had needs as well. Two sturdy dark shapes emerged from the woods, and Robert and Sally ran quickly over the field. Neville continued to bark orders in rapid-fire succession.

"Robert, come man, and help me lift Mr. McMillan. We need to carry him to the cabin so Skinner can see him clearly. Sarah, go on ahead and clear off the kitchen table. We'll lay him out there. Do you have another lantern on hand?" She nodded. "Good. Light it and be ready. Sally?" Neville's kind, worried, face turned toward his house help. "Take the mule here and unhitch him. Make sure he's got plenty of water and is well fed before you make your way to the cabin. You can leave the plow here in the field."

"Yas, sir," she nodded, her coal-black face hidden in the shadow of the trees.

"Alright? Sarah, go on, child. We will have him there shortly."

Turning on her heel, Sarah ran back across the field and into the path as quickly as she could without the light of the lantern. Unlike the others, though, she knew her way, and it only took a few seconds to get her bearings.

When she reached the back of the cabin, she half expected to see Mr. Skinner's horse tethered nearby, but apparently he had yet to make it. Leaving the front door open for extra light, Sarah moved inside and felt for the spare lantern kept next to her father's bed.

Once it was lit, the small room leapt to life, and she cleared off the table with speed, expecting any minute to have Mr. Neville and Robert there, carrying her father's lifeless body. Yet when that was completed, she found herself at the door, staring blindly down the path – still waiting. Silence. There was no sign of them. For the first time in hours, she began to think. Her emotions swung from one extreme to the other. There was no doubt her father treated her horribly and if anything serious happened ... she would be free. Perhaps this is what God intended?

Yet how could she in good conscience wish such a fate on the man who was her own flesh and blood, who had cared for her in his own perverse way? And what would God think about her taking joy in his downfall?

The temptation surely was there, but she could not find it within herself to wish ill towards him, no matter how despicable he had been. She had left Muddy Creek this morning – was it only this morning? – with the intent to obey God's direction. She would not give in now by allowing her father to succumb to an illness without a fight. She knew it was part of riding this road to its finish. "Lord God," she prayed into the dark, "bring him out of this, and let it be for Your glory. Show me what I must do and redeem my father's life."

Robert's heavy panting alerted Sarah that the two men approached the cabin. Simultaneously, Mr. Skinner rode into the yard, a lantern swinging in his free hand. He leapt from his mount as the other two men hefted Matthew through the cabin door and onto the table.

Sarah stood to the side, staring at the ghostly pallor of her father's face. Half of it was covered with fresh dirt; Robert leaned over him, brushing it off gently then setting her father's head back on the table. He, too, stood back then, allowing Skinner to draw near.

"Tell me what happened, Neville," Skinner spoke quickly.

As Neville relayed the information, Sarah watched the blacksmith probe, bend, touch and thump her father's body. Mr. Skinner was the closest thing Port Royal had to a doctor. Sarah could only hope the years of wilderness infimities and accidents had given the man much medical knowledge.

Her father still mumbled every once in a while, but the periods of ranting seemed to be farther apart than they were in the field.

"Sarah?" Skinner turned toward her, wiping sweat off his forehead. "Can you tell me anything else about your father's constitution? Had he been ill today? Vomiting? Did he eat anything different than you did?"

"Not that I know of," she responded, thoughtfully. "We rode all the way from Logan County, and we never really stopped to eat. When we arrived here, he went directly out to the back field to plow."

"Hmm," he looked back at his patient. Leaning down, Skinner laid his head on Matthew's chest, listening to the rhythm of his heart. Matthew's mumblings began again, and Skinner moved his ear closer to his mouth. While everyone else in the room only heard grunts and moans, Skinner's face began to lighten then shift in confusion. He jerked up straight, looking directly at Sarah again.

"Has Matthew been to a religious meeting today?"

"Pardon?" Sarah stared blankly.

"Meeting house. Has Matthew been to a meeting or some such religious exercise?"

"He, uh, he found me at a Presbyterian meeting house this morning, why?"

"Strange."

Skinner glanced at the others standing around the table.

"He was saying something about Jesus Christ and the power of the cross. A heavenly light. That sort of thing. Couldn't make out much else."

Neville, Sarah, Robert and now Sally, who had just entered the room, looked at one another in confusion. Sarah's heart beat rapidly, and her mouth felt dry as cotton.

"What, uh, why do you think he is saying that?" she worked out.

"I have no idea, child, but I can find no problem with him physically. He is unmarked. There are no abrasions on him. He seems as healthy as a horse. The only thing I know to tell you is to get him comfortable, perhaps in his bed, and try to get something wet down his throat. Do you have any whiskey in this place?" She nodded. "Good. Other than that, you will have to wait this one out." Skinner turned away, repacking his small carry bag. Slinging it over his shoulder, he stood straight again, now smiling at the close-knit group. "I think all will be well, but I will return after first light. Take care, young one." He lightly touched Sarah on the arm as he walked out their front door, leaving the four of them staring after him in a stupor. Neville finally broke the silence.

"To bed he goes, then. Sarah, is that your father's place over there?" He pointed to Matthew's corner of the cabin, and Sarah nodded dumbly, suddenly feeling fatigue falling on her like a rock. Automatically, she moved out of the way as the men picked Matthew up from the table and transferred his limp body across the room. Sally watched carefully, a thoughtful frown furrowing her brow.

Once Robert and Neville had him positioned, they turned to go.

"Sarah, I am leaving Sally with you for the night," he nodded to Sally as he spoke. "I am sure Mrs. Neville would agree with my decision. As soon as first light approaches, I will send Hagar over to help you both out – perhaps bring some breakfast already prepared – and then I or Robert will check in later in the morning. Does this sound agreeable to you?" The kind gentleman gazed at Sarah with tenderness and concern.

To Sarah, his voice was like a rope descending toward her as she sank in a deep well. She grasped hold as best as she could but felt as though she still might drown.

"Yes, sir. I believe so," she eked out.

"Sally," Neville turned toward his house help, "get Miss Sarah into her bed. I believe the events of the day are catching up with her, and if we are not careful, she may derive some ailment worse than that of her father."

"Yas, sir. I see that, too," she spoke firmly, grabbing Sarah's arm.

As Robert and Neville left, drawing the heavy cloth back over the cabin door, Sally steered Sarah toward her bed, whispering kindly as she laid her down. Before her head hit the pillow, Sarah was asleep.

Chapter Twenty Nine

It was shouting that woke her. Sarah sat up straight, trying desperately to throw off the blanket of sleep that wrapped around her mind. Arms swinging, she slung her legs to the side of the bed, both feet hitting the floor solidly then she was standing. She felt for the stable log wall as she steadied herself.

"It be alright, Miss Sarah," Sally's calm voice shot out from the other side of the room. "It's just yo' pappy. I gots him. You jest lay yoself back down."

Sarah shook her head, trying to remember. Her father. The field. Night. Muddy Creek. It all came rushing back. She gazed intently into the half-lit cabin, barely making out the shape of Sally sitting beside her father's bed. The woman was waving her hand at her, motioning for Sarah to leave her be. But that wasn't to happen. Sarah was awake. And her father had cried out. She walked closer.

"What is he saying?"

"I surely don't know, child. He been cryin' out a little all night, but he don't seem to be in no pain nowhere. Jest a'cryin' out ever once in a while."

"Is he calling any names?"

"Only Jesus," Sally smiled at the frazzled girl. "Like Mr. Skinner say, he call out on the name of the Lord ever now an' then, but nuthin' else I can make out."

Sarah bent over, examining her father's countenance. He appeared quite serene and peaceful, as though he slept in a warm, safe place. She continued to stare, gazing steadily, when suddenly, his eyes flew open and he gasped like a man who had been drowning.

Sarah cried out and jumped back, almost falling over Sally, who shrieked as well — the two women staring at him as though he rose from the dead.

Matthew's eyes began to focus on the room, the women standing beside him, the slow light of dawn coming through the slits in the front door's cloth, the morning sounds from the woods surrounding the cabin – he took it all in within seconds; and then he came to himself.

"Sarah?" he whispered. "Is there water?"

"Yes, oh glory hallelujah, yes," Sally broke in, reaching for the pail beside his bed. Holding the gourd scoop close to his lips, he drank deeply then lay back with a sigh. Sarah stood dumbstruck, her heart racing.

"Am I ... uh ... what day is it?" His voice was stronger now.

Again, Sally replied. "Wednesday, Mr. McMillan. It be early Wednesday morning."

"Wednesday? Are you sure? Only one night then? Only one night have I been gone."

"That'd be right, sir. Yas, sir. Twas last night Miss Sarah done found you out in yo' field. Gone from this world, you was, Mr. McMillan," Sally nodded firmly, as if her expression would add the needed weight to her words.

His heavily-lined, gruff face lightened as he smiled at the woman, showing a row of straight, white teeth. Sarah wasn't sure she had ever seen his teeth. She wasn't sure she had ever seen her father smile.

"You are quite right, Sally. I was gone from this world and in another – of sorts. Sarah?" he turned toward her now, the smile gone from his countenance. As he shifted his weight, he motioned toward her. "Grab that chair and come closer. I have much to say to you."

Obediently and without a word, Sarah did as he said, sliding as close to her father as she dared. She was thankful for Sally's sure presence by her side.

Before camp had broken up at Muddy Creek the day before, McGready had gathered the saints for an impromptu prayer meeting specifically directed toward God's protection over Sarah and for His salvation to be extended to Matthew. While both Daniel and Charity were thankful for the prayers of the saints, they couldn't help feeling anxious and nervous. They rode out of Muddy Creek together, the two families again following each other in wagons, as McGready and McGee watched.

"Seems a mighty heavy way to end the meeting," McGee spoke around the grass sprig he chewed on. "I mean to say, fifty-five souls is fifty-five souls – a bounteous crop of heavenly bound people, for certain. Yet my heart grieves for the McMillan girl and her situation."

McGready gazed at his friend and associate thoughtfully. "Yes, I feel the weight as well, but if God be for us, who can be against us? We can only pray, William. Continue to cry out that the hound of Heaven will pursue the man and bring him to the light."

"Oh I have surely been praying, but I must tell you, James, I wanted to do more than pray this morning. When he hauled off and dealt Daniel Townsend that blow on the chin? Well, it was all a man could do to keep his hands to himself." McGee spit out the grass in frustration. "If he had raised any part of his hand toward the girl, it would have been a different story. But he is her father – I knew I had to take care."

"You did right, William. Although I will admit it was a tough decision." McGready waved his wife over to their spot. Nancy had seen off the last wagon full of people and now turned to get their own wagon and provisions loaded. The three McGready girls still ran and played in the clearing. After the morning rains had passed through, the day had grown bright and hot. The moisture in the air only sealed in the heat tighter, making it almost difficult to breath.

"James," Nancy puffed as she labored over. "It is time to pack up if we have any hope of getting home before nightfall."

"As usual, the misses is right," McGee smiled broadly, tipping his hat. "'Tis the wise ant who works steadily and makes it after harvest has come and gone."

"Indeed, Mr. McGee," Nancy tilted her head up, laughing at the man. Her pink-and-white plaid ribboned hat had shifted from her head, revealing the shimmering blonde hair McGready loved. "Perhaps you might come to our home and repeat that saying at least ten times a day, preferably in the presence of the girls?"

"Alas, Mrs. McGready. I have my own whip to crack at my homestead – and I fear no one listens there either."

Laughing, McGready put his arm around the petite shoulder of his wife, nodding to McGee as they parted ways – McGee walking toward

Rankin to make sure the meeting house was closed up properly, the Mc-Greadys toward their wagon and camp. Nancy wrapped her arm around her husband's waist, leaning her head against his muscle-laden arm. She stood a full head shorter.

"Girls!" he called to the three scampering children running in the woods. "Time to come help pack up." Three blonde heads stopped their play at his words then conferred briefly. As their feet brought them running toward camp, Nancy looked questioningly at her husband.

"Are you pleased with the meeting, then?"

"Most pleased, Mrs. McGready. And yet, not satisfied at all," he smiled down at her, his typically furrowed brow light and open.

"Ah, 'tis as I expected then. What will you do now?"

"We will continue this week. Friday, the ministers will gather at The Ridge in Tennessee for another set of sacramental meetings."

"The Ridge? Is that anywhere near the McMillan girl?"

"Alas, no. I think not. Her home is farther west in Port Royal. Remember, McGee explained The Ridge is quite south of us – almost a direct line south into the state."

"Oh, too bad then. I had hoped …"

"That we might see how the McMillans fare after this day?"

"Indeed," Nancy chewed her bottom lip thoughtfully. "It is strange, James. I do not fear for the girl for I truly believe the Lord is her strength and is her protection. And yet, I hate that she has to endure that insufferable man. However will she manage?"

"As the Lord wills, so she will abide. According to Mrs. McPherson, the girl has come a long way spiritually in a short time. God will not let her falter."

"I pray not," Nancy whispered to herself as the three girls reached them, shouting out who won their race from the creek. The laughing tumble of girls rolled wildly into their father's legs, practically dragging him down. Reaching down, McGready snatched up the youngest and threw her over his shoulder.

"To work, girls!" he bellowed in his Son of Thunder voice. "To work!"

Chapter Thirty

The rising sun had illuminated the tiny cabin second by second since Sarah had awakened so abruptly. Now she could clearly see her father's face, every expression, every nuance. Sally's brown skin glistened in the early morning heat, and Sarah already felt a line of sweat forming on her own brow. Her father seemed oblivious and his dark eyes were unnaturally bright. Sarah wondered if he was feverish, but she wasn't about to put her hand on his brow while he was awake. She clasped her hands in her lap as if they might move toward him of their own accord.

Sally had been mumbling about Matthew not talking, it not being good for him to sit up so after such a strenuous night, how he needed food – but Sarah thought it all a ruse to keep him from holding this sort of meeting with Sally present. The Neville's house slave appeared quite unnerved and jumpy. Sarah completely understood and held no ill will toward her for it. She would do the same thing if she could.

"Mebbe I jus' need to go on and get Mr. Skinner since you is awake, Mr. McMillan," Sally was saying, standing by her chair. "Seems to me he ought to be the one to make sure you's alright to talk and such." Her feet began inching toward the door as she talked, almost without taking a breath. She had just about reached the heavy cloth that hung over it when Matthew stopped her.

"Sally, come back and sit."

His voice allowed no room for argument. Sally came back and sat.

"I realize what I have to say is really for Sarah's ears, but because of our history together, I feel she would be more comfortable with you here as witness. And since you are the only one available, you will have to do. Understand?"

"Yas, sir," Sally nodded blankly.

"Now, my daughter, let me begin by saying that for the first time since your birth, today I feel as if I live. For the past sixteen —or is it seventeen? – years I have walked this earth as a dead man, pulling boots on over feet that are merely part of a rotting carcass. Therefore, you have had the weight of living with death, day in and day out. You have fed death, slept in the same room with death, traveled with death, talked to death. I began stinking of it when your mother passed, and it has only become more and more rancid. So, first, I owe you an apology for your life. I have never been a true father to you and that stands before me this morning as a burden I must bear forever."

Sarah sat stone cold, her mind telling her she should show some form of gratitude for his confession, at least say a word. But nothing would come out. Her eyes were dry. She simply stared. Matthew smiled a little, as if he understood.

"Perhaps I should tell you what I experienced last night," he said, almost to himself. Looking back at Sarah, he sighed and nodded. "Yes, I think that would be best. Otherwise my remarkable, complete change rings hollow in your ears." He laughed abruptly. "I can scarce fathom it myself." Drawing in a deep breath, he began.

"You know, of course, that I railed insults at you in the yard yesterday evening —how can you ever forgive me? Ah, Lord. You may not – and once I had spewed yet more venom your way, I moved to the back field with the mule. I plowed like a man possessed, driving the poor mule harder than I ever have, practically running up and down the rows, turning the soil over like some kind of demon. My mind was filled with images of your Aunt Charity's face, of the boy's face after I had hit him, of your face all the way home. The sound of that minister's voice rolled in my mind as well, though I had heard little of his message before I interrupted the meeting yesterday morning. Still, the sound of his voice ..." Matthew shook his head.

"Then I came to the place where I had almost completed the field, and the sun was lowering in the sky when I felt a heavy presence fall upon my body. Today, I cannot tell you what it was, but suddenly I was no longer in our field; I was back in Carolina, transported back in time to the day Matilda was taken from me.

"As nightmares go, it was familiar. Once again I faced the burning cottage where the Williams family lived. Once again I ran toward the door to attempt to retrieve the baby, knowing all the while that your mother was at our house in the throes of labor. I felt the urgency to complete this task that God had assigned to me before I attended to my own wife." He stopped then, gazing intently into Sarah's face. "I assume your aunt has told you of this?"

Sarah nodded hesitantly, fearfully.

"Yes, I knew she would. It is just as well." He leaned forward, pointing to the water pail. Sally filled the gourd again, and he drank deeply. Sitting back, he continued to speak.

"I have dreamed this thousands of times since it happened, over and over I replay the events, trying desperately to concoct a different ending; yet it always ends the same, and I would awake as though Matilda just died again. The feelings were fresh and new.

"But last night was different. As I lay in the field — I suppose that's where I was at this point in my dream – my mind began to take me to the familiar places. Inside the Williams' cabin, I reached for the baby's form in the cradle, just as she had been, but this time there was a realm of bright light around the child. I still was able to grab her, but even as I crawled from the burning cabin, the light remained in my arms, surrounding the child as though she were on fire – yet a different sort of fire. In my mind, I heard a voice like that of many waters, but not loud, just very … full, complete. It said, 'I was there.' And I continued to carry the baby.

"The threshold fell in on me, and I felt the pain again in my leg. Williams dragged me from the door while Mrs. Williams attended to the child who was still enveloped in the light. She began to weep and swaddle their baby girl, rocking back and forth, and I felt afresh her grief. My heart began to wrench when … again … I heard the voice, 'I was there.' The light continued to hover over the child." Matthew stopped for a moment, seeming to gather himself to continue. Sarah glanced at Sally whose face was filled with grief and anguish. She had known nothing of Matthew's agony.

"The dream sped ahead as it always did," he continued, "and your Uncle Billy was riding in to tell me of Matilda's struggle. The light that surrounded the dead child also surrounded your uncle as he dismounted. His mouth told of your mother's condition, and I reached for panic. As I stretched out my hand, the voice spoke, 'I was there.'

"Then I was transported to our cabin and saw my Matilda stretched out on our bed, the bedclothes bloody and soiled, her face a glorious, beautiful, pale image of what she was. All life was gone from her, and I felt a despair rise in me, that familiar, agonizing despair. But the light surrounded her as well and the voice spoke again – the same message.

"And lastly, I saw you, daughter, held in the arms of my mother, a squirming, red-faced little thing, crying lustily at being so dragged into this hard world. The light hovered over you as well, child, and the voice spoke yet again, 'I was there.'"

Tears began to stream down the hard, calloused cheeks of Matthew, and Sarah's heart cracked ever so slightly.

"It was at that point in the dream that I felt His love – for I have no doubt it was the presence of the Lord that abided with me – I felt that love swim over my body. When I began to accept that love, the light of His presence shifted from Matilda's dead form and your live body to me. It enveloped me and brought such a warmth and kindness that I have never felt. I could have stayed there forever in that place." He laughed briefly. "I know not where I was in the physical, whether still in the field or here in my own bed, but in the Heavenlies, I was with the Lord. His presence was enough for me. More than enough. I felt all the grief and anguish and bitterness over Matilda's death leave me as a bird flies from her nest. Gone in a matter of seconds. And in its place is a tenderness and kindness that I have never known.

"I do not know how long I stayed in that state of … I suppose I was reveling in the presence of God … but it seemed only a short moment. All too soon, the dream ended, and I awoke to the bright, serious, loving green eyes of my daughter, peering into mine." He reached out as if to touch her face, but Sarah hung back, watching. He dropped his hand, sighing deeply.

"And so, daughter, I present to you a father who confesses his sin to you, a lifetime of sin, and repents of his bitterness and hatred, though I never really hated you, you know. Your Aunt Charity was right. Oh, she was so right. My love for you – that I fought every day I breathed – threatened to overtake me if I allowed it. I knew I could not open my heart to you and love you truly for then … then I might lose you as well.

And that I could never survive." His tears continued to run, unchecked, down his face. "I vow this day…" he paused then glanced at Sally to make sure she was listening. There was no doubt of that. Tears also coursed down her brown cheeks. "I vow this day to treat you as the Godly daughter you are, to provide for you, to love you, to cherish you as you deserve to be cherished. I beg your forgiveness but know I have no payment to give. Forgiveness can only come from the hand of God, and you may choose to withhold it from me. I would not blame you if you did for I have fearfully wronged you, and I will suffer every day of my life for it."

His words ceased – the most words Sarah had ever heard him speak at one time in her life. The crack she had felt in her heart grew wider and wider as the reality of what he said soaked in her mind. She already had sensed the presence of God in the cabin, and now it overwhelmed her. Tears that she had held in since childhood began to fall, slowly at first then with increasing freedom. She felt her shoulders begin to heave as she fell to her knees beside her father's bed. He placed his hand on her head as she wept.

Chapter Thirty One

Thanks to travelers that had passed through Port Royal on their way to Logan County, the letters from Sarah to Charity and Daniel reached them both within a week. Obediah had returned to his family only a few days prior and immediately had learned of Matthew's trek to Muddy Creek and his subsequent reclaiming of Sarah. Obediah had held Charity as she wept in his arms; she never doubted God's goodness but suffered for what she knew Sarah must be experiencing.

Daniel, in his effort to manage his emotions, had spent the week clearing trees at the back corner of his father's property. From sunrise to sunset, he chopped and dragged down huge tulip poplars, cedars and oaks in order to clear an area for a future homestead. When night fell, he barely had enough energy to get back to his family's home before falling exhausted into bed.

Each day he threatened to go to the barn, saddle the horse and ride to Port Royal; and each day, he released the notion, still feeling in his heart that he must wait, that perseverance must complete its work to make him mature and complete, as the apostle James had written.

And so it was that two people in Logan County felt enormous relief upon receiving letters from Tennessee, explaining what had happened and, indeed, the miraculous salvation of Matthew McMillan. Within minutes of reading the missive, Daniel saddled his mare and rode to the McPherson home. Charity sat outside under the elm tree shucking the last of the fall corn as he tore into the yard.

"Did you hear?" he called out from the road.

"Yes, Daniel," Charity laughed, waving her letter in the air. "She wrote to me as well."

In dismounting and removing his hat, Charity could see the joy planted in Daniel's eyes, the relief on his countenance. She was sure her face was a reflection of his.

"It's such an amazing tale, although I know we prayed for such a thing. Still ..."

"Oh Daniel! You have no idea. I lived through Matthew's grief and anger. Truly only the Lord can turn a heart that was so hurt and bitter to Himself. He heard our prayers and the prayers of the saints at Muddy Creek. God heard!" Charity reached out, shaking Daniel's arm in emphasis. He laughed heartily.

"And to think, God struck the man down in the middle of his own field. It is almost too strange to comprehend," he shook his head. "No one will believe it, except perhaps those who have attended meetings this summer. Still, it is good that *something* happened. At the rate I was going, I would have killed myself chopping trees before I could ever wed Sarah!"

They laughed together, immense relief intermingled with joy.

"What does she advise to you, Daniel? Has Matthew said anything of your relationship with Sarah?"

"He has said he is willing to hear me and meet me again, as though for the first time. For that I can only be grateful. After blurting out my intentions at Muddy Creek, I could scarcely hope for more," he shook his head regretfully. "I do not know what came over me. I saw him, his anger and rage, and simply wanted to rescue Sarah from such a horror. Blast my foolheadedness!"

Charity patted his knee as he sat down beside her. "No worries, Daniel. God had it under his control all along. Now tell me, when do you go thence?"

His brown eyes sparkled again, anticipation lighting them.

"Right after the fourth Sabbath of the month. You have heard of the meeting our ministers held at The Ridge in Tennessee last week?"

Charity nodded, tossing another ear of shucked corn in the basket to her side.

"According to Rev. McGready, between fifty and sixty souls were brought to Christ, and they all – McGready, Rev. Hodge and McGee — say the Spirit has begun to move down in Tennessee. They have planned a sacrament meeting the fourth Sabbath at Shiloh, the meeting house where Rev. Hodge and his wife are now settled. Already I have promised my help and presence at this meeting – they anticipate great crowds; and then after, I plan to go home by way of Port Royal." He smiled at the thought. "May it be that I am so full of the Spirit by then that Mr. McMillan cannot help but feel I am the perfect man for his perfect daughter."

"May it truly be so, Daniel," Charity agreed, waving as Obediah walked toward them from the field. Millie trotted at his side while baby Matthew sat securely in his father's arms.

"Daniel Townsend, as I live and breathe," Obediah bellowed from a ways off. "Did you, too, receive a letter from our Sarah?"

"Yes, sir, Mr. McPherson, and it was a welcome correspondence."

"I am sure of that, my boy," Obediah laughed as he approached, shaking Daniel's extended hand with force.

"Did Sarah write that she loves you?" Millie asked, a twinkle in her eye.

"Milliford Anne McPherson, you watch yourself, young lady!" Charity reproved.

Daniel merely laughed and tousled her head. "Well, she had better write that she loves me if she wants to be Mrs. Townsend, right?"

"Really, she did write that?" Millie's eyes were wide.

"Millie, I mean it," Charity's countenance grew more severe.

"Never fear, Millie, my dear," her father broke in. "I am sure you will have many opportunities in the future to speak to Sarah of her love. Yet for now, you had best button that lip before your mother buttons it for you."

"Buttons," Matthew said, tugging at his vest. "Big, blue buttons. I got buttons."

"Have, Matthew. I have buttons," Charity turned her gaze upon him.

"Yes, Mama. I got buttons."

Charity's tender eyes turned serious as she returned her gaze to Daniel. "When do you plan to leave for Shiloh?"

"I will ride down with Rev. McGready. We will meet at the Red River Meeting House Thursday after dinner and will ride together."

"I see," she pondered. "Then come Monday or Tuesday, depending on the move of the Spirit, you will head toward Port Royal?"

"That is my plan," Daniel retorted. "Pray for me. And pray for the people at Shiloh. God continues to move, and I would that I beheld it."

"Agreed," Obediah nodded vigorously. "I only hope that I can attend some of the meetings later this fall. I feel as though I have missed an awakening of sorts. Thanks be to God, there is enough of His Spirit to go around. I may not miss it yet," he smiled, showing a small gap between two straight front teeth.

"Surely you will not, sir," Daniel retorted.

"And I am praying, Daniel," Charity said, standing and stretching her back. "I must tend to supper, but know that we will be crying out to Heaven for you." She tapped Millie lightly on the head and waved her toward the cabin while Obediah took her tree-stump seat, placing Matthew on the smooth ground at his feet. The two men sat together and continued talking while Charity's mind slipped easily into supper preparations.

Looking back at her father, Millie dragged her feet. She would much rather stay with the men than join her mother over a hot fire.

"Millie, come quickly. There is much to be done."

Sighing heavily, the tiny girl ran to catch up, dreaming of the day when she could stay outside and play while someone else prepared supper.

Shiloh, Tennessee, stood about fifty miles south of Logan County. McGready was glad to make the trip, if only to see William Hodge again. Hodge, his wife Charity, and their children had been in Shiloh a few years, feeling the leading of the Holy Spirit to oversee this congregation when they left the Carolinas. That didn't mean that he didn't travel as a minister with McGready, but it was certainly easier for Hodge to help cover the southern portion of McGready's expanding area while Rankin oversaw the northern portion. McGee had stretched toward the west, taking on congregations such as Montgomery's Meeting House in Tennessee.

As the fall of 1800 fully enveloped them, each man had settled in his portion of the region, but all still met when possible to assist the others. Word of the Shiloh meeting on this fourth Sabbath of September had spread far and wide. McGready was anticipating huge numbers; Hodge was prepared. McGee was planning to assist, and McGready hoped Rankin would make it, but he had his doubts.

Leaving Daniel to ride to Hodge's cabin and alert him of their presence, McGready stayed on his horse at the edge of the clearing, gazing resolutely at the Shiloh Meeting House. As was his nature, Hodge had the grounds immaculate. Not a stray weed, not a mud hole dotted the landscape. The road was as smooth as a baby's bottom, and the grass was neatly shorn, McGready considered with a smile. Some things never change.

Taking care to dismount slowly (his stomach had been giving him no rest for the past fortnight), he stood large and authoritative beside the mare. Ironically, he felt weak and tired. When the anointing of the Lord came upon him as he preached and ministered, he was full of strength and power. But when that lifted – for lift it must; no one can sustain such a thing — when it lifted, he seemed to feel his frailty more deeply than before.

Cupping his hand over his eyes, McGready searched out as far and wide as he could see. The land around Shiloh lent itself more to flatlands than did Logan County, yet still McGready saw no wagons on the horizon, no signs of the avalanche of people that would descend on this place tomorrow. Now, all was still and quiet, the chirping of a blue jay signaling the only sound of life.

He dropped to a knee, grimacing as he went down.

"Lord God in your most high Heavens, I beseech You to stretch out Your hand over this place as You have done in days past. Pour out Your mighty Spirit, once again, on Your people, by holding out Your hand in compassion and grace, for You are a loving God, full of mercy and compassion, slow to anger and rich in love. Hear the prayers that have arisen from Your people in Stone's River, Cedar Creek, Goose Creek, the Red Banks of Ohio, Fountain Head – all these societies that continuously pray for revival, for Your Spirit to move over Your people.

"And give me the strength as Your humble servant to fulfill that to which You have called me. For the glory of the Father, the Son and the Holy Spirit – this I pray."

Leaning heavily against the foreleg of his mare, McGready rose from the ground and stood again, panting a little from the exertion. Two dots rose over the horizon from the west, and he knew Daniel Townsend had fetched Hodge. Drawing his tired mare over to a shadier spot, he loosely tied her to allow her to graze while he stood silently, waiting for the men to approach. The sun was dipping low in the sky. Tomorrow would come quickly.

Chapter Thirty Two

Daniel couldn't pinpoint the exact cause of his excitement. All he knew, as he rode steadily toward Port Royal on Tuesday afternoon, was that his spirit was jumping and spinning like a top. Certainly, his nerves were raw. Facing Matthew McMillan, albeit a converted one, still gave him great angst. And, of course, the thought of seeing Sarah filled his mind constantly. How would she look? Would she be glad to see him? Anxious as well?

He absentmindedly directed his horse through a shallow creek, the hooves splashing water up to his boots.

He couldn't deny that what he had seen in Shiloh also filled his mind to capacity. Five thousand people, Rev. Hodge had said! He had roughly counted five thousand people! Unheard of. In all his lifetime, he had never seen five thousand souls gathered at one place. They came from everywhere – north, south, east, west –he had heard so many stories of their arrivals that he couldn't keep them all straight anymore.

And then the move of the Spirit of God. Just as it had been at Muddy Creek, Red River, Gasper River. God's Spirit had moved over them in majestic power, striking both children and adults. At one time he counted fifteen people lying beside each other, weeping, groaning and crying out for mercy. The days and nights blurred together in a filmy memory.

In reality, Daniel was also exhausted. He had helped McGready, Hodge and both McGee brothers minister well into the night from Friday through Tuesday. Perhaps what he felt was merely anxiety mixed with fatigue mixed with anticipation. He shook his head to remain alert as he approached the road connecting Nashville to the Port Royal settlement.

Turning northwest, his spirits and energy level began to rise as he encountered various people up and down this busy roadway. Everyone from a scattering of Indians going south to trade – no danger with them now, Daniel thought with relief – to fur traders to families traveling in wagons. Strangers all of them, but Daniel felt an unusual connectedness, a warm compassion for their souls that he had never experienced. He could only assume it was the heart of God in him, placed in his spirit from the Shiloh meetings.

He recalled one of the gentlemen he met who had come to the meeting to see what all the talk was about. Daniel had been standing nearby when Hodge began preaching the last sermon of that night. McGready had been in the crowds, ministering and praying, when this stranger moved to the outside of the group and mounted his horse. Daniel, being the closest person in proximity, approached him.

"Are you going away without the blessing?" Daniel had asked.

"I live at a great distance," the man had replied. "I must go."

"How can you go away without Christ?"

At that point, the man sunk to the ground, his horse's reins still grasped tightly in his hand. He began to cry out for God's mercy, and conviction fell heavily upon him. Within a few minutes, he was able to stand but wanted to speak to McGready as quickly as possible. Daniel pointed out the location of the minister and watched as the man weaved his way over, staggering as if he had drunk too much whiskey.

Seeing his approach, McGready waited then listened as the man told his story. They spoke together for a few minutes as Daniel watched from afar. Once again, the man sank to his knees, crying out for mercy and generally making a great commotion in the midst of the assembly. McGready had looked up then, spotted Daniel, and waved him over.

"Can you get some help and move this poor soul to the edge of the assembly?" McGready whispered.

Daniel nodded, found a willing assistant and transferred the stranger to a corner spot of the clearing. The man was powerless to move and continued groaning and crying even as they dragged him to the side. He lay there until the middle of the night and eventually found deliverance.

Daniel shook his head as he remembered. He didn't know when the man had finally come to his senses, but he must have because by Tuesday morning's light, both he and his horse were gone. Hopefully, he left as a converted soul who had met the Christ.

The experience reminded Daniel somewhat of Matthew's conversion in the field. He wondered if he would be able to talk with Sarah's father about it, or if he would close himself off since Daniel had so brashly told him of his intentions with Sarah.

The hard jolt of his horse stumbling brought Daniel back to the present. Looking around, he noticed that the land had begun to rise and fall more, the woods thickening as he drew closer to Port Royal and the Red River. Rounding a corner, he came upon three men resting their horses in a clearing. Pulling up on his reins, he called out, "Good day!"

"And to you, sir," the tallest of them responded.

"Would any of you gentleman happen to know how much farther it is to the Port Royal settlement?" Daniel questioned as he pushed his hat back on his forehead.

"Indeed. You will travel another ten miles and a bit and will run upon it. Cross over the Red River and you are past it."

Daniel glanced skyward, assessing. Half to himself, he said, "Then I would certainly make it before nightfall."

"Most assuredly," the tall stranger agreed, having heard him. "We are bound there as well, myself having a sister who will board us all for the night. Would you want to travel together and share news? We have come up the Natchez Trace and have reports from the Mississippi River and Alabama."

"I would indeed enjoy some company," Daniel replied. "I come from up Shiloh way, east of here, and have been amongst a great revival of God's Spirit in this area. In fact, I have enjoyed little sleep these last three days and having lively conversation would be a welcome boon."

"Truly? There have been meetings in these backwoods? I have heard nothing of such things, have you two?" He glanced toward his traveling companions, both quiet and solemn. They shook their heads in unison. "Then by all means, join us. We would hear of these things."

So Daniel pulled to the side to wait as the men untethered their horses and mounted. The four rode together in companionable conversation as Daniel spread more seeds of the Gospel along the road.

Sarah thought she might burst. For the one-hundredth time, she went to the open door of the cabin and gazed down the path, listening intently for any sound of a boot or a horse's hoof. Nothing.

Sighing heavily, she moved back in and poked the embers on the fire to keep it burning slowly. The days were bright and beautiful, boasting a sky so blue it almost hurt her eyes to gaze upon it. But the late September nights could be chilly, and Sarah spent much time regulating the heat emanating from their hearth fire.

"How much longer must I wait, Lord?" she spoke out loud to the empty cabin. "I feel as though my heart would leap from my chest if he does not arrive soon."

She moved back to the table, picking up Daniel's letter again, reading the few words scribbled upon the paper. "Tuesday afternoon," she whispered. "I should leave Shiloh by noon and would arrive at Port Royal sometime late in the day. Please thank your father for his graciousness in agreeing to see me and host me in his home." Sarah lifted her eyes to the ceiling, "I would thank *You,* Lord God, for my father's willingness to host Daniel. Were it not for Your pursuit of him, in spite of my own lack of belief and faith, this would not be happening; and I would be a most miserable woman."

A sound of tumbling logs thumped against the side of the cabin, but Sarah didn't flinch. Her father had been hauling firewood all afternoon, and she had become accustomed to his noises. She walked to the door again, peering down the path.

"He still tarries then?" her father rounded the corner, wiping his hands on his pant legs.

Startled at the sound of his voice, she jerked a bit. "Yes, Father. But he should arrive any time now."

Since Matthew's return to the Lord as a true prodigal son, he and Sarah had been much like two strangers that meet up on a road. Assessing one another, being cordial above all things, deferring to one another, but they hadn't truly talked of the happenings of a week ago since that time. It was all very awkward, Sarah thought. Not horrible. Much better than life had been. But she still wasn't sure how to relate to this stranger she lived with.

Certainly, his repentance toward her had been a beautiful thing, but was that all she would receive? Was she to release seventeen years of pain in the snap of a finger for the "I am so sorry" from her father? So much time had been lost – an entire childhood gone – and had it not been for Grandma McMillan, Sarah would have lived an entirely loveless life.

Often she thought of the Scriptures and the Christ telling Peter to forgive seventy times seven. She was trying, really trying, but her heart still felt cold and bitter.

Matthew's strong, stocky frame stood firmly planted in front of their cabin. He was solid and muscular, the effects of his night visitation completely vanished now. He was as healthy as a horse and – as intimidating in body as he always had been. Hands on his hips, he turned to survey the path that opened up into the clearing around their cabin.

"You gave him good directions, then?"

"I wrote it out as clearly as I was able. This morning, I tied a small ribbon around the dogwood tree at the end of the path next to the trace to Port Royal. I do not see how he could miss that, especially as he will be searching for it."

"No...I would agree," he sighed then, walking toward the rain barrel to the side of the cabin. Taking the gourd hanging on the side of it, he filled it and drank deeply. As he was wiping his mouth, they both heard the approach of horse's hooves. Sarah felt her heart drop to her knees, and she laid her hand on the doorpost for support. Into the clearing rode Daniel, his countenance hidden by the brim of his hat, his body sagging in fatigue. Sarah spotted that immediately, though her father probably did not. She knew every line of his body so well, that she felt she could read his mind if he would sit still long enough.

"Daniel!" she called out.

Kicking his horse into a trot, he pulled farther in.

"Sarah! Praise be to God, I found you," he smiled, dismounting and stopping in one motion.

"And here's my father," she quickly blurted out as he walked out from under the shadow of the cabin.

Daniel halted immediately, a quick passing of anxiety shadowing his face, then turned toward Matthew with hand outstretched.

"Good day, sir. Daniel Townsend at your service."

"Good day to you, Mr. Townsend. I see you found our humble home. Was it a profitable trip?"

Daniel took off his hat to reveal straight, neat hair plastered to his head. Sarah stood, her hands clasped tightly together.

"It was most profitable. I met up with three men in Robertson County who also were traveling to Port Royal. We shared news and companionship. It made the last hour or so speed by." Daniel stopped abruptly, afraid he was talking too much. Sarah smiled encouragingly.

She left her cap off today and had her hair, unruly as usual, pulled back. The trademark tendrils escaped everywhere, framing her face with a soft, auburn glow. Her green eyes sparkled with life, and Daniel thought she had never looked so beautiful or alive.

"As much as I hate to ask it, I wonder if you might assist me with a few big logs before we retire for supper and before Sarah shows you your place for the night? Unfortunately, we must place you in the barn, but it will be comfortable, and Sarah has outdone herself in preparing a clean area for you to sleep."

Daniel met Matthew's eyes without flinching.

"I would be most willing to help, sir."

"Then let us be off. Sarah? Would you take his horse and see to her while we work? It should not take more than an hour at the most, and we will be ready for supper."

Matthew's tone gave no room for argument, and indeed, Sarah would have offered none. She knew that Daniel and her father must have this time together without her presence, and she would rather it happen right away than have to wait around in an anxious stew. She nodded, gave Daniel a brief, encouraging glance, and led his mare toward the barn where she would find a good grooming, a small bucket full of tasty grain and hay aplenty. As she led her inside the small structure, she turned to watch the backs of her father, strong and stout, and Daniel, tall and lean, disappear down the path to the creek. She began to pray.

Chapter Thirty Three

Sarah was surprised at how comfortable she felt after their supper of stew, biscuits and tomatoes. The two red vegetables she sliced tonight might be the last of the season, but they were just as juicy and succulent as the first tomatoes in June. Using her handkerchief, she wiped her mouth in satisfaction, looking across the table again at Daniel, hardly believing he was actually here, in her home, seated at their table. Glancing up, he caught her gaze and smiled, a similar thought running through his mind.

Matthew appeared not to notice the unspoken communication as he buttered the last biscuit with intense scrutiny.

"And so, that many people came to Shiloh?" he spoke, directing his question to Daniel.

"Indeed. Five thousand, Mr. Hodge estimated."

"Remarkable. And God's spirit moved in a way similar to that which He moved over me?"

"He seemed to, sir. Many people were outside of themselves, apparently wrestling with religion – or perhaps they wrestled against religion – I know not." Daniel tore his eyes from Sarah to respond to Matthew. She began clearing the table, her ears bent fully toward the conversation.

Matthew laughed abruptly.

"Wrestled is certainly a good word for how God can move over a man. I told you of my dramatic tale. How did you find the Christ, Daniel?" (Sarah noted that formal titles had been dropped after the men returned with freshly hewn logs.)

"Well, sir, it was more of a journey with me, as opposed to a dramatic event. Nevertheless, the power of the Lord weighs upon me just as heavily as it does on any man, I would suppose." Matthew waved Daniel over to the fireplace and began taking off his boots. Although they had not housed many guests in their home over the years, Sarah knew her father intended to continue the conversation while she cleaned. It was a task she didn't begrudge. Simply being in the room with Daniel and hearing the cadence of his voice brought her great joy. She glanced toward the two men, listening to her father question again about the revival meetings. How could one woman be so happy?

She shook her head, smiling, as she moved the three plates toward the keeler and reached under the shelf for the water bucket.

Daniel stayed on with the McMillans for two full days. Sarah thought she had never heard the birds chirp so beautifully or seen the skies display such vivid shades of blue. She would have stated that no mosquitoes or bugs bothered her, although she had bites on her arms and ankles. She felt strong and healthy. In short, it was Paradise and nothing could pull her from this state of perfection.

Surprisingly, she found her father and Daniel had many things in common and worked well together during the day. On Wednesday morning, Matthew had asked Daniel to come with him to the barrel-making shop, and Daniel had been honored to accept. While Sarah visited with Mrs. Neville – a visit that was long overdue – Daniel had met townspeople and learned some of the rudiments of barrel-making.

It was while the men were at the warehouse that Sarah heard of the Logan County meetings stretching west, into this area of Tennessee. Mrs. Neville had been the mouthpiece for the news. They had been drinking hot tea on her front porch, sharing memories of Ann, when Mrs. Neville mentioned McGready. Yet, within seconds, her conversation had circled back to her sorrow and loneliness without her daughter.

"And how is Esther?" Sarah hoped a change of topic would comfort the lady.

"Esther? Oh, she is very well. You know she is thirteen now and has, almost, fully grown out of her impetuosity. Almost, I say," she laughed a bit. "She still is the most hard-headed child, but her father insists that will bode her well in the future. I pray often for her husband." The two women laughed together, looking out toward Spring Street.

In truth, it was still painful for Sarah to speak of Ann as well. While the comfort of the Lord had filled her heart, she knew she would never fully heal from the absence of her friend. Aunt Charity would call it a scar, healed, but still marked.

As she enjoyed listening to Mrs. Neville's news of Port Royal, part of Sarah's mind wandered. If she had a scar, then certainly her father would have a hosts of scars from his experience. Make no mistake, she was still amazed, relieved and stunned by his return to the Lord, but she still had yet to fully open her heart to him. Perhaps she was afraid this would end, and, one day, he would come home from work yelling, screaming and throwing things again. She had been watching from the side, not engaging with him.

She vaguely heard Mrs. Neville's story of last Sabbath's picnic. The Lord was pricking her heart as she sat, and she determined to be more open to her father and begin living as though she forgave him. It was a matter of will, was it not? She willed to forgive and therefore, she did. Perhaps it must start as an act, a forced emotion. Surely God's love would pour out and enfold her in this thing? She sighed deeply.

"Are you alright, dear?" Mrs. Neville's direct question broke into her thoughts.

"Pardon? Oh, yes, ma'am. You were saying something about the picnic and the Baptist meetings."

"That's right. And the word about a Presbyterian meeting coming our way in the next few weeks."

"Oh?" Sarah's ears perked up. "I apologize. I did not catch what you said about that."

"Well, our reverend said he heard that Mr. Montgomery is opening his meeting house for your Rev. McGready to come in mid-to-late October."

"Are you certain?"

"Most assuredly. Of course, weather permitting, but I know Mr. Montgomery is preparing the place as we speak – for there is a mighty mess to clean up there if a crowd of people is to descend upon it."

Sarah's mind was jumping. "Perhaps my father would attend those meetings, then," she said, half to herself.

"You do admire Mr. McGready?"

"Admire? Oh, most certainly. He is a forceful preacher, full of God's Holy Spirit. A powerful man in both body and spirit. But very common,

Mrs. Neville. He puts on no pretentions. I would that he would meet my father now for he is so unlike what he was a few weeks ago."

"Yes … that would be most satisfying. Well," she leaned forward, placing her hand on Sarah's arm, "then we must pray, should we not? Now. We have tarried long enough, tell me all about this Daniel Townsend. As Ann would say, I want to know everything." Mrs. Neville's smile broadened, and Sarah couldn't help laughing.

"Gladly," she said, and began to recount to Mrs. Neville all that had happened during the summer with Daniel.

Sarah wasted no time in telling Daniel and her father about Mc-Gready's plans to hold meetings at Montgomery's Meeting House in Tennessee. Having spent the past few days with McGready, Daniel already knew about it.

"Why have you not told me?" Sarah chastised him that evening after their supper. She, Daniel and her father sat outside, the two men whittling in the shade.

"I am sorry. I just have not thought of it, I suppose. Is Montgomery's close to here?"

"According to Mrs. Neville, it is just down the road a piece. Father?" Sarah turned her eyes toward Matthew. His brow was furrowed as he rounded the bottom of a wooden bowl. "May we go to Mr. McGready's meeting? I would that he may know you now, how you have changed and what God has wrought in your heart."

Matthew raised his eyes toward his daughter.

"Do you say I have changed, daughter? Indeed. You have merely been watching for a few days now. Is there a change?"

Sarah dropped her gaze, embarrassed.

"Yes. I am sorry I have been detached, I suppose. There has been a mighty change. You are a different person."

Matthew smiled broadly, reaching for Sarah's hand. She allowed him to grasp it, but it was difficult.

"I do not mean to rush you, child. How does a person release seventeen years of pent up feelings in a mere week? I am merely pleased that your heart is thawing toward me."

Daniel had continued to whittle, his head down.

"As to your question, I would go to this meeting, most assuredly. I believe I have some apologies to make, and it is my heart to see some of the wonders you both have spoken of. I would, also, if he would permit, like to be baptized in water."

"I, too, would like that," Sarah spoke.

"You? Have you not been baptized in Logan County? I would assume you had seen to that a year ago," Matthew's strong face was puzzled.

"I set to do it, but something kept me back."

"Is that so?" Matthew paused, struggling. "I know it is much to ask – much to assume – but would you consider our being baptized together... as a family?" The strong man's voice choked on his last words, the earnest hope in his face so fierce it was almost painful to see.

Daniel raised his eyes to gaze at Sarah. He prayed silently as he watched the emotions roll across her countenance – anger, resentment, compassion, hurt. Lowering his head, he continued whittling. Her voice broke into the silence so quietly it was almost a whisper.

"I suppose so."

The compassion won out, Daniel thought. He smiled as he met Sarah's eyes, and she tremulously held his gaze.

Matthew's stern features fell into a radiant surprise as he gazed upon his daughter. He shook his head, laughing quietly. "How can a man be so blessed? So forgiven?"

"Sir?" Daniel spoke up. "I know how Sarah loves the Red River. What if the two of you were baptized right here, in Port Royal at the crossing place? I would think we would only have to ask Mr. McGready, and he would be glad to do such a thing. He comes near here anyway on his trek from Logan County to Montgomery's Meeting House."

Sarah's eyes opened wide at the prospect. A baptism right here in Port Royal settlement, with all their neighbors watching? Sammy and Hagar would be beside themselves, she smiled to herself. But her father would never agree to that. It would be too much.

"I think that idea might be from the mouth of God," Matthew said thoughtfully. Sarah gaped. "What would I need to do to search that out?" he continued.

"I would imagine a letter to Mr. McGready, a letter I would be most happy to deliver when I leave tomorrow for home."

"Yes. And one to Obediah and Charity. If we were to do such a thing, they must attend, yes, Sarah?"

Her eyes wide in disbelief, Sarah could only nod. This change. This new creation of her father. It was almost too much to take in at times. Daniel and Matthew appeared not to notice her struggle.

"Yes...well, then. Tonight I will write and you, Daniel, may deliver those letters. We will hear of their responses, but in the meantime, we will make plans to attend the gethering at Montgomery's meeting house. My heart leaps in anticipation."

Night sounds fell upon them then as the crisp September evening darkened. It wasn't long before the chill ran them back inside the cabin, and while Sarah was preoccupied knowing this was Daniel's last night, she also found her mind tugged toward the things of God, toward baptisms and forgiveness.

Chapter Thirty Four

Port Royal, Tennessee
October 1800

McGready's eye fell on Port Royal with interest. He had simply by-passed the settlement the week earlier on his way to Montgomery's Meeting House in order to reach it before the crowd arrived; he knew he would see the town when he came back through to baptize the McMil-lans.

Port Royal seemed a busy place, he thought, though not as active nor as big as Russellville – he would put it on the same scale as Keysburg. But the river was nicely situated as it joined with Sulphur Fork Creek. The junction of the two made for wider water and allowed the warehouse traffic to thrive.

He saw all this within seconds before fatigue settled over him like a heavy dew. While the salvations at Montgomery's meeting house were numerous – forty at last count – the weight of these last few months had begun to take its toll. He would continue meetings as long as weather would allow because, above all things, he didn't want this incredible dis-play of God's power to cease. Everywhere they went, everywhere they met now, there were hundreds, if not thousands, of people who attended. Just the week before at Clay-lick in Logan County, more than eighty peo-ple experienced the saving grace of God. And this happened at a tiny cabin, not a meeting house proper. It was as though the tide of God could not be stopped or slowed. It flowed like a rushing river, pouring out and capturing everything in its path. It had rolled first to Red River Meeting House, then northeast to Gasper, then northwest to Muddy Creek, south to Shiloh and now west to Tennessee.

"Mr. McGready!" a voice bellowed out. "Welcome to Port Royal, sir."
He sat on his horse on the north side of the Red while the man ad-

dressing him called from the opposite river bank. Tilting back his hat to see better, he raised his hand in acknowledgement.

"We will send Mr. Anderson over to bring you and your horse across," he yelled. "Meantime, I will let the McMillans know you've arrived, then." And he turned his back to walk back toward the settlement. As Anderson readied the ferry to cross, McGready dismounted and allowed himself time to think.

Apparently, Obediah and Charity McPherson were here somewhere, waiting for him to arrive for this impromptu baptism. Ordinarily, he tried to gather the faithful at one time to hold multiple baptisms, but as Nancy had said when the letter had arrived requesting this thing, "You must do this, James. It is as though God's hand grips me through the very words and compels me to urge you."

And if truth be known, he agreed completely. Matthew McMillan's apology had been complete on paper, then two days ago when he and his daughter came to Montgomery's meeting house, he had immediately sought McGready out to apologize "properly" for barging in at Muddy Creek. McGready, along with all the other ministers, was merely grateful for God's heavy-handed conversion of Matthew. Forgiveness had already been extended.

Ah, but what a difference in the man's countenance!

"Here, sir," Anderson had pulled the ferry up to his side of the bank, interrupting his contemplations. "Can I help you with your horse?"

"I have her, many thanks," McGready responded, gently drawing his mare on the wooden ferry. It was still morning yet, though barely, and the late October rains had not begun. The Red River ran slowly and was fairly low. It was not a treacherous crossing.

Already a small crowd had gathered on the town side of the river. Any ferry crossing was sure to bring watchers – he saw children and some of the ladies shading their eyes in curiosity. When he had almost landed, he heard the booming voice of Obediah McPherson tumbling out of the warehouse. The man was hatless with red hair flying wildly.

"Rev. McGready, as I live and breathe! It is good to see you in Tennessee!"

"And it is good to be here, Mr. McPherson," McGready smiled, leaping off the side of the ferry. Anderson drew his horse gently after him.

The two men shook hands heartily. "Matthew and Sarah told us of the success of the Montgomery house meetings. About forty salvations, you estimate?"

"As best as we could discern."

"Glory be to God!"

The watchers from town had begun to slip away, and the children resumed their games as McGready and Obediah walked up the bank.

"Charity, Sarah and the children are on their way – along with some of the townspeople who have befriended them. Matthew is here," Obediah pointed into the darkness of Wilcox's warehouse, "finishing up a barrel before the baptism. " He stopped, hesitating. "I cannot thank you enough for agreeing to this, Rev. McGready. It means so much to the girl to have you do the baptism."

McGready's tall form halted along with Obediah, his furrowed brows bent in reflection. "Perhaps, Obediah, it means much to me as well."

The sounds of approaching laughter and children's voices pulled the men's gaze toward Spring Street. Two children, one dark-skinned and the other a tow-headed white boy, raced together toward them both. Behind them was a procession that included all the McPherson children and a family of well-dressed people, accompanied by a few more dark-skinned folk.

"Well, then. Here's our flock now," Obediah spoke, eyes catching on Sarah's tall form heading the line. "Sarah blooms like a flower these days. Gone is the quiet, withdrawn girl I met two years ago." They watched as she caught up with the two children and wrapped them both in a hug.

"She and Daniel Townsend have come to an understanding, have they not?" McGready questioned quietly.

"Indeed. Matthew gave his blessing a few weeks ago, and the two plan to be wed in the spring. She is beside herself with joy, but continues to put the Lord first in her thoughts and actions."

"Ah. It is well then for I know Daniel will do the same."

Even as he spoke, Daniel and Matthew emerged from the shaded doorway, Matthew wiping his hand on his heavy apron, a broad smile on his open face.

"Greetings to all!" Matthew waved them over. "Are we come to the time of baptism, then? Rev. McGready?" Matthew turned toward the man with a question in his eyes. "I know you hope to reach Logan County before dark. Can I try to persuade you once again to stay with us this day?"

McGready shook his head slowly.

"I must reach Mrs. McGready by day's end, sir, though I appreciate the offer. I have much to do on our own homestead and am planning another sacrament meeting a week hence in Mr. Rankin's territory. It is of the utmost urgency that we continue to gather God's people as weather permits."

Matthew nodded in understanding.

"Well, then," he said, clapping his hands, "we are off to the river's edge. Sarah?"

As her father held out his hand, Sarah felt almost dizzy. Daniel stood beside him, tall and strong, holding such a smile of peace and contentment on his face. In her wildest dreams, she never imagined this moment. Hagar and Sammy, who had been constantly at her side since she had returned to Port Royal, stood by watching with unaccustomed solemnity. Hagar's lips were moving quietly, her prayers flowing to Heaven unencumbered.

She reached out toward him, feeling her father's strong grasp, and the two followed McGready back down to the river's edge. Trailing them was their small entourage — Mr. and Mrs. Neville, Esther, Sally and Robert, Hagar, Sammy, Mr. Wilcox, Charity and Obediah, all the McPherson children, and quite a few of the townspeople who had heard rumors of a river baptism to occur that day.

Sarah didn't notice any of them. As she and her father approached the water hand-in-hand, she only saw him, Rev. McGready, in front of them, taking off his outer garments, and Daniel, standing to the side.

McGready's boots hit the water, the splashing increasing as he stepped farther and father into the river. She and her father followed without missing a step, easing their bodies deeper into the cold water. She felt her body heat flow out, the chill creeping up her feet, to her legs, to her waist. They stopped when she was waist-deep, the brackish water flowing slowly around her. Obediah waded in after them, stripped of his outer garment, to assist. The four of them turned and faced the crowd standing on the shore.

Sarah gazed unwaveringly at all those who had become more dear to her than life since she arrived in Tennessee. Mrs. Neville stood to the right, tears coursing down her cheeks, and – Sarah knew – she was thinking of Ann, wishing she were here. Mr. Neville and Esther looked like sentinels at her side. Aunt Charity held Matthew while the other three children stood silently beside her.

Sammy and Hagar had moved to Robert and Sally, who had placed their hands on the children's shoulders. Mr. Wilcox had walked out on the porch of the warehouse, leaning slightly against a post, tamping his pipe.

And Daniel? Her husband-to-be. Such peace emanated from his face.

"Ladies and Gentlemen," McGready's voice boomed out, echoing over the water like thunder. "We have joined together to witness a sealing of God's powerful work in the lives of Matthew and Sarah McMillan, father and daughter who are come to the throne of God together. In the Bible, Christ holds out the only terms upon which salvation may be expected. 'If any man will come after me, let him deny himself, and take up his cross and follow me.'

"In these words, we have, first, the character of the genuine Christian — him that is a saint indeed – He follows Christ. To follow someone means to pursue the footsteps of a person who has gone before; by this means coming to the place where he is, and finding him. Sometimes it signifies the conduct of a careful and industrious student, who loves his master – who places the highest confidence in his rules and instructions, and pursues his directions with diligence and attention. Sometimes it signifies an exact copying the example of some amiable and respectable character. In every sense of the word it implies that Jesus has gone to Heaven to prepare a place for His followers; He has marked the way with His blood and His footsteps; and all His spiritual children are walking in the 'narrow' way of holiness and endeavoring to tread in His footsteps."

In the back of her mind, Sarah realized she could no longer feel her feet. The icy water had sucked away all awareness, yet she was fully engaged with McGready's words.

"I present before you today these two who are walking in the 'narrow' way of Christ, who have determined that they would express their devotion to their Lord by participating in the ordinance of baptism. Matthew McMillan," McGready's right hand reached out, touching the man on his shoulder, "and Sarah McMillan." He lightly placed his other hand on Sarah's shoulder. "By their profession in Jesus as the Christ, the Son of God, and by their acknowledgement of His Lordship in their lives, they would call on you to be witnesses of this public profession of faith."

He turned to Sarah first. Obediah sidled up beside her as best as he could, the current tugging at his shirt.

"Do you, Sarah Elizabeth McMillan, proclaim that Jesus is your Lord this day?"

"I do," she tried to answer loudly, willing her teeth not to chatter.

"Have you acknowledged to Him that you are a sinner in need of a Savior?"

"I have," her voice grew stronger.

" And have you accepted the washing of His blood over your conscience, thereby making you righteous and able to stand before God the Father under the covering of His Son?"

"I have." Sarah's green eyes sparkled in determination and joy. Those watching from the bank saw a fierceness in her that was new, a strength that belied her frailness as a woman. A few even unconsciously stepped back.

"Then I baptize you today in the name of the Father, the Son and the Holy Ghost." McGready gently lowered Sarah back into the gently flowing Red River. She felt the icy water rush up her back and into her hair as she closed her eyes and descended into darkness and cold. Quickly, she shot back to the surface, gasping for breath, the water feeling like icicles as it streamed down her face. Hands pushed her toward the riverbank as she struggled with her weighted skirts. She willed her feet to move – one step, then another – even though she couldn't feel the ground at all. Charity stood by the water's edge, holding out a warm blanket, waiting for Sarah to reach it. Daniel eased out into the water, taking her extended hand and pulling her in the rest of the way.

Teeth chattering and hands not able to grasp properly, Sarah found herself wrapped tightly and held by both Charity and Daniel. She turned back toward the river to watch her father. Matthew stood solidly, about six inches shorter than McGready, but he still looked like a rock. His warm gaze rested on his daughter as he listened to McGready's questions and responded as Sarah had.

Within a minute, he, too, disappeared beneath the reddish-brown surface of the water, emerging with a gasp and a shout of joy. Sarah heard people clapping and cheering up and down the river's edge as even more of the townspeople had come out to see this miraculous thing. Some, of course, thought it nothing but foolishness and wondered how Matthew McMillan of all people – a sensible man if ever there was one – had come to this place of ridiculous religion. But for the most part, the folk in Port Royal celebrated with the McMillans and their friends.

After Matthew was on the bank standing beside Sarah, McGready prayed and sealed what had been done in the Spirit on this day.

"Let us, then, try to be Christians in reality," McGready concluded. "To have the knowledge of God and His Son Jesus Christ, which is eternal life – that faith which beholds the divine glory in the face of Jesus – that faith which feeds and lives upon Christ the bread of life, which came down from Heaven. Then we will be able to come to God in Christ, as children to a father – then we will be able to wrestle with God in prayer like Jacob, and prevail like Israel. Amen and so be it."

Turning to his left, McGready reached out and shook Obediah's hand, and the two men waded their way back to the riverbank. Charity stood silently, holding out two more large blankets as the men inched their way up.

The Red River continued to flow toward the west, moving slowly and silently past the small crowd on its banks.

Epilogue

It was the last time she ever had the dream.

Once again Sarah found herself on the edge of the Red River, standing exactly where she had the week before when she and her father were baptized by Rev. McGready. There was no water in the riverbed, and the familiar dead fish stared back into her face, its unwavering eyes stuck open.

Slowly and surely, the trickle of water began, coming from the east, first as a thin line of fluid, then growing a little larger and longer. Her father stepped up beside her and smiled at her. She smiled back as he reached out his hand to grasp hers. Gone was the fear in his face. He turned with her toward the increased tide, his eyes wide open.

The two of them stood together, holding hands, as the water increased exponentially. The trickle had become a stream.

As before, Sarah first knew it had peaked by the sound. A rushing, rolling, cascading noise of many waters encircled her. She glanced at her father again. His gaze was fixed toward the east, a strange smile of acceptance on his face.

As she looked back toward the descending river, she felt her right hand lift in the grasp of her father's. Like him, she lifted her other hand and the two stood watching the roiling water as it hurled itself toward them. Their arms were lifted, their faces expectant, as the river poured over their heads and bodies, completely engulfing them in its wake.

Sarah woke abruptly — but not in fear. Her coverlet lay crisp and clean over her without any sign of dampness. Her heart beat steadily. She glanced over and saw the figure of her father still asleep in his bed as the morning sun barged its way into their cabin. Breathing out a sigh of satisfaction, she nestled back under her covers for a few more minutes of sleep. The day would begin soon enough.

With Heartfelt Gratitude

When I felt the call to write about the Second Great Awakening, I knew I would need help. How does one even go about writing historical fiction? Although my last book was set in the 1960s South, it was more fiction than history. I also knew I would be writing on my usual home-schooling mom/pastor's wife timetable – not many spare minutes in a day. Yet in His gracious goodness, the Lord had it all figured out.

Mark Swann, a local historian in Port Royal, Tennessee, was my first contact. As a former park ranger of Port Royal State Park, he was a wealth of information and the first person to read the entire novel. You have Mark to thank for many of the 1790s tool, farming and vegetation information. He was invaluable and is a dear friend! I am blessed to know him.

As I moved toward Logan County, Kentucky, I tripped up on Mrs. Evelyn Richardson. She is the county historian and just happens to volunteer at the Logan County Public Library. I believe she was the first person I spoke with over the phone, and I would like to think we have formed a friendship. Her mountain-sized file of papers on McGready, Red River Meeting House, Gasper and Muddy River meeting houses — not to mention maps — was a God-send. I simply couldn't have written *The Waking Up* without her help. Along with Mark, she agreed to read the entire manuscript before printing, just to make sure my facts were correct. That's over and beyond the call of duty!

Darlynn Moore, one of the members of the Red River Meeting House and Cemetery Association, met me at the old Red River Cemetery, which is adjacent to the Meeting House replica. It's open to the public and is right off Highway 663 in southeastern Logan County. Darlynn has beaucoup of documents detailing happenings at Red River. She was most gracious and generous with her research. For more information on the RRMH and its annual events, go to the website at www.redriverrevival.com. It would be worth your time to see it firsthand.

Also, my monthly writers' group gals suffered through numerous grammatical, spelling and consistency errors while encouraging me to keep on going. Thank you, Ellen Kanervo, Sharon Mabry and Ellen Taylor!

Several folks suffered through initial "read-throughs," and I am much beholdin'. Thank you Miz Audrey Johnson, Michelle Fraley and Tami Fraley.

David and Teresa Elder, the brains and brawn behind RA Publishing, kept me accountable, serve as editors, critiquers, cheerleaders and wise counselors. For all you have done, and so much more than you know, thank you.

My husband and boys put up with a sleep-deprived woman for six months while I wrote in the early morning hours. They deserve some sort of award. I am crabby when I'm tired.

Most of all, I'm incredibly grateful to my Lord and Savior Jesus Christ who, I believe, called me to write this nation-changing history in novel form.

Also by Melanie M. Meadow

It's the summer of 1968 -- the Rev. Martin Luther King, Jr., was recently assassinated, Nixon is about to become president, and 12-year-old Mildred Juniper Rhodes is in a quandary. Her Daddy got a wild hair to move to Piedmont Ridge, S.C., to pastor a church filled with coloreds and whites -- which isn't making much of anybody happy.

ColorBlind is available at:

www.melaniemeadow.com
or in paperback and e-book at
www.amazon.com

"